Nick Oldham was b
1956. He has been a police officer since the age of
nineteen, spending the majority of his service in operational roles. His previous novels – *A Time for Justice* and
Nightmare City – are also set in the world of policing in
north-west England. He is married and lives with his
wife and son on the outskirts of Preston.

'For sheer grab-you-by-the-throat readability, *A Time for
Justice* takes some beating. Policeman Nick Oldham's
high-speed thriller is the genuine article – a tale from the
cutting edge of law enforcement that is utterly authentic.
I think this new author is a real find!'

Mystery and Thriller Guild

'Sergeant Oldham has put his experience to good use to
turn thriller-writer . . . he looks set to have a bright future
as a best-selling author'

West Lancashire Evening Gazette

'Chilling authenticity . . . a gripping tale'

Manchester Evening News

'Nick Oldham makes a superb start to his career as a
novelist . . . *A Time for Justice* is a good yarn and well
worth a read'   *Sunderland Echo*

'A rattling good crime saga'   *Bolton Evening News*

'Every detail in this gripping, fast-paced story of police
corruption and gang warfare has the ring of truth'

Bradford Telegraph and Argus

One Dead Witness

Nick Oldham

HEADLINE

First published in 1998
by HEADLINE BOOK PUBLISHING

First published in paperback in 1999
by HEADLINE BOOK PUBLISHING

10 9 8 7 6 5 4 3 2 1

ISBN 0 7472 5855 4

Printed and bound in Great Britain by
Clays Ltd, St Ives plc

HEADLINE BOOK PUBLISHING
A division of Hodder Headline PLC
338 Euston Road
London NW1 3BH
www.headline.co.uk
www.hodderheadline.com

This book is dedicated to my son,
Philip Joseph Oldham.

Acknowledgements

Many thanks to John Drury and Steve Little, both consummate police trainers, for sharing their knowledge of paedophiles with me, and to Carol Woodcock for pointing me towards the Internet.

Author's Note

Although certain passages in this novel may be disturbing to some readers, the incidents and feelings portrayed are based on the day-to-day realities with which police officers have to deal.

PART ONE

Prologue

Trent knew they were coming long before they arrived.

He could smell it in the air – sense the unnatural quietness, the electric tension which pervaded the prison.

They were coming for him. *Again.*

Suddenly it was very hot.

His throat became dry and he swallowed with some difficulty. A bead of sweat scuttled down his temple like some sort of insect, leaving a glistening silvery trail in its wake. He closed his eyes and gritted his teeth, willing himself to have the courage to face up to what was about to happen.

He was laid out full-length on the lower bunk in his cell, alone, his head propped up on the iron-hard pillows. He had been reading one of his well-thumbed, tatty magazines called *13-Plus*, aimed at young teenage girls. When he felt the atmosphere change, and his spine tingled in response, he closed it, tossed it to one side and let it flutter to the floor.

He lay there for several minutes, eyes staring upwards at the empty bunk above him.

Then he heard the footsteps.

Distant at first . . . rather like listening to a piece of music and honing in on the bass line, separating it from the rest of the instruments. The footsteps clattered more loudly as they mounted the iron steps and reached the landing on which his cell was situated.

Trent's heart began to pound remorselessly. His breathing became shallow.

He knew there would be four of them.

Three were always the same – the swaggering trio of tough guys who ruled the whole prison between them with their violence and intimidation. Then there would be a fourth one, the one who was about to be treated, the one who was desperate, and had paid in cash or dope or tobacco, whatever the acceptable currency happened to be, to satisfy his pent-up frustrations and cravings.

So far it had been a different man every time. Trent had a fairly good idea who it would be this time.

He considered screaming the place down. Then decided not to bother. He had screamed the first few times. A waste of breath. His squeals had gone unheeded, proving that everyone was in on it, including the screws . . . as had been so painfully demonstrated on the last occasion, some two weeks earlier, when the fourth member of the party, the paying member, had been wearing a prison officer's uniform.

The steps were closer now.

He also considered putting up a fight.

He'd tried that before, too. Though he was a man of reasonable stature, the three hard men had loved his resistance and risen to the occasion. After they had overpowered him and held his squirming body down to be abused by the fourth member, they had then beaten him senseless. A cold-hearted, clinical assault which put Trent into the casualty department of the local hospital overnight and then into the poorly-equipped prison hospital to recover for four days.

Trent swung his legs off the bunk and sat up.

The ominous sound of footfalls on the metallic landing grew even nearer.

He swallowed once more, this time to keep the vomit down. He attempted to regain control of his breathing and his shaking. Not a chance.

4

He swore between gasps.

They were now only yards away.

On jittery legs he got to his feet. He groaned pathetically.

Somewhere in the distance he could hear the laughter of men: prisoners on association, playing cards, or table tennis, reading, chatting, watching TV. All fully aware of what was about to take place in cell number one-six on landing four. And not one of them with the courage to make a stand because not one of them cared a toss.

Trent was alone. No one would help him.

By the time the four men reached the door, Trent had unfastened and unzipped his trousers. Anything to save time and get the nightmare over with more quickly.

They barged into the tiny cell, their stench and presence overpowering him, their size terrifying him.

Their leader – Trent's main tormentor – was called Blake. His mouth was crimped into a cruel smile as he regarded Trent with contempt.

Trent glanced beyond Blake's shoulder, past his two regular accomplices, to the fourth man. He had been correct in his guess, recalling the knowing looks the black man – a violent rapist whose MO was to break into houses owned by single females and subject them to brutal attacks – had been giving him for the last couple of days during mealtimes.

'What's it gonna be, Trent?' Blake growled. He raised his eyebrows questioningly, but his hard grey eyes glowered dangerously as he spoke. 'Wanna give us a hard time – or are you gonna grin an' bear it like a good child-molester should?'

In reply, Trent allowed his trousers to fall to his ankles. He stepped out of them, hooked his thumbs into the waistband of his grimy-grey underpants and shuffled them down his legs.

'You're learning,' remarked Blake triumphantly.

5

By lights out the bleeding had stopped. A whole blood-stained toilet roll had been flushed down the inadequate loo.

Fortunately, Trent had been able to reduce some of the excruciating pain. By exchanging some loose tobacco for half a dozen aspirins with another inmate and then raiding his own secret stash of cannabis, he had taken the pills, waited for them to have some effect, then smoked a joint. It helped a little, but for some things the pain never goes away.

When darkness came, he was lying on his bunk, holding his breath so as to infuse the smoke from his lungs into his bloodstream. The hot smoke burned his throat, but he resisted the temptation to cough. That would have been a waste of a very precious substance.

The squelching from the above bunk indicated that the man there was in the throes of masturbation. Trent ignored it and concentrated on other distasteful matters that were more relevant.

Firstly there was the all-consuming hatred he harboured for the people responsible for putting him into this hell-hole. The cops, the barristers, the judges – yeah, he despised them utterly – but his worst rage was reserved for the little people he had once loved and cared for. They were the ones who had turned on him and told all those lies. Betrayed him. How could they? *After all he had done for them?*

And secondly, he thought about his bitter hatred for Blake and his other tormentors here in prison. Trent growled in his throat, fantasies of terrible revenge whirring around and around in his mind. One thing was for sure: they had all taken on much more than they had bargained for.

As he lay there brooding, the cannabis on its mercy dash through his system, he decided that one day in the not-too distant future he would mete out a very painful revenge on every single bastard who had either hurt him, turned against him or had in some way been responsible for his plight.

The man in the top bunk moved, rolled to the edge of the bed and with a gasp of ecstasy concluded his act of self-gratification by ejaculating onto the cell floor, narrowly missing Trent's head.

Chapter One

It was obvious from the way in which she was driving that Detective Constable Danny Furness was one very pissed-off woman.

She changed gear jerkily and jabbed at the accelerator, even though it was her own car, not a police car, and it was her pride and joy – one of the few major indulgences she had allowed herself in the whole of her life. The car surged out of the rear yard of Blackpool Central police station with a screech. Danny threw a right down Richardson Street, followed by another right up Chapel Street towards the traffic lights at the Promenade, which were on red.

She braked, nearly upending the car, then took a deep breath and forced herself to relax into the comfortable driver's seat of the ten-year-old Mercedes 190. Then she lambasted herself mentally for getting so riled up about the plight and the 'up yours' attitude of just another of her customers.

No doubt about it: the job was getting to her.

No, scrap that. The job *had* got to her.

She thanked the Almighty that last Thursday she had paraded in front of the Chief Constable and had been promoted to Sergeant with effect from the following Monday; this meant she had only a week more to work on the Family Protection Unit (FPU) before she transferred onto the CID and became a Detective Sergeant. She couldn't wait to go.

She squinted at the sullen figure in the passenger seat next to her. The eleven-year-old girl clung miserably to the door-handle, having refused on a point of principle to put her seat belt on. She wore a scowl of pure loathing splattered across what was actually a very pretty face and stared angrily ahead through the windscreen, refusing to even acknowledge the detective next to her.

Danny sighed impatiently – at the girl and the unchanging lights.

'Look, Claire, let's face facts: you can't go around doing exactly what you wanna do all the time. You're well old enough to realise that you need to consider other people's feelings besides your own. Your mum has been frantic, really worried about you.'

Claire's lips curled cynically at Danny's reasonable words. She continued to stare dead ahead through the rain, her eyes unrelenting pools of liquid steel. The little speech had gone in one ear and out the other.

Danny shook her head in frustration.

The lights changed. She turned left – south – onto the Promenade, smack into the fiercely driving rain and howling gale-force wind which had virtually cleared the sea-front of all pedestrians.

She had spent most of the last two hours trying to get underneath Claire's tough facade – in the presence of the girl's nineteen-year-old cousin, who had been as useful as a verruca in a swimming pool – and failed. Danny would have preferred to have had Claire's mother present, but she had been uncontactable.

'You've gone missing from home six times in the last two months and the last two times you've been nicked for shoplifting. You're bloody lucky we've decided to caution you again; next time we might put you before a juvenile court. Is that what you want? The court might even decide to place you in a home . . . Do you want to be sent away?'

Danny knew it was only a remote possibility, but Claire didn't need to be aware of that.

Not that Danny's words had much effect. The kid exhaled in a manner which suggested she'd heard all this garbage before, turned haughtily to face Danny and with a sneer said, 'I don't fucking care.' She drew her right knee up and wedged her foot on the seat.

Danny had an urge to lurch across the gap between them and give the young lady one almighty slap across the chops. Instead she snapped, 'Feet off!'

Claire insolently let her foot thud back onto the floor.

'Six times in the last two months, eh? Why? What's behind it? You unhappy at home?'

Claire winced and quickly looked out of the side window at the passing Promenade which was being lashed by a combination of the heavy rain and the waves which crashed over the sea wall, driven by high winds.

Danny missed the reaction. She expelled an exasperated breath and thought, Sod you, you little cow! If you don't want to open up, I'm not sure I want to be bothered with you.

And yet she was concerned. Which is probably the reason why Danny had been such a success on FPU. She cared.

Why should a kid like Claire, from a good, apparently stable background, doing well at school, popular, likeable, suddenly veer off the rails? There was a multitude of possible reasons, none of which Claire seemed willing to divulge.

It didn't add up.

And Danielle Louise Furness, soon to be a Detective Sergeant, didn't like things that didn't add up.

The remainder of the journey was completed in deathly silence, Danny knowing from experience when she was banging her head against a brick wall. She didn't have the time or the energy to pursue things further. So instead of trying to draw Claire out, she concentrated on driving, enjoying the car, which despite its age handled and responded beautifully.

Claire, glad of the respite from the pressure, closed her eyes and rested her head on the seat, exhausted.

★ ★ ★

A few minutes later, Danny pulled up outside the sea-front hotel on South Shore Promenade which was Claire's home.

'Here we are,' she announced, and killed the engine. 'Home sweet home.'

With a start, Claire opened her eyes. She had almost dropped off to sleep for the first time in thirty-six hours. She looked quickly – wide-eyed, like a trapped rabbit – at Danny, who saw the expression on the youngster's face; but it was only on later reflection, much, much later, that she recognised it as fear. There and then, Claire's reaction to her arrival home did not really register with the detective. It just seemed to be a rude awakening. Nothing more.

'C'mon lass,' Danny urged her into action.

Claire's shoulders slumped. The corners of her pretty mouth curled down and she pouted with a quivering bottom lip. With resignation she opened the door and climbed out of the car.

Danny unfastened her seat belt and got out too. The rain washed over her immediately, as if someone had thrown a bucket of water at them.

Side by side they walked across the paved parking area outside the small hotel towards the front door. Danny knew Claire's parents were now home. Apparently they had been out at the Cash & Carry warehouse when Claire had been picked up, which was why the police had been unable to contact them. Danny was anticipating the very real pleasure of depositing the uncooperative little brat back into Mummy's open arms.

She looked down at the grubby 'misper' – missing person – by her side.

Claire was dressed in raggy denim jeans, an 'Oasis'-style anorak and a pair of multi-coloured Reeboks.

By contrast, the older woman was dressed in a practical but elegantly tailored longline suit in a colour described as 'soft-grape' and sling-back court shoes with three-inch heels on her feet. Ideal attire for office work as well as the wide range of other activities she carried out on the FPU; completely inappropriate, however, for pursuing a young lady who decided on the spur of the moment that there was no way in this world that she was going to be returned home.

About four yards from the door, Claire twisted unexpectedly. She legged it around a parked car and vaulted over the low wall separating the frontage of her parents' hotel from the one next door. Then she shifted quickly into top gear.

Danny lunged for her. Missed. Grabbed an armful of fresh air. Swore with words from a vocabulary that could only have come from seventeen years' police service. And without a second thought, gave chase.

'You little bitch!' she screamed, yanked her skirt above her knees and cleared the low wall with only millimetres to spare. Claire was fast and agile, as an eleven-year-old girl should be. But Danny was determined not to lose her, even though she was not in the peak of physical condition. It was a matter of pride.

She landed awkwardly, going over onto her left ankle, feeling it crick out of shape with a pop. She gasped, regained her footing and belted after the fleeing kid.

Claire looked over her shoulder, saw how close Danny was, and reacted by veering right, skittering round the front of a parked car and bounding over the dividing wall onto the next hotel forecourt. She lost her footing, skidded over, rolled, and was up and running again.

Danny followed.

This time she caught the top of the wall with the heel of her shoe and crashed down on the opposite side, landing on her hands and knees in a deep puddle of rainwater.

Her work suit was now ruined. The cuffs of her jacket sleeves were soaked in dirty water, the skirt was completely drenched and she had laddered her tights. Eyes

13

burning with irritation, she scrambled to her feet, slithering and sliding, then was back in pursuit, determined not to lose her quarry.

Seconds later, Claire realised she would have to do more than simply leg it in order to escape from Danny. Despite her present lack of fitness, the detective was built with the loose-limbed athleticism of a cheetah and, in days gone by, before the evils of cigarettes, booze and late nights, she had been a superb sportswoman who had represented the county at running, tennis and netball. She was still pretty good over short distances.

Danny lunged for Claire a second time.

And would have had her if the girl hadn't glanced over her shoulder at that exact moment, seen Danny's fingers stretching out for her, ducked left behind a car, then shot towards the Promenade.

The road was busy, the traffic heavy, the rain making it worse.

Without even looking, Claire flung herself dangerously in the path of an oncoming van.

Panting now, Danny ran after her round the same parked car, only to hear an ominous ripping sound as her skirt caught on the bumper and tore.

This, however, was not something which immediately bothered her because she had seen Claire's reckless dash into the road and the van bearing down on her.

Danny shrieked the girl's name.

Claire stopped immediately. She became rooted to the spot on the tarmac and turned to face the van.

Her mouth dropped open in a silent scream.

Everything slurred down into slow motion.

The driver had been motoring along, not concentrating particularly, listening to some very loud classical music and exceeding the 30 mph speed limit by a dangerous eighteen miles per hour. His windscreen wipers were working hard against the sluicing rain. The last thing he expected to see was the ghost-like apparition of a young girl darting out directly in front of him and stopping stone dead.

'Jesus!'

He gripped the steering-wheel tightly enough to crush it and literally stood on the brake pedal, his backside lifting off the seat. The classical music pounding in his ears lost all form and substance, becoming a deafening, blare.

The brakes slammed on. The wheels locked. The tyres vainly tried to grip the surface of the road which was a river of rain. The back end slithered round towards the front end as the van entered a skid and lurched towards the petrified Claire.

On the roadside Danny watched the scene unfold with a kind of morbid fascination. Even as she stared at the inevitable accident-to-be, her mind told her she would be the one to blame; she was the one who had chased a frightened eleven-year-old into the path of a vehicle; the one who would have to answer all those awkward questions in a Coroner's court.

Claire was only inches away from the front grille of the van. A fraction of a second from being mown down.

Then, amazingly, she moved.

She leapt out of the way and ran across the road, over the tram tracks towards the sea.

Everything clicked back into real time.

The van shuddered to a skewed halt over the spot where Claire had been standing a second before. The driver was white-faced. His heart had stopped momentarily. His fingers were still wrapped solidly around the wheel. His eyes bulged in their sockets like someone had whacked him with a spade on the back of his head. He wasn't sure whether or not he'd hit the girl and she was underneath the front wheels, whether it had been some sort of spiritual apparition or whether he needed to see an optician.

With one last judder, the engine stalled.

He watched in fascination as a tall, slim woman, drenched to the skin, hair plastered to her head, dressed in a filthy suit with a tear right up the back of her skirt to her knickers, dashed past his vision.

The Promenade was being bombarded by a fusion of crashing waves and heavy rain, supported by the strong wind.

Claire was running along, perilously close to the railings next to the sea wall. Danny was behind her, leaving more space between herself and the angry sea. She was finding it increasingly difficult to make up any ground on Claire. The elements didn't seem to want her to catch up – running against the gale-force wind was like swimming in porridge – she was approaching the limit of her fitness and also by now her ankle was hurting like hell.

All rational thoughts were then purged when a huge wave burst over the sea wall and landed on her, almost drowning her in an ice-cold sheet. For more than a few moments Danny had to fight against the terrifying elemental force of the water as it retreated back to the sea. It tore at her, trying to unbalance her and drag her back, pulling at her legs and ankles. It was all she could do to remain upright against such power which had knocked all the breath and spirit out of her.

She was worried about Claire: if the foolish youngster should get hit, would she be able to resist the strength of the sea?

With that in mind, Danny stopped chasing, giving Claire the opportunity to get away from both herself and the sea. Nothing was worth putting lives in danger.

Up ahead, Claire ceased running. She turned and faced Danny, looking like a half-drowned squirrel.

Some thirty yards separated the two females.

Claire shouted something which was whisked away in the wind and the water.

Danny took several paces towards her.

'Don't come any closer!' Claire yelled in warning.

Danny stood still. She could see utter anguish on the girl's face.

'I won't, I promise,' Danny shouted in reply. 'Just come away from the edge, it's very dangerous. Then we can talk.'

'I'm not coming home. You can't make me go home. If you do, I'll run away again.'

'Okay, okay, just move away from there . . . Claire! LOOK OUT!' Danny bellowed out the last two words of warning as she saw a massive swell build up and then break like a huge claw right over Claire.

The crushing weight of the water rammed the youngster to the ground as effectively as if a sack of coal had been dumped on her shoulders. When the water rushed back, its tentacles took her with it. She screamed and writhed in a fight against it, but it was no use. She was hauled across the concrete back towards the sea like a fish on the deck of a trawler, her screams muted as the bitter salt-water filled her nose and mouth and lungs, choking her.

For the second time in less than two minutes, Danny was compelled to watch in horrified fascination as the fate of the young girl was enacted in front of her eyes.

Then Danny moved into action. Drawing on her last reserves of strength and energy, she flung herself towards the pathetic figure.

She knew she would not make it, though.

Claire was too far away and being pulled too quickly. She would be gone in seconds . . . *and explain that one, Detective Furness*. Not now a fatal road traffic accident, but a drowning victim . . .

Claire slithered towards the precipice of the sea wall and was dashed sideways against one of the perpendicular posts of the railings – which she grabbed instinctively – but still the sea pulled her backwards and tried to unwrap her fingers from the post. She clung on desperately, but with failing strength and great pain inside her chest where she had slammed against the iron post. At the same time a new, even more powerful swell was building up behind her, one designed to finish the job started by its predecessor and claim a victim. Or two.

Danny saw it rise. She also saw that Claire's progress had been halted by her collision with the railing post. But not for very long.

She weighed up the odds.

If she did reach Claire and grab her, the chances were in favour of them both being sucked into a watery grave. If she didn't, Claire was definitely dead. The poor odds did not prevent her from flinging herself across the last few feet and risking her own life to save Claire's.

At the precise moment Danny got hold of her sleeve, Claire lost her grip and her legs went over the edge of the wall. The sea boiled only inches away from the soles of her shoes. Danny wrapped herself around the post and shouted, 'Hold on tight.'

The new wave rose like a monster from the deep and exploded spectacularly over them, twice as savage as the previous one. Through it all Danny and Claire held grimly onto each other, their eyes locked into each other's gaze, looks of solid resolve on their faces as they fought to live, whilst the Irish Sea did its utmost to separate them once and for all.

'Don't let go, don't let go,' Danny chanted as much for herself as Claire.

The water whooshed back past them, battering them, trying its damnedest to draw them into the sea and almost succeeding. Had it continued a few more moments, Danny would have had to let go.

Suddenly the water all drained away, leaving them clinging to the edge of the Promenade. Alive. The wind had changed its angle ever so slightly and the tide whipped away to a point further south.

Danny did not hesitate. She knew from past experience

just how fickle the sea was – she had pulled four bodies out of it in her time – and this respite would only be brief. They had to make use of it, even though their natural reaction would be to stay put and get their breath back.

'Oh God, oh God,' Claire spluttered.

'Come on, we've got to move!' With one last effort, Danny heaved Claire back onto the Promenade. 'Come on, get up, we can't hang around.'

Claire was on all fours, coughing and retching up the water which had cascaded down her gullet. Danny yanked her up. 'Run!' she shouted.

The howling wind changed again. The sea was about to make another attempt on their lives. The burgeoning swell looked enormous.

'I can't,' Claire wept.

Danny grabbed her roughly by the collar and hoisted her bodily away from the edge. They reached the comparative safety of the tram tracks just in time to turn and watch the next monstrous wave explode against the sea wall.

Had they been underneath it, they would have been fish food. For sure.

Danny pulled a blanket around her shoulders, brushed her damp straggly hair back from her face and said, 'Claire seems to be unhappy for some reason.'

'I can't think why. God knows, we give her everything she wants,' said Claire's mother, Ruth Lilton.

'She's spoilt rotten,' her stepfather grunted, a tone of real nastiness underneath the words. Joe Lilton was a big, brusque individual who intensely annoyed Danny. She thought she knew him from somewhere – way back when – but could not quite place him. 'She's going through a rebellious phase, that's all. Needs it knocking out of her.'

And you're just the one to do it, obviously, Danny nearly said. Instead she ignored him, turned back to Mrs Lilton and commented: 'Well, this phase seems to be

19

pretty extreme, wouldn't you say? Shoplifting? Missing from home? Ruth, if you'd like to bring her down to the police station, I could spend some time with her, interview her again, maybe less formally. Perhaps that'd get to the root of the problem.'

'That's a good id—' the woman began, but her husband butted in rudely.

'There's no call for that,' he interrupted. 'We'll sort her out. What she's short of is a good old-fashioned leathering. No need for you lot to be involved any further – you've done enough. Family matter from now on.' He seemed to brighten suddenly. 'Thanks anyway.'

Danny shrugged. 'Whatever.' But to Mrs Lilton she said, 'I'm always available if you need me.'

Mrs Lilton said a quiet thanks.

The three of them were sitting in one corner of the crowded waiting room in the casualty department at Blackpool Victoria Hospital. After the fright on the seafront, Danny and Claire had stumbled back across the road to Claire's parents' hotel. From there Danny had driven her immediately to BVH because Claire had been creased double with an agonising pain in her chest. Mr and Mrs Lilton followed in their car.

After an interminable wait, an X-ray had confirmed two cracked ribs, caused when Claire had been smashed against the railing post.

Danny herself had been given a swift check-up by a very dishy doctor and been declared fighting fit. He had rather sensuously eased a tubi-grip bandage around her ankle which, from X-rays, was diagnosed as being sprained. All Danny had wanted, though, was a double vodka-tonic and a drag of a Benson & Hedges Gold. But she didn't have any spirits to hand and her ciggies – which had been kept in her jacket pocket – were a sodden mush.

'Here she is,' said Danny, looking up.

A nurse was guiding the still-bedraggled young girl down the corridor towards the waiting room. Claire was shuffling rather than walking. Each step looked painful because other than the broken ribs, she had suffered a multitude of other bangs, cuts and bruises during her sea-front ordeal.

She looked exhausted and ready to drop. She was in need of a good meal and a rake of sleep.

'Sweetheart,' cried Mrs Lilton. She stood up. Open-armed, she went to Claire and embraced her gently.

'Little cow,' Joe Lilton muttered under his breath. He got up and put on a false face of concern. 'C'mon girl, let's get you home.' He rubbed her head with his hand in a fatherly gesture. Claire reared away from him, fireballs in her eyes. He withdrew his hand. His mouth became a hard line.

Danny rose wearily, aware that the tear up the back of her skirt was hanging open like a pair of curtains. She didn't have the energy to care who saw her knickers any more.

Claire walked up and murmured a meek, 'Thank you,' to Danny, who nodded. She could not fail to see the expression of absolute desolation on the youngster's face as her parents led her away. She looked as if she was going to the scaffold. Danny heard Mrs Lilton saying, 'The first thing we'll do is get you into a hot bath and then . . .' Her voice faded.

Danny wondered how long it would be before Claire Lilton went on the run again.

The Detective Constable limped into the ladies' loo. After she had relieved herself, she studied herself in a mirror over a wash basin, stunned by her reflection. Talk about the witch from Hell City. She looked appalling!

Her pretty ash-blonde hair had dried like strands of thick, coarse string. Most of her make-up, which she always took great pride in applying, had been washed away. The remnants of her eye-liner and mascara made her look like the victim of an assault. Her suit was ruined beyond cleaning or repair and she knew there would be no earthly chance of the police footing the bill for its replacement. Her tights had more ladders in them than a board game and her shoes, which had partly dried out, had gone all crinkly.

But worse than that, she looked and felt her age.

She was aching all over, having used muscles that hadn't been stretched for years when she'd chased and rescued Claire. This must be how an arthritic eighty-year-old feels, she thought. And frankly, you don't look much less than eighty.

It was as if the seawater had scoured away the last vestiges of her youth. She held up her chin and could see the lines of ageing running down her neck, giving her the likeness of a scrawny chicken. There were also deep lines at the edge of her mouth which seemed to put ten years on her and needed filling.

Her shoulders sagged; she experienced a wave of nauseating depression.

'Darlin',' she said to herself critically, 'if you don't watch it, you're going to become an old slapper.' She blew out a long breath. 'Shit.'

Then she stood upright, forced a smile onto her face and tried to be positive. The sea might have revealed the Danny underneath the make-up, but it also showed that her best features couldn't be washed away – her lovely slanting green eyes which were almost oriental; and her lips, which despite the lines at the edges, were full, soft and very definitely kissable. Nor had the sea done any damage to her figure. She still had firm, beautifully formed breasts which provoked many a second glance from passing men, a slim waist and hips which were only just beginning to broaden.

Suddenly the cloakroom door burst open and a couple of noisy teenage girls entered, giggling when they clapped eyes on the state of Danny. She brushed regally past them and stormed – limp and all – out of the hospital.

The rain was still bucketing down but the wind had

eased off. By the time Danny reached her car she was soaked to the skin again, hair plastered down her forehead.

If only she had been returning home to a husband or loving partner and some TLC. That would have made things much more bearable. But to go through all this and skulk back to an empty house, pleasant though it was, and wait, usually with disappointment, for her married lover to call by or ring, made her want to cry.

All she craved was some uncomplicated love. Was that too much to ask?

Chapter Two

As Danny Furness accelerated tiredly out of the hospital car park onto East Park Road, it was 11 p.m. British-time. Three thousand miles to the west, all the way across the Atlantic Ocean, in Miami, Florida it was 6 p.m., five hours behind. The weather in Dade County that day could not have been more of a contrast to its British counterpart. At its height the sun had pounded down an unbearable 90 degrees, making the city of Miami airless and oppressive . . . but now a light breeze whisked in across Biscayne Bay and promised a pleasant evening.

Perfect for dining out on the terrace, thought Steve Kruger, who had just wrapped up a day which had started eleven hours earlier. He was looking forward to getting home, throwing off his work suit and changing into baggy shorts, busting open a bottle of Hurricane Reef Lager and preparing the barbecue ready for the arrival of his son, daughter-in-law and their two kids.

It had been a long, tedious day at the office. Because it was the month-end and not a zillion miles away from the end of the financial year, Kruger had spent most of his time stuck behind his desk in air-conditioned splendour, neck-tie discarded, locked into strategic and tactical planning with his secretary, accountant and three company directors. Specific plans for next year and outline plans for the next three had been thrashed out.

Some of the more nuts-and-bolts stuff had also been finalised. Such as tidying up some files and putting together a huge batch of bad-debt bills which the secretary had posted off today. If they were all paid by return, Kruger's cashflow would be $150,000 to the good. In reality he knew he'd be lucky to get 30 per cent of them paid off within six weeks. He'd been chasing one debtor's ass for seven months – a lawyer, of all people – who owed over ten grand. Kruger had sent that son of a bitch a final FINAL demand, together with a mildly threatening letter which intimated – subtly – that no one ever welched on a Kruger Investigations Final Demand notice with success.

It had been a pleasure to dictate that letter, safe in the knowledge that it didn't matter whether the guy paid up or not, because the one positive thing to emerge during the day was that Kruger Investigations' net profits were going to be very healthy indeed. Five per cent up on the previous year. Somewhere in the region of two million dollars.

Not bad for a firm which had only begun operating five years earlier, employing only himself and his second wife (now ex) as a secretary. She had long gone, but Kruger had stayed at the helm and after a very worrying first eighteen months had built up a business employing forty people and fast approaching inter-state expansion time.

With these happy thoughts in mind, Kruger, bulky, muscle-bound, ex-Marine, ex-cop (Homicide), qualified lawyer, married and divorced three times (his third wife had also split), and the boss of one of the country's fastest-expanding security agencies, whistled tunelessly whilst walking across the secure parking lot, jacket slung casually over his shoulder, to his Chevrolet Astra Van. Professionally speaking he was a very contented individual; in personal terms, though, at the age of forty-six, with three wrecked marriages behind him and no one in his life at present, he was nowhere near.

His van was a 1989 model which he'd owned from new. He also owned a Porsche and a Corvette, but preferred to drive the Chevy around the city. It gave him

26

the advantage of height, a necessity in the Miami traffic, which had been described as worse than Rome, New York or Calcutta. He swung his lightweight jacket off his shoulder and fumbled in one of the pockets for the keys as he got closer to the vehicle.

Out of the corner of his right eye, Kruger caught the shadow of movement behind another parked car. A pair of feet belonging to someone crouched down, trying to hide. Kruger's guts reacted with a little twirl. The peculiar bitter taste came into the back of his throat that was the first flush of adrenaline washing into his system.

Two possibilities immediately sprang to mind.

Robbery; or the angry husband of some client out for revenge.

The first option was the most likely. Kruger knew of two people who'd been rolled in this parking lot in the last month – even though it was advertised as *Safe 'n' Secure – 24 hours a day* and the only way in and out was through barriers and past a gatekeeper.

Well, let 'em try, Kruger thought. His eyes shone. The prospect of a tussle fired him up.

The man rose from his hiding place, brushing down his suit. His suit? Didn't look like any normal street mugger. Young. Smartly dressed. A touch of Hispanic somewhere in the blood. Could easily have been one of Kruger's own operatives. Maybe he'd simply been tying his shoe-laces and maybe Kruger was putting more into the situation than was really there.

Until Kruger saw he was wearing loafers.

Okay, maybe he'd dropped something instead? Aw, what the hell, Kruger thought. Lemme get home. He fished out the van keys and the remote alarm, pointed and pressed. The vehicle responded with a high-pitched squawk and a double flash of the indicators. He opened the driver's door, tossed his jacket across to the opposite seat.

'Hey, man,' the guy called to him.

Kruger raised his eyebrows. He was still feeling uncomfortable, but at least there had been no attempt to approach him.

'Lost ma keys, wouldya believe it? You seen any?'

'No. Sorry, pal.'

'Damn – thanks anyway.'

The brief conversation had been just enough to put Kruger offguard, keep his attention fixed for a vital few seconds and allow the guy's running partner to slip out from behind the Chevy, take two long strides so that he was directly behind Kruger and ram the muzzle of a .22 right up under his left ear.

'Hands up, fella. Put 'em on the roof of the car.'

Kruger knew he could have easily turned, swept the gun away and disarmed this man, grounded him with a blow to the neck and probably one to the chest – but the position of the first guy and his unknown abilities made Kruger wary of trying anything rash.

He dropped the keys onto the tarmac and failed to keep a sneer of self-contempt off his face for missing the second guy who must have been just as easy to spot as the first one. If he'd been switched on enough.

Getting old and stale, he thought to himself.

He laid the palms of his hands obligingly on the burning hot metal roof of the van. 'I've got sixty dollars and one credit card in my wallet,' he explained calmly. 'There's a state-of-the-art cell-tel in my jacket an' I don't carry anything more with me.' Then he thought, Shit, I hope they don't notice my watch.

It was a Rolex Oyster Day-Date Chronometer in 18-carat gold with the President bracelet. He had bought it in London on the honeymoon of his third marriage, eighteen months before. Buying it had been one of those 'Big Life Moments', or 'BLMs' as he called them. Ever since he'd been a teenager reading *National Geographic* and seeing the Rolex ads in there on the wrist of some great adventurer or explorer, he'd promised himself that

28

one day he would buy one. And when the time came, thirty years later – just as the firm was beginning to make real money – he had cherished the moment. In a grand, rather tacky gesture, he had paid hard cash. Truly a moment to remember and savour. Apart from when he made love (and sometimes even then), the Rolex had never left his wrist.

Kruger dropped his head. Looking down underneath his armpit he saw the shoes of the first guy almost directly behind him. He was puzzled for a very brief moment when he saw the shoes crease as the man stood on his tiptoes. Then, ironically, it all became clear when everything went black as a hood was thrown over his head and tightened with a drawstring around his neck.

Kruger gagged. 'What the hell . . .?' He lashed out blindly but without effect. He was punched twice in the kidneys, driving him down to his knees. A pair of hand-cuffs were ratcheted tightly on his wrists.

Once again he felt the muzzle of the revolver rammed against his head.

'You fucker – you do what we say, or we kill ya, okay? You bein' dead don't make no odds to us.' It was the first guy talking, Kruger was sure.

'Fine, fine,' Kruger growled through gritted teeth.

'Now get to yo' godamned feet.'

No one assisted him, but a few seconds later he was standing shakily. 'Now you gonna get inna the back o' yo' Chevy, okay? And we're gonna go fo' a little ride . . . and I suggests you keep it schtum, otherwise I'll gets really pissed with yo' and I'll put a few slugs inna yo' brain.'

Danny eased herself inch by glorious inch into a hot bath so full of foam and water the tub almost overflowed. She groaned with sheer ecstasy as her bottom, then her back and finally all of her, was covered. She reached for the glass of vodka on ice from the top of the loo and took a life-saving gulp, shivering as the liquid burned down to her stomach. Then she picked up a ready-lighted Benson & Hedges, put it to her lips and pulled a long, deep drag as a chaser to the spirit.

Oh God. Heaven!

A heaven which lasted approximately four minutes, curtailed by the chimes of the front-door bell.

Danny's heart dropped. She knew who it would be.

A decision had to be made tonight – one way or the other.

Kruger lost all track of his whereabouts almost as soon as the Chevy rolled out of the parking lot. He tried to keep with it for a few moments, but the pain from his kidneys distracted him. It was like someone poking a red-hot needle straight through the middle of his lower back. He'd been whacked there a few times in the past, but the effects had worn off quite quickly. Today the pain was hanging in there, making him think he might have a stone or something. Depending on the outcome of this little shake-down, which was obviously not a robbery, a visit to the doctor was only a day away.

Eventually the pain dissipated.

'Where are you taking me?' Kruger demanded.

'Shut the hell up,' one of his captors grunted and skewered the muzzle of the gun into the skin at the side of his neck.

'Okay, okay, I'll be quiet.'

Was he being kidnapped? And if he was – why? Most of his money was tied up in the business. Maybe he was being taken to be wasted somewhere. And maybe the idea that this was the work of some disgruntled husband of a client was not so far-fetched after all.

But if that was the case, why hadn't they done him in the parking lot? That would've been nice and easy. This was complicated.

No matter how many questions he asked himself, he could not work any of it out.

So here he was, bundled up like some damn amateur in the back of his own van after all he'd been through and survived in his life so far. Taken by two spunkless punks who were young enough to be his sons.

How the mighty are fallen.

The sound of the tyres on the road changed to a high-pitched hum which Kruger recognised. The van was travelling over one of the causeways which linked the city with Miami Beach, South Beach or possibly Key Biscayne.

So they were travelling east. Not that the knowledge helped Kruger in any way.

The van slowed. There was a series of twists and turns. Kruger sensed he was near to the end of his journey.

The van stopped.

He became very frightened.

His two captors manhandled him out of the back of the Chevy, pushed, prodded and almost dragged him across a gravel surface. He stumbled up a short flight of what he imagined to be concrete steps. He heard a door open and then he was inside a building, still being roughly pushed, cajoled, pulled and directed. Finally they brought him to a halt. He was told to stand still. They held onto his biceps with firm grips.

He was completely disorientated.

He had no idea where he was.

No idea why he was there. Abducted off the street like some millionaire tycoon.

He did as instructed and stood completely motionless, wrists cuffed in front of his groin. It was hot beneath the black hood, which was made from some sort of thick polythene, like a garden refuse sack. He sweated. Standing there in silence, it became even hotter, unbearable, made even worse as his imagination ran riot. He ground his teeth and dilated his nostrils whilst the tension began to build up in him like a geyser.

31

Something told him very bluntly, 'This is it, Buddy Boy. This is where you buy it. The end of the line – and you don't even know why.'

He fought hard to control his heartbeat and his bowels and prepared himself for the bullet. The third one he would have taken in his life.

The fatal one.

A female voice Kruger thought he recognised said softly, 'Handcuffs.'

His hands were bent outwards in order to get the key into the locks. The ratchets swung back, his wrists came free. In the confusion and fear of his predicament Kruger had not realised how deeply the steel rims of the cuffs had been biting into his flesh. As they were opened, the blood rushed back into his hands with a surge of pins and needles.

His biceps were still in the grip of his captors.

He became suddenly aware of someone standing very close in front of him. Very close indeed. Almost touching. He could smell a scent, a familiar perfume. Couldn't quite remember its name. He shook his head. Must be dreaming. Then he felt a hand on his chest and jumped as if he'd been electrified. The grips on his arms tightened.

The top button of his shirt was already undone. The fingers of the hand at his chest slid up to the second button and skilfully tweaked it open. Then the third and fourth. The hand slid under the shirt and rested on Kruger's left breast, playfully pinching his nipple.

. . . At which point Kruger bellowed and exploded without warning.

Almost like Samson escaping from shackles, he lifted his arms and pushed outwards at the same time, driving the back of his fists against the men on either side of him, sending them staggering away.

He ripped the hood off, ready to fight for his life.

And the nightmare continued because standing in front of him trying to control her giggling was one of the worst mistakes of his life: his third wife, stage name Felicity Snowball. Real name, Felicity Bussola. Born plain Jane Creek.

'Jesus Christ, you godamned bitch!' screamed Kruger. 'What the hell you playin' at?' He lurched towards her and grabbed her shoulders. His arm drew back and he was about to lay one of his mightiest slaps across her cheeks when for the second time that day, a gun was poked in his neck. His hand screeched to a halt in mid-arc. He allowed it to flutter down uselessly to his side.

He stood upright, breathing heavily.

'Stevie baby,' cooed Felicity. 'Baby, baby . . . you don't wanna hit your honey-pie, now do you, sweetie?'

'Yes, I do.'

The muzzle of the gun was ground into his neck.

Felicity's face became serious. ''Cos I ain't foolin' around here, Stevie. You touch me, babe, and I'll waste you.'

Kruger nodded.

The gun was withdrawn. He glanced briefly at the two men who'd brought him here and said, 'No trouble – promise.' He felt obliged to put it into plain English because if the two goons were connected to Felicity's new husband, they would have no qualms in filling him full of lead then dumping his concrete-encased body in the foundations of a new apartment block somewhere in the city.

He turned to face Felicity. 'What the hell d'you want?'

She shooed the men away. 'I'll scream if he touches me,' she told them, 'then you two boys come runnin', okay?'

When they were alone she tiptoed up to Kruger and kissed him on the lips. What began as a friendly peck suddenly developed into a passionate embrace. She ran

33

her arms around his neck, yanked him towards her, forced her tongue into his mouth and ground her hot sex into his groin.

Despite himself, he responded . . . until common sense prevailed. He eased her away.

'Hey, what about hubby? If he strolls in here, I'm dead meat.'

'Aw, fuck him,' she said dismissively.

Which was not a sentiment Kruger shared. Mario Bussola was a very feared and respected individual in Florida's low-life, widely recognised to be the number one mobster in the state following the blood-soaked demise of Tony Corelli a couple of years before, who was then tops.

Bussola, it was rumoured, had people put to death for far less contentious issues than French-kissing his wife.

Joe Lilton rolled slowly over onto his back. He held his breath and listened. Next to him in bed lay his wife, Ruth. She was breathing heavily in a very deep sleep induced by several large glasses of wine and a couple of strong sleeping pills. 'The worry's over now,' Joe had cajoled her earlier on their return from hospital. 'Claire's back home. You can relax, chill out. You deserve a good night's rest. After all, you haven't slept a wink for the last two what with worrying about Claire. Come on, off to bed now. Tomorrow we'll get everything sorted out.'

Once Ruth had supervised a hot bath for Claire, some supper and tucked her up for the night, she had been easy to manipulate by Joe. She had willingly supped the wine, almost a full bottle of Hock; easy to drink, cheap and extremely effective.

Joe had had a few stiff brandies himself, whilst acting the concerned husband and father.

When he'd suggested sleeping tablets and shown Ruth the box of Nitrazepam, there had been no resistance. She was already woozy as her jaded body had been an easy target for the alcohol.

It didn't take long for the combination to take effect. Less than fifteen minutes later, Joe steered her to bed, helped her undress and eased her under the covers. After checking the hotel and briefly chatting to the night porter, Joe had also gone to bed in the family annexe at the rear of the ground floor.

When he entered the bedroom, a bedside light was still on, but Ruth was fast asleep. Just to make certain, Joe had purposely crashed round the room, deliberately dropping things.

Ruth did not even flinch.

As he climbed in next to her, naked, Joe had smiled dangerously to himself. From past experience he knew she would be out of it for at least ten hours. Not even a bomb could have woken her. Joe had free reign.

Just to be on the safe side, he prodded her. There was no reaction. Ruth was as good as dead.

He lay by her side for a few more minutes, slightly concerned when she shifted, though all she did was flip over onto her back, mutter something incomprehensible, open her mouth and commence to snore gently.

Joe even closed her mouth with the tip of his forefinger and then let her jaw drop open again. She stayed asleep. A feeling of elation zipped through him, coupled with a tight feeling in his throat.

He reached down and grabbed his penis. It was already rock hard with expectation. He drew back the foreskin and squeezed his damp glans, drawing a stuttering breath.

Carefully he peeled the duvet off himself, and sat up on the edge of the bed. The hardness of his curved erection pressed into his stomach. He stroked the length of it proudly and caressed his balls with his fingertips.

He was feeling good. Alive. He stood up. It swayed in front of him. It was huge, throbbing urgently. She would love every painful inch of it.

He glided out of the bedroom, his feet creeping along the deep carpet. Moments later he was at the far end of the hallway outside Claire's bedroom. He pushed the door open.

Claire's teddy-bear nightlight glowed in the darkness, casting enough of a dim glow to allow Joe's eyes to see into the room. Claire's petite figure was curled up in a ball underneath the quilt. She moved when Joe opened the door, lifting her head to see.

She had not been asleep, but had been ready, waiting fearfully for this moment.

'Claire, you're awake,' Joe whispered, as if surprised. 'I was checking to see if you were okay, darling.'

'I am, so go away please.' Her voice trembled.

Joe stepped into the room, clicking the door closed behind him.

Claire stiffened and drew the cover up to her chin. Joe took two steps across the room to the bed and settled down on the edge of it. Claire emitted a little whimper of fright.

'Its okay, sweetheart,' he reassured her. He reached over and stroked her hair. 'It's okay, don't worry.' The whimper metamorphosed into a despairing groan. 'Now be quiet, honey . . . come on, don't be afraid . . . you know you like it as much as I do. Give me your hand.' She drew away from him, but he grabbed her with great strength. 'That's it, come on . . . touch me here – and don't forget, it's our little secret, so let's make sure we don't wake your mummy up.'

This was the first time Kruger had been into one of the homes Felicity shared with Bussola. It was the one on Ocean Drive, South Beach, facing the Atlantic. The other two houses were too far away for Kruger to have been driven there in such a short space of time.

Had he been less inclined towards wringing her neck, Kruger might have enjoyed the Grand Tour of the house that Felicity gave him. Impressed to see what crime could buy in terms of material possessions. As it was, the whole shooting match passed him by; even the less-than-subtle pause in one of the bedrooms when Felicity's body language screamed out the word 'screw'. When he didn't respond to the invitation she gave him a look like he was a piece of shit and carried on with the tour.

He dutifully followed, brooding intensely, aware that the two goons were lurking in the background shadows, ready to pounce should Felicity give the signal.

Eventually they sat in a huge conservatory overlooking the outdoor pool (there was an indoor one, naturally). She poured him a very colourful drink which tasted like paraffin.

'Why the hell have you dragged me out here?' he wanted to know.

'You've been avoiding me, Stevie.'

'I haven't. I've just not got round to returning your calls.'

'Same as,' she said childishly.

'And anyway, what earthly reason would I have to call you, Liss? As far as I'm aware, our marital business has been finalised. You stung me for more than you deserved, I paid up, we're even, you married Bussola.'

'Aw, it's not about money,' she said with a flutter of her hand. 'I got more money now than I ever had in my life. I'm rollin' in the stuff.'

'In that case,' Kruger cut in, not one to miss a chance, 'how 'bout giving me back that quarter of a mill your shyster lawyer screwed outta me?'

Felicity snorted dismissively. 'Spent it. Every last godamned cent – as a gesture to our short, momentarily sweet, then very sour marriage.'

'That figures,' Kruger responded with a bitter tone, recalling a marriage that had been pretty much a shambles from day one.

They had met at a point in time when both of them

had been at a low ebb in their lives. Kruger was in a deep rough patch following the disappearance of his second wife with some creep of a Disney executive in Orlando. Kruger felt he had been struck by lightning because he had been truly, madly, passionately in love with the woman, worshipped the ground she glided over, even. For all that, she had dumped him with all the ceremony of taking the trash out, leaving a gaping hole in his heart.

His response had been to throw himself into his work in a big way. Often he worked fourteen hours per day, never less than eleven. Then, because he had problems sleeping even after such exhausting hours, he found himself drifting through Miami nightlife; clubs, bars, strip-joints, often finding solace at four in the morning, clutching a half-empty bottle of bourbon.

Since the age of fourteen, Felicity had been trying to make it big as a singer. She was always on the periphery of a big break and had been the backing singer for several big acts. She had released one single which sold a couple of thousand copies before sinking without trace.

When she hit her thirties her agency dropped her like a hot fajita; it became apparent that despite her good looks and superb voice, she lacked that certain 'something' to set her apart from the crowd. And she had passed into that dangerous decade in life when women do not become stars.

She gravitated south, following club and hotel work, hit the bottle, dabbled in dope, and managed to eke out a reasonable living as a hotel singer around Miami and Ford Lauderdale. It was in a hotel in the latter town at three in the morning that she met Kruger, clinging precariously to a bar stool.

After exchanging their tales of woe, the next logical step for two lonely people was obvious. That same night they booked into a suite, ripped each other's clothes off, fell onto the bed and humped way past dawn. They emerged three days later, much the worse for wear.

A whirlwind romance followed, with little thought for future compatibility. Marriage seemed the natural progression, though each soon discovered that a relationship based solely on mutually-attracted genitalia does not make for a lasting partnership.

Living together as man and wife proved to be a horrendous experience for both.

Felicity was naturally a slob. She kept late hours, slept all day.

Kruger, on the other hand, was a well-ordered man who liked routine and tidiness. When he eventually got himself back on an even keel and out of the bottle, he realised that returning home to an apartment which looked like it had been burglarised and a wife who was still in bed – usually full of crumbs – was not what he wanted.

The disputes between them were out of this world.

Then one night Felicity was singing in a grotty hotel in Lemon City owned (although she did not know this at the time) by Mario Bussola. He happened to be in the audience and became smitten by her gravelly voice and curvaceous appearance. After her set, he summoned her to a private room and they almost immediately began an adulterous relationship; Bussola also gave her a fat contract to sing in his chain of six hotels.

She fell in love with the overweight gangster.

It was the end for her and Kruger. Though she was technically responsible for the downfall of the marriage, that didn't mean she left the relationship without a fight for a huge percentage of Kruger's stash.

Kruger wasn't sorry to see her go.

Back in the present, Kruger glanced down at his gold Rolex. With a quick grin he thought maybe he was being too harsh. A few good things had come from the brief relationship: the London honeymoon, the Rolex, the sex – which had been tremendous – and he had recovered his self-esteem.

He smiled at her and sighed. She did look good sitting there in her work-out gear, the spandex clinging tightly to the shapely outline of her body.

'So, c'mon, what's all this about? I didn't return your calls and you have me kidnapped by two extras from *Goodfellas*. It's a federal offence, honey.'

She shrugged and took a sip of her multi-coloured cocktail through a wiggly straw which looked like a piece of spaghetti. 'So go to the fibbies, ya big cry baby.'

'Liss,' Kruger said firmly, using the pet name he had always called her, 'stop assin' around and tell me what's goin' on.'

'How's business?'

'Good to booming.'

'I wanna hire you for some detective work.'

'Such as?'

'I want somebody followed – to see what they're gettin' up to.'

'Is that it?' Kruger growled. 'You drag me here for that? Why in hell didn't ya tell the fucking telephonist? She woulda sent someone round.'

'I don't just want someone, Stevie . . . I want you.'

His eyes narrowed, suspicion growing in him like a cancer. 'I'll send one of my best guys round in the morning. I don't follow people any more.'

She shook her head stubbornly. 'No, honey. I want you.'

Kruger leaned back in the cane chair. It creaked under his weight. There was the remnant of an ache in his back where he'd been punched.

'Why?'

She pouted. 'It's Mario.' Her eyelids flickered, eyes moistened. 'I think he's being unfaithful.'

Kruger staunched a belly laugh. At last – something to brighten up his day again. 'Expand.' He interlocked his fingers around a knee and bowed forwards like a counsellor whilst trying to keep a straight face.

'Oh, it's just – oh, I don't know – something, y'know? The hours he keeps, the times he doesn't come home, how we ever only seem to screw maybe once a month, if that. God, I feel so horny. I think he's got someone else, Stevie,' she concluded desperately.

'Felicity,' Kruger stated. 'Your husband, as you well know, is one of the biggest and most feared gang bosses in the United States of America. The fact that he has time to come home at all is a blessing. He's a busy guy. He's got fingers to break, debts to collect, people to blackmail and intimidate . . . and all those groupies hangin' around. It must be very tempting for him. He's only human – like you once were. And if you think he married you for any other reason than to have a good-looking woman on his arm, you're kidding yourself.'

'You're a son of a bitch, Steve,' she said tightly.

'I tell the truth, that's all. And to be completely honest with you, Liss, I hope he *is* seeing someone else. It'll teach you a lesson.'

'Our marriage was over long before I slept with Mario,' she protested.

Kruger looked at her pityingly for a few moments, tutted, slapped his thighs and said, 'Gotta go, babe.'

'I still want to hire you.'

'Naw – it's company policy not to get involved in anything which remotely stinks of the mob. Mario Bussola is very definitely mob. I don't like to find my operatives with their brains blown out, so the answer's no. Now, if you'd be kind enough to beckon your human Dobermans back here, I'd like my vehicle keys.' He stood up.

'Sit down, Steve,' she ordered him, a hard edge to her voice, an uncompromising expression on her face. Something made him obey. 'You *will* work for me – and you wanna know why? I'll tell ya – because if you don't I'll put you out of business like that.' She snapped her fingers with a crack. 'I can ruin you, Stevie babe, because I know

41

things about you, don't I? Things you would hate the Feds to know.'

A trickle of sweat rolled down the valley between Danny's breasts. Her whole body was on fire, every nerve-end tingling, overloading her with pleasure. She could feel her toes against the sheets, the skin on her inner thighs holding and moving over the skin on the outer thighs of the man underneath her. His fingers kneaded into her backside, his hands then caressed her breasts, fingering and rolling her dark, purple nipples, tugging them gently so they became long and hard. But above all she could feel every inch of him deep inside her and the growing sensation radiating out from her clitoris as she ground hard against his pubic bone.

She shuddered, threw back her head, arched her spine, rising and holding him there, the tip of his penis wedged at the entrance to her throbbing vagina. It was coming. They were coming. She could keep him positioned there and not move and know she would climax, but he was there too and she could feel he was hard and big and ready for his orgasm.

She gazed down at him. They locked eyes.

'I think you've hit the button,' she moaned.

She rammed herself down onto him at the same time as he thrust upwards and they collided in an intense, writhing, wild orgasm which seemed to go on for ever.

When it was eventually over and Danny had got her breath back, she rolled languidly off him and reached for her cigarettes on the bedside cabinet. She lit two simultaneously and handed one across. He took it gratefully from her fingers.

Danny inhaled the strong smoke deeply, held it in, then blew it slowly out. Her heart slackened its pace as the magical sensation of just having had great sex ebbed away.

'That was fantastic.'

Danny sighed. She turned to look at him, brushing her hair away from her eyes. 'I know, Jack . . . but it's going to have to stop. This can't go on. This is definitely the last time.'

Words she had said many times before.

The difference was – this time she meant them.

Felicity's mouth turned into a wicked smile of triumph. She sat back, took a long draw on her straw, and watched her ex-husband's face turn deep red.

She did not have to spell it out for him. He knew exactly what she meant. A shiver of fear rippled down his spine. He licked his dry lips.

'*Things you would hate the Feds to know.*'

The words echoed around in his head.

In truth, what she'd said was an understatement. Not only would Kruger *not* like the Feds to know, he'd be darned upset if the CIA got to know, absolutely desolate should the State Department ever find out, or for that matter any godamned person walking the streets.

What Felicity was referring to was the time when he left the cops and started out in business, and the first six months of trading were hell on earth. He struggled to make any sort of living, was on the verge of giving up and becoming a security guard in a shopping mall.

Then, out of the blue, he was approached by two different people on the same day.

One had goods to sell.

The other wanted to buy.

Knowing that no such circumstances could be purely coincidental, Kruger sussed he had been targeted because the parties obviously didn't want to be seen doing business directly with each other. They needed the buffer or an agent and Kruger, down on his luck, seemed the perfect man.

He had wrestled with his conscience, his mind in a turmoil.

It was possible he was being set up by the authorities for some reason. But if he wasn't, it was just the piece of luck he needed. One which would kick-start his business to the tune of two hundred grand in fees.

With both eyes wide open, conscious that if the deal went belly-up he would become an inmate of Dade County Correctional Institute, not just a visitor, he took the chance.

He arranged to sell over two million dollars' worth of 18-inch electric shock batons to a Middle Eastern buyer, knowing full well the end user was Iraq. Which, twelve months after the Gulf War, was a very naughty thing to do.

Although he lived on a wire for several months after, there were no repercussions. No midnight raids by SWAT squads. No visits by men in black suits. Nothing. The surge of money was accounted for creatively and Kruger's business went through the roof. He had never since, to his knowledge, made any illegal deals.

All was well.

Until now.

Felicity, his ruthless, unfaithful ex-wife, had plucked it right out of the mist and slapped it across his face like a wet fish.

Kruger rubbed his eyes. His knee began to ache. He recalled telling Felicity the story of his dubious deal one night early in their relationship, in the days when he confused lust with love. He had vowed her to secrecy. She had, of course, promised silence. Damn pillowtalk, he thought bitterly. It always ends up biting your ass.

'What d'you want me to do?' he asked with an expression of resignation on his countenance.

Danny looked directly into the eyes of Detective Inspector Jack Sands, the man who was her boss. The man who had become her lover.

'No, Jack, I really mean it this time. There's no future

for either of us in this . . . unless you leave your wife, that is. You know how many times you've promised to do that and never kept your word.' Her voice was shaking with emotion as she spoke, delivering a speech she had practised over and over again in the last few days, but which at that moment she struggled to remember. 'You'll never leave her, will you? I accept that now and that's why this has to stop. Now. Whilst no one else knows, whilst we're still in a position not to hurt people.'

Sands stared blankly at her. Then he blinked rapidly as the meaning of the words sank in. As she finished, he sighed and closed his eyes. 'But Danny, I love you,' he pleaded pitifully. 'It's just the kids . . . you know? I can't walk out on them.'

'In that case, you obviously don't love me,' Danny retorted rather cruelly. In truth she did not want to wreck a marriage, though on the other hand she thought she loved Sands deeply. It was a love that was tearing her apart. She knew it had to end now, once and for all. That was the best way for both of them. To be able to leave the relationship with some dignity, try to be adult about it, part as friends if that was possible in the circumstances. 'So get dressed and go, please, Jack. It's got to end now. It's as good a time as any, with me getting promoted next week. We won't be under each other's feet all the time, won't be in adjoining offices, won't be able to look at each other all day, every day.'

She clenched her teeth and hardened her jawline, feeling absolutely gutted by what she was doing.

'But . . .'

'No! Just get up and go,' she said sternly. 'It's over. Accept it and then we can both get on with our lives.'

Sands dressed silently and very, very slowly whilst Danny stood in one corner of the room in her dressing gown, cigarette in hand. It was all she could do to prevent herself grabbing him and dragging him back into bed.

45

Dressed, he paused at the bedroom door, gazed back at her.

She looked down at her fingernails, refusing to meet his eyes. That would have snapped her resolve in a second.

Jack closed the door softly.

Danny heard his footsteps descending the stairs. The front door opened and closed.

She broke down and wept.

And not many miles away, in a tiny bedroom in a sea-front hotel in South Shore, another female cried quietly to herself, but for a completely different reason.

Claire Lilton was folded up into a tight ball, her arms hugging her knees, nightdress pulled securely around her. She rocked herself with the steady motion of a disturbed person. She had once seen Polar Bears in a zoo, not long ago on a school trip. She had watched one of the huge great beasts rock backwards and forwards whilst it stood there, trapped in its tiny enclosure. She had looked on in empathy because all she could think was, That's me. That's just me. Rocking, and can't get away.

God, how she hated the man. The stepfather who abused her right under her mother's nose since coming into their lives two years before. The man her mother loved so much, who could do no wrong in her eyes. The bastard, the fucking two-faced bastard. Claire's mother would never have believed it, even if she'd been told right to her face that her stepdad was doing things to her, making her do things to him, forcing himself into her until he jizzed, sometimes up her bum. Claire didn't even know the words for some of the things he did to her, but she knew she was being 'shagged' because she had heard other, older girls talking about it, describing it. Saying how some of the lads did it to them.

But not their fathers.

Claire stopped rocking. Her eyes stared into the darkness. The rain beat down against her window.

46

She also knew enough to understand she might have a baby – because that was how people got babies, by shagging – especially now she had started her periods.

The thought terrified her.

But what frightened her even more was the threat that, should she ever tell anybody – *anybody* – her stepdad would kill her.

Chapter Three

Trent was awake long before the cell lights flickered on the following morning. He had watched the darkness of the night slowly fade to the dull greyness of dawn and eventually the brightness of day. He saw these changes take place through his cell window from 4 a.m. onwards, lying there on his bunk with his hands clasped behind his head.

His mind was very clear by the time the key turned in the lock and the screws barked to the residents that the new day had dawned.

Trent had reached two conclusions.

The first was that if he stayed in prison, whichever prison it happened to be, this or any other, he would continue to suffer at the hands of mad bastards like Blake and his cronies. His miserable life would be continually made worse. Therefore, in order to make his existence more tolerable, Trent knew he had to do something to make everyone acknowledge he could not be messed about with.

The second was that he'd had enough of being in prison. He promised himself that if the opportunity ever presented itself, he would escape. He needed to do this because he had vowed to bring retribution to the people responsible for putting him in here. There was no way he could even out that score with another eight years still to serve.

The sooner the better for both ideas.

And, Trent thought as the cell door was pushed open, if the two could be combined . . .

The sea, the sex and the emotional turmoil of the day before had taken its toll on Danny Furness. She managed to rise at eight and slope into the shower, but hardly had the strength to dry herself, put on her make-up to the usual high standard and then eat breakfast. She did all three in a state of extreme lethargy.

She drove into work with a jittery feeling in her belly. There were several busy days to go before her promotion and transfer to the CID, which meant it would be impossible to avoid Jack who, if he so chose, could make life very uncomfortable for her.

She hoped he would be okay about the split. She knew, however, he had a stubborn, sometimes nasty streak to his nature. A smooth ride was not a foregone conclusion . . .

. . .which was confirmed with a vengeance when she drove into the police station yard, found a parking space in the covered car park and spotted Sands in her rearview mirror just before she was about to get out of the car. He must have been lurking in the shadows, waiting for her to arrive. She snarled and swore under her breath. He wasn't even giving her the chance to get into the office, for God's sake!

She pounded the steering-wheel in frustration, got a grip on herself and clambered slowly out of the Mercedes, mentally preparing herself for an unpleasant encounter.

Sands stalked up to her, positioning himself between her car and the next one along, effectively blocking Danny's path.

He looked far worse than Danny had ever seen him. His eyes were sunk in their sockets. His skin hung loosely off his cheekbones as though he'd lost weight overnight. His hair was in disarray, his suit crumpled as if he'd slept in it, which he probably had. He was a million light years distant from the normally immaculate Jack Sands, dapper Detective Inspector.

For a fleeting moment Danny's heart reached out to him. She had an urge to hug and squeeze him, tell him she was wrong, that everything was hunky-dory, that yes, she'd continue to be the other woman. The one he visited twice a week for sex – if he had time; the one who waited stupidly for his call, the one madly in love with him, dreaming of being his wife yet knowing for sure she never would be.

The moment whizzed by and Danny found her will-power. Being on the pointed end of the eternal triangle was not going to be her future. Once again, she looked coldly at him.

'Danny,' he gasped, the smell of stale intoxicants on his breath, 'don't do this to me.'

She shook her head. 'No, Jack – don't do this to *me*. Let me pass.'

He drew himself up to his full height, almost six-three. He was a big, powerful man. Danny saw a look come into his eyes which made her shiver. That of a desperate man, capable of anything.

Suddenly she felt queasy. Her legs almost buckled.

'Jack, it's over. I'm sorry, but it's best for both of us.' She tried to sound reasonable. She ducked to one side and made to walk through the narrow gap between Sands and her car.

His arm shot out, preventing her passing. He side-stepped smartly to block her with his body.

'No,' he croaked. He was on the verge of either tears or hysteria. 'It's not over. Not unless I say it's over. I love you, Danny. You can't just end it like this. I need you.'

'More than you need your wife?' she rejoined bitterly.

'I've told you why I can't leave her,' he hissed.

'Then it is over, isn't it? Don't be a fool. Let me pass. We both have work to do. This is just silly.'

51

They were the wrong words to say. Some inner demon overtook Sands as these last words left Danny's mouth. He seized her coat by the lapels and rammed her painfully back against the Mercedes as though she was a prisoner he was trying to subdue.

Danny's literal knee-jerk reaction floored him. He emitted a howl and doubled over. His hands shot down to nurse his groin. Danny pushed past and walked smartly away whilst he supported himself on the boot of her car with one hand, the other gingerly massaging his balls.

Then he spoke the words, which for Danny, finally nailed the coffin lid on their relationship.

'You fucking bitch!'

As the day wore on, Trent's thoughts about combining an escape from prison with a revenge attack on Blake became all-consuming. He could think of nothing else. Escape and revenge, escape, revenge.

But how, he wondered.

As he strolled around the prison, ignored by virtually everyone, a few ideas seemed to slot into place as he thought long and hard about the problem.

Blake and his two colleagues had blighted Trent's life ever since their arrival as inmates eighteen months earlier; they had done the same to every other sex-offender in the place. They had systematically rooted out all the 'pervs', as they referred to them, and made their whole existence a misery on a grand scale.

For some solace, and so they could exchange information on Blake's intentions and movements, the pervs banded together. About eight of them formed a sort of club, though Trent tended to keep his distance from them. Apart from holding them in a kind of contempt, he didn't want to be seen to be too pally with them because he actually felt superior.

But that morning, Trent purposely sought one of them out – an insipid worm of a man who had been convicted of a series of indecent assaults on boys in the local authority children's home where he was Head Warden – and the deaths of two of them. His name was Victor Wallwork.

Trent found him sitting alone at breakfast, shunned by the other inmates who were eating at that time. He sat down next to him and spooned sugar into the grey, lifeless porridge in the bowl in front of him. It looked more like wet cement than food.

Wallwork did not acknowledge Trent. He munched toast, slurped loudly out of a mug of tea, his unfocused eyes stuck somewhere in the middle distance.

Between mouthfuls of his own stodge, Trent said through the side of his mouth; 'They got me last night, the bastards. Blake and his crew. Bastards!' He spat out the last word.

'I know,' grunted Wallwork. He shifted uncomfortably on his chair.

'You next,' Trent informed him casually.

Wallwork choked on his tea and toast. He broke into a paroxysm of coughing and spluttering whilst he tried to clear his throat. He turned to face Trent. At the best of times Wallwork's face had a deathly-grey pallor. Now, what blood there was had seeped away into his boots, leaving him ashen-white.

'True. I heard 'em talking after,' Trent whispered. 'I heard your name. "Gonna get some of his own medicine" I heard 'em say. Mentioned your name, Vic.'

Wallwork could not even get his mouth to form and project a single word. His lips opened and closed a few times, making a popping sound like a fish out of water.

'They buggered me until I bled,' Trent continued, laying it on thick.

'When?' Wallwork managed to croak. 'When will they come after me?'

Trent shrugged. 'Could be any time. Suddenly they'll be there.'

Wallwork closed his eyes hopelessly.

'We need to fight back,' Trent said. 'We need to make a stand, otherwise our lives won't be worth shite.'

Wallwork snorted derisively, but there was a touch of hysteria in his voice. 'Yeah, like sure. They'd kill us if we did anything.'

'Are you at the farm today?'

'Yeah, why? What's that got to do with it?'

'Plenty.' Trent sounded mysterious. He laid his spoon down, turned his face close to Wallwork's and lowered his voice a couple of degrees to no more than a hoarse whisper. 'We need to sort those bastards out once and for all and you can help me by bringing something back with you.'

'Oh, like a pitchfork, you mean? Don't be stupid. We get searched going out and coming back. I don't want to lose my privileges by being caught with something I shouldn't have.'

'You'd rather have eight inches up your arse, would you? Probably followed by a broom-handle?' Trent's voice grated ferociously. ''Cos I'll tell you now – it hurts. It fucking hurts. If you want to do anything about them, you'll find a way of bringing what I want back in . . . won't you?'

Danny was tied up that morning with the bane which afflicts all police officers: paperwork.

For once, though, she was uncomplaining about it, kept her head down and tried not to look up when Sands came into the office for any reason. Out of the periphery of her vision she couldn't help but notice him banging about, making everyone else's life a misery. However, he studiously ignored her, for which she was grateful.

She guessed he might try to tag onto her at lunch, so when the chance came and he was otherwise engaged, she slipped out of the office and made her way to the canteen where she collected a sandwich and sat down opposite the

54

man who was destined to be her next boss, Detective Inspector Henry Christie.

'I heard about your problems yesterday,' Henry said to her, partway through the meal. He was eating a light salad. It looked like he was on a diet.

Briefly Danny was puzzled. How on earth did he know about Sands? Then it dawned on her. He was referring to Claire Lilton.

'Oh yeah. Little cow.'

'You did well. You deserve a commend,' Henry said genuinely. 'I hear some poor sod got blown off the prom in Morecambe, so you were lucky.'

'I should've let her drown.'

Henry laughed, changed the subject. 'So – next Monday? You'll be with us?'

'Can't come quick enough. Really looking forward to it,' Danny said with sweet expectancy. Working for Henry Christie, it was said, was a great pleasure. She knew his CID team was well-motivated and got results. She was eager to be a part of it.

She bit into her tuna-mayo sandwich – granary bread, no butter or margarine, no salt, light mayo. Having her back to one of the canteen doors meant she didn't notice him come into the room so it was consequently a surprise when Jack Sands sat down next to Henry, bearing a plate of spaghetti bolognese. He glared at her and his expression morphed into an evil smile. She attempted to respond with a pleasant greeting but it stuck somewhere in her throat.

Henry glanced quickly between the two of them. He immediately picked up the tension. It was like a crackle of static. His brow creased. Something was not quite right, the vibes informed him.

He nodded at Sands and they fell into an easy conversation to which Danny strenuously declined to contribute.

The phone on the other side of the room rang and was answered by an officer nearby. He clamped his hand across the mouthpiece and called across: 'Danny – for you.' He held up the phone.

She couldn't have left her seat any faster, Henry noted.

Danny took the call, hung up and returned to the table where she collected her shoulder bag. 'Someone at the desk to see me.'

Henry watched her leave, then glanced sideways at Sands whose eyes fixed on the door she had gone through, like he was in some sort of trance. His face had become hard and angry.

Henry speculated whether the rumours were true about Sands and Danny having a 'liaison'. Maybe they'd just had some sort of lovers' tiff, he thought.

Trent's next target was another member of the small clique of sex-offenders, a man called Coysh who had been virtually conscripted by Blake to be a manservant for him and his team. Coysh had willingly accepted this role of 'fetch-me, carry-me' because it kept him reasonably safe from the gang rapes organised by Blake. Even so, he had been subjected to a couple to keep him in his place and he was often ritually humiliated by Blake. Just for sport.

Trent went to Coysh for two reasons.

Firstly he worked in the kitchens and secondly he was generally up to date with Blake's whereabouts – knowledge Trent would need in the near future.

They were out in the sunshine of the exercise yard when Trent accosted Coysh.

They conversed as they walked around. Coysh nodded at Trent's requests. Easy – on both counts.

A couple of minutes later they parted.

Trent smiled. It was coming together quite nicely.

Danny was relieved to get away.

Once outside the canteen she breathed deeply, thanked God for the phone call and tried to stop herself shaking.

She did not bother to wait for the lift because sometimes it took ages to arrive and the last thing she wanted was to step into it and turn to find Jack behind her, trapping her.

Instead she chose the stairs, trotting quickly down them to first-floor level where she headed for the back of the enquiry desk.

'Hiya, Danny,' the public enquiry assistant said. 'It's that Claire Lilton waiting for you. She's in the foyer.'

'Cheers.' Danny walked out through the security doors, into the waiting area. Unusually it was completely empty.

Claire Lilton had vanished.

Trent spent the remainder of his afternoon engaged in trading his stash of cash, sweets, cigarettes and cannabis around the prison.

He knew he could easily have approached one single person – a guy called Connor, the most powerful drugs dealer in the institution – to get what he wanted, but a one-stop strategy wasn't in line with his plans. He considered it more important to get around as many people as possible, act manically depressed following last night's violent rape, and even mention the word 'suicide' a few times. That way as many people as possible knew of his intentions. He knew that in a short space of time the word would spread up to the screws who, he knew, would do nothing. Not that he cared. He wanted them to do nothing. Just to know.

By tea-time, Trent had bought enough tablets to kill an elephant, never mind a human being.

He inserted them one at a time into the hole in the waistband of his jeans. Towards the end of this process he had to push quite hard to get them in. He counted 162 assorted tablets, many of indeterminate origin.

The offices of Kruger Investigations were situated on the seventeenth floor of an office block in downtown Miami. This was the fourth relocation of the business which had begun its existence in a one-roomed grot-office above a rent-a-car place in Wynwood, north Miami. Each move had been to a larger premises, but never quite large enough to house the ever-expanding business. Finally Kruger had decided on impulse to take the whole floor of the current premises some two years earlier. It had proved to be a good move but once again, business had boomed to fit the available space. Another move was imminent, something in the business plan for the next year. He hoped to be able to take some space in the floor above as the company installed at present looked as though they were going bust. The only drawback to the place was the lack of spaces available in the underground parking facility, which was presently hogged by the finance company on the first two floors.

At midday Steve Kruger walked nonchalantly around the various offices, chatting to staff and laughing whilst munching a baguette packed with beef and sipping a Diet Coke.

He was pleased to see there were only a couple of people sitting around in the department which conducted what he termed 'real investigations'. This meant they were busy on the streets, following adulterers, compiling reports for insurance companies, and doing all the stuff connected to real detective work. The department dealing with the recapture of bail jumpers was also sparsely populated too, indicating that a few unfortunates would be in the custody of the courts that night.

The offices which were busy were the ones dealing with the sales of specialist security equipment. Kruger sold anything connected with bomb disposal and search equipment, any sort of kit – excluding firearms – for police and special forces, surveillance and counter-surveillance, communications, personal and property protection.

On being invalided out of the cops, Kruger had originally intended to set up a one-man operation. Having been introduced at an early stage to the scope and potential profits associated with security and surveillance (albeit illegal) he decided to move forwards in two directions – the private investigations side and the security side.

Although the detective side was moderately profitable, its drawback was it was manpower intensive. The sales side, however, only needed a bank of phones, faxes, e-mail facilities and a nucleus of highly trained sales executives to bring in millions for very little effort. It was also fairly safe, whereas there was always some danger associated with being a detective.

Having been a cop, Steve loved that side of the business because it was in his blood and he would never downsize it. Besides anything else, it enhanced the reputation of the firm and kept him in good with the local cops and Feds.

He finished his Coke and sandwich, ditching the bottle and wrapper in a trash can. He nipped into a restroom, freshened up. Then he made his way to the conference room where three people waited for him. Not impatiently, just talking quietly to themselves.

Kruger entered and seated himself at the circular table. They shut up.

'Mario Bussola,' he announced, instantly getting their full attention.

Trent queued up for his evening meal, plastic tray in one hand, plastic cutlery in the other. Coysh was serving. He paid Trent no more heed than any other inmate, slopping the watery food onto his plate and handing it across the hatch with no more than the merest of nods.

Trent collected his chocolate pudding and mug of tea, then wandered to a dining table where some others were eating. He wanted to be in a crowd. He slid the plate off the tray, placed it on the table and surreptitiously removed the four-inch kitchen knife Coysh had loosely taped to the underside of the plate. He looked around cautiously, relieved no one seemed to be taking any notice of him. The two screws on duty in the dining hall were having an animated conversation with a couple of old lags, probably about football. None of his fellow inmates were remotely interested in him. This was not unusual because few people actually ever spoke to him, a manifestation of the low regard in which he was held in the prison hierarchy.

He ate with his usual lack of gusto, leaning on the table with one elbow, forking the food into his mouth. His other hand rested on his thigh, fingers touching the slim blade. One edge of it was serrated, as he had requested. With his index finger he touched the tip of the knife. It was sharp. He pushed the pad of his fingertip harder down, almost to the point where he was about to draw blood. He stopped before this happened. Yes, it was sharp. It was only a small knife, but if used swiftly, accurately, it would be deadly.

Trent quivered with pleasure. He grasped the blade in his fist and held it tightly, knowing that if he drew his hand upwards very quickly, the blade would slice the palm of his hand wide open.

It was an ideal weapon.

Coysh had done good.

Trent put another unappetising forkful of corned-beef hash into his mouth. He glanced triumphantly around the dining room as he ate it.

Using only one hand, Trent eased the knife inch by inch up his sleeve and placed his watch strap over the blade to keep it in place.

He continued to eat his meal, feeling very, very happy. So happy in fact he rocked on his chair, but not so much that people might see him. After all, he was suicidally depressed and people like that don't go about with stupid grins on their faces.

After returning his empty plate and plastic cutlery to

the appropriate pile and bucket, he nodded discreetly to Coysh who was now eating his own meal and wandered back to his cell. He tried to look as though he might kill himself at any moment.

His pillow was foam-filled. He had prepared a hole in the foam into which the knife slotted perfectly. He bunged some foam back into the hole to plug it and slid the pillowcase back over. It was, he believed, good enough to withstand a cursory check by a screw.

Bursting with happiness, Trent sat on the bed and delved into his pile of magazines. He picked one called *Girl Power* which was aimed at thirteen- to sixteen-year-old girls – a little old for his tastes, but beggars couldn't be choosers. It was full of photos of young girls and often contained articles about sex, some of which had caused uproar in the national press for their explicitness. Trent settled back to read about fellatio, dreaming that very soon this would be a reality for him.

One of Kruger's company directors was a woman called Myrna Rosza. She was a trained lawyer, but Kruger had known her originally as an FBI agent. He had offered her a job once Kruger Investigations got kick-started and she had grabbed it with both hands, having had her fill of endless FBI bureaucracy. She was black, in her early forties, married to a surgeon, no kids. She was also wiltingly beautiful and possessed more assertiveness than all Kruger's employees put together. She was his conscience and wasn't frightened of saying no to him.

Kruger paused.

He had told the three members of the board his story, obviously leaving out certain elements, and knew he had them eating out of his hand – emotionally, if not intellectually . . . with one exception. The fly in the ointment, he noted glumly as his and Myrna's eyes fused across the table.

'No,' she said stubbornly. Her perfect mouth pursed

61

into a little 'o'. Kruger had often thought he could have kissed that mouth. Right at that moment he would have preferred to drive his fist into it.

And with that single word, Kruger saw she had unleashed everyone else from his spell. He cursed her big brown eyes.

Although technically he could have made any damned decision he wanted – after all, it was his company – the reality was that he needed the backing of the board on any controversial issues. Which is what this was.

'We have agreed time and time again that we will never become involved in any way in any sort of investigation or work which smells remotely of the mob. And Steve,' Myrna said patronisingly, 'you of all people should know why.'

Kruger winced. The memory of the slug tearing into his thigh just above his right knee jolted him vividly. Yes, he should know why – because he almost got himself killed once over. But he had good reason for going against company policy on this one.

'I understand what you're saying, honey,' Kruger responded, 'but we're talking about my ex-wife here, a woman I still have deep feelings for.'

'Not what you once told me,' Myrna rumbled.

'Well, I do – and when I saw her yesterday I realised I'd been hiding those feelings from myself.' Kruger reddened, feeling idiotic, saying words which were a complete lie. 'I figured that if we do a good job and find Bussola cheatin' on her, she might just come back to me.' He almost choked to death on the words, but kept a straight face.

'So, for the sake of your ex-wife,' Myrna said, outraged, 'you're suggestin' we mount a surveillance on a mobster, when even the joint forces of the Feds, local cops, DEA and AFT haven't managed to sniff him out, despite their resources?' She looked around at each of the board members. 'I suggest we all say no.' There was a general nodding of heads, though no one made direct eye contact with Kruger who was, after all, the boss man. 'Bussola is a dangerous guy,' Myrna boomed in conclusion. 'If he finds out we're tailing him, he'll react in his usual way. I don't believe any of our operatives should be put into such danger.'

Kruger leaned forwards. His face was thunderous.

'Okay, okay,' he breathed angrily. 'I won't overrule you, though I really want to, but I will tell you something you should know.' He took a deep breath, wondering how he should phrase the bombshell. 'If we don't take on this assignment – and this is the truth – everyone in this room, everybody sat out there in those offices, every one of our teams out on the streets will be out of a job tomorrow.'

Trent was disturbed a short time later by Coysh who was wearing a loose-fitting blouson jacket zipped up to the neck. He was holding the hem tightly. He stepped into Trent's cell, found him to be alone and unzipped the jacket. Almost a hundred styrofoam cups fell out onto the floor. He emptied all his pockets and produced another fifteen, crushed and broken.

Trent gathered them up delightedly and began to stuff them underneath his mattress.

'I'll probably need another load – maybe more,' he told Coysh. 'Can you do it?'

Coysh nodded but eyed Trent uncertainly. 'What d'you want them for?' He was completely befuddled. 'I thought you wanted to sort Blake out, not give him a tea party.'

'I do – and I will. You'll see.'

'What, with styrofoam cups?'

Trent winked. 'Method in my madness. Now, there is something else you can do for me . . .'

'You bastard, Steve Kruger.'

Myrna's countenance was set hard as granite as she faced him across the office. The others had left, cowed by

Kruger's shock announcement and the brief conversation afterwards. Myrna wasn't to be railroaded though. When they were alone together she powered into him like a prize-fighter.

'You cannot make a statement like that, then say no more, refuse to give us the "why". That's treatin' us all like imbeciles, Steve. How in hell are we even supposed to believe a word of what you said – that we'd all lose our jobs? It's preposterous.'

She was a very fine-looking woman, Kruger had to admit. Standing there in front of him, hands on hips, feet shoulder-width apart, she was pretty darn intimidating. He weakened for a moment, then rallied.

'Myrna, I'm not lyin' to you.' He sat down heavily on a chair and his head dropped into his hands. He blew a farting noise into his palms, then looked up at her, allowing his fingers to stretch his facial features. 'But you were right about one thing . . . Felicity does absolutely nothing for me. I hate the goddamned sight of her. I definitely do not harbour any affection for her.'

'Thought not.' Myrna's voice held a wisp of triumph. 'So what then, what's this all about?'

Kruger snorted a short laugh.

'She's got a hold on me, Myrna. Something stupid I did a few years ago, something so completely idiotic you wouldn't believe it.' He closed his eyes. 'Damn . . . and I think she's got the paperwork to prove it.'

'Tell me – now,' Myrna insisted.

He made the decision to admit to only the second person in his life about the illicit weapon-dealing which had provided the foundations on which the successful enterprise known as Kruger Investigations had been constructed.

Trent was in the TV lounge watching a documentary about the fire brigade, unable to keep a smirk off his face. A couple of other inmates were in the room but the majority of the others were packed into the main association room where a big-screen TV had been erected and onto which a satellite beamed a live Manchester United game. Trent could hear 'ooh's' and 'ahh's'.

Vic Wallwork sauntered in, looking ill and as worried as ever. He sat next to Trent. They ignored each other for a few minutes as the firefighters on TV tackled a very nasty blaze by which several people were trapped.

When everyone was rescued – to an appropriate but unconnected cheer from the football audience – Trent said, 'Well?'

'Yeah, done it. But never again, never a-fuckin-gain.'

'How much?'

'Just what you ordered.'

'Well done, Vic.'

'When are they gonna get me, Trent?'

'I don't exactly know, but if I were you, Vic, I'd keep my arse right up against the wall . . . not that that'll help, you understand, because they'll still fuck you.'

Danny's day concluded about seven that evening.

After having put the puzzlement of Claire Lilton's disappearance out of her mind, she spent most of the afternoon interviewing a young lad who had been the subject of repeated indecent assaults and buggery by the head teacher of the primary school he attended. It proved to be a pretty harrowing afternoon, made all the more difficult because the boy was only six. Whilst interviewing him Danny felt like a fraud for thinking she had problems. At least they were solvable . . . but the youngster, unless he was something very special indeed, had a lifetime of nightmares ahead as well as medical problems. Danny's predicament melted into insignificance.

In the end she obtained a first-class video statement which would hopefully get the teacher put away for many years.

Her brain was the texture of cottonwool balls when she

rode down in the lift and walked out into the rear yard of the police station. Night had fallen early, rain was splattering down and it was dark even though the yard was illuminated by electric lights. It became even darker as she walked into the covered area where the car was parked.

She swore to herself.

It was only at that moment she remembered Jack Sands and the little episode from the morning. She realised as she approached her car that she had not taken any precautions against the possibility of a repeat confrontation.

Even though she was in a police car park, it was poorly lit, she was alone and feeling vulnerable. No one was around to hear her screams.

The hairs on the back of her neck prickled. A tight feeling, as if her skin had been super-frozen, spread across her face.

Suddenly she was on guard, holding her breath.

Every shadow was Jack Sands, waiting to pounce.

Her trembling hand snaked into her bag. Her fingers sought, fought and withdrew the remote locking control and keys for her car.

She quickened her step . . . and of course she had parked at the far end of the car park.

In a matter of seconds she had reached the rear of her car – safely. Then she was inside the car, slamming the door, desperate to slide the key into the ignition. She was okay. She had made it. She giggled a little at her stupidity.

The key went in . . . and her door was yanked open. Sands reached in, grabbed her and dragged her out in a split second before she could react. He dumped her onto the concrete and the base of her spine crashed on the hard surface, sending a shock wave up to her cranium.

She opened her mouth to scream – but Sands was quickly on top of her, hand clasped over her mouth, forcing her back, smashing her head against the ground. He pinned her down and straddled her chest.

'Bitch. Don't ever think I'll let you get away with kneeing me in the balls.'

He struck her open-handed across the cheek as hard as he could, whipping her face sideways.

Then, miraculously, his weight was lifted from her chest and he seemed to be flying through the air in a flurry of limbs.

Quickly Danny got to her knees, spun round, saw it was Henry Christie who had pulled Sands off, but that now Sands had recovered, gained the upper hand and was laying into Henry, pummelling him with a series of blows. Henry defended himself like a boxer, hands protecting his head, forearms his chest. He rolled with the onslaught, saw a minute gap and launched a rock-hard fist onto the point of Sands's chin. His head jerked right back on impact.

The blow knocked him stone cold. His legs crumpled underneath him like a drunken man. He went down with a groan and a thud.

'Damn!' yelled Henry, rubbing the knuckles of his fist, doing a little jig. It felt as though the cap of the knuckle had been dislodged. 'Yow! That effin' hurts.'

Danny got to her feet. Her lower spine throbbed painfully. Her face was smarting and she could feel a lump growing like a tumour on the back of her head. She stared speechless at her stunned ex-lover who was squirming around on the floor, then looked at Henry.

'You okay?' he asked.

She nodded dumbly, muttered a thanks of sorts.

'No probs. Look, you go home. I'll deal with Jack. If you need to talk, we'll talk – later.'

'Yeah . . . yep,' she said unsurely, still dazed. She rolled back into her car and started the engine.

Henry took hold of Sands's lapels and heaved him out of the path of her rear wheels.

Seconds later she was gone, leaving Henry with a fast-recovering Detective Inspector Sands who had a good bit of explaining to do.

Chapter Four

Steve Kruger fidgeted, trying to make the radio harness a little more comfortable beneath his armpit. Though allegedly 'body moulded' and well hidden by his jacket, it was tight and unwieldy, as though he were carrying a set of books. It was a psychological problem Kruger had always had on surveillance, right back to his undercover cop days; he always thought that the equipment would be completely obvious to the public and constantly expected to be approached and exposed.

He had begun to sweat already.

Myrna came into the office wearing a smart, stylish suit in beige with a very short skirt displaying her excellent legs. She had been in the ladies' restroom fitting her radio harness underneath her blouse, next to her skin. Kruger peered at her chest – for professional reasons, obviously – and was relieved to find he could not detect any bulges there other than legitimate ones.

She executed a pirouette for him.

'Can't see a thing,' he admitted.

He slid the miniature encrypted radio into the pouch, then threaded the fine wire of the press-to-talk button down his sleeve and into the palm of his left hand. He secured it with flesh-coloured Band Aid, adjusting it minutely so he could grip it and comfortably press the button with his thumb. A wire-free earpiece was already implanted in his ear and a microphone – doubling as a tie pin – was pinned to his tie. In order to transmit he had to talk down to his chest without falling into the trap of mumbling his words.

He stood to attention and tugged down the hem of his jacket. He cocked his head at Myrna.

'Obviously I can see the bulge when you do that,' she said witheringly.

Kruger let go. The jacket bounced back to its normal shape.

'That's better.'

He picked up the pistol from his desk top – a Sig Sauer P230 in .765 Browning calibre, the standard blue-black version with an eight-round magazine capacity. It was the gun all his operatives were issued with whenever necessary, and had been chosen by Kruger following his Army and police experience. A lightweight weapon, rugged and very simple to handle and a good size for concealed carrying.

He clicked the magazine out, emptied and re-loaded it so he was satisfied. After slotting the mag back into the butt, he placed the gun into the holster on his belt at the small of his back. Another piece of equipment hopefully hidden by his jacket.

Myrna had done exactly the same.

She smiled at him.

'Sorry about all this,' he said with a pathetic shrug.

'We all make mistakes. Let's just hope this puts yours behind us all.'

There was a light knock on the door. The three other members of that night's team sauntered confidently into the room.

There were the two brothers, Jimmy and Dale Armstrong – two ex-cops with a lot of SWAT and undercover experience behind them. Then there was Kelly Marks, former employee of Bell in the area of Communications Engineering. All three had been fully briefed.

They were bang on time. Kruger greeted them warmly. They had been approached for their expertise and trustworthiness . . . and, of course, they were volunteers because Kruger would not make anyone act against Bussola against their will.

'Ev'rybody a-rarin'?' Kruger asked.

He received assent from all.

'Let's go then,' he said.

Danny stirred uncomfortably in her double bed.

She had been there six hours, had trouble getting to sleep initially, and once there, had problems remaining. She tossed and rolled, sweating uncomfortably into the pillow and duvet. Too hot, then too cold. Never in quite the most comfortable of positions.

She was feeling sore from her encounter with Sands. Physically and mentally.

Her face smarted from the open-hander he had given her. The blow the base of her spine received when he'd dropped her onto the ground had jarred the whole of her body and her lumber region throbbed. The bump on the back of her head had transformed into a tender swelling the size of a ping-pong ball and was giving her a roaring headache despite the Anadin.

And she was angry – deep down and all over. Why had she let herself get taken by surprise like that! She should have known what a sneaky, low-down bastard Sands could be – after all, hadn't he been having an adulterous affair for several months? And why hadn't she fought back? She was perfectly capable of it. And now, damnit, she was indebted to Henry Christie. For God's sake, she could fight her own battles, didn't need a man to come to her rescue.

Danny sighed as she remembered the heavy figure of Sands straddling her and admitted to herself that she had been well and truly beaten. It was a good job Henry *had* come along, but (and here she thumped her pillow with frustration), she did not want to be beholden to anyone, let alone a man, even if he was a nice guy. The frustration

71

turned to a giggle as she pictured Henry dancing about, holding his sore fist . . . and then the laugh faded. A feeling of dread seeped into the pit of her stomach when she recalled Sands's body out cold on the garage floor . . . and she knew it wasn't over.

She rubbed her eyes, squinted at the digital alarm clock. 4.03, the green figures informed her. Time to get up in just over three hours' time.

She cursed, gingerly resettled herself in the bed, eyes wide open, all senses switched on full blast.

'Sleep . . . sleep . . . deep sleep,' she willed herself rhythmically.

From outside she heard a noise which sent a shock right through her. A kind of scraping that put her teeth on edge. Metal on metal. Then a cracking, snapping sound, like a dry twig being broken in two.

She listened hard. Her body tensed up.

Silence.

She relaxed, breathed out, certain she was hearing things that were not there.

It came again, the scraping.

She flung back the duvet and shot out of bed in an instant, crossing the room, drawing the curtain back just far enough to see out. Her car was parked in the short driveway in front of her house, partly obscured by a tree in the garden.

She put a hand over her eyes to eliminate the glare from the nearby street lamp.

Nothing. No movement. Bugger all.

Just imagination. Or cats screwing.

She uttered an expletive, let the curtain fall back, trotted to the loo, then dropped wearily back into bed.

At 4.10 she closed her eyes and was immediately asleep.

At 4.11 a full house brick, expertly aimed, exploded through her bedroom window, shattering glass with a sound like a shotgun blast. It powered its way past the curtain and landed on Danny's pillow, only inches from her face, showering her with glass.

A particularly nasty shard sliced into her left cheek.

'This is nice, Steve, I'm really impressed,' Myrna nodded approvingly. She heaped another forkful of the excellent *Arroz con pollo* into her mouth and licked her lips after she had consumed it.

'Yeah, and it's also owned by Mario Bussola,' he said, adding begrudgingly, 'and every damn cent we spend in here goes from our accounts into his. We are helping to support his lifestyle.'

'Aw, it don't stop it being nice though,' Myrna said through another mouthful of chicken. 'We might as well get something good out of this before we all lose our jobs,' she concluded wickedly.

Kruger frowned, unhappy at being unable to relax. Had the circumstances been different he could really have enjoyed the evening and no doubt have chanced it with Myrna, even though she was strictly a 'no no' on his list as far as women were concerned – i.e. married and employed by him. A very uncool combination.

He tried to chill out and soak in the atmosphere. It wasn't easy, not least because of the radio under his left arm, gun at his back, earpiece in his ear and transmit button stuck to his palm.

The Club Montoya was a nightclub situated in the basement of the Hotel Montoya. The hotel was perhaps one of Bussola's finest establishments, if not the finest of the seven hotels he owned. It was also one of South Beach's hottest locations. The hotel was Art Deco done to death, all the rage with the young business end of Miami, with four themed restaurants, two pools, a sports complex and very, very superior-priced rooms.

The nightclub, open from 6 p.m. to 6 a.m. every day, and soundproofed from the hotel, had become very much the place for everyone who was anyone to be seen in. Gays,

Latinos, cross-dressers. Even white male heterosexuals.

It had a dozen bars and two restaurants, one of which clients had to skirt through to enter the nightclub proper. This was the one in which Kruger and Myrna were sitting. It served expensive, but highly palatable Cuban food.

Kruger hoped the information given by Felicity about her wayward husband's whereabouts 'sometime tonight' was good gen. Otherwise it would be a wasted evening and Kruger wanted to spend as little time and effort on a case which would bring his company nothing in terms of money or kudos.

He hoped to end it tonight by jumping onto Bussola's trail, finding him with a piece of unofficial ass, reporting the news back to Felicity, together with some evidence, and then – *zap!* – calling it quits.

Kruger was enough of a realist, though, to know things were unlikely to turn out as smoothly as that.

'You told hubby you're dining out with the boss tonight?' Kruger smiled.

'Of course. He's away in Salt Lake City for a couple of days at a seminar. We spoke on the phone earlier.'

'Is he very liberal?'

'He trusts me, Steve.' She leaned forwards, elbow points on the table, and rested her chin on her thumbs. 'He knows I would never be unfaithful with you.' She stressed the last two words with a light sneer.

Kruger raised his eyebrows. But before he could respond with a feisty remark . . .

'He's here!' Their earpieces blurted into life, making them both jump out of their skins.

It was Kelly's voice, broadcasting from the back of the comms van parked a little way down the street outside the hotel. She commanded a good view of the entrance of the Hotel Montoya through the lens of a high-powered night-intensifier camera mounted in the side of the vehicle. She was sitting in the back of the van in a cosy little room with a bank of miniature TV screens and radio equipment. 'He's getting out the back of his car . . . accompanied by another guy and two bodyguards . . . they're going into the hotel . . . they're out of my line of sight . . . now!'

'And coming into the foyer,' Jimmy Armstrong said, taking over the commentary from his position half-hidden by a huge marble pillar near the reception desk.

'I hope the two assholes with him are not the two who were with Liss yesterday, the ones who kidnapped me,' Kruger mused, thinking out loud. 'If they are, we might as well call it off right now. Damn, shoulda thought about that.' He wasn't too concerned about Bussola slapping eyes on him because Kruger believed the mobster had never seen him before.

'Now he's headin' towards the club entrance,' Jimmy continued. 'It's his usual firepower,' he added, referring to the bodyguards, meaning they were Bussola's regular minders.

Kruger sat upright. He reached out, gently took Myrna's hands and held them across the table. He looked into her bright brown sparkling eyes.

'Kruger received,' he said into his radio. He tried to give Myrna a look of love tinged with lust.

Myrna eased herself into her role. She leaned further forwards, making the scenario seem more intimate, but also giving herself a good, unobstructed view over Kruger's shoulder to the club entrance.

Bussola, A.N. Other, and two bodyguards came into sight.

'Here he is,' she whispered to Kruger, fluttering her eyelids. 'Got him,' she said into the miniature mike which was positioned, secured by tape, between her breasts. In her present lean-forwards position, Kruger could see it there. By angling his head forwards a few more degrees he could have spoken into it. He caught his breath and concentrated on the task in hand.

'He's coming towards us,' Myrna warned, seeing that

75

Bussola and his small entourage had entered the club.

Myrna lifted an arm languidly and placed a cool hand around Kruger's neck. She scratched him naughtily, drew his face a little nearer to hers, then suddenly pulled him even closer across the small table so that her mouth was next to his ear and his mouth was only millimetres away from her cleavage. He became very hot.

She pretended to whisper love things into his ear.

'He's only feet away now,' she said. 'I confirm he's with another guy and two goons.'

Kruger was content to receive the information from his present position.

'Now walking around the perimeter of the restaurant.' Kruger felt Myrna's big soft mouth brushing his ear. Her voice became very husky. Her lips tickled him as they moved. 'He's right behind you, babe,' she murmured. 'I didn't realise he was such a big, fat bastard, and the guy he's with is enormous too . . . I could reach out and touch them . . . now he's gone past . . . approaching the entrance to the Tropicana Bar.'

As Bussola and company went through the doors to the bar, a roar of loud music boomed out.

'And now I've got him,' Dale Armstrong confirmed from his position inside the bar.

Myrna leaned back and pushed Kruger gently away.

He blew a long breath and loosened his neck-tie, sadly aware that he had been as close as he would ever get to Myrna's breasts.

'Enjoy, big boy?'

'Not in the slightest,' Kruger lied, wiping his forehead with his napkin.

Danny held the flannel tightly against her bleeding cheek. Though some thirty minutes had passed since the brick had crashed through the bedroom window, she was still shivering with shock.

She had dressed in a tracksuit with her dressing-gown

over it and wrapped tightly. Even so she was very cold and numb.

She eased the flannel away from her face to inspect the damage in the mirror. No doubt about it, medical treatment was required. The cut was only about three-quarters of an inch long, but was quite deep. She prayed it would not need stitches.

Blood oozed out of it immediately.

She replaced the bloody flannel, stared blankly at herself, thinking what a god-awful-tired-weary mess she looked.

'Dan?' came a voice from the foot of the stairs. It was the night-duty Patrol Sergeant, Lesley Elvin, one of Danny's best friends. She, along with two of her PCs, had attended Danny's 999.

'Yep?' Danny came out of the bathroom and teetered unsteadily down the stairs towards Lesley who waited at the foot, a concerned expression on her face.

'You okay, honey?'

Danny nodded, knowing she wasn't.

'You look as white as a sheet.'

'I'm okay,' she insisted.

Lesley shrugged. 'A twenty-four-hour glazier will be here soon to board up the window. Once it's done I would not recommend you sleep in that bed until you're sure all the glass has been removed . . . and you need to go to hospital to get that cleaned up. There could be some glass in it.' She pointed at Danny's face.

'I don't think I'm very likely to go back to bed now. I'll probably drop in to Casualty before work.'

'Do you want a lift? I can arrange one.'

Danny placed a hand on her friend's shoulder. 'No, it's okay. I'll see to it myself.'

Lesley's personal radio crackled, requesting her to attend the custody office at Blackpool to assist with processing some prisoners.

'Gotta go, hun.'

'Yeah, thanks.'

'The lads've had a good look around . . . can't see anyone. I'll tell 'em to keep a passing eye on you until we go off-duty at six, though I doubt there'll be a problem.'

'Mmm.' Danny sounded unsure.

'You got something to tell me?' the Sergeant enquired. She was usually pretty intuitive with things like this.

Danny shook her head.

She went to the front door with Lesley, offered her thanks, watched her walk away up the driveway past the Mercedes. Something in the light, the shimmer of the trees against the street lamp focused Danny's eyes on the front radiator grille of the car. For a moment Danny could not see what it was that made her look. Then she groaned out loud and rushed to the car.

Lesley spun round.

'The bastard!' Danny uttered.

She stared down at the top of the radiator grille and the jagged stump of metal upon which the famous three-pointed star used to proudly sit. It had been snapped off.

Danny's mouth tensed angrily. Anger boiled up inside her.

When she checked the rest of the car, she found what she feared. A track of scratches had been gouged down both sides, from front wing to rear, making some sense of the noises Danny had heard earlier.

Kruger thought it pointless to leave Kelly outside in the comms van whilst everyone else was inside the club and they knew the precise whereabouts of their target. Accordingly he teamed her up with Jimmy Armstrong and, as a couple, they came into the club after a lengthy period of queuing.

Dale played the part of a single, unattached male, targeting various females throughout the evening. It was a part he played well.

Meanwhile, Kruger and Myrna danced the night away.

He began to enjoy himself, despite sweating profusely because he was unable to remove his jacket for obvious reasons.

Keeping tabs on Bussola was easy.

The mobster, his fat friend, and the two bodyguards occupied a table in one corner of the room, constantly being attended by waitresses. The two minders remained detached and alert, whilst their boss and his buddy were fawned upon by a stream of sexily-clad women, who mostly looked like hookers. The two men spent some time on the dance floor, gyrating as rudely as their bulk would allow with a number of these women who all seemed to be very impressed with them.

Kruger hazarded an educated guess that if Bussola was playing away at all, it was probably with prostitutes or women who were only interested in screwing him because of his exalted position in low-life. Having been fucked by the biggest mobster in Florida was probably quite a thrill, Kruger assumed. They were probably not any sort of threat to Felicity, other than by way of sexually transmitted diseases.

Myrna enjoyed herself too. This was the first time in years she'd been to a nightclub and although it was work which brought her here, she decided to get full value.

She moved slinkily to the beat. So slinkily that Kruger often found himself transfixed by her mesmeric gyrations. The sweat poured down from her scalp, temple, neck, shoulders and cleavage, making Kruger's tongue flicker in anticipation of being able to lick it off her body.

So near yet so far.

It was just as well he was a man of high moral values, otherwise he could easily have been driven by lust.

Just before two o'clock, Bussola and company made a move to leave.

Kruger and his employees left quickly, discreetly, ahead of him.

Kelly returned to the comms van; Dale and Jimmy

went to a car each. Kruger and Myrna got into Myrna's Lexus.

They had only a short wait.

Bussola's stretch limo drew up to the hotel entrance. A doorman opened the rear door in readiness. The two bodyguards appeared ahead of Bussola, checking.

Moments later the man himself emerged from the hotel. His friend – or whoever the hell the other guy happened to be – was at his shoulder. They squeezed into the limo and the bodyguards got into the front seat next to the driver.

'No women,' Kruger observed. 'He's had plenty of opportunity to pick one up.'

'Perhaps he's faithful after all,' Myrna suggested.

'And lions don't have big teeth.'

The limo pulled smoothly away into the night.

Kruger's team began to follow.

Despite the early hours, tailing the limo through Miami was an absolute breeze because Miami is one of those cities which never sleeps and the amount of traffic about was phenomenal. Kruger found the experience exhilarating, though he would have preferred to have been behind the wheel rather than passenger. It was too many years since he had been involved in mobile surveillance. He'd almost forgotten how much fun it was. He was also pleased to note that his people had following techniques off a 'T' – because he'd taught them all he knew.

The limo worked its way out of South Beach, down to MacArthur Causeway, over the Miami Channel and into the city. From there it meandered south. For a few blocks Kruger thought the tail had been spotted, particularly when the limo executed a series of U-turns, sudden stops and block-loops. The team held its nerve and after five minutes of these anti-surveillance manoeuvres continued its journey. Bussola was obviously going through the motions as he probably did on every journey he undertook. However, they were moves that a good following team should be ready for and act accordingly.

The limo hit the Latin Quarter and eventually landed in Shenandoah where it stopped outside a parade of rundown shops and offices. Jimmy Armstrong just happened to be the eyeball at the time and the rest of the team, following his instructions, parked discreetly in an arc 200 to 500 metres away, but not in visual contact with the limo – which was intensely frustrating for all concerned. They had to rely totally on Jimmy's commentary.

'It's like some sorta shop,' Jimmy said over the radio, trying to describe the place where Bussola's limo had pulled up. 'Lowrise . . . dunno . . . difficult to see properly without getting much closer.'

'Roger,' Kruger acknowledged.

'Well, boss, what we gonna do?' Myrna asked with a yawn. Since leaving the club her energy had dissipated and she needed her bed quite badly. Suddenly she felt her age.

'Sit tight, I suppose.'

Myrna slid down her seat, reclined it and closed her eyes.

Jimmy watched all the occupants of the limo, with the exception of the driver, get out and go into what was probably once a shop with a couple of floors above which could have been storerooms, offices or apartments. The shop at ground floor, with a massive plate-glass window white-washed from the inside, seemed to be derelict.

Jimmy reported there was definitely a light on at both ground-floor and first-floor level.

To Kruger it sounded like it could be some kind of illegal gambling joint, but he had heard lots of things about Bussola from his time as a cop and never was there a whisper of gambling. Everything else imaginable in the criminal line, but not gambling.

Still, you never could tell. Money was money to people like Bussola and where it came from was immaterial.

'Update,' Kruger snapped into his radio. It had been a good thirty seconds since Jimmy had finished speaking and Kruger was getting crabby.

'Very little going on . . . hang fire, the limo's pulling away without our man. He could be settled here for a while.'

'Is there much other traffic?'

'Naw – quiet as a grave.'

'Pedestrians?'

'Nope.'

'Anything else?' Kruger said desperately.

'An all-night drugstore at the end of the block.'

'Dale – did you receive that?' Kruger asked the other Armstrong brother.

'Affirmative.'

'Go check the place over, will ya? See if you can find out anything – discreetly, of course. Treat yourself to a packet of Jiffs while you're in there. Put 'em down to expenses.'

'Roger. I need to renew my supply . . . the last ones I bought have gone right past their "best before" date.'

Kruger and Myrna chuckled.

A few seconds later, Dale's car cruised slowly past.

Kruger settled back to wait for an update.

Five minutes later Dale was back on the air.

'The guy from the drugstore thinks it's a telephone sales place now. Used to be a barber shop. Closed down about eighteen months ago. Guy didn't have anything else to say voluntarily. I got the impression he knows who owns the place and he ain't too happy about divulging. And I've walked past and tried the front door. Locked.'

'Idiot,' Kruger said to Myrna before replying over the radio to Dale. 'Received and understood. Now you pull outta there and don't try any more stunts.'

Dale acknowledged.

Kruger was puzzled. 'Telephone sales?' he said with

82

disbelief. He looked thoughtfully at Myrna. 'Telephone sales at this time-a day?'

She shrugged . . . and something dawned on Kruger. He sat bolt upright and thumped the dash triumphantly. 'Not tele-sales – tele-*sex*! Let's check it out. I'm intrigued.'

Tracey was hot stuff. She was one of the favourites on the sex-line. This was because of her northern English accent, now so familiar to millions of Americans through the medium of the sit-com *Frasier* and the character of Daphne, whose dubious vowels are supposed to originate in Manchester.

Tracey was in constant demand from a stream of men who happily jerked themselves off with the assistance of her voice, a telephone and whatever aids they had available.

She had just finished a particularly horrible call with one of her regulars who purported to be a Texan billionaire. He was on the line every night and if he was calling from Houston, as he claimed, it would be costing him a fortune . . . which, of course, was the whole idea, with Bussola and the phone company splitting the revenue.

Easy money. Big profits.

'*Keep 'em on the line!*' one poster proclaimed on the wall in front of Tracey.

'*Premature ejaculations we don't need!*' said another.

And Tracey kept the Texan on the line. Right from the moment she allowed him to rip her clothes off, unpack the whip and vibrator and gently eased the latter up her ass. Thirty-five minutes later, as decreed by the customer, Tracey changed her mind about sex and entered the 'rape' phase where the Texan beat up on her – and still managed to make her come at the same time as he did. Except that he really did come all over his belly and she faked a multiple orgasm whilst at the same time chewing on a slice of pepperoni pizza.

She slammed the phone down, closed her eyes wearily and sniffed up through her cocaine-damaged nostrils.

A line of lights flashed on her little switchboard, demanding her attention. She frowned and ignored them, leaning back in her telephonist's chair and glancing down the row of booths. There were a dozen in all, each one soundproofed from its neighbours, around the walls of the former barbershop which still smelled of hairspray.

Each booth was occupied by an experienced sex-telephonist busy handling calls. Leaning a little further back, Tracey could hear some of the things going on. Grunts, panting, screams of pain and passion, loving whispers, sexual demands. The noises were like the combination of a zoo and a blue-movie soundtrack.

The telephonists – two male, the remainder female – came from a range of backgrounds, each with their own personal reason for being there, not least of which for all of them was that they were paid tax-free. There were single mothers, supermarket cashiers, a former prostitute with a tongue of silk, and a couple of out-of-work actors trying to make ends meet whilst 'resting'.

And they were all good at sextalk: chat which could make the customer – always a man – ejaculate whilst imagining a vivid sexy scenario. They could ad lib at will, immediately adopting the role required by the caller, always giving their best shot.

'Answer yer fuckin' lines,' Tracey's earphones informed her.

She looked over her shoulder and shot a sneering glance at the supervisor who was sitting behind a large switchboard on a small raised dais at the back of the room. From there, the supervisor could dip into all the workers' calls, keeping a check by listening in . . . and also being able to tell when a telephonist wasn't working.

And work they did. This was no easy option. It was draining, emotional toil. Twelve-hour stints. Continuous, consecutive calls. Constantly talking and listening to the weirdest fantasies imaginable and having the ability and imagination to match them. It was beginning to take its toll on Tracey that night as she suddenly found she needed the lift which only one thing could give her.

Bitch, she thought. She gave the supervisor a one-digit salute, ensuring she didn't see it, of course. She ripped the headset off and stood up. 'I need a piss,' she announced and picked up her purse.

At that moment the front door opened.

Bussola, his two meat-head bodyguards and the other guy came in. They walked straight inside, completely ignoring the telephonists, went through a door at the back, down a short corridor and up the stairs beyond.

One of the bodyguards stayed at the door and sat down in a plastic chair.

Tracey watched the entrance of the men, completely astounded. She shook her head, hardly able to believe who had just walked through the door.

Two people she thought she would never see again.

Bussola and the man accompanying him.

Charlie Gilbert.

Charlie Fucking Gilbert.

The man she had once trusted. The man who had promised her the earth. Her guts coiled with the hatred she harboured for him.

Because look where she had ended up. At the age of nineteen she was working on a sex-chatline, verbally masturbating guys over the telephone wires.

Tracey walked numbly towards the seated bodyguard. He looked tiredly at her and stood up as she approached the door through which his boss had just gone.

'Where ya goin', girl?'

'I need to pee,' she said truthfully. 'The toilet's through there.' It was – down along the ground-floor hallway, last door on the right.

The bodyguard raised his big square chin and dark

bushy eyebrows in a kind of acknowledgement and nodded slightly. His eyes bore down the length of his broken
nose. 'How much d'ya cost, babe?'

'I'm too fuckin' expensive for you, ya greasy dago,' she
responded, and tried to push past him. He grabbed her
arm and pulled her roughly towards him, raising her up
onto tiptoe so that her belly was at his groin level. He was
already hard. She could feel it through her clothes.

'Don't push your luck, babe. If I want you, I have you.'
His breath was enhanced by garlic.

Tracey uttered a short laugh of contempt, even though
she was fully aware that she was very close to annoying
him. Her eyes traversed slowly down to his hand, the big
fat fingers squeezing like a vice around her bicep. 'Let go.'

He eased his grip slowly. His mouth was open and his
nostrils were dilating. Long hairs grew out of them. His
ears also sprouted a bushy forest. He had blackheads on
his nose and around his mouth. Specks of perspiration
were dotted all over his face.

All these things Tracey saw as she regained her proper
footing.

All these things made her cringe and find him utterly
repulsive.

She edged past, through the door.

'And don't go upstairs,' he told her. 'Or else.'

Kruger looked down at the object he held between his left
forefinger and thumb.

It resembled a doll's eye with a sty in one corner of it
and was surrounded by a rubber sucker rather like the tip
of a kid's arrow, though it was half the diameter. In his
right hand was a palm-sized portable TV which he flicked
on. The tiny screen, four centimetres square, was fuzzy
for a few moments then gradually cleared and came into
focus, giving him a clear, monochrome, slug's-eyeview of
the underside of his chin and his nostrils, transmitted
from the lens he was holding in his fingers.

He pointed the lens towards a shop doorway and saw that image reproduced on the screen. Kruger was impressed. He could see why this was one of his top-selling lines. It was like having an extra eye on the end of your fingers.

He was standing at the rear of the comms van which was parked in a quiet street. Myrna and Dale stood next to him. Kelly was in the van, the back doors being open. She peered over Kruger's shoulder, looking at the tiny TV.

'Excellent,' she said. 'The lens has a powerful night-intensifier built into it which self-focuses and adjusts to the available light. There's a mike fitted in the lens too which can give pretty good results, even through glass.'

Kruger nodded approvingly. He was not sure if there would be any call to use the surveillance kit tonight, but decided to take it along just in case. 'Are you receiving okay?' he asked Kelly.

She turned into the van, switched on a monitor, made a couple of minor adjustments and the screen blinked into life. She saw exactly what Kruger saw on the mini-screen. 'Yep – no probs.'

Kruger looked at Myrna and Dale.

Like himself, they had changed into more appropriate clothing for the little foray ahead, having ditched their party gear for all black – jeans, T-shirts, jackets and sneakers which had been kept ready in the van for such an eventuality. 'We play it by ear – literally,' Kruger said. 'We don't know what the hell's going on there. They could just be playing cards. We'll leave Jimmy watching the front. Myself and Myrna will go to the rear of the property to see if there is any way of getting a view inside. Dale, you be our lookout, okay?'

Both nodded.

Myrna was now raring to go, having got her second wind.

'Anybody any further suggestions?' Kruger asked.

They shook their heads.

'Let's go then – and take care.' He picked a set of aluminium extending ladders which were part of the van's equipment store and hauled them over his shoulder.

Tracey took her time in the restroom. Her mind was in complete turmoil. She had never expected to see either of the two men again, particularly Gilbert. He had conned and tricked her, and used and ultimately abused her, then discarded her into the clutches of people who did it all over again. It was only through her strength of character that she had risen from the gutter to her present position – on the kerb of the sidewalk. But at least it was upwards.

She finished peeing and washed her hands carefully, soaping them thoroughly whilst she continued to think about Charlie Gilbert in particular.

She looked up from her hands and caught sight of her reflection in the cracked, dirty mirror above the wash-stand. She closed her eyes quickly, not wishing to see the ragged reflection of someone who had been a drug abuser from the age of thirteen. The skin sagging off the bone, sunken eyes, dried-up, wrinkled lips.

The reflection of a drug addict who had not yet died, but would do so, in the not-too-distant future. She opened her eyes and sneered at herself, briefly able to see the discoloured gums in her mouth.

She sniffed and blew her leaking nose on a paper towel.

Above her was the sound of clumping feet moving about.

Her watery eyes rose towards the ceiling.

The alleyway behind the shops was pitch black. Briefly Kruger regretted not taking Kelly up on her offer of night-vision goggles. However, he took his time, allowed his eyes to adjust and used the night-eye in his fingers to assist himself and Myrna as they walked down the alley, monitoring their progress on the tiny TV screen.

She stayed at his shoulder, a cool hand gripping his bicep.

The extension ladders hung off his other shoulder.

He led the way without incident to the rear of Bussola's place.

The building was pretty much as Kruger expected it to be, making him glad he'd brought the steps. This was a high-crime neighbourhood and the rear of the disused shop was boarded up with sheet steel, riveted for the rest of time – or until demolition – into the brickwork.

Fortunately, the first-floor windows were just that – windows. There were two, quite large, both with drapes drawn across and lights on behind, indicating occupation. Running below the windows was a metallic catwalk which formed part of the fire escape. The folding ladders which were an intrinsic part of the escape were secured at that level, out of reach from below.

Kruger swung the set of ladders off his shoulders and gently leaned them against the shop wall. He gazed upwards at the underside of the fire escape. Slowly, quietly, he eased out the ladder extension.

The rubber tips of the ladders rested on the outer edge of the fire escape.

'Hold 'em tight,' he whispered to Myrna. He slid the night-eye and TV into his pocket and started to climb, rung by careful rung. When he was almost at the top, he hoisted himself onto the fire escape and dropped silently onto the catwalk.

He reached through the rails and held the top of the ladders as Myrna ascended.

She came up nimbly, leapt over the rail and landed next to Kruger, crouching down without a sound. Kruger relayed their progress to the team via the radio, whispering his message.

The two of them shuffled along the catwalk on all fours towards the first window. They stopped underneath it and listened. No noise emanated from inside; nothing seemed to be going on. Kruger took a chance. He eased himself up and tried to see in by way of a minute crack down the edge of the drapes. He saw nothing. He sidled along to the centre of the window and peered in through the small aperture where the drapes hadn't quite met.

Instinctively he dropped back down.

'One of Bussola's bodyguards,' he whispered to Myrna. 'He's sitting reading. I couldn't see anything else.'

Myrna helped herself to a quick look, confirming Kruger's observation. The guy was reading a hard-core porn magazine.

Kruger pointed to the next window, some ten feet along the catwalk. Myrna nodded. Again on hands and knees they set off. Myrna stayed right up Kruger's ass and almost kissed it when he suddenly stopped in front of her and rose to listen at the next window.

This time he could clearly hear voices.

He could not see into the room, but there was a crack of light where the drapes met carelessly in the middle and the possibility of a view. This time, instead of chancing a look for himself, he reached up, using his hand rather like a periscope, and pointed the nighteye into the room.

What he saw on the TV screen nearly made him fall off the fire escape.

Although the most common method of using cocaine is by snorting, it is alleged that the subsequent rush is not quite as intense as that produced by mainlining. But Tracey knew that if the purity of the drug was high enough, the buzz was just as good.

The coke she used that night was first class.

She opened her purse, unzipped the small inside pocket and removed a twenty-dollar bill she had already prepared. It was rolled up tight as a straw, both ends expertly folded over after the required amount of the finely grained white powder had been sifted inside the tube.

With extreme caution, Tracey unfolded one end of the note and inserted this end into her left nostril. She closed the other nostril with her thumb to bring about better suction.

She tilted her head back and snorted.

Immediately her nostril froze up, showing just how pure the stuff was. Before the real buzz hit her, she quickly shoved the note up her other nostril and sniffed up the remainder of the coke from the tube, instantly freezing that one too.

She gritted her teeth as tiny particles of the drug were taken down her passages to her throat; other particles of it were transported by the small capillaries in the mucus membrane and delivered speedily and efficiently to her brain.

The rush slammed into her seconds later. Like an express train smashing into her cranium.

She staggered, dropped the twenty-dollar bill and grabbed the wash-stand to steady herself.

Her eyes rose to her reflection. She no longer saw the scrawny, drug-abused female; instead there was a transformation. She was beautiful again. Full of confidence and sass, raring to confront Charlie Gilbert and Mario Bussola. The two men who had promised so much and given so little.

Kruger angled the TV screen in the palm of his hand to enable Myrna to see the picture properly.

She stared down at the tiny set. Horrified, her face creased into a mask of anger. She looked quickly at Kruger. 'The bastards,' she uttered. 'What are we going to do?'

'Call the cops, I imagine,' he said. His heartrate had increased in pace to about a million beats per second. He stared back down at the sordid tableau which was being delivered to him by the latest in hi-tec. 'Kelly?' he hissed into his radio. 'Are you receiving this picture?'

'I was, but it's gone blank for some reason. I'm trying to get it back, but there's interference on the screen from somewhere,' she responded desperately.

'Get it fixed and get it recorded,' Kruger ordered her, knowing there were video-recording facilities in the comms van.

'Yes, boss.'

'And call the godamned cops and tell 'em to break their asses gettin' here.'

'Okay, boss.'

'Cops could take for ever,' Myrna said. 'We can't let this go on, Steve. If that's not rape and that kid is older than ten years, my name's not Myrna Rosza.'

'PI's watch – they don't get involved,' Kruger baulked.

'Not in this case, Steve. Otherwise we might find ourselves accessories to murder.'

'Yeah, you're dead right.' He looked at the TV screen again and made a decision – but before he could translate it into words and action, something else happened on-screen and he gasped, 'What the hell's this?'

Tracey crept out of the restroom and stepped quietly down the hallway towards the foot of the stairs, feeling as though she was walking on air. She paused briefly, checked over her shoulder to ensure that the door to the telephonists' room was still closed, then began to slowly climb the stairs. On the landing at the top she was faced with one door, which she opened.

Beyond was a sparsely furnished room, with simple, whitewashed walls; it had been a storeroom previously. There was a door in the opposite wall next to which sat Bussola's second bodyguard, an overweight guy with a heavy moustache but hardly any other hair. His ample ass was stuck in a plastic stacking chair, his nose in his porno mag. At the sound of the door opening he looked up and an expression of vague annoyance crossed his face.

He thought it was his buddy from downstairs and was

ready to give him a roasting for leaving his post.

The sight of the thin, waif-like girl puzzled him.

'I've come to see Charlie Gilbert,' Tracey said.

'Who?' As he said the word he remembered it was the name of Bussola's pal. 'Get the fuck outta here,' he said, dismissing her with a gesture.

'No.'

He stood up and walked towards her. Tracey timed it right, ducked to his left and darted to the door, skimming past him with ease. He made a grab for her but ended up embracing himself.

Before he could stop her, she was through the door.

The bodyguard swore and roared at her.

The commotion caught the attention of the two naked men in the second room, but the third person in the room continued to struggle to try and free herself from her ordeal.

Bussola was situated at the rear of the young girl, slamming into her. He yelled angrily, 'What the hell's going on? Get her outta here, you fool!'

Gilbert was positioned at the other end of the girl. He held her head down in a vice-like grip, forcing her to fellate his flaccid penis. He simply looked up, unconcerned at the interruption; his eyes were glazed over a drug-induced euphoria.

Tracey didn't hesitate.

She flew across the room at Gilbert, screaming, 'Bastard! Bastard!' Her arms flailed like some sort of medieval instrument of war.

Then she was on Gilbert, punching and pounding him madly, five years of hatred which had been growing inside her like a malignant tumour, now given a cathartic release.

Gilbert rolled with the blows. Other than to raise his forearms defensively, thereby letting go of the girl's head, his brain was unable to coordinate a proper response; within seconds Tracey had punched him over a dozen times around his head and chest.

However, Bussola, who always kept a clear head, disengaged his cock from the girl's anus and threw her roughly to one side. She sprawled awkwardly to the floor where she immediately scuttled to one corner of the room, cowering, shivering with fright and pain.

Bussola and his overweight bodyguard both laid hands on Tracey at the same time. They dragged her away from Gilbert and flung her against the wall, her light weight proving no problem for them. The bodyguard moved in and laid into her, landing a devastating punch on the bridge of her nose. Her coke-frozen nostrils flattened as easily as crushing an empty match-box. She gurgled, blood gushing down her face and chest, and sank to her knees, holding her face in her hands.

Once down there the bodyguard kicked her in the side of the head, making her jerk as if he was kicking a marionette. He continued to boot her remorselessly around the head and upper torso, watched by Bussola and Gilbert.

'Everyone! Front door now! Go, c'mon, move it!' Kruger growled urgently into his microphone.

He had quickly considered and discarded the idea of trying to force an entry through the window, mainly because it was thick glass and would take a long time to break – and he didn't have the right equipment anyway.

He ran back along the catwalk, leapt on the fire-escape ladders and heaved them from their fastenings. He put a foot on the bottom rung, stepped on and the ladders dropped quickly through the walkway to ground level. He jumped off.

Myrna was right behind him. She jumped the last five feet, hitting the ground running.

They sprinted side by side down the alley, Kruger silently cursing his knee which clicked loudly every time his foot jarred down, sending a searing pain up through his thigh.

By the time they reached the front of the shop, the other three had arrived. They looked cool and ready for anything. Kruger knew there and then his recruitment and selection process was spot on.

'No time for a detailed explanation, people,' Kruger shouted as he approached them. 'Assault and battery taking place in the upstairs back room. You may need your weapons drawn – but nobody's obliged to follow me,' he finished off.

He rammed his right shoulder against the front door of the shop and tried to burst it open. It didn't budge. He measured a few steps backwards, eyed up his target area and flat-footed the door by the lock. Still nothing. He increased his effort and on the second kick it gave a little; on the third the door splintered open with a crack. Kruger rushed through like a charging rhino, having drawn his Sig which he held high in his right hand.

None of the team took the decision to hang back.

They followed him, guns drawn.

Kruger's cold experienced eyes flitted around the room as he entered, instantly taking everything in: the phone booths, the raised dais of the supervisor – and more importantly, Bussola's bodyguard who was still in his chair by the door at the back of the room.

Kruger dismissed the telephone side of things as no threat. He focused in on the bodyguard. Kruger was surprised to note the guy hardly moved. Their entry, which had taken three kicks and probably only ten seconds, had been long enough for any self-respecting bodyguard to prepare for appropriate action.

This guy, however, made a sloth look slick.

He rose from his chair and reached underneath his jacket for his piece. His eyes were wide with horror and a silent scream of, 'Oh fuck' was on his lips as he thought, This is it. This is what I get paid for. And I'm too slow and I'm gonna die at the age of thirty-six.

He was right in one respect. He *was* too slow.

Kruger launched himself across the last six feet of space, driving his left shoulder into the guy's lower belly, bundling him over, flattening him with a football tackle to be proud of.

All the air gushed out of the bodyguard, all his strength with it.

Kruger and Dale quickly heaved the man over onto his stomach, wrenched his hands behind his back. Dale knelt down in the middle of the guy's back, driving his right knee down hard between his shoulderblades, forcing his whole weight onto him, pinning him down.

Dale then jammed the muzzle of his gun into the man's ear and said, 'Don't move.'

'You take care-a him,' Kruger said, rising. 'Rest of you, with me now.'

With one last flicker of his eyes around the room of stunned telephonists – most of whom were well into sex-chat – Kruger opened the door and stepped through.

He took the stairs three at a time, creasing his knee in agony.

Jimmy, Myrna and Kelly were right behind.

When faced with a situation, it had always been Bussola's policy to act first and ask questions afterwards. This was one of the reasons why he joined in beating up Tracey even though she had been overpowered within seconds. His other reason was that he was extremely annoyed at the interruption. He had been having a good time – and no one had the right to spoil that. This little bitch had to be made to realise that. Then he might talk to her. As for his bodyguards . . . if the stupid bastards couldn't keep a little girl out, what chance was there of keeping someone out who meant business?

Bussola reached down. He wound his fingers into Tracey's hair, got a grip and banged her head repeatedly against the wall.

The time for talking started. 'Now then, you little

shit-for-brains, what's all this about?' he screamed into her bashed-up face. Blood was being flicked everywhere.

Even if she could have replied, she did not get time, because Kruger stepped into the doorway, Sig in hand. His presence was menacing.

'Stand back,' he shouted. 'Leave her alone.'

Bussola stopped what he was doing, letting go of Tracey's hair. Her head slopped to one side. The mobster stood up to his full height and coldly turned his big, fat nakedness to Kruger. Despite his predicament, his erection was still rampant and twitching against the folds of his big belly. 'What the fuck?' he sneered.

'I said stand back and leave her alone,' Kruger reiterated.

Jimmy appeared behind him, Myrna and Kelly behind Jimmy.

Bussola shot a glance to his bodyguard who was standing next to Tracey, looking impassively at Kruger, weighing up the odds. 'Shoot him,' Bussola said.

A smile crossed the bodyguard's fat lips. Kruger realised he was about to be tested. The guy's hand went for his gun, but Jimmy took the initiative. He weaved past Kruger and pointed his Sig directly into the bodyguard's face. 'Yeah, that's right,' he breathed. 'You pull that weapon out nice 'n' slow, thumb and forefinger on the butt, then you throw it across the floor. If you don't, I'll pop ya, babe.' Jimmy's finger tightened visibly on the trigger.

The bodyguard looked at Bussola for guidance. He got none.

Bussola was too busy eyeing Kruger.

The gun was extracted slowly as per instructions.

The silence of the moment was punctuated by the young girl sobbing in a corner of the room and the sound of Tracey spitting blood on the floor by the bed.

The gun clattered to the floor.

'I hope you know what you're doing,' Bussola said. 'Steve,' he added.

97

A jolt, like electricity, whipped through Kruger. It must have shown on his face.

Bussola smiled. His erection wilted slightly. 'Yeah, I know who you are. Surprised? That bitch I married talks of no one else.'

'Move over to the wall,' Kruger said, feeling somehow that his advantage had been taken from him. He indicated to Bussola where he wanted him to stand. The mobster did not move. Just stood there with a taunting smirk quivering on his lips. 'Move, Mario,' Kruger repeated. 'The cops're coming and I'll tell them all sorts of lies if I have to. Y'know – about how I had to save a wretched girl's life, how you turned on me with a gun . . . all that kinda shit, and you won't be able to say anything 'cos you'll be ashes and so will your fatso pal here.' Kruger's gun pointed to the bodyguard, then flicked back to Bussola. 'All because you refused to stand next to the wall. Very intelligent.'

'What . . . what's going on?' Charlie Gilbert blurted from the bed. He had been watching the events unfolding with incomprehension. He then vomited spectacularly down his chest, stomach and genitals, fell forwards on the bed with a groan, huge ass in the air, and started snoring.

Kruger raised his eyebrows at Bussola. 'Well?'

Reluctantly he edged towards the wall. His eyes lasered into Kruger with a fierce anger. 'You'll regret this, Steve.'

It was a statement of fact. It told Kruger nothing he didn't already know.

'In fact you'll all regret this,' Bussola declared blandly.

'Get the girls out of here,' Kruger said to Myrna and Kelly. The two women entered the room, careful not to step into the line of fire between Kruger, Jimmy and their two targets. Bussola watched them through veiled lids, lingering over Myrna. His face turned back to Kruger. 'Why the hell are you here anyway, Steve?' Bussola mused out loud. He licked his lips. The ex-cop felt himself begin to weaken underneath the tough exterior.

Even naked and exposed, Bussola was every inch a gangster. He'd paid his dues on the mean streets of New York and Chicago, punking around with the gangs, terrifying neighbourhoods, but always thinking about expansion and the future. In his thirties, with a well-established criminal organisation in those cities, he decided to move the centre of his operations to Miami where it expanded to epic proportions. He orchestrated some bloody – and a few bloodless – coups and continued to grow, though he only ever made the number two spot. Number one was held by a mobster named Tony Corelli. Corelli's unexpected demise at the hands of two armed women – a case still unsolved by the cops – opened the way for Bussola to claim top spot. Which he did, ruthlessly taking over Corelli's flourishing empire.

Bussola was widely believed to be a billionaire.

He was also widely believed to have personally killed several people on the way to amassing his fortune. Legend had it that he once chainsawed a rival to pieces. This was never proved, but Kruger believed it.

And Kruger was frightened because he believed everything about Bussola, and frightened because he believed Bussola's words.

He was also totally disgusted at a man who had so much wealth at his disposal that he could have bought anything legal in terms of sexual pleasure, yet resorted to a sordid back-street room where he, together with another man, got his kicks by raping a girl who did not look twelve years old.

Maybe that was part of the thrill. Doing something which, no matter what the circumstance, was unlawful – and getting away with it. The ultimate middle finger stuck up at a society he despised.

Except this time he would not get away with it.

Kruger found he could not prevent his mouth curling into a sneer of contempt as these thoughts went through his mind.

'What choo lookin' at?' Bussola growled.

'Scum.'

Bussola nodded, then winked at Kruger. 'I'm a very bad person to have as an enemy.'

'So am I,' Kruger responded. He could see Bussola was not convinced, whereas Kruger honestly believed the Italian would be a very bad adversary.

Myrna and Kelly escorted the two girls out of the room, the younger one of them covered up by a large, soiled towel Kelly had found on the floor.

This left Kruger and Jimmy facing Bussola, the bodyguard and the big fat guy spread-eagled on the bed in a sea of vomit.

Their guns never wavered.

'What now, Steve?' Bussola raised his thick bushy eyebrows.

'Cops.'

'And what do you expect to happen?'

'Arrest and conviction.'

Bussola blinked as though he could not believe his ears. Then he roared with laughter, throwing his head right back. His penis, now limp, jiggled with merriment. Then the laughter stopped. He became serious. 'I very much doubt it, Steve. Very much.'

A cop siren wailed not too distantly. A flood of relief passed through Kruger. 'We'll see, Mario.' Inside he already had his doubts.

'How about letting us get dressed?'

'No – stay as you are,' Kruger said, not wanting to lose any forensics. 'Just as we found you – naked as jailbirds.'

Chapter Five

Although British prisons have had a bad press over recent years for their allegedly liberal regimes, it is true to say that even a prison run along the strictest of lines would not be able to control inmates 100 per cent of the time – unless they were banged up in their cells twenty-four hours a day.

And however tightly policed the prison inside which Trent was incarcerated had been, there is a better than even chance he would still have been able to plan, prepare and execute the course of action he had decided to take.

As it was, the fairly laid-back way in which the prison was run meant that with just a little care and common sense, there was no earthly chance of him being caught.

Once again he was awake early.

He watched the darkness of night become the brightness of morning, willing the time to pass, eager to get going.

By the time his cell door opened he was shaved, dressed and ready for breakfast. He did not show any enthusiasm to the warder for the day ahead, however, but sloped dejectedly out of the cell and walked slowly along the landing. He stared blankly ahead of himself, dragging his feet, trying to give the impression of a dead man walking.

He joined the queue to the breakfast servery. Coysh was one of the servers, Trent noticed, and the man sloped wet scrambled eggs and bacon swimming in grease onto people's plastic plates.

Coysh clocked Trent's imminent approach and surreptitiously selected a few prime rashers for him.

The two men exchanged a knowing glance. Trent said, 'Everything okay?'

Coysh nodded.

'Keep me informed.'

Coysh turned his attention to the next one in line.

Trent moved on, smiling secretly, grabbed a mug of tea and sat down at a table. Alone.

'I heard about what happened last night, Danny,' Henry Christie said. The two of them were in Henry's office, the door closed, his phone on divert.

He saw she looked tired and worn-out. Not just because of the problems of the early morning, but for lessons far more fundamental. The white, narrow strip of plaster over the sutured cut on her face did not help matters.

Danny, in turn, eyed Henry. She bit her bottom lip to stop it from quivering because she wanted to cry. But not here. Not in front of her future boss. The last thing she wanted was to be tagged as a pathetic, weeping woman.

She drew in a deep, juddering breath and braced herself.

'Think it was Jack Sands who smashed the window and damaged your car?' Henry asked. He leaned his elbows on the desk.

Danny shrugged noncommittally. In herself she knew damn well it was Sands. Evidentially, though, she could not prove a thing.

'Want to discuss it?' Henry offered.

She closed her eyes, shook her head. She was perilously close to bubbling over. She had spent the last two hours since coming to work avoiding both Henry and Sands in an effort to steer away from the problem. She knew that if she encountered either one of them, the bubble would burst with a messy flood of emotion all over the carpet. With Sands it would have been anger. With Henry, tears.

Henry had been the first one to collar her and beckon her into his office.

'No, not really, Henry. I just want to get on with my work. I've got loads of things to get boxed off before I join you. I don't want to talk about my private life, if you don't mind . . . with respect.'

Even as she said the words, she knew they weren't true. More than anything she wanted to share her predicament with someone. But not here, not now. She placed her hands on the chair-arm and started to stand up . . . about to run away.

Henry stood up quickly and waved her to be seated. He came round from behind his desk and sat down on the chair next to Danny.

He said, 'I'll bet you're thinking you're making one hell of a bad impression with your new boss, aren't you?' She opened her mouth to say something; Henry held up a silencing finger. 'I'll tell you this, Danny. All I'm interested in – bottom line – is how you perform in the workplace. However, I know from my own experience that personal issues often cloud professional judgments. I know that for a fact, Danny. I've been that person in that situation more times than I care to remember. So what I'm trying to say, dead clumsily, is that I realise people are more than machines, more than what they are for eight hours a day at work, and I'm interested in my team as individuals who have thoughts, feelings, aspirations, problems . . . whatever . . . and these are the things I have to deal with to get the best out of my people.' He blew out his cheeks and said, 'Phew! That was a long one. So, if I can help you Danny, let me. Okay? Totally confidential.'

She slumped back, regarding Henry's face slowly. Letting her eyes take his features in. It was a kind, concerned face. She felt instinctively she could trust him.

'And not only that,' he reminded her. 'As you said, I am involved already. I have some right to know about what happened in the garage last night . . . at the very least.'

'Yeah, you're right Henry.'

She looked away, gathered her thoughts and decided to tell him the lot. 'Me and Jack have been having an affair for about six months. I fell in love with him, I guess. All that lonely female baloney. But it was going nowhere, except down the tubes. I've tried to end it a few times now, but he's so overbearing and clinging and possessive – horrible, really, if I'm honest – and I just let it go on and on. Night before last I'd had enough and told him it was over, for good this time. But he won't let it lie and I don't want to hurt his wife. I'm sure she doesn't know yet. I feel a complete bitch and I'm not happy at all with the situation . . . I'm so bloody depressed, actually. I'm dying to get out of that office onto CID.' She stopped talking abruptly because she realised the babbling had started. She swallowed and wiped the beginning of a tear out of her eye. 'Sorry, Henry.'

'It's okay.'

'What did Jack say last night, after I'd gone?'

'Nothing, other than to abuse me.' Henry leaned forwards, elbows on knees. 'What do you want to do, Danny? What's the best thing that can happen now?'

She considered the questions a moment. 'For him to accept it's over, leave me alone, and let us both get on with our lives.'

At eleven-thirty that morning, Trent swigged down the last dregs of his morning brew. He was alone in his cell, sitting on the edge of his bunk, leafing idly through one of his teen-girl magazines. He closed it, slid it onto the pile underneath his bunk and got to his feet. He walked over to the steel toilet in the corner of the cell and urinated, his back to the door.

As he finished he heard a movement behind. He zipped up and turned.

Blake leaned nonchalantly against the door. In his grimy nicotine-stained fingers he held a self-rolled cigarette from which a single whisper of smoke rose.

'Okay, nonce?' he sneered. He slurped his tongue around the inside of his mouth, then spat on the cell floor.

Cold icicles of fear spread rapidly through Trent's veins. Literally, his blood ran cold.

'What do you want?'

There was a strange, deadly look in Blake's eyes which Trent immediately interpreted. When the answer spilled out of the villain's mouth, Trent was not surprised.

'You . . . I want you – but you've always known that, haven't you?'

Trent nodded. He could scarcely breathe.

Yes, he had known that one day Blake would want to have him too. But it would not be from a loving desire, it would be from hatred.

'I want to give it to you, Trent,' Blake said. 'Everything I've got – and I want to make you suffer just as much as you made them little girls suffer . . . and after that I'm gonna make you suffer ten times more so they'll never ever properly repair you.'

'You've already done that.' It was a hoarse, strained whisper that grated out from Trent's dry throat.

'I haven't even started.' Blake pushed himself upright and took a menacing stride into the cell. Trent almost screamed, though it was more of a whimper. He recoiled, stepped backwards, caught the back of his knee on the toilet, causing the joint to fold. He grabbed thin air in an attempt to prevent himself from falling backwards, failed, and next thing he knew he was sitting on the lavatory, looking meekly upwards at the towering menace of Blake.

The big man burst into laughter.

'You pathetic twat.' He reached for Trent's throat with

his right hand. The fingers curled around his windpipe, digging in, hoisting him to his feet. Blake pivoted and slammed Trent against the cell wall. 'You haven't got an ounce of fight in you, have you? I'm going to really enjoy raping you, so you'd better prepare yourself, 'cos I won't be long. Maybe today, maybe tomorrow, you little piece of shite.' His face was only inches away from Trent's. He reeked of smoke and body odour. His breath made Trent gag. 'Who knows?' he snarled. 'But it'll be soon and you won't know what's hit you – because I intend inserting more than just myself up your backside. So let yer imagination run riot.'

He opened his fingers, releasing Trent, who, choking, slithered down the wall, tears streaming out of his eyes. 'See ya.' Blake gave a friendly wave and spun out of the cell. Trent could hear him laughing all the way down the walkway.

Trent quickly removed his trousers and underpants and dashed to the toilet, plonking himself down only just in time. The terrifying encounter had taken its toll on his bowels. They opened up immediately.

With his head in his hands, he realised he would probably have to act sooner than later.

Talking to Henry had proved to be a nice release for Danny. She left his office feeling better having dumped such a heavy burden from her shoulders. It helped her greatly with the mental side – a trouble shared, and all that – but the physical side was another matter altogether.

Danny would be the first to admit she had allowed her fitness to deteriorate over the last ten years, but it had happened in such slow stages that she had been unaware of just how unfit she had become because it had been masked by her sedentary lifestyle.

It had taken the exertions and batterings of the last forty-eight hours to demonstrate what a blob she had become.

Firstly, chasing Claire Lilton and rescuing her; then being assaulted by Jack, coupled with the early-morning incidents at her house. Everything had accumulated in such a short space of time so that when she sat down at her desk she felt so creaky she should have had her pension book in her bag.

Yet she knew that if she had been only slightly fitter, she would not have felt half as bad.

She leaned back in her chair and took a quick evaluation of her body, from feet upwards.

Actually her toes did not feel too bad.

Everything else above and beyond was in pretty poor condition though.

The ankle she'd twisted throbbed meanly away underneath the tubi-grip bandage and was swollen like a football. She rotated her foot carefully and winced.

Her long legs were stiffening up. Running after Claire – all of what, 200 metres? – had made her use muscles which had lain dormant for ten years, despite the most robust lovemaking, and there had been plenty of that. They ached all the way up to the cheeks of her bum.

During the buffeting on the sea-front, she only now discovered she must have taken a few knocks which went unheeded at the time, probably due to adrenaline. Her chest was painful around the ribs, and the outer point of her right elbow felt like it might have been smashed against the ground.

The base of her spine was still damned sore, making every other movement of her body a chore. The back of her head was agonisingly tender and her face smarted from the blow Jack had delivered to her. And, of course, there was the cut on her left cheek, stitched with such precision by the same drop-dead gorgeous doctor who'd tubi-gripped her.

Sod Jack, the bastard, she thought bitterly. She wondered whether or not to make an official complaint of assault, as suggested by Henry, who had voiced the opinion that if Jack had the capacity to do that to someone he allegedly loved, he deserved to face the consequences.

Danny shook her head. No.

That was the last thing she wanted. Muck-raking, grievances, courts, ruining reputations, marriages, professional relationships. She simply wanted it all sorted out as amicably as possible.

Danny's fingertips touched her cheek, gently moving across the two stitches inserted at Casualty earlier that morning.

Two stitches. A serious assault by any standards.

And yet she did not want Jack to get away without facing any consequences – especially if he had smashed her window and damaged her car in a fit of pique. He should be forced to admit it, pay restitution – then get out of her life.

She moved in the chair to ease the pain in her back.

She knew she could at least make one decision about her life there and then. That would be to drag herself, unwillingly, to fitness classes a couple of times a week. Then, she reasoned, if she was feeling physically better it would make it easier to get to grips with other more nebulous aspects of her life.

Such as cutting out smoking – although as she thought about that one, a deep longing for a cigarette pervaded her body like an insistent spirit. Maybe that would have to wait.

The phone on her desk rang. It was the public enquiry assistant (PEA), down at the front desk.

Claire Lilton wanted to see her. Could Danny come down, please?

It is not necessarily the prison hard men who know everything there is to know about the institutions in which they are forced to lead their lives. In fact, more often than not, these are the people who know the least. They may control things like drugs, screws, booze, cigarettes and violence, but they were wrapped up in their own comfort zones, insulated and smug. They know what they feel they need to know and little else. Only when they want to escape, perhaps, or cause a riot, do they get to know it better.

It's usually the more harmless inmates, the trusted ones, the pathetic ones, the listeners, the shadows, who know everything there is to know.

They are aware of the full picture as regards the comings and goings of the prison staff. They know the complete geography of the buildings; all the little nooks and crannies; the hidey-holes where they can disappear for a while if necessary. They know where everything is kept, locked away, stored.

These people are the ones who can, seemingly, move around unchallenged because they are not worth challenging; float around, creeping, watching all the time.

Trent was not one of those people.

But Vic Wallwork was.

Fifteen years behind bars had made him so. Turned him into an acquiescent, simpering inmate who said yes to everything, never let the authorities down, yet at the same time watched, learned, listened, explored.

This was his third prison. He knew it intimately.

Which is why he was able to lead Trent through places he never knew existed.

He guided Trent out through the back of the kitchens, past a series of storerooms, down a doom-laden corridor with low beams and little light, out through a door and into the glorious open air, somewhere – Trent could only guess – near to the back of the Governor's offices.

They had to race across this space, around the corner of a redbrick building Trent had never seen before, and into a narrow ginnel no more than three feet wide. It twisted at right angles and ten yards further came to a dead end. But in the dead end was a door with a huge rusting padlock securing it.

Wallwork produced a key from his pocket, inserted it and forced it to turn. The lock released itself. He removed it and pushed the door open. Beyond was a dank, dark room. Wallwork reached around the door jamb and flicked a switch. A single naked bulb flickered uncertainly, casting a dim light into the room.

Trent followed Wallwork inside, closing the door behind him. He gazed around, sniffing, trying to speculate what the room was for.

Wallwork second-guessed the question. 'Part of an old boiler area . . . course, it's all gas now. Through that door is where the main boiler is.' He pointed a crooked finger at the far end of the room. Trent saw a door which looked as if it hadn't been opened for years. Wallwork's index finger then pointed downwards at a petrol can on the floor.

'That's what you wanted, isn't it?'

A surge of pure pleasure beat through Trent. He knelt down by the can and touched it lovingly. 'Yeah, great. How much is in it?'

'A gallon. Like you asked for – at great risk to me, I might add.'

'Excellent.' Trent pulled two milk bottles Coysh had given him out of his jacket pockets and stood them up on the concrete floor. He looked at the petrol can, head cocked, and did some calculations, as well as visualising a spectacular future. 'Mmm,' he murmured thoughtfully, biting his bottom lip.

Wallwork watched him with a certain degree of puzzlement, although having now seen the milk bottles, things were a little clearer to him now. What was still foxing him, though, was why Trent was also carrying a pillowcase stuffed with the styrofoam cups Coysh had stolen for him. Didn't make any sense to him. Trent placed the pillowcase on the floor.

'Need more bottles,' Trent said. 'Four more, to be on the safe side.' He exhaled through his nose. 'And I need another container of some sort, like an open can – something I can pour the petrol into.'

Both men considered the matter for a few seconds.

'I know just the thing!' Wallwork declared, raising a finger. He went to a dark corner of the room where he rooted about amongst some debris. He picked something up and returned. It was a lidless metal toolbox, old and misshapen.

Trent grabbed it greedily from Vic's grasp and inspected it closely, holding it up to the light, carefully rotating it. All the seals, corners and edges appeared to be intact. There was a lot of rust, some of it flaking off, but nothing which would cause a problem in the short term. In fact, a bit of rust would be quite nice, Trent thought.

'That's good.' He looked at his companion. 'That's very, very good.' His eyes glazed over as he spoke; once again he was seeing the future.

Wallwork's blood froze for an instant. A tremor crawled all the way down his spine like a serpent. The expression on Trent's face was one he knew well. He recognised it from himself, a look which had crossed his own face just over fifteen years ago. Twice. And each time it had resulted in the brutal slaying of a young boy. After which – here Vic Wallwork thanked God – they caught him and incarcerated him for the rest of his life before it happened again.

It was the killing look.

Trent's eyes refocused and he came back to his own brand of normality. He squatted down by the petrol can and poured petrol into the two milk bottles until each was about a third full. Not being an expert, he guesstimated that would be enough.

He placed the bottles out of the way, next to the brick wall.

'By the way, Vic,' he said conversationally. 'I bumped into Blake again.'

'Oh?' Wallwork swallowed.

'Soon, he told me. Soon. He's going to get you and stick a broom-handle right up your arse so it comes out of your mouth. Exact words.' And Trent continued with his task, pouring the remaining petrol from the can into the toolbox, slowly, checking for leaks as he did so.

Wallwork watched the activity, virtually catatonic because of what Trent had just said. Without even seeing Wallwork's face, Trent realised the devastating effect he'd had on the man. He smiled wickedly to himself.

Next he emptied the pillowcase, making a small mountain of the styrofoam cups next to the toolbox. He sat down on the floor and picked up one of the cups. He tore it into little stamp-sized pieces and began dropping them into the petrol, like confetti. Bit by bit.

'What are you doing?' Wallwork asked. He had shaken himself out of his moment of terror.

Trent stopped. He raised his head slowly. His eyes once more became glassy.

The killing look.

'Ever heard of napalm?'

Once again Claire Lilton had disappeared.

As soon as Danny received the call she dashed down to the front office of the police station, although the dash was more of a hobble. Even so, she was there within a minute.

The PEA shrugged her shoulders. She had been too busy to do anything about Claire leaving.

Danny checked the area just outside the foyer. No sign of the girl.

A troubled and frustrated DC Furness returned to her desk, wondering what the hell it was all about. Obviously Claire wanted to talk, but maybe didn't have the courage. Perhaps if Danny visited her home she would be able to talk privately . . . although that might prove difficult with Stepdaddy Lilton around.

And that thought struck a chord in Danny's mind.

The stepfather – Joe Lilton.

When she had met him at the hospital, Danny had been positive it was not the first time. The face and voice were familiar, yet had been impossible to pinpoint. Someone from many years ago.

Danny picked up the phone, spoke to the PNC operator in comms and requested a body check on Joe Lilton.

He came up on the screen immediately. Not because he had any previous convictions, which was the usual case for people on the Police National Computer, but because he was the holder of a firearms certificate issued by the Chief Constable of Lancashire.

Danny thanked the operator, hung up.

Yet still nothing registered with her.

She trawled deep into her long-term memory . . . and there it was, filed away neatly and nicely in the attic storeroom of her brain cells. The firearms certificate was the key, the reason why Danny knew him.

She had been the police officer, all of fifteen years before, who had visited Lilton at his home address somewhere in Blackburn following his application for a certificate. You had to check for previous convictions, visit the house and ensure there were safe storage facilities for the weapons. It was a routine procedure. Routine but necessary. Then you had to make a recommendation as to whether the applicant was suitable to hold a firearms certificate.

. . . It was all coming back as she thought long and hard.

The petrol ate up the styrofoam until it was sated and could devour no more. Finally, Trent was left with a thick, syrupy substance.

'There we are,' he declared happily. 'Whatever you do, don't touch it,' he warned Wallwork, who had helped him to mix the styrofoam into it, 'or it'll burn your skin off.'

'We'd better get going,' Wallwork said. 'They'll miss us soon.'

'Yeah, you're right. Will this be safe here? Anyone likely to come noseying in?'

Wallwork shook his head. 'Doubtful.'

They locked the door behind them and made their way back through the prison, emerging at the rear of the kitchens. Wallwork guided him unobtrusively into the main body of the prison without mishap.

'Make sure you get a shower,' Trent advised, painfully aware they both reeked of petrol. Wallwork said he would.

Fifteen minutes later, refreshed and changed, Trent descended into the association area and found Coysh in the TV lounge, sitting in a chair at the back of the room, away from the other inmates who were watching the box.

Trent sat in the empty chair next to him.

Neither man formally acknowledged the other.

'I wanna know their plans for the rest of the day.' Trent spoke just loud enough for Coysh to hear.

'In the gym between two and three. After the brew they'll be in Blake's cell up on level two. Card-game arranged. The three of them and the nigger – you know, your big pal.'

'That'll be handy.'

'They'll be there until evening meal. After that, don't know.'

Trent relaxed in the comfortable chair, his eyes looking at, but not focusing on the TV. He placed his fingertips together and made a steeple with his fingers. He placed the tip of it underneath his chin.

It was an ideal situation for his proposed course of action.

Level two was the prison equivalent of a high-class housing estate. Anyone who was anyone had a cell up there; the movers and shakers of prison society. The remainder of the inmates were on the other landings. If you were found on landing two and didn't have a cell

114

there, you needed a damned good reason for your presence. There was no wandering through, no nosy-parkering – unless you wanted your face smashed in. Or worse.

Which would probably make it all the more easy for Trent because the likelihood was that between the hours mentioned by Coysh, there would be few people up there anyway. And the ones who were, such as Blake, would be busy in their cells, conspiring.

'Keep me informed,' Trent said. He made to stand up, then had a thought. 'Did you fulfil my other request?'

Coysh reached down the side of his chair and picked up an open can of Diet Coke. He handed it to Trent who found it to be quite heavy.

'Don't drink it, for fuck's sake,' Coysh laughed.

Trent smelled it, winced. 'What is it?'

'Just what you wanted. Pig's blood.'

'I want to thank you all for last night's effort.'

Steve Kruger surveyed the faces of the team which had successfully put themselves up against Bussola – and won so convincingly.

Since the cops had arrived at the scene and arrested Bussola, Kruger and the team had stayed up and given witness depositions. Now it was ten in the morning. None of them had had any sleep for over twenty-four hours. All were shattered and showed it.

Myrna nodded. 'Yeah, everyone worked well.'

'But now we have a problem,' Kruger said with caution. 'And I don't think I need to spend a great deal of time expanding on it. I'm talking about Bussola's organisation. We need to be watching our backs – and fronts – from now on. Bussola doesn't like people who go against him, but I doubt whether he'll be stupid enough to do anything too soon. However, be wary.'

When they were gone, with the exception of Myrna, Kruger sat down heavily and rubbed his tired, red-raw eyes.

'What are you going to tell Felicity?' Myrna asked.

He shrugged. 'Doubt if I'll have to tell her anything.'

Myrna yawned; Kruger saw a mouthful of perfect teeth. 'You realise,' he said, 'you spent a whole night with the boss. What'll hubby think about that one?'

She was about to make a smart-ass reply when Kruger's cell-tel chirped.

'Steve Kruger.'

'Steve, it's Mark Tapperman here.'

'Hi, Mark.' Kruger and he went back many years. Tapperman was now a Lieutenant in the Miami Police Department.

'Bad news, I'm afraid,' Tapperman said. Kruger knew what it would be even before he said it. 'Bussola's walked. No charges. Nuthin' we could do about it. He's free as a bird again.'

Chapter Six

Trent, Wallwork and Coysh made the trip out to the old boiler-room.

Trent poured a few inches of petrol into two more milk bottles and then half-filled three more bottles with the home-made napalm, pouring it carefully from the toolbox into the mouths of the bottles, not spilling a drop of the thick liquid. He was totally concentrated; his hands were steady, his eyes focused. The sticky substance did not run easily, but Trent was not worried about that. It wasn't supposed to. That part of the job finished, he covered the tops of the bottles with tinfoil.

The pillowcase in which the styrofoam cups had been transported was torn up by him into strips which he dipped in petrol. He folded the strips into an empty, clean and dry baked-bean tin which he covered with a square of tinfoil.

'Yeah, good, I'm right,' he said, bouncing as he surveyed his handiwork with a gleam in his eyes. 'Let's get this stuff back to the kitchens.'

He had brought along another pillowcase which he folded carefully around the bottles; then he placed them into a sports bag which he zipped up and hung over his shoulder, keeping it level.

'You're sure the cell next to Blake's will be empty?' he questioned Coysh again.

Coysh nodded.

'Right, good. Once we get back, you look after this gear

in the kitchens, then when I give you the nod, take it up to that cell and shove it underneath the bunk, got that? Think you can do that?'

'Yep,' said Coysh.

'And you know what you're doing?' Trent turned to Vic Wallwork.

'I know.'

'Good. Right – let's go.'

Wallwork led them uneventfully back to the kitchens where Coysh placed the sports bag in a cupboard underneath a sink.

Trent went back to his cell. He knew it would be empty because his stupid cellmates always watched *Fifteen-to-One* on Channel Four at 4.30 p.m.

It was now 4.20 p.m. They always got there early for the front-row seats.

He stole a pillowcase from one of their beds and tore it into fairly wide strips. After this he filled the wash-basin with cold water and dropped the strips inside to soak them.

Next he helped himself to a pair of trousers and a shirt, both prison issue, belonging to the cellmate he judged to be more or less the same size as himself. He put both items into the water and made sure they were waterlogged too.

From the waistband of his jeans he popped out the pills he'd bought on his spending spree around the prison the day before and dribbled them out into a nice pile near the pillow on his bed. Just for the hell of it he wolfed a few of them down, even though he did not know what they were. They tasted foul, but did nothing for him immediately.

He was nearing readiness.

Sitting down on the edge of the bed he rolled up his shirtsleeves and exposed both forearms. The skin was criss-crossed with old scars, poor attempts at previous suicides.

118

Time for the knife.

He reached into his foam pillow, pulled out the bung and extracted the knife from its hiding place.

It looked, and he knew it was, shiny, sharp and deadly.

Firstly he ran his thumb down the sharp blade, just to test it. He smiled maliciously, knowing if he pressed harder his thumb would have been sliced in two halves.

Next he placed the blade against the soft skin on the inside of his left forearm, just above the wrist. He applied a little pressure, the blade indented the skin. He pressed a little harder and slowly, deliberately, drew the knife across the skin which parted easily, leaving a thin red line. Breath escaped through his teeth. The pain was almost unbearable pleasure. He pulled the knife away and stared at what he had done. Nothing happened for a few seconds . . . then little blobs of blood appeared down the line of the cut. They burst and began to trickle.

He inspected the cut and clenched his fist, tightening the muscles and sinews of his forearm, forcing more blood to seep out of the wound.

Trent's face had an expression of grim satisfaction on it.

It had been a finely judged cut.

Just deep enough to draw blood, not too deep to do any real damage.

He placed the blade a further two inches up his arm, gritted his teeth and sliced the skin open. A sensation went through him that was almost sexual.

Again, the cut was perfect.

It bled, but was not serious.

Trent was enjoying himself.

His heart was pounding.

He had a sudden urge to do more, in a less controlled, more frenzied way . . . and in fact he could not stop himself as half a dozen more times he slashed the razor-sharp blade across his forearm, each time gasping orgasmically as the skin opened.

Suddenly, breathlessly, he knew he had to get a grip and stop.

He looked at his arm and licked the blood from it with a slurping, drain-like noise, tasting the hot, salty liquid on his tongue, covering his teeth with it. It tasted good and he groaned. 'I'm good, yeah, good.' He shook his head, crossed the knife into his left hand and quickly repeated the process on the skin of his right forearm, leaving eight slash-lines across the lily-white skin, but not one of them deep enough to cause him any problems.

He rolled down his shirtsleeves and buttoned them at the cuffs. He stood up and walked smartly out onto the landing, his arms folded across his chest. He went to a point which overlooked the association area.

Coysh and Wallwork were sitting huddled over a chess-board.

Coysh looked up, saw Trent and nodded.

He moved a bishop. 'Mate,' he said, and stood.

Trent walked quickly back to his cell where he immediately stripped naked, bar his footwear, and re-dressed in the cold wet clothes which had been soaking in the wash-basin. He took the torn pillowcase and squeezed out some of the excess water.

Before leaving the cell he grabbed the knife.

He knew from experience that the chances of meeting other prisoners or maybe even a screw were pretty scarce at this time of day. Most people were down on association or beginning to form an early queue for the evening meal. Screw activity was focused on those areas with the occasional officer prowling about . . . or, as Trent knew today, in a cell with a drug dealer sampling some wares. Trent's luck would have to be pretty low for him to meet anyone who mattered on the journey between his cell and level two.

He saw no one.

Quietly he mounted the metal staircase which led up to level two, peering ahead of him down the walkway in front of the cells, checking the all-clear.

A second later he was on the landing. Level two. Home to Blake *et al.*

The cell Trent was interested in was the fourth along. The other cell which interested him was third along.

He crept quietly, hearing Blake's raucous laughter and voice from the fourth cell. There were other voices too. Trent recognised them all. They belonged to his tormentors and the black rapist, and because of what they had done to him, they were all going to die.

He sneaked into the third cell – empty, as promised – knelt down by the first bunk and reached for the sports bag which had been placed there by Coysh just a few minutes earlier. Trent dragged it out, unzipped it and carefully unwrapped the pillowcase from around the milk bottles. He placed them side by side on the cell floor, removing the tinfoil tops.

He picked out the petrol-soaked strips of cotton from the baked-bean tin and pushed them into the mouth of each bottle.

Last, but not least, he found the Zippo lighter which he had previously ensured was safely stored in the side compartment of the sports bag.

Before lighting the strips, he wrapped several of the water-soaked strands of torn pillowcase around his head for protection against any possible backdraught.

The lighter flared first time. He moved the flame towards one of the bottles.

'What the hell y'doin'?'

Trent dropped the lighter, spun round and saw the shape of the large black man standing at the cell door; it was the one who had raped him. He had been involved in the card-game next door for almost two hours and had come out to stretch his legs.

Trent reacted instantly.

His right hand flew round to the back pocket where he had put the knife and whilst he reached for it he rose and hurled himself towards the black man with more speed than he knew he had. By the time he reached him, the knife was in his right hand and executing an unstoppable upward arc towards the man's chest. It entered just below the sternum with such force and at such an angle that Trent was able to drive the point of the blade into the heart. He actually felt it enter that organ. Felt the resistance of the muscle wall, felt it burst through into the right ventricle.

The man was astounded by the speed. He didn't have time to react in any way at all.

Trent double-forced the blade and screwed it horribly as though he was wrenching the handle of a table football game. At the same time he grabbed the man's curly hair and pulled him into the cell.

He was dead.

Trent eased the limp body down onto his knees, then onto his face, withdrew the knife, wiped it clean on the man's back and returned to the milk bottles and cigarette lighter.

Time was running out.

He lit each bottle. The blue flames faltered slightly until they took hold.

He picked up two bottles, one petrol, one napalm, and weighed them thoughtfully in his hands as he wondered just how he was going to do this.

He decided to take a chance.

The landing was clear, so he quickly placed the burning bottles in a row outside the cell door.

Then he took two petrol bombs, a deep breath, spun into the doorway of Blake's cell and announced, 'Your time has come, you bastards!'

The three men inside were sat on the edge of two beds with a small table between them. Halfway through a card-game, they looked up, annoyed by the interruption.

At which moment Trent acted.

With all the force he could muster he aimed the first

bottle at a point on the floor in front of the table and smashed it down.

It burst on impact. With a whoosh of flame the petrol splashed up and ignited.

Trent immediately bowled the second bottle in.

It crashed and exploded, engulfing the cell in flame.

Trent bent down, picked up two napalm bombs and they went the same way as the others – smashing on impact, their contents being sprayed all over the men in the cell – with the added effect that the home-made napalm clung and burned fiercely.

Blake avoided the full blast of the first two bombs, but could not avoid the napalm. He screamed as gobs of fire splattered all over him. One shot down his throat and burned him from the inside.

The other two men were victims of the first firebombs.

One managed to run out of the cell, a demented, writhing fireball, screaming in agony as he burst his way past Trent. He stamped frenziedly across the walkway and flung himself over the railings into space, dropping like a comet into the safety netting below. Here he thrashed about wildly, suspended twenty-five feet above the association area, watched by stunned, open-mouthed inmates and staff. All helpless to assist him.

Without watching this, Trent lobbed the remaining bottles into the cell, ducking as the heat and flames bellowed out. The fingers of fire caressed and singed his protective clothing.

The last bottles did not have a great effect because most of the damage had been done, the first explosions having sucked and burned up most of the available oxygen.

Trent did not wait. As the last bottle left his hand he turned and hared for the steps which would take him down to his level. He knew the majority of people would make their way up onto level two from the opposite direction, from the steps nearest to the association area.

In order to aid his passage, he ripped the wet protective strips off his head and screamed, 'Help! Fire! Get some help! People hurt!' as he tore down the walkway, pointing frantically in the direction from which he had come.

He pushed his way through the gathering number of people running towards the scene of the inferno. No one seemed to take a blind bit of notice of him.

He landed back in his cell probably forty seconds after the last petrol bomb had exploded. He was breathless, shaking. He ripped his clothing off and stuffed the wet garments underneath his mattress, jumped into his own clothing, pulled up his shirtsleeves and sat on the bed.

His arms were bleeding nicely.

They needed to bleed some more.

He reached for the tin of pig's blood.

Danny had been a naughty policewoman over the years. In more ways than one.

Regulations state that all officers must hand in their pocket-books for safe storage purposes each time one is completed. Danny had only ever handed pocket-books in during her two-year probationary period. She preferred to keep them in her locker and now, fifteen years on, she had a stackful on the top shelf which she would be hard-pressed to explain if called to account.

It was, in essence, a complete history of her police service, minus the first two years.

She reached right to the back of the shelf and found the one she was looking for. Pocket-book number 12. The twelfth book issued to her in her third year of service, showing how busy she had been in those days when she had been bright, keen and conscientious. Twelve in less than three years was pretty good going.

Of late, Danny recorded little in her pocket-books, just the bare necessities. The book she was using at that moment was over two years old.

She smiled when she saw the pink-covered, dog-eared

log. Her memories flooded back fifteen years to those simple, uncluttered days of her first posting at Blackburn police station in the east of the county. Flicking the book open to the last page she glanced down the index of names and incidents she had attended. As she read them to herself, standing in a locker-room at Blackpool police station, she found she remembered each one.

Amongst the names were:

Loughlin: Burglary (he'd broken into a sweetshop on Eanam.)

Alexander: Parking offence (that bitch had been a real cow to deal with.)

Allcock: Prostitution (one of the many Blackburn hookers.)

There were numerous other names, all invoking their own particular reminiscence.

Eventually she saw the name she had been searching for.

Lilton: F/arm cert.

Danny rifled to the entry on page 21. Her memory was now well and truly jogged. She read the entry, then her eyes became misty as she visualised the day.

Visiting people who had applied for firearms certificates was a routine job usually carried out by more experienced officers. That particular day Danny's shift was 2 p.m.-10 p.m., and the guy who usually covered the outer rural beats of Blackburn had reported in sick. Much to Danny's surprise, the Sergeant allocated her his beat for the day. She had been expecting to spend another eight hours trudging round the town centre, picking up shoplifters and drunks. The chance to work a mobile beat was pretty rare for a woman in those days, especially at her length of service. It was a beat usually given out to the older 'lads' as a bit of a sweetener.

She was handed the keys to the Panda car and the stack of routine enquiries and told to come in for her refreshments at six.

Danny could see herself marching confidently down the corridor. Twenty-two years old, slim as a beanpole. A non-smoker who hardly drank at all but enjoyed lots of uncomplicated sex with a variety of guys, mainly detectives. Fit as a flea and a regular member of the County Athletic Team.

What great days.

As she went out to the car she collected her PR from the comms room. Whilst fiddling with the radio harness she accidentally dropped the pile of enquiries onto the floor. The Constable who had issued her radio, and who was desperate to find his way into Danny's knickers, picked them up for her, like the gentleman he was, or purported to be.

He noticed the Lilton firearms enquiry on top of the pile.

Danny could not quite recall the exact words. They were along the lines of, 'I wouldn't trust him with a catapult, never mind a thirty-eight.' A remark which set Danny's alarm bells ringing.

She asked why.

The PC told her. 'Always beating his wife up. Real volatile git.' He handed her the enquiries and changed tack to a more favourable subject. He asked Danny out for the tenth time.

And for the tenth time, she politely refused.

He sighed despondently and waddled his short twenty-two-stone frame back into the radio room.

So that afternoon, before going out on patrol, Danny sat in the report room and leafed through all the messages, reports and any references whatsoever to do with Joe Lilton of Head Bank House, Osbaldeston, Blackburn.

She got the impression the overweight Constable had a point.

After she turned out from the station, she enjoyed half an hour tootling round the country lanes, not having a single deployment. Then she got bored and made her way to Osbaldeston, a quiet village close to the River Ribble.

There was a fair smattering of wealth in the area and Head Bank House was a large, detached building surrounded by a couple of acres of landscaped gardens. Danny knew from his firearms application form that Lilton described himself as a self-employed trader. Further digging had revealed he owned six shops which sold High Street seconds at knock-down prices.

Danny drove down the wide, arcing driveway laid with white chippings crunching under the tyres of the battered Ford Escort. She drew up outside the front door next to a brand-new Jaguar and a slightly older Mini. Danny was calling on spec. It looked as though she'd struck lucky.

As soon as she stepped out of the car she heard raised voices from inside the house. A big argument. Man and woman. She stood and listened and tried to work out what it was about. It seemed to be about infidelity.

She walked confidently to the front door and jammed her thumb on the doorbell. The shouting continued. She kept her thumb on. It rang loudly. The shouting stopped.

Footsteps. The sound of crying. Footsteps getting closer to the door. The door opening.

The woman was very glamorous in a tacky sort of way. She was in her mid-thirties. Her mascara had run, making her look like a surprised owl.

This was Mrs Lilton, Danny assumed. She looked puzzled to see a uniform at her door. 'What d'you want?' she asked sharply. 'No one's called the police, have they?'

Danny shook her head. 'I'm here on another matter . . . but are you all right? Do you need some help?'

The woman stared disgustedly at Danny. 'Yeah, I'm okay – no thanks to you lot. As if you care.' Her breath reeked of alcohol fumes. 'You've never cared yet, have you? So what d'you want?'

'To see Joe Lilton, please.'

'Why? Won't it wait?'

'Not unless he doesn't want to get a firearms certificate.' As she finished the sentence, Joe Lilton appeared behind the woman.

'Come in, come in,' he said graciously to Danny. 'There's nothing going on here but a little family disagreement.' He looked at Danny and their eyes locked ever so briefly and he knew she knew he was lying to his back teeth.

Danny remembered that face well, now, fifteen years later. Those pinched, mean features, now fleshed out by ageing.

At the door of the house in Osbaldeston, he had placed his hands on his wife's shoulders. She had juddered visibly at the touch. 'Come on,' he said gently to her. To Danny he stated, 'A misunderstanding, that's all.'

Yeah, no mistaking it, Danny thought, closing her pocket-book.

It was the same Joe Lilton who was now Claire Lilton's stepfather.

What a small world.

'Oh, fucking hell, he's bleeding like a stuck pig, for God's sake!' the young, blood-covered prison officer screamed to the paramedics. 'And he's got internal bleeding too, for some reason,' he blabbered. 'Christ!' he mouthed. 'The bastard puked a whole gob-full all over me!'

The young man looked down his chest. He retched at the sight of the thick red globules all down the front of his uniform shirt which had once been white.

'God, I've never seen anything so foul. Taken a load of pills too.'

He was blithering these words to the green-jacketed paramedics whilst they stretchered the supposedly dying Trent expertly through the twists and turns of the prison, along walkways, down steep stairwells.

Finally they emerged at the yard behind the front gates of the prison where three ambulances, a couple of fire tenders and two cop cars were drawn up.

Trent was dumped in the back of the nearest ambulance.

Having listened to the screw babbling on, Trent was having difficulty keeping a straight face. He desperately needed to belly laugh, sit up and say, 'Fooled you, you stupid set of cunts.'

Instead he continued to play the part of someone who has just tried to end his own life with a concoction of drugs and the old opening-of-veins ceremony.

When he heard the ambulance doors clunk shut, he was satisfied. Then more so when he experienced the forwards motion of the vehicle. Then orgasmically so, when through his rolling eyes, he saw the blue lights begin to flash and rotate.

He was on his way to freedom.

It had worked perfectly.

The prison officers, as Trent had rightly predicted, had reacted to the crisis like a bunch of headless chickens, running around the prison, not knowing whether they were coming or going. The fire in Blake's cell, the discovery of the four bodies – two burnt-out in the cell, one knifed to death in the adjacent cell and the other toasted alive whilst suspended above an audience – had thrown them into utter confusion. No one seemed able to take control of the situation. Having a suicide attempt thrown in on top of all that was the last straw.

When they had seen how bad he was, Trent was certain they would not mess about by transferring him to the woefully inadequate medical wing. It did not have the staff or facilities to deal with someone who had tried to shred his arms and taken such a lethal dose of junk he was bleeding internally and puking blood.

He knew their reaction would be to get him out of the way, cart him off to the nearest Casualty unit.

Which is exactly what they did. And to speed things up in the chaos, they cut corners. Obviously they could not handcuff Trent because of his injured arms, but nor did they search him. They seemed happy to believe that the small penknife they found next to the bed was the one with which he had mutilated himself.

An absolute dream.

Having said that, the task of keeping a mouthful of pig's blood ready to cough out onto a screw had created a few trying moments. That had been a case of mind over matter. It was a good job the screw had raced into the cell when he did (urged by Vic Wallwork, playing his part in the scenario), because Trent was about to puke anyway.

And now he was in the rear of the ambulance.

He moaned. He groaned. He writhed and twisted his body in agony, ensuring they could not quite find his pulse or clamp an oxygen mask on him or stick a tube up his arm.

'OOOARH – urgh,' he uttered with deep pain, loving every moment of it.

'Come on, pal, keep still, you'll be okay,' the paramedic fussed caringly and tried to clean him up.

Less than thirty seconds later the ambulance had negotiated its way through the narrow prison gates, accelerating away smoothly, then screeching around a roundabout onto a dual carriageway.

The prison officer who had been tasked to remain with Trent – the one covered in pig's blood – looked on with an expression of worry and repulsion. Over the paramedic's shoulders he said, 'I hope the bastard's not got HIV, with all this fucking blood over me. He's an arse-bandit, you know.'

The paramedic put him straight immediately. 'If you've had unprotected sex with this man and drunk a pint of his blood, you might have cause for concern. If not, don't worry.'

Trent continued to squirm realistically, feeling the need to put more distance between himself and the prison before he took matters to their logical conclusion.

When he judged the moment right, he suddenly sat up with a scream as though a great pain had burned through his abdomen. He reached behind himself, his hand went underneath his shirt and his fingers closed on the hilt of the knife fastened to his spine with a couple of Band Aids.

He ripped the instrument from its moorings.

The paramedic, surprised by the sudden sitting up, stepped back. The roll of the ambulance unbalanced him slightly.

Without hesitation, Trent drove the knife into the unfortunate man's neck. The razor-sharp blade pierced the jugular vein as Trent dug it in and rived it round and round. He withdrew the blade as the man screamed dreadfully and a glorious crimson fountain flowered into the air, splattering the inside of the ambulance with deep red swathes of blood. The paramedic's hands reached instinctively for his neck to try and stop the flow.

Trent grabbed the man's overalls at the chest and threw him sideways. Then he jumped to his feet and leapt across the small space at the prison officer. That man's senses had not been capable, in those brief seconds, of taking in what had just happened to the paramedic.

Trent was on the officer, yelling, 'I'm not an arse bandit, I'm a fucking paedophile, you pig-bastard.'

He plunged the knife into the officer's right eye which burst with a pop as the blade entered the pupil, its watery contents spurting out. Trent pushed the blade further in, right up to the hilt, angled it upwards into the brain, killing him the instant the soft tissue was pierced.

Trent held the knife in there, grinding it round. The dead man's jangled nerves reacted by making him dance like someone possessed by the devil. Then Trent extracted it as the man's legs gave way.

Trent slid casually next to the ambulance driver, reached for the radio and ripped the handset out. He leaned across to the driver who had not even realised what was going on and pushed the point of the knife into his neck. A trickle of blood popped out from the prick.

'Taxi,' Trent said with a smile.

Chapter Seven

Lieutenant Mark Tapperman was a very big guy, even in comparison to Steve Kruger who was no midget himself. Tapperman was six-four, built like the frontal elevation of a very substantial building and kept himself incredibly fit – necessary qualifications for policing the crime-ridden streets of Miami where a cop needed all the edge he could get . . . and then some.

Despite these credentials, Tapperman looked sheepishly at Steve Kruger as the ex-cop walked towards him with a slight limp and an expression of seething anger stamped across his face.

'Oh shit,' Tapperman mumbled under his breath. 'He's mad.' He suddenly had the thought that maybe coming to this particular restaurant for lunch was not the best of choices. Granny Feelgood's was not the right place for someone who probably wanted to rip a twelve-ounce steak to shreds; it was more suited to a person on a diet who wanted to pig out on tofu or spiced tea. Arbetter Hot Dogs would've been a more appropriate place to meet and eat, Tapperman thought too late.

'Mark,' Kruger nodded curtly. He slumped down on the chair opposite Tapperman and slung his jacket across the back of another. He loosened his neck-tie and unfastened his collar, his face distorting as his fingers eased the button out of its hole. He tugged the collar loose.

Once again Miami was like a fan oven and that, combined with his tiredness – for Kruger had not yet had

133

any sleep – meant he was mega-irritable.

It showed in his body language.

'Herb tea?' Tapperman enquired hopefully.

Kruger eyed the detective critically for a moment. 'Nooo,' he said quietly with an exaggerated pursing of the lips. 'Just tell me what you've got.'

Tapperman sipped his Perrier to clear his dust-dry throat.

'Nothing we could do about it,' he said helplessly. 'Bussola's lawyer, Ira Begin, was waiting at the station-house when we arrived. Couldn't stop Bussola talking to him – y'know, prisoner's rights and all that crap; couldn't stop his lawyer makin' phone calls either, could we?' Tapperman sighed. 'Anyways, we got the process going . . . then we find out there ain't no process to get going.'

Kruger waited impatiently.

'Somehow, probably through the lawyer, he'd got to the girl's parents.'

'So?'

'Well, that little girl he was ridin' when you found him was only eleven years old. She'd been on the run from home 'bout three weeks and somehow got herself sucked into Bussola's porn system. Thing is, though, the reason why we got nowhere, was because there ain't no complaint. Bussola's organisation got to her parents before we did – and this is only an assumption, Steve. I think they were paid off and delivered a bottom-line threat at the same time. "You're dead if you testify". They're poor people from Homestead. Ain't recovered from Hurricane Andrew yet. In those circumstances, Bussola's money is as good as anybody's.'

'Even if he raped your daughter?' Kruger was incredulous. He went on, 'Why not indict without them? It's serious enough. Do it on the girl's behalf.' Kruger's voice was cold, hard. He had not liked one word of what had been said.

'If we did, Steve, Bussola would kill the family. You know he would, and that would not achieve anything.'

Kruger began to hiss steam. He wanted to overturn the table and rant and rave about injustice.

'Let me get this straight: he's got away with anally raping – and probably kidnapping – an eleven-year-old girl, and you're powerless to do anything about it?'

'You're sayin' we should force her to testify? The DA wouldn't have any part in that, and you know it. A hostile witness, a terrified witness, and a kid at that. No way.'

'What about all my corroborative evidence? My team's evidence? Surely that would go a long way to proving the case?'

Tapperman uttered a snort of a laugh.

'What's so goddam funny?'

The detective raised a hand placatingly when he read Kruger's face. 'Hey, I ain't laughin' at your suggestion, buddy. It's a good idea. Only thing is, Bussola's legal team are goin' to sue your ass for' – here Tapperman began to count on his fingers – 'unlawful entry, invasion of privacy, breakin' an' enterin', unlawful arrest, assault and battery . . . you name it, he's gonna try an' plug ya.'

'Shit,' breathed Kruger. His head dropped wearily. He had been very tired up to that point, but that extra bad news simply swamped him with weariness. 'What about the other girl – the one he was beatin' up on?'

'What girl's that?' Tapperman responded. 'She's gone, vamoose. *Disparue*. As soon as we turned our heads she was away. I think she was warned off, too.'

Kruger rubbed his eyes with his knuckles. He looked bitterly across the table at Tapperman, who shrugged apologetically. 'So all in all, the Miami Police Department have made a complete fuck-up. Is it true to say that?'

Tapperman nodded happily, feeling that an opposing viewpoint would have been detrimental to his health.

'Who was the other fat guy, the one who passed out? The one at the head end of the girl? The one who was forcing her to suck his cock?'

Heads turned. Several touchy customers made 'tutting' noises.

Tapperman coughed nervously. 'A British guy, name of Charles Gilbert. One of Bussola's business associates in the leisure industry. Operates out of the north of England. The little we know about him suggests he's clean. He was high as a kite but because Bussola acted so quickly we didn't even get a chance to speak to him. Apparently he's flying out early tomorrow, back to Manchester.'

'What a complete mess,' Kruger groaned. He churned over the prospect of civil litigation together with the words Bussola had spieled out about having regrets. 'Fuck that bitch Felicity for getting me into this.'

Tapperman was vaguely aware of the reasons why Kruger had been watching the mobster. Gravely, he said, 'If I were you I might be bothered about Felicity's safety right now. If Mario adds this up and starts asking questions, he'll get mightily pissed with her answers, I reckon.'

Kruger's eyelids snapped shut with an involuntary spasm as the implications of Tapperman's words hit him. He hung his head despondently. 'You're right,' he said quietly.

Although Danny believed she had amassed enough evidence, most of which was hearsay, to recommend that Joe Lilton should be refused a firearms certificate, she did not succeed.

She presented a very detailed report about Lilton's ongoing violence towards his wife which had been logged over a period of several months. However, the powers-that-be decided it would be too much trouble and cost to refuse the application because if Lilton appealed against the decision he had immediate right of appeal to a Crown Court.

In those days – the early 1980s – the ownership of firearms was not seen as too big a deal. The horror of Hungerford had yet to happen and the tragedy of Dunblane was completely unthinkable. People didn't do such things, did they?

Therefore Lilton got his certificate, got his guns – a thirty-eight and a forty-five – joined a gun club and to all intents and purposes, became a model gun-owner.

Danny knew that not long after her visit to Lilton's house in Osbaldeston, he and his wife split up and later divorced. Beyond that she knew nothing more – until now, here in the present, because she had bumped into Joe Lilton again.

Remarried to Ruth – who seemed decent, if highly strung – and stepfather to Claire, runaway and deeply unhappy child.

Nor was Danny happy. There was something at the back of her mind, niggling away. Something from all those years ago . . . yet she could not pinpoint it.

At least she was up to date with Joe Lilton and feeling smug that the new government had decided to ban private ownership of handguns. In a couple of months' time, Lilton, along with thousands of others, would be obliged to hand in his weapons to the police.

She stretched her arms and sat back.

It was eight o'clock. Time to go home.

She had spent more or less the whole day at her desk – with the occasional excursion to research Joe Lilton – head down, beavering way, trying to clear her work so there would be no earthly reason for her ever to return to this office once she had been promoted.

She had seen nothing of Jack Sands. He might have been in his office, might not. She did not care. All she wanted to do was forget him and the last couple of days, and get on with her life. Hopefully he had got the message and would leave her alone in future.

When he walked into the office at that very moment, as

cocky and cool as she had ever seen him, her heart juddered.

Fortunately a couple of other people were in the office too.

Sands addressed everyone.

'Just thought you'd like to be informed – for those who know him, that is – I've just received a preliminary message from Control Room.' Here he looked directly at Danny. 'And you'll be very interested in this, Dan: Louis Vernon Trent has escaped from prison and in the process he killed two paramedics and a prison guard, and is suspected of a firebomb attack on another inmate's cell which killed four people. He could well be making his way back to his home town. Here. Blackpool.'

Danny gasped.

That was all she needed.

To Steve Kruger it seemed almost a lifetime ago since he had been walking across that parking lot, eagerly anticipating the planned barbecue and beer with his son and grandchildren. The barbecue had obviously been cancelled and they had all taken a raincheck. At least, for now, Kruger could achieve one of his ambitions, and that was to get his mouth round the neck of a bottle of Hurricane Reef Lager.

He screeched the Chevy into the driveway of his Bal Harbour villa, gearing himself up to the coolness of the beer working its delicious way down his throat. He tapped in the alarm code and went in through the front door of his home, of which he was extremely proud.

He tossed his jacket and tie onto the staircase, kicked off his shoes, and loosening everything else, made his way directly to the kitchen. He almost fainted with pleasure when he opened the refrigerator door and a burst of frozen air hit him. He stood there a few moments, basking. Then he grabbed a beer. A second later it tumbled down his neck like an ice-cold mountain stream.

Most of the contents went down in that first pull.

'Jeez, that's wonderful.' He rolled the bottle across his sweaty forehead.

Next he stripped off where he stood.

He made his way through the living room, to the patio door which led out to the pool. He took a few steps across the hot concrete and dived naked into the water, secure in the knowledge the garden was not overlooked.

He did a graceful length underwater, turned whilst submerged and swam back. With bursting lungs he surfaced at the point where he had entered.

He did not expect to see the long black pair of female legs standing on the poolside, slightly astride. The view stopped him dead. He gulped, recognised them from previous discreet observation, and his eyes travelled slowly up them to see that the groin was covered by a pair of very tight shorts.

He looked further up.

There was a gap between the top of the shorts – exposing a lovely flat stomach with a belly button to die for – and a button T-shirt tied with a knot underneath the breasts.

'Myrna,' Kruger said, puzzled. 'What you doin' here?'

She shrugged. 'Couldn't sleep, I guess. Too much goin' on in my head. Needed some sort of debrief. Mind if I join you?'

'Be my guest.' He realised she must be able to see that he was completely naked.

Myrna undid the knot in her T-shirt and dragged it over her head. She shimmied out of her shorts, discarding them and her panties to one side. Then, for one beautiful moment, as she raised her hands to a point above her head, Kruger was treated to a sight he had only ever dreamt about. He had to admit, the reality was far better than the imagination. The breasts tauter, the nipples bigger, the tummy flatter and the legs longer.

She dived over him, and entered the pool with hardly a ripple.

Kruger turned, ducked under the surface and pushed himself away from the poolside, wondering what form the debrief would take.

Everything going on in Danny's life at that moment seemed to be connected with ghosts from her past. People she thought had been laid to rest.

First there was Joe Lilton, from fifteen years ago.

Then Jack Sands, a nightmare from her very recent past.

Now here was Louis Vernon Trent a mere nine years in her past.

Trent had been the first major criminal Danny had ever arrested and put away for a long time. She had locked up plenty of burglars and petty drugs dealers but Trent had been her first biggie. He wasn't a master criminal in the usual sense of the phrase. He wasn't driven by greed or the need to show off. He was driven by a perverted and uncontrollable lust. Mainly for young girls and occasionally for boys.

Because of this he was considered a danger to the public.

That was why Trent was a biggie.

His arrest had been Danny's passport to any specialist department she chose. She plumped for Family Protection because she felt it was the area in which she could do most good.

It had probably been the near-fatal injuries caused by Trent to two young girls in one frenzied attack that had driven Danny in the direction of the FPU. It gave her a burning desire to catch and convict people like Trent who ruined young lives without a thought for anything but their own sadistic pleasures.

Trent had been sentenced to seventeen years' imprisonment, with the Judge's recommendation he serve the full term.

It wasn't enough for Danny, but it would have to do.

Seventeen years did not give back to even one of those girls the chance of enjoying a healthy family life when she reached adulthood. Nor did it give the other little girl the chance of ever going to the toilet and not screaming in agony. Nor did it repay the other thirty children he had molested in a reign of terror lasting eighteen months.

But seventeen years would have to do, because the justice system said so.

Seventeen years for thirty-two ruined lives.

Now he was back on the streets, no doubt with the intention of resuming his activities.

Danny shivered at the thought.

She prayed he would not return to Blackpool, but knowing he probably would – because he had unfinished business to attend to – Danny decided that tomorrow she would make it her task to ensure every police officer within a twenty-mile radius of Blackpool was carrying an up-to-date photo of Trent.

Danny left her desk and walked to the lift. Whilst waiting for its creaky arrival, she stared blandly at the buttons, picturing Trent's evil eyes.

Hearing clearly the voice that went with them. At the conclusion of one of Danny's interviews with Trent, nine years before, he had said, quite blatantly at a point when Danny's interviewing partner had left the room briefly, 'Guilty or not guilty, Danny, one fine day I'm going to come back and kill you for this.'

Her partner came back into the room to find Trent smiling pleasantly at him, then at Danny for whom he added a salacious wink.

She had nearly wet herself there and then, because she believed him.

The lift arrived, the doors slid open, she stepped in and pressed the ground-floor button. The doors began to close.

At eighteen inches apart, Jack Sands contorted sideways through the gap and a second later the doors were

141

shut. Only he and Danny were in the lift.

She cowered away from him in the confined space.

'Danny, I need to talk to you.' He held out his arms. His face had a look of total desperation and misery on it.

'Get away from me, Jack,' she warned him. 'I'll knee you in the balls again.'

'Whoa, okay, honey. But we need to talk. You know I love you and I know you love me. You're denying yourself. I need you and you need me, so let's stop pretending and get back to what we were.'

'It's over,' Danny stated through gritted teeth. 'Now leave me alone.'

The lift clattered to a halt at the ground floor.

'Please, God, let there be someone waiting to get in,' Danny grovelled in her mind. Sands's finger was pressed on the button for the fifth floor and he was standing across the doors. He wasn't going to let her go anywhere.

Danny's legs became wobbling strips of blubber when she thought that somehow Sands had succeeded in preventing the doors opening. An agonising couple of seconds passed. She eyed her ex-lover fearfully . . . until, thankfully, the doors opened. Several people were in the corridor, waiting to get in. A gush of relief flushed through her system.

Sands glanced over his shoulder, a look of rage on his face. Danny took advantage of the moment to duck past him, shove her way through the waiting people with a strained, 'Excuse me,' and head for the exit.

Her legs, having turned back from blubber into muscle, carried her swiftly down the corridor, past the entrance to the custody office, out of the back door and into the rear yard.

Head high, vision tunnelled, she commenced what had become a very long walk to her car.

She sensed, rather than saw, felt or heard, Sands by her shoulders. Walking with her. Slightly behind.

'Fuck off, Jack,' she hissed without turning her head.

'We haven't finished.' He sounded breathless. 'You can't cut me out like this, Dan. It's not on. You owe me more.' His voice was pleading and threatening at the same time.

She refused to rise and make a reply, and carried on walking. As she wheeled into the parking area where her car was parked, she saw it was dark, badly lit. Making a quick decision, she stopped abruptly and spun to face Jack.

'Don't come to my car, Jack. I've let what happened pass, but I'm not prepared to do that again. Next time you touch me, you'll get locked up. I won't have any hesitation whatsoever – and if you want the hassle of our affair finding its way to your wife's ears, then so be it.'

Sands said nothing, simply stared unemotionally at her.

She nodded quickly and made towards her car. The walk seemed to take an hour. Each footfall reverberated around her skull. All the time expecting Sands to pounce and drag her to the floor.

Nothing happened. She reached the car unmolested, but her hands were trembling wickedly.

Next thing she was reversing out of her spot, engaging 'D' and driving out of the car park.

Sands lounged against a wall near to the exit. He was holding his right fist out towards her. The consideration of running the bastard down quickly entered her head. As she drew alongside him, he opened the fingers of his fist, showing Danny the palm of his hand . . . in which was a Mercedes three-pointed star.

Danny's foot rammed down on the gas. The car surged ahead with a squeal of tyres. She gunned out of the yard, glancing fleetingly in her rearview mirror, catching a glimpse of Sands's face. He was laughing uproariously.

Danny yelled something incomprehensible as the implication of what she had seen smacked her with the force of a slab of concrete coming through her windscreen.

It was now confirmed. Jack Sands was the person

143

responsible for smashing her bedroom window, nearly causing her serious injury and damaging her beloved car.

Sands turned on his heels and slid the badge into his pocket. He walked back into the police station, a smirk of superiority on his face.

He failed to notice the lurking figure of Henry Christie in the dark shadow next to the police van.

'That was a one-off – two-off, actually, I suppose – but having said that, it was definitely the nicest two-off I've ever experienced,' Myrna Rosza admitted to Steve Kruger. 'It can't happen again. It's just that we seem to have gone through so much together in such a short space of time that my head was spinning with it all. I needed some sorta relief . . . but with someone who understood.'

Kruger uttered a kind of reply from deep in his throat.

He understood completely. It was one of the reasons why so many cop marriages failed. Non-cop partners didn't fully comprehend some of the situations and emotions that only other cops could. Usually those of the opposite sex, although not necessarily so. Too often, when he'd been a cop, he'd found himself in similar situations, one of which was responsible for the demise of his first marriage.

Kruger and Myrna were lying askew his king-size bed. He was on his back, an arm thrown lazily around Myrna's wonderfully soft-brown shoulders. She was tucked under his armpit, his fingers playfully curling the thick hairs on his chest.

Their legs were entwined, toes playing with each other's toes. The heat of Myrna's sex pumped against his thigh.

It had been incredible.

From the shallow end of the swimming pool, right through the house, taking a few moments to dry each other off before hitting the sack. Then an unbelievable fuck in the greatest tradition of the word.

Even though all the time he had been telling himself what a stupid fool he was being.

Firstly by breaking rule number one – never ever fraternise with the staff.

Secondly because he knew Ben Rosza, Myrna's husband. A soft, gentle man who wouldn't hurt a fly. A decent hardworking doctor who Kruger quite liked and whose wife had just mounted him from several directions.

But hell, it had been good, the second one even better. And good sex was something Kruger had been short of recently. Actually he had been short of sex, full stop.

She ran her long nails lightly down his stomach, making him quiver.

'I love Ben,' she said. 'He's a good man. I don't want to do anything to harm him or hurt him, okay?'

Kruger caught her hand. He pushed himself up onto one elbow and gazed into her eyes, aware that in the periphery of his vision he could see her breasts and nipples pressed into his ribs and beyond that her legs wrapped around his.

Her eyes were serious. Kruger was suddenly aware he was looking at a vulnerable individual who had just taken a big step in her life. Gone was the facade of the sassy, cheeky woman.

'No one will ever know about this,' he reassured her. 'No one. This is between me and you alone. What happened here happened for a reason and for a brief moment in time we needed each other. And that's the end of it. When you walk out of this house, we're back to square one, okay? End of story.'

He knew it was a lie. Even if they never jumped into bed again, their relationship would never be the same in the future. But he did not feel bad telling her what she wanted to hear.

She nodded, also knowing it was a lie.

Their eyes stayed in contact, holding onto the moment. Kruger fought it, so did Myrna, but suddenly they both

145

knew they needed each other again.

Kruger pulled her up towards him. Their lips mashed together, parted and tongues darted together. Kruger became short of breath as his manhood sprang back to life again. At the same moment, Myrna curled her long fingers around it.

She broke away from the kiss, her breathing heavy. She pushed herself down the bed, taking him into her hot mouth.

Kruger groaned and flopped back onto the bed luxuriating in the pleasure. When the bedside phone rang he nearly leapt out of his skin.

Myrna was not phased by the interruption. Her head rose and fell.

Kruger fumbled for the phone, answering it with a little squeak which came as the result of a flutter of Myrna's tongue. 'Yep?' he managed to say.

He listened for a few moments, 'Jeez, no . . . That can't be right.' He tapped Myrna on the shoulder and indicated for her to stop. Reluctantly she did. 'This has got to be some kinda joke,' he said, sat up, his mind nowhere near sex now.

'Okay . . . okay. I'll be there soon . . . yeah, no problems. Thanks for phoning.'

Slowly he replaced the receiver and looked at Myrna with an expression of deep shock.

'What is it?' she asked worriedly.

Kruger rubbed a hand down his face. It was many seconds before he found the words to tell her.

Danny reached home within the space of a few minutes. The Mercedes jarred to a springy halt in her driveway. She darted quickly, like a fugitive, to the front door of her house and wasted no time getting inside, slamming the door shut with such force that the frame rattled. She slid the security chain on, drew the bolt and fell against the back of the door. She closed her eyes tightly and tried to get hold of herself. She was shaking uncontrollably, but she fought it. In the end she lost, seemed to burst out of herself and dashed down the short hallway, ripping her outer jacket off and leaving it discarded in her wake, splayed on the carpet. She veered into the lounge and headed directly for the drinks cabinet in the sideboard.

With trembling fingers she unfastened a bottle of vodka, poured a large measure with a spit of tonic and drank it very quickly. It was the only drink capable of calming her shattered nerves.

She lit a ciggie and sank down into an armchair, gratefully feeling herself take control again. The drinks cabinet was now at her eye-level and she could see its contents. There were several bottles of whisky, a drink she detested. She snorted with contemptuous derision when she recalled the reason for its presence.

For Jack.

His favourite tipple. After about ten pints of Boddington's Bitter, that is.

Anger washed over her.

She grabbed the bottles, stormed into the kitchen and emptied them down the sink. Four half-full bottles of good quality single malt guggled away. She wasn't sorry to see it go, even though her money had purchased it. She tossed the empty bottles into the swing bin.

The bastard, she thought. The cheeky bastard.

She then descended on the house like a hurricane, whooshing through all the rooms, collecting every piece of anything Jack Sands had left behind. Twenty minutes later she placed a black plastic bin-liner in the middle of the kitchen floor and wiped her hands with satisfaction. Everything had gone into it. She had been surprised at how much the adulterous sod had accumulated in a house that wasn't his home.

That sorted, she was still perplexed about what to do about Jack himself. It did not make a great deal of difference that she was a police officer with all that experience behind her. She was still a woman – a lone woman – with a problem, experiencing all the anxieties that lone women suffer.

She had to weigh up the odds.

By taking it further, and possibly getting nowhere due to lack of evidence (Jack would never be stupid enough to let anyone find the Mercedes star on him), all that would happen is that Jack would be further incensed.

She decided to leave it. Let it ride. Accept what had happened and hope Jack would see sense. He'd had his last laugh, made his point. Maybe that would be enough for him.

Maybe.

A long sigh cleared her lungs. She felt happier now. From the fridge she took a swig of fresh orange to take away the lingering flavour of the vodka and poured herself a very cold glass of Chablis. The fresh, icy-sharp taste revitalised her senses. She came alive again.

In the hallway she picked up her jacket, turned to go upstairs for a shower. On the first step the phone rang.

'Yep, Danny Furness.'

There was a hollow silence on the line.

Danny went as ice-old as the glass of wine in her hand. 'Jack, I know it's you. Stop messing around.'

Silence. Possibly some breathing.

'Jack, just fuck off.'

'Bitch.' One word only. Growled. Frightening.

She slammed the phone down, immediately picked it up again and dialled 1471.

The electronic voice said, 'You were called today at 2017. We do not have the caller's number to return the call. Please hang up. Please hang up. Please hang . . .'

Mark Tapperman raised his bushy eyebrows in surprise when he saw Kruger and Myrna arrive together in the same car – her Lexus. Kruger ignored the reaction. 'What've you got for us, Mark?'

'Come on, I'll show you, but I'm not sure Myrna will want to see.'

'She wants,' Kruger said with a tone that brooked no argument. 'She used to be a Fed. She's seen some shit in her time.'

Kruger and she had discussed it on the way over. He had not wanted her to come, let alone visit the actual crime scene. She insisted; he didn't argue.

'It ain't nice,' Tapperman warned her.

She sighed and looked at him like the dumb chauvinistic cop she imagined him to be. He got the message and acquiesced. 'Your decision, lady.'

They walked across the sidewalk from the car towards what was the front of a four-storey apartment building in Greenwood Heights, north-west of central Miami. A police crime-scene cordon tape was stretched across the front doors, supervised by a uniformed cop with clipboard. Tapperman approached the uniform and gave him a few details which he entered on the log which recorded persons in and out.

Tapperman lifted the tape with a forefinger, Kruger and Myrna ducked under, followed by the cop.

'The whole building's been sealed for the moment. When we're satisfied we'll draw the cordon in,' Tapperman explained. 'We'll use the stairs,' he said. A forensic team of three were crouched down in the elevator, dusting for prints and traces of anything.

'Try not to touch too much,' Tapperman said. 'We ain't had a chance to do the stairs yet.'

'Okay,' nodded Kruger. He slid his hands into his pockets and meekly followed Tapperman. Secretly he was dreading what he was about to see. His guts fell as though they'd been filled with a bucket of cement.

They passed a couple more uniformed cops guarding the stairs. On the third floor all three of them were required to don a pair of paper overalls and plastic shoes which would have to be bagged and tagged for evidential

149

purposes when they left. Then they went up onto the top floor where they emerged on a carpeted landing. A hallway ran off to their left, doors on either side, entrances to apartments. There was a mass of police activity from the landing all the way down the corridor.

Tapperman turned to them. 'We've managed to work out a way down the corridor without disturbing too much evidence, so can I ask you guys to follow exactly in my footsteps. It's important.'

Numbly they both nodded.

Tapperman glanced at Myrna. Her horrified face sent a shiver down him, reminding him it was one of the worst crime scenes he had ever visited. He took a deep breath, began to lead the way.

Kruger steeled himself. Perspiration rolled down his forehead.

Before following Tapperman, he allowed himself a couple of moments to cast his eyes down the hallway ahead. He pursed his lips. He too had seen some awful things in his life, but this wasn't far off taking the biscuit.

Blood was everywhere.

Splats of it.

Gobs of it.

Swathes of it.

The carpet was saturated in it. Some parts of the floor looked deep enough to float a toy boat in it. The walls were covered, as though some would-be modern artist had opened a tin of red paint and gleefully thrown it everywhere with artistic abandon.

Tapperman walked a couple of yards before noticing he was alone. He stopped, looped his chin over his shoulder. 'Coming?'

Kruger and Myrna caught up. He walked on, held up his hand to halt them and pointed down to his side at something on the carpet by the wall which both of them had seen already anyway.

A severed hand.

Cleanly cut off at the wrist. Lying there, palm up, like a gruesome ashtray. It was a right hand and there was a gold ring on the little finger.

Myrna touched Kruger. He reached back and squeezed her hand.

Tapperman moved on. Two yards further he stopped again, pointed down to his right. Was it a leg this time? Kruger wondered initially. Then, no. It was a forearm, cut from elbow to wrist. A hairy, muscled forearm.

Behind him, Myrna uttered a pitiful squeak.

'You okay, honey?' he asked gently.

Her hand was over her mouth. She nodded, wide-eyed.

Their journey progressed, avoiding pools of blood, stepping over them like a nightmarish game of hopscotch. Tapperman pointed out all the sights of interest along the way, like a tour guide taking a party around the Museum of Horrors.

Another severed hand – again a right one. Palm down, fingers spread wide looking like one of those huge bird-eating spiders but with three of its fat legs amputated; a pair of feet removed from the rest of the body at the ankles, standing there side by side. Could have been a pair of bookends. Obviously placed there with care by the offender.

All the while, the bile rose inside Kruger's stomach as the journey down the corridor became increasingly akin to a ghoulish fantasy. His ears pounded, bass drums rattling his eardrums. He was light-headed and slightly 'out of it'; he fully expected to wake up, bathed in a cold sweat.

There was no such luxury for him.

Tapperman reached one of the doors in the corridor which led to an apartment. It was open. He stood slightly to one side and indicated for Myrna and Kruger to have a looksee.

They did.

That was enough for Kruger.

151

Fuck the evidence.

He lurched past Tapperman down the hallway and sank to his knees, supporting himself against the wall. He regurgitated his stomach contents in one violent vomit. It looked just like wet cement.

Behind him, and ringing in his ears, was the ear-splitting petrified scream of Myrna. She had hit hysteria within a milli-second and showed no signs of coming back to earth until Tapperman gave her one almighty crack across the chops.

'Fuckin' civvies,' he said under his breath. Maybe it had been a mistake inviting them to the scene. On reflection, though, perhaps he should've warned them.

It's not every day that a person gets to see two severed heads, plonked side by side, ear to ear, on a coffee table. Eyes wide open. Mouths gaping. Tongues lolling out. Set in their own coagulating blood, like candle wax.

The heads of the two brothers, Jimmy and Dale Armstrong. Now former employees of Kruger Investigations.

Tapperman had a further thought. Jeez, they look like a matching pair of candles. If there had been a wick coming out of them, he would have been tempted to light it.

Chapter Eight

The phone rang twice more before Danny even made it upstairs. Each time she answered, it was the same as the first call. Nothing . . . then one word which took a further step towards obscenity.

The fourth time it rang, Danny lifted the receiver, replaced it and threw it down, off the hook.

Before going upstairs she checked all the doors and windows were locked, curtains drawn.

Only then, when she felt completely safe, did she go for that long bath to soothe her jagged nerves.

In the deep, hot, soapy water, she had time for reflection.

Over the years she had dealt with many women – and some men – who had become victims of obsessive behaviour by their former partners or other people, who for some reason became attracted to them in a sick way. In the past she had given normal, routine advice. See a solicitor. Get an injunction. Ring us when he's here. Keep a log. You'll have a hell of a time proving it, you know. Stop being such a softie. Pull yourself together.

Only now did she begin to really understand just something of what those poor people must have been going through. Now it was real to her. It may have only just started, but it made her afraid, alone and isolated. And much, much more.

Without even knowing what was coming, Danny burst into tears.

Her initial reaction was to choke them back, but she

realised she needed their release. Accordingly, she howled in anguish, smashed the bath brush on the water and went with the flow.

When they subsided, she felt slightly better.

Ten minutes later, refreshed, skin buzzing, hair clean, in her bathrobe and slippers, she trotted downstairs, filled up the wine glass and pointed the remote at the telly.

Tentatively she picked up the phone and bounced it in her hand. She replaced it, held her breath, bit her tongue.

Nothing happened.

She breathed out and sat down.

When the ring came it sound like an explosion in her ears.

Inside herself, something crumbled.

Louis Vernon Trent sat prim and proper across from the old lady. He smiled at her occasionally. She thought he looked like a thoroughly decent young man.

Most of the time he watched the world go by from the train window, gazing at the landscape which he knew so well. Particularly once he had changed trains in Manchester, he recognised every inch of the towns and country of East Lancashire, eventually merging into mid-Lancashire at Preston, then west as the train headed towards the coast.

Whilst the train was stationary in Preston, he had a few torrid moments when a couple of uniformed British Transport Policemen came into the carriage. They worked their way down the aisles, closely scrutinising passengers, in particular lone males.

He knew they were looking for him.

He kept his cool, eyed their approach with confidence and leaned forwards, almost with an intimate gesture to the old woman.

'So how're you doing, Mum?' he said. He stressed the last word loud enough for it to be picked up by the approaching cops.

'I'm very well, son,' she responded brightly, glad of the opportunity to say something. 'For my age, that is.'

She laughed. So did Trent.

'What did you think of my birthday present to you?' he asked as the policemen came alongside. They ignored Trent and his mum. After all, they were seeking a single man, probably still in prison gear. Not someone travelling with his mum.

'Eh?' said the lady.

'Nowt,' he said. 'Go back to sleep.' He relaxed and allowed himself a smug smile as he closed his eyes and recalled the final moments of his escape.

He had forced the ambulance driver to take him towards the outskirts of the nearest town where he knew there was an out-of-town retail park. The ambulance was driven behind the retail park to an industrial estate, where they parked up in the back yard of a deserted warehouse.

At knifepoint, Trent forced the driver out, made him open the rear doors of the ambulance and stand there looking at two dead bodies, soaked in blood. The foot of the brain-skewered prison guard still twitched.

Trent made the ambulance-driver undress and fold up his clothes in a neat pile. He took the man's wallet which contained sixty pounds and a credit card. He shoved the knife underneath the man's ear and made him divulge the PIN number for the card which Trent memorised.

Then it was time to dispose of him.

Both knew the moment had arrived.

'Look, pal, I won't talk. I'll stay here for as long as you say. Anything. Whatever you want. I don't wanna die. I haven't done anything wrong. I've got a wife and kids.'

Trent sneered at him. 'I hate kids,' he chided. 'Do you fuck them?'

The man swallowed, shook his head.

'Get down on your knees.'

He descended slowly. He was on the same eye-line as

155

his dead colleague in the ambulance, whose eyes stared sightless at him.

'Shall I take mercy on you?'

'Yes . . . please . . . Look, you can trust me . . .'

'Oh, fucking shut up whining,' shouted Trent. He'd had enough of the man. He grabbed his hair and pulled his head back, exposing the neck. He sliced the knife across his throat, forcing the blade deep with a sawing action, severing the arteries.

The man gurgled, slumped onto the back step of the ambulance, clutching his neck, trying to stem the flow.

Six feet away, Trent watched him writhe and begin to bleed to death.

When the man no longer moved, Trent stepped over him and climbed into the back of the ambulance. He cleaned up the self-inflicted wounds on his arms with antiseptic wipes and dressed them with bandages. He undressed himself, towelled himself clean, and got into the ambulance driver's gear which fitted him well – a green overall and trainers. Over the top of this he put an anorak from which he cut off the epaulettes. He threw his prison gear into the ambulance and then helped himself to the wallets belonging to the dead paramedic and prison guard. This added another forty-five pounds to his stash of cash, four credit cards and a driving licence.

He briefly considered setting fire to the ambulance, but realised all that would achieve would be to draw attention to the fact he would not be very far away. It was a good decision because the ambulance was not discovered until after midnight, giving Trent ample time to do what he had planned.

He strolled boldly towards the retail park, posing as an off-duty paramedic; he knew he would find an ASDA store open until ten. Before entering the store he went to a hole-in-the-wall cash machine on the outer wall where, using the ambulance-driver's card, he withdrew the maximum allowed that day.

Three hundred pounds richer and armed with a nice, new, non-squeaky trolley, he went shopping.

In the 'George' clothing shop within the store he selected a couple of smart new outfits and two pairs of shoes, with underwear, socks and shirts to match. Next he bought a selection of tasty food and drink which could be consumed on the hoof and finally a few toiletries and a large holdall.

Feeling his luck was still in, he pinpointed the busiest check-out with the most harassed-looking till operator and joined the queue. He presented the ambulance-driver's credit card and looked the young girl directly in the eye. There was no problem. Being under severe pressure, the girl swiped it through and couldn't even be bothered to give a cursory glance at the signature on the receipt as opposed to the card. It was as well she didn't. Trent's was nowhere near that of the man he had murdered.

He sailed through on a high, bearing two hundred pounds' worth of clothing. He went directly to the toilets and changed into a new outfit, washed, brushed his hair, cleaned his teeth, emerged a new man.

Clean. Unruffled.

Even with the time to buy a newspaper at the kiosk and linger over sausage and chips at the in-store café.

Twenty-five minutes later a taxi dropped him off at the railway station where he boarded the next train north.

And here he was, only minutes away from his home town, his old stomping ground, Blackpool. It had gone like a dream.

The old lady had nodded off.

Trent smiled indulgently at her. Bitch.

Next stop along the line was Poulton-le-Fylde, the last one before the end of the line at Blackpool.

Guessing, rightly, that there were likely to be cops waiting at the terminus, he decided not to push his luck too far. He looked slyly around the almost deserted railway carriage – no one was paying any attention to him – and dipped his hand into the old lady's shopping bag, helping himself to her unguarded purse.

It went straight into his pocket.

He hit the platform running as the train pulled into Poulton-le-Fylde and trotted away, carried by his own momentum.

In a cubicle in the public toilets he examined with glee the contents of a well-stocked purse. Trent blessed the stupid old woman who probably did not have a bank account and kept all her savings underneath her bed. There was almost five hundred pounds stuffed into the purse, plus a large handful of loose change.

He transferred the money into his pockets and wedged the purse behind the toilet block.

A few minutes later he was settled in the snug of a nearby pub, a pint of bitter in one hand, a cumbersome-looking sandwich in the other. He estimated he probably had about half an hour before he needed to move on. When he did he would simply catch a cab into Blackpool, book into one of the thousands of guest-houses, and disappear amongst the great unwashed.

Home and dry.

A dithery Steve Kruger put the plastic cup to his lips and took a sip of the scalding-hot black coffee.

With Tapperman and Myrna, he was out in the sultry street, about a hundred yards away from the Armstrong brothers' apartment building. The trio were leaning on a semi-permanent burger stall from which they'd bought their drinks.

Myrna looked very ill. Her normally lovely golden-brown skin had developed a tinge of grey and her eyes were tired and sunken.

Tapperman was talking at the same time as inserting a greasy onion-laden cheeseburger into his mouth.

'Fuckin' incredible.' He shook his head and wiped the

dribble of fat from his chin. 'To do that to somebody. I mean, hell, *Texas Chainsaw Massacre* eat yer goddam heart out.' The last of the burger disappeared.

'Okay, Mark, we get the picture,' Kruger cut him short. He breathed out long and hard and tried to manage the memory of what he'd experienced in the last hour.

On recovering from his vomiting fit in the corridor, Kruger had gone on to witness the rest of the carnage in the apartment which had belonged to the Armstrong brothers. After edging past their heads on the coffee table, he was treated to a tour so he could see where the remaining parts of their two bodies had been scattered.

Their limbless torsos had been dumped in the bath; their arms and legs were distributed around the living room, kitchen and two bedrooms. The final, nice touch, was that their private parts had been sliced off and placed side by side on a plate in the icebox.

Kruger didn't linger. His experienced eyes saw everything they needed to see. He urgently required fresh air. But the atmosphere of the late afternoon in Miami was clammy, making pleasant breathing a difficulty, even on the sidewalk. The air from the apartment stuck in his lungs; he seemed unable to expel it.

'They were good boys,' croaked Myrna, the first words she had spoken for some time. 'Good boys and good workers. They didn't deserve to die, not like this.'

Kruger looked at her. Some of the colour was flowing back into her face now that anger was beginning to replace shock.

'Yeah, they were,' Kruger agreed. The Armstrongs had been two of his first employees and had stuck with him through the early days. Both had been tough professionals and superb investigators. Both were good friends to Steve Kruger. He had spent many nights in their company, particularly during the dark days of divorce, and had crashed out several times at their apartment when he'd been too drunk to get home. The apartment, therefore, held fond memories for Kruger. The three of them had hit it a few times with willing ladies.

Kruger's eyes returned to Tapperman. 'Any leads?'

The big cop shrugged. 'I guess you an' me are thinking pretty much along the same lines.'

'Yeah – Bussola. He's supposed to be a whizz with a chainsaw.'

'Only rumours,' Tapperman cautioned.

'No smoke without fire.' Kruger frowned. 'Anything from the other tenants? To do that with a chainsaw must have made a hell of a racket.'

'So far, no one's heard a mouse's fart and no one saw nuthin'.'

'But a chainsaw in that place! Must've been like a lion roaring in a cookie jar.'

'Nuthin' – yet. But these state-of-the-art chainsaws can run almost silent.'

'Forensics?'

'Again – nuthin' yet. Crime-scene guys reckon whoever did it was wearing plastic gloves and overalls . . . which'll all be destroyed by now.'

'It was Bussola,' Myrna blurted out. 'He warned us we'd regret it – and now we do.'

'Myrna, honey . . . I know it was Bussola, you know it, and so does Steve here . . . but provin' it's gonna be one helluva godamned difficult thing to do.'

'In that case, Mark – "honey" – you'd better get your ass into gear,' Myrna retorted.

In the dream Danny had been transported back in time. Fifteen years to be exact. She was on-duty and attending the Liltons' address in Osbaldeston. It was all very clear, as though she was actually there again. She drew up in the car, stopped outside the front of the house and got out. She could hear the argument in progress. Joe Lilton versus his then wife. Danny walked towards the house. She could hear the words being shouted, but she wasn't really listening. They were going into her brain, but not registering . . . then the dream changed and went black and she was being pinned down. A face appeared above her, grotesque features, but it was definitely Jack Sands. His breath smelled of spermicidal cream. He held her down and tried to force her legs apart.

There was an interruption. A metallic sound, followed by a sort of shuffling noise.

Danny woke with a start.

The noises were not in the dream, they were reality.

She sat bolt upright, sweat pouring off her, heart pounding, her senses switched on, acute.

There it was again. The click of metal followed by the shuffling noise.

Danny cursed.

Jack was back.

Once more she recognised just how vulnerable she was. The phone was downstairs – off the hook – and there was no alarm on the house with a panic button right where she needed it – next to the bed.

She rolled off the bed, wrapped her dressing-gown tightly around her.

Time check: 1.30 a.m.

Out onto the landing to the top of the stairs. No lights. Don't switch the lights on. Be brave. Catch the bastard.

That metallic sound again. This time she recognised what it was. Her imagination ran riot. It was the sound of the metal flap on the letter box. Christ! He was pouring petrol into the house! He was going to torch it, burn it down and kill her at the same time.

Danny emitted a mad scream of anguish and threw herself at the double light-switch on the landing. Both hall and landing lights came on. Scaring him away was now her priority, before that lighted match came through the letter box. She raced downstairs, bellowing words which were incomprehensible.

She leapt down the last five steps, twisted into the

hallway and faced the front door.

It was not petrol which had been pushed through.

A dozen red roses, several with broken stems, lay there forlornly on the mat.

Danny sank to her knees and picked one up. She crushed the flower in the palm of her hand and allowed the creased petals to drift onto the carpet.

Steve Kruger sat silently in the passenger seat of the Lexus whilst a trance-like Myrna drove him home. There was nothing of value to say. Kruger had been warned about the dangers of dealing with the mafia and the warnings had proved to be accurate. Two of his employees had been butchered and no doubt he, Myrna and Kelly (who he had phoned, found to be safe and well, and warned to get out of town) were probably still in grave danger. All because he had been frightened by his ex-wife's big mouth, threatening to reveal things which might destroy him.

'I'm sorry,' he said meekly.

'I'm sorry too – for everything,' Myrna replied, stressing the last word. The meaning was bluntly clear to Kruger. 'Everything' included their sexual encounter.

He sighed and screwed up his face, sick to the stomach, disgusted with himself for having been so weak-kneed as to accede to Felicity's demands. He should have called her bluff. After all, she was the one who would have had to prove he sold restricted weapons to an unfriendly country.

He rubbed the base of his thumbs into his eyes.

The Lexus drew up outside his house.

Kruger wrapped his fingers around the door-handle, paused before alighting and glanced sideways at Myrna. 'Drink? Coffee? Anything?'

She did not look at him. 'Not a good idea,' she said, addressing the steering-wheel. Her voice was like stone and her body language gave Kruger the impression she hated him. She tapped the wheel and after a moment she relaxed. She looked sadly at Kruger. Her voice became soft. 'Not a good idea,' she repeated. 'I need to get home.'

'I . . .' Kruger began to speak with a stutter.

Myrna reached across and placed a forefinger on his lips. 'Don't say something you'll regret. We need to get back to square one – and get our revenge for Jimmy and Dale.'

Kruger was startled. It was apparent the old Myrna had returned.

'Yeah, you heard right. I said revenge. I want revenge on Bussola, and one way or another I'm gonna get it. And if I can't do it by fair means, I'll sure as hell do it by foul.'

Kruger nodded. 'Look after yourself,' he said.

'I'll be okay and so will Kelly, I guess. He won't do anything against us . . . but you'll need to be careful, Steve. He might well come after you.'

Moments later, Myrna pulled away from the kerb. Kruger let himself back into his house, totally exhausted.

It was 10 p.m. After pouring a beer down his throat and setting the house alarm, he crawled into bed, unmade since he and Myrna had been writhing ecstatically around on it.

The last thing he did before sleep was to reach out to the drawer in his bedside cabinet. He fumbled under a couple of paperbacks and his fingers found the butt of his .38 police special. He pulled it out and placed it carefully on top of the cabinet, pointing away from his head.

Then he slept, secure in the knowledge that only another matter of feet away, in his wardrobe, were several other guns of various calibre and design which he could reach in seconds if necessary.

Trent openly cruised the bars and clubs of Blackpool, enjoying his newfound freedom, savouring the taste of alcohol and getting very drunk indeed. He was sure no one would recognise him. After all, he was nine years older, thinner and much more gaunt than he had been; his hair had shaded to grey and his facial features become narrow and pinched.

Nine years before he had looked like a predatory owl, now he looked like an evil weasel.

He drifted into a few pubs where he knew he could get some good information on where to go later. As it was his first night out of jail he wasn't too bothered with the quality. All he wanted was a taster to whet his appetite.

Eventually he got word of something happening in the secure back room of a stripjoint near to North Pier. He wasn't sure what it would be – it was difficult to pin people down to specifics – but it would do.

When the clubs closed at two, he went to a cash machine and because it was another day, he was able to withdraw another £300 from the dead ambulanceman's account.

With cash almost bursting out of his pockets, none of it his, he strolled to the club specified. He had been directed to go up the fire escape and knock gently on the first door he came to.

It would cost him fifty dabs.

He knocked, the money ready in his fist. The door opened. A gorilla/bouncer took the cash and counted it carefully. He directed Trent to the second door along a poorly lit corridor.

Trent went into a darkened room, illuminated by lights which had been dimmed almost to black. He paused on the threshold, allowing his eyes to accustom themselves to the gloom.

He saw four rows of chairs arranged in a horseshoe shape facing a huge TV screen at the far end of the small room. About a dozen people, all men, were seated. Some conversed in a subdued way. Others were completely alone.

Trent weaved his way through the chairs and sat down on the front row to have an unrestricted view of the screen.

164

He checked his watch – stolen from the ambulanceman – and saw the digital figures flicker onto 3.00 a.m.

What light there was in the room doused to black. Everyone's attention focused on the screen, which flickered.

The image of a child, wide-eyed and beautiful, appeared.

A frisson of excitement captivated Trent's body.

The films Trent saw that night were about half an hour each. They originated from Holland and had been dubbed poorly into English. The quality of the camerawork was shoddy, but the pictures were fairly sharp. The editing was questionable.

Both told much the same story.

One was based around a little boy who looked to be about nine years old.

The other was about a little blonde girl who looked slightly older.

They were both very graphic tales.

Each film began with what appeared to be the abduction off the street of the child. The story carried on with the captivity of the children, both of whom were tied naked to a bed. The story progressed to the sexual abuse of the kids. Sometimes by one person only, more often by a group of people. All men. During these scenes the children screamed and were allowed to do so. This seemed to fire the depraved lust of their captors and tormentors.

The climax of each film was the rape of the child by one person, who with a noose around the neck of the child reached orgasm at the same time as apparently strangling the child to death. The deaths looked very real. Probably were.

Trent left the viewing room tremendously excited by what he had seen. It had been worth every penny.

He knew he had to go and repeat it.

Less than two miles away was the sea-front hotel on South Shore which belonged to the Lilton family. The hotel was quiet and in darkness. Outwardly it looked peaceful at four in the morning.

Inside was a different matter.

Ruth Lilton was in a deep, coma-like sleep on her bed. She lay on her back, mouth open, snoring. A cocktail of carefully administered alcohol and sleeping tablets had put her there. Virtually nothing could have woken her. Not even the whimpering cries and the deep male groans escaping from under the closed door of her daughter's room.

Claire cried out in pain and shame each time her stepfather rammed his unprotected self into her. It was almost a blessed relief when he roughly turned her over, adjusted her loose limbs so she was on her hands and knees and carried on from the rear. The pain increased with deeper penetration, but at least she did not have to look up at his face, wasn't obliged to inhale the intoxicant fumes he breathed all over her, or smell the sweat and body odour of him. She could bury her face in the pillow.

It was also a relief because she knew he would finish quicker in this position.

He did. With fearsome, violent strokes.

It was all over. He collapsed exhausted across her, squeezing her young breasts roughly with his big, hard hands.

'That was great,' he breathed.

He got off the bed and leaned towards her ear. 'Don't tell your mum, or I'll fucking kill you,' he warned her quietly. Then he left the room and returned to his marital bed.

Claire cried for a long, long time.

Finally her sobs subsided. She rolled off the bed and packed her bag. This time she wasn't going to return.

'I thought you were never gonna answer,' Steve Kruger's

166

voice boomed down the phone-line.

Mark Tapperman had had a busy day and night and was only an hour into what was going to be, at best, four hours' sleep. He tried to force open his groggy eyelids. His wife uttered something unrepeatable next to him and dragged the single sheet over her head.

'Steve, what the hell do you want?' Tapperman asked with some difficulty. Two reasons for that: his throat was bone dry (a sure sign he'd been snoring loudly) and it was hard work to coordinate the brain-speech function. 'It's . . . damn, I can't even open my eyes to see the clock.'

'Four in the morning,' Kruger informed him.

'Steve, you asshole, I'm shattered here. I've been on the go for twenty-four hours, as have you. In fact, why the hell aren't you asleep? Anybody with any sense would be.'

'Okay, so I've woken you. Sorry and all that, but I couldn't sleep and something came into my mind I needed clarifying.'

Tapperman sighed with reluctance. 'Fire away.'

'You said that English guy, Gilbert, was catching a plane out of Miami. When, exactly?'

Tapperman shuffled his brain cells and sorted through them. 'Er, gee . . . five or six o'clock this morning, I think it leaves . . . I'm not completely sure. Why?'

'Thanks for that,' Kruger said brightly.

'Why, Steve?' the detective insisted.

'Gonna pay the bastards a call.' Kruger hung up.

Tapperman leaned back against the headboard, wondering what the hell that was all about. He closed his eyes as his thoughts evaporated and he fell asleep immediately.

Chapter Nine

Detective Inspector Henry Christie read through the long and detailed message switch which had arrived in the early hours of the morning at Blackpool nick. It concerned the escape from prison of Louis Vernon Trent, a man born and raised in Blackpool. The story had been all over the daily newspaper Henry read before coming to work, but the nitty-gritty detail of what Trent had done in order to effect the escape was spelled out starkly in the police report in front of him. What the media could only guess at was laid out, blow by blow.

To Henry, the rather formal language of the message made Trent's exploits seem much more callous and evil than the sensationalism of the newspaper articles.

He read the story once more, then picked up a copy of a message received from the Royal Bank of Scotland, informing him that the bank account belonging to the dead ambulance-driver had been plundered twice since his death. The second time – and the time that interested Henry – was at two thirty-five that morning, from their cash-point at the branch on Talbot Square in Blackpool.

Two thirty-five! The bastard had obviously been walking around, bold as brass, through the streets of Blackpool.

Next Henry read a crime report concerning the theft of a purse belonging to an old woman; it had been stolen from her bag whilst she was on the train to Blackpool. The description of the offender fitted that of Trent, who

169

had been seen to get off the train at Poulton-le-Fylde.

He was definitely in town. That much was obvious.

Henry laid the crime report down and looked at the fax next to it from the prison service. It showed a two-year-old photo of Trent. Much of the quality had disappeared during transmission, but Henry could see from the image that the man had a piercing pair of eyes; they made him shiver.

'Shit,' he breathed.

Underneath the fax was a copy of Trent's previous convictions.

His telephone squawked. He answered it on the second ring.

'Henry, I hope you're looking at the reports I'm looking at, otherwise I'll have your effin' guts for shoelaces!' the voice shouted rudely down the line. The person did not have the courtesy to introduce himself, expecting to be instantly recognised. Henry knew it was the newly promoted Assistant Chief Constable (Operations), Robert Fanshaw-Bayley, known generally as FB and in particular as 'that Fucking Bastard'.

Although FB's responsibilities covered the whole range of police operations in Lancashire County, FB's main love and interest was crime. He'd been a detective for most of his service.

He and Henry went back many years. However, Henry did not like him.

In response to FB's opening broadside, Henry said, 'I assume you mean our friend Mr Trent?'

'You assume dead-fucking-right. This is very much your pigeon, Henry, so what the hell are you doing about him? I've had the press crawlin' right up my arse already this morning and also the Chief Constable of Staffordshire where the prison is located; she is not a happy woman with seven murders on her patch, I can tell you, and she wants this bastard catching. So, what're you doing to catch him?'

170

'Actually nothing,' should have been Henry's truthful reply. 'I've done bugger all but sit here, scratching my backside and trying to look moderately intelligent while I wonder what the hell to do.'

'Well, sir,' Henry began, when there was a light tap on his office door and Danny poked her head round. Henry's eyes lit up as a thought struck him. He beckoned her in and waved her to sit down.

'Well, sir – *what*?' FB demanded, annoyed by Henry's hesitation.

The DI's voice remained calm whilst underneath he paddled like mad. 'I was just this minute chatting to DC Furness from Family Protection about this very matter. She's the one who caught Trent originally and got him sent down; obviously, she knows quite a bit about him. We were discussing the possibility of her transferring onto CID a few days early – as you know, she joins us as a DS next Monday anyway. If she came early, she could coordinate the operation to nail Trent. We're bringing in some Divisional Support Units to assist ours . . .' Henry cringed at Danny and closed his eyes desperately '. . . and I've arranged a briefing at eleven.' Henry hoped he sounded convincing. He crossed his fingers.

'Good, good.' FB was impressed. 'Trusted you to be ahead of the game . . . I expected nothing less.'

'There is a slight hitch,' Henry interjected.

'Go on.'

'Regarding DC Furness joining us early. It might be, er . . . politically sensitive, so will you sanction it in writing?'

This time it was Danny who crossed her fingers.

The expression which broke over Henry's face told her the news was good.

He put the phone down at last. 'Hope that's okay with you?'

'Okay is a bit of an understatement. I'd say ecstatic.

171

Jack won't like it one little bit, though. He'll dig his heels in.'

'In that case, we'll present him with a *fait accompli*. He won't have any choice in the matter. So, Danny,' Henry raised his eyebrows, 'have you come to talk to me about Jack again?'

She nodded sadly.

Steve Kruger drove recklessly to MIA with little or no thought about what exactly he was doing. He didn't know the number of the flight Bussola's friend was due to catch; didn't know where in the airport he was likely to find them (and Miami International Airport is a very big place) and, most stupid of all, he hadn't a clue what he was going to do if a confrontation took place with Bussola.

Remonstrate nicely with him? Be politely assertive? Explain just how deeply peeved he was feeling because Bussola had managed to wriggle out of child-abuse indictments and subsequently chopped up two Kruger Investigations' employees with more skill than a meat butcher and decorated a hallway with their body parts?

He didn't know. He just didn't fucking know.

But what he *did* know was that the chances of actually coming face to face with Bussola in future would be minimal. The gangster led an existence shrouded in secrecy and protected by guards, however useless they might be. It wasn't often he stepped into public, and when he did so no one usually knew when or where it would be. Kruger had only learned of Bussola's whereabouts the other night because Felicity had told him. Kruger guessed that in future Bussola would be even more careful following the shock of his arrest.

This might be Kruger's last chance to get right into Bussola's face and let the bastard know he meant business; that he was on his case and wouldn't be off it until a grand jury sat there examining him.

Once parked up at MIA, Kruger made his way into the terminal building. The place was extremely crowded, making Kruger step back when he saw them.

He checked the departure screens and saw that the first flight to the UK was to Manchester; apparently it was delayed for an hour, which gave him some heart. Yet finding Bussola amongst all these folks would be like looking for a proverbial needle.

And that assumed Bussola hadn't simply dumped his fat friend Gilbert and gone straight home. Kruger hoped the two men – partners in sexual abuse – would be spending a little quality time together, maybe chewing the fat, before the Englishman caught the big bird. Maybe having a drink, or a meal . . .?

The police constable found that, try as he might, he could not dredge up any great sympathy for this misper. Seven times now in the last two months was enough to try anyone's patience. He, personally, had taken four of these reports.

As far as he was concerned, she was a nuisance. A silly, headstrong little kid who needed a good belting.

Nevertheless, he smiled patiently at the mother, took out his pen and the appropriate forms and wrote down details he knew almost off by heart.

Full name of missing person: LILTON, Claire Jane.

After making some hurried phone calls between them, using FB's name as a lever, Henry and Danny gradually put together enough police officers to form a team big enough to kick-start a manhunt.

Weary after this flurry of activity, they made their way up to the canteen to grab a cup of tea and some toast. Henry guided Danny to the far corner where they sat out of earshot. He looked expectantly at her, waiting for her to begin, and noting the dark rings around her eyes.

'He's driving me absolutely nuts,' she commenced,

calmly enough. 'Now he's started phoning me and not speaking . . . really babyish. But it's getting to me; making me a nervous wreck. I'm beginning to feel like a prisoner in my own home . . . God, I hope I don't sound like a hysterical female.'

'No, you don't,' Henry reassured her. 'But are you sure it's him phoning?'

'I tried 1471 and got no joy, but it could have come from a phone on a switchboard . . . so, no, I don't know, but I'm sure it is.'

'We can check out the phone in his office.'

'And then twelve red roses came through the letter box at half-one this morning. I'm sure it's him.'

'Any proof?'

She shrugged thoughtfully. 'I could possibly check something out.'

'Do it,' Henry ordered her.

'I'm also positive he's the one who damaged my car. When I drove out last night he was holding the badge for me to see.'

'Oh, that's what it was.'

'You saw him?'

'I was in the vicinity, shall we say? Purely by accident.' Henry opened his palms. 'Okay, Danny, what do you want to do? I know we've had this discussion before, but now things have moved on a pace.'

She looked glum. She sighed through her nose and rested her elbow on the table, her chin on her hand and gazed out of the window towards the Tower. There was a huge inflatable gorilla climbing up it which made her smile briefly. 'He'll no doubt have dumped the badge somewhere, so I don't see any future in court proceedings. He's not stupid enough to have kept it, is he?'

Henry raised a finger to interrupt her. He smiled wickedly. 'Yes, he is stupid enough. I sneaked in behind him last night and followed him to his office. I think he hid it in there somewhere.'

Danny's mouth fell open. She was silent for a few moments. 'Do you know how much those things are?' she blurted. 'Criminal damage,' she ruminated as the implications dawned on her. 'He could lose his job if he got convicted.'

'He deserves to.'

She shook her head decisively. 'No, I wouldn't want that. I simply want him sorted out. I'm not even bothered about compensation – just get him off my back.'

Henry took a deep breath. 'Right,' he said with finality. 'In that case, let's present him with *fait accompli numéro deux de la jour*. Okay?'

'It's a deal.'

'And while we're doing that, let's do our level best to catch Louis Vernon Trent . . . an old friend of yours, I believe.'

Kruger meandered around the shops and bars and poked his head into the VIP lounges he knew of.

Nothing.

He realised he could be wasting time better spent in bed. Then, as he passed the meeting point Location and Information Center on concourse E, he had an idea.

The pretty lady behind the counter was called Julia.

'Hi, my name's Steve,' he said disingenuously. 'I dunno if you can do this for me, but I'm supposed to meet my buddy, Charlie Gilbert here . . . about twenty minutes ago. We seem to have missed each other and I don't know where he is. He's due to board the Manchester flight an' I'm Seattle-bound. It's our last chance to get together before he leaves the States. We probably won't see each other again for years.' He sighed, looking upset. 'I was wonderin' if you could page him, maybe tell him there's some urgent information for him. Could you do that, honey?'

Julia smiled. 'Of course, sir.'

She leaned forwards and opened her mouth to speak

close to the mike in a way which made Kruger's heart palpitate, when out of the corner of his eye he saw Gilbert actually walk past. He was accompanied by a guy Kruger placed as one of Bussola's minders.

'Forget it, babe.' Kruger placed his hand between her mouth and the mike and smiled. 'Some other time, maybe.' Then he was gone, tailing Gilbert at a discreet distance.

The pair walked into the main shopping mall on the first floor and made a beeline for the Disney Store. With a bored-looking bodyguard lounging idly by the door, Gilbert spent about twenty minutes browsing before reappearing, bearing a large carrier bag stuffed with a giant Mickey Mouse.

He did a little more shopping and, suitably laden down, left the shopping area. He went to concourse E, turned up some steps and disappeared through a door marked *Private – Executive Lounge*.

The minder followed and so did Kruger. He had already made up his mind to follow Gilbert wherever he went, positive he would be led to Bussola.

Kruger burst through the door and found himself in a privately rented room with a small bar, waitress and a few tables and chairs.

Bussola sat at the bar, drinking whisky.

There were four bodyguards in all. As soon as Kruger came through the door, they reacted. He was faced with the muzzles of three pistols, all held in very steady hands.

Bussola smiled broadly at the intruder.

Kruger knew then what it must have been like to step into the lion's den, particularly when an ebullient Bussola shouted, 'Hey, Steve! Wondered when you'd show up. Come in and have a drink. You look like you need one. Siddown, let's have chats.' He glanced at the bodyguards. 'Search him,' he barked.

It was not so much a VIP lounge as a cosy VIP living

176

room. Kruger had not known such things existed. Most of the flying he had done had been on the cheap; waiting with hundreds of other poor unfortunates, then being crammed with a shoe-horn onto a pencil-thin plane to sit in seats with hardly any recline, leg space or comfort.

This, he decided, was the way to travel in the future.

Kruger's eyes surveyed the bodyguards again.

Two stood near the door. The other two were slightly to one side of him, positioned to judge his every move and react should he do anything stupid.

But he'd already done about the most stupid thing he was ever going to do by turning up at the airport with some half-baked notion in his brain.

Now he knew he'd be lucky to leave here in one piece.

He looked narrowly at Bussola.

Mark Tapperman jerked into wakefulness. The telephone was still in his hand. The bedside light was still on. His wife still asleep. He blew out his cheeks and wondered if it had been a dream, the phone call from Kruger. With a further rude start, he realised no. He sat up quickly, re-set the phone and dialled Kruger's home number, hoping his friend would not be so stupid as to . . . No, Tapperman reassured himself as he waited for Kruger to answer, he couldn't be that stupid. *Could he?*

'You gotta lotta balls,' the Italian was saying, 'coming out here. Either that or you're a complete jerk.'

'The latter, I think,' Kruger said dryly.

'Well, whatever, Steve, you're here now and we can talk like two grown men.'

'Do grown men cut each other to pieces?'

Bussola stuck a large cigar between his fat lips and lit it with a silver lighter. It had the diameter of a trashcan lid and took a lot of flame to get going. Once lit, he squinted at it, blew on the end and replied, 'Sometimes, Steve . . . when it's really necessary.'

'Bit of an overreaction, wouldn't you say?'

'For me? Naw . . . pussy cat stuff. So, c'mon Steve, I'm hellish curious. What did Felicity want to see you for? Is that the reason you turned up unannounced the other night and caught me and my friend *in flagrante delicto*?'

The questions threw Kruger slightly off-balance. They meant that the two goons who had kidnapped him weren't so loyal to Felicity as she believed them to be. They had blabbed to Bussola, something that didn't surprise Kruger. However, she was still technically a client even if she hadn't paid a dime yet, and Kruger always retained confidentiality except when ordered to talk by a court of law.

Additionally, she had once been his wife and though he hated her with a volcanic intensity, he did not really want any harm to befall her.

'Not sure what you mean, Mario. Felicity?'

'Steve, don't piss me off. The two guys who hauled your ass off the street informed me. And what's more, I have a video-tape of you entering and leaving the house. I am very security conscious, for obvious reasons.' He looked expectantly at the increasingly uncomfortable Kruger.

'More drinks, sir?' the waitress interrupted.

Bussola glared at her for a fraction of a second, before his face softened and he said, 'Not just now, honey.' He patted her ass and rubbed the back of her leg. She didn't seem concerned. 'Make yourself scarce . . . this is business.'

'Okay, sir.'

She turned and disappeared out the back of the bar. Kruger and Bussola watched her retreat and their eyes slowly returned to each other.

'Nice, huh?' Bussola asked.

'Yeah, sure.'

The Italian leaned forwards confidentially to Kruger who could smell, nay taste, the guy's cigar breath. 'Too

178

fuckin' old for me, Steve. I like 'em young and I like 'em tight and I like to hear the bitches scream . . . but you know that, don't you?' He smiled.

Kruger's face hardened over. Through gritted teeth he said, 'You disgust me.'

Bussola rocked back and laughed. 'D'ya think I give a shit, you stupid asshole? Now, where were we?' He brushed some cigar-ash off his pants. 'Oh, yes – you and Felicity.'

'She missed me and we had to catch up with things. That's what exes often do . . . much to the chagrin of their current spouses.'

'Baloney! Did you ball her?'

'Uh-uh. No way.'

'What did you really want, Steve?' His eyes glittered. 'That's the last time I'll ask that question, bud. If I don't get a satisfactory answer, you can consider yourself a very dead human being.'

This situation was the other exception to Kruger's client confidentiality rule. When his life was threatened, he had no qualms about talking over any aspect of the client's business. His sense of responsibility to the client went out the window as self-preservation kicked in. 'She thought you were cheating on her. She hired me to find out. I did it because of our past.' The words tumbled out of Kruger's mouth with no further prompting.

Bussola guffawed and almost choked on his cigar smoke. 'Almost the right answer.' Without warning, the mobster's left hand shot out in a blur and gripped Kruger's wrist with fat fingers. At the same time, he plunged the smouldering end of the cigar hard down into the back of Kruger's trapped hand.

Kruger emitted an unworldly scream of agony. He attempted to yank his hand away, but Bussola held on. Kruger's next response was to draw back his free hand, curl it into a fist and propel it towards Bussola's fat face.

The fist got nowhere.

Two of the bodyguards grabbed him and held on tight as the gangster continued to grind the cigar into the flesh whilst leaning forwards with a look of pure unadulterated glee.

Kruger gritted his teeth as the torture continued. Blobs of sweat burst from his hairline, raced down his forehead into his eyebrows. The smell of his flesh burning wafted into his nostrils.

It probably only lasted a few seconds. Kruger's perception was that it seemed to go on for ever until the cigar was lifted away, having been effectively stubbed out. A black-grey-red welt was left sizzling on the back of his hand.

Bussola leaned back, satisfied by his handiwork. He immediately re-ignited the cigar. With a wave he indicated for the guards to release Kruger.

'You bastard!' cried Kruger, He leapt up and raced to the bar, watched curiously by Charlie Gilbert who was sat on a stool, drinking. He ducked as Kruger approached, but need not have worried. Kruger veered past him and thrust his throbbing hand into the bucket of ice cubes on the bar top.

Breathless, he turned and glared at Bussola, holding himself back from doing or saying anything he might not live to regret.

The ice worked well, numbing the pain like an anaesthetic.

All four guards had their handguns drawn, gazing indolently at Kruger who could see they were totally different material to the ones he'd encountered the other night. Those two dickbrains were probably delivering pizzas now.

With a waggle of his fingers, Bussola beckoned Kruger back to his seat.

He carried the ice-bucket wedged under one arm, keeping his hand shoved deep into the ice. He sat shaking. Fear, mainly, being the cause. Pain too.

'Yeah, almost the right answer, Steve,' Bussola said in a level conversational tone, as if nothing had happened. 'But let's stop beating about the bush: I have the whole of your meeting and chit-chat with Felicity down on tape.'

'You tape what goes on in your house while you're not there?' Kruger asked in disbelief.

'Absolutely. I like to know what she gets up to while I'm away. I have some very heavy footage of several of her sexual encounters with a succession of personal fitness trainers. I say succession because each one has met with – how shall I say? – an unfortunate set of circumstances. Gotta say, I prefer videos featuring younger people, though.'

'You're a whizz of a hubby, Mario.'

Bussola's face set for a moment; Kruger thought he'd made a remark too far, then the big man relaxed again, did not rise to the bait.

'In that case,' Kruger pushed on quickly, 'you know I didn't screw her and she had me by the short and curlies.'

'That shock-baton stuff?'

'Yep.'

'Looks as though I have the privilege now, doesn't it?'

'Looks that way,' Kruger admitted. His world collapsed at the prospect of having a Mafia godfather playing executive games with his testicles. Despite the ice, his hand started hurting again.

'Hey, you're worried. Can see it in your face. No need. I don't propose to use the knowledge of your past shady dealings in any way to influence you or blackmail you. As far as I'm concerned, you're not worth it, Steve. You're just a piece of dogshit on my shoes and I wanna wipe you off. Basically I'm gonna have you executed and I'll tell you why. You' – he leaned forwards and held the newly lit burning tip of the cigar perilously close to Kruger's face; Kruger felt its heat. Instinctively he jerked back. 'You have severely annoyed me. Firstly by being so weak-kneed as to give in to the petty demands of your nympho ex-wife

181

and then,' his voice rose a few tones, 'having the effront-
ery to go up against me. You have caused me consider-
able pain and aggravation AND cost me money. These
guys,' he waved to indicate the bodyguards, 'will accompany you back to your car, pump several big fucking holes
into your skull and then dump you in the Everglades, but
before you go, just hand me your Rolex, please. It's too
nice for an alligator to swallow.'

Kruger handed over his most treasured possession. He
squirmed inwardly whilst he watched Bussola strap it
onto his own wrist.

'Nice,' he said admiringly, 'very nice.'

Once again, the big man moved faster than Kruger
could have anticipated. He rose from his seat, wrapped a
huge arm around Kruger's neck, holding him there in a
vice in the crook of his elbow, then stubbed the cigar out
on Kruger's face. When it was extinguished, he pushed
Kruger away. The ice-bucket spilled and Kruger went
down onto his knees, covering his horrendously injured
face with his hands, moaning loudly.

'Take this fucker away and ice him,' Bussola ordered.

Just how Danny managed it, Henry Christie wasn't sure.

He could not conceal a smile when he entered the
first-floor briefing room at Blackpool police station and
saw the room packed with the officers she had managed
to pull together for 'Operation Trawler'.

The operation which, Henry hoped, would lead to the
capture of Louis Vernon Trent.

There was a full police support unit from Preston (one
Inspector, three Sergeants and twenty-one Constables).
Not bad going by any standards. In addition there were
six PCs from Blackpool and three Detective Constables
from his own office. Danny had also managed to turn out
seven Special Constables. There was a dog-handler and
four PCs from the mouthed branch, dogs and horses
being excluded from the room. Six plainclothes officers

from the Targeting Team made up the rest.

All were swigging tea, coffee or orange juice and scoffing biscuits, thoughtfully provided by Danny. She stood by the briefing lectern at the front of the room, shuffling papers, happily taking charge of the whole kit and caboodle.

Henry was impressed by the turnout. It was just one of those days when everyone seemed to be at the other end of the phone. There were not many of those days in a year.

'Okay, people,' he began, sliding in next to Danny. He rubbed his hands together. 'Can I have your undivided attention, please?' The room fell silent. 'To those of you from outside the Division, welcome to Blackpool. Whilst you're here, we'll try to look after your needs to the best of our abilities; to our residents, we'll try to look after you shower, too. For those of you who don't know me, I'm DI Henry Christie and this is Danny Furness who'll be running the show. And, not to put too fine a point on it, you're here to hunt down a very, very dangerous individual indeed . . .'

By the time Henry Christie was saying those words, that dangerous individual had been up and out of bed for an hour. Although he had only got to bed at 5 a.m., the few hours' sleep he'd had were adequate. Several years behind bars had whittled away his need for sleep. He woke bright and cheerful.

The owner of the guest-house, Mrs Mitcham, a lady in her early fifties, was extremely happy to cook Trent a late breakfast . . . at a price. Not being his own money, Trent paid gladly.

Outside, the weather was glorious.

Trent's first objective was to extend his wardrobe again by buying some light summer gear. Then he intended to drift round town and go into a pub where he knew he could off-load the credit cards and driving licence he'd stolen from several unfortunate people the previous day. He'd take whatever price was offered. Probably about a hundred quid, he guessed – but before all that, he had a more urgent need to fulfil.

He used the phone in the guest-house to order a taxi which subsequently deposited him in Blackpool town centre just as Henry handed the briefing over to Danny.

Two behind. One either side. That was the formation. Each of them with a hand resting inconspicuously on the butt of some type of firearm or other, concealed by well-tailored clothing from the prying eyes of the outside world.

Kruger was the man in the middle.

Before they left the room, he was given instructions by Bussola.

'Okay Steve, you walk out of here nice and cool, okay? You walk them to your car and they'll do it there, nice 'n' quick – promise. Bam! Bam!' He pointed his forefinger at Kruger's head and cocked his thumb. 'Over in a jiffy . . . Now, you might well think that before you reach the parking lot you'll try some fancy footwork as you walk through the airport, or even do something really rash – like attract some cop's attention. Now, Steve, I gotta warn you, if you do, these nice guys will blow you away there and then – and any other simple fucker who so much as steps towards them. There'll be a real bloodbath, at the end of which they'll simply fade into the background.

'Just to reiterate: by behaving yourself and leading these fine gents to your wheels, you'll save innocent lives.'

Bussola nodded at his men. 'Okay, away you go.'

Kruger's face and hand hurt bad where the burning cigar had been screwed into his skin, but these injuries were right at the back of his mind as he tried desperately to figure a way out of this predicament.

Whatever he did, it seemed, he was destined to die.

184

There was no time for niceties any more. There would be no building up of rapport. No sweeties. No laughter.

No love.

That was all in the past, before the betrayals had sent him to prison. Now the little ones he had loved so much had to suffer and feel the pain he was feeling. It did not matter that they would not actually be the ones who had gone to court and damned him. It was the principle that mattered now.

He had to make a point.

No one betrayed or hurt him and got away with it.

No one.

Trent was sitting on a green park bench in the recreation area adjacent to Claremont Road in the North Shore of Blackpool. Watching, waiting, listening, his senses buzzing, anticipating. Soon, he knew, his opportunity would come.

His eyes took in all the activity. Several youngsters were playing on the swings and slide. Most were accompanied by adults.

Trent's lips snarled at the inconvenience.

He lifted up his newspaper, reckoning to be engrossed in it.

He could wait, despite the urges inside him.

They began the journey from the lounge to airport parking. Kruger felt as though he was walking on the moon. His legs became light and bloodless. The same pretty much applied to his brain.

Everything was completely unreal. Being walked through Miami International Airport to be executed – how real was that?

Everything blurred at the edges. His ears pounded like his head was inside a bass drum. People drifted by in a mist. Sound distorted, like a tape being eaten by a Walkman.

Kruger shook his head, opened his eyes wide. Then his

mind picked up the pain again from the burns on his skin, a sensation it had been suppressing. This brought him back to sharp focus.

Back to the real world.

Suddenly the unreality of before seemed much more preferable.

Without doubt, Kruger was about to experience another of those Big Life Moments.

Chapter Ten

The shop was on Dickson Road, Blackpool, the road
which runs behind the Imperial Hotel which is used each
year as a base for political parties during conference week.
The shop was one of those grocery-cum-everything shops
which opened from 7 a.m. until extremely late. It was
owned by an Asian family who had turned it into a
thriving business by their sheer hard work.

Claire Lilton had the straps of her sports bag over her
left shoulder, holding the bag underneath her armpit. She
had a metal shopping basket in her left hand, leaving her
right hand free. The zip of the sports bag was open about
six inches and if she squeezed the bag in a certain way, a
hole appeared when the zip parted.

In the basket were a couple of items from the shelves.
In the sports bag were even more items from the shelves,
none of which she intended to pay for. She paused near
the sweet display, picked up a Kit Kat, looked closely at
it, replaced it on the shelf. Her eyes moved to the corners
of their sockets and she checked the aisle. Apart from a
doddering old woman, Claire was alone.

She picked up half a dozen Kit Kats, squeezed the bag
and dropped them expertly into the hole. Casually she
dawdled along the sweet display and dropped a 10p
chocolate bear into the basket. She moved on.

By the time she reached the till, her basket contained
six cheap items. Her sports bag, which began to weigh
heavy, contained a great deal of contraband.

At the till she paid for the stuff in the wire basket and even asked for a carrier bag.

Then she stepped out of the shop, only to be dragged back in by an irate Asian man, no taller than herself.

'Get your dirty hands off me,' she screamed.

The man did not let go. 'You steal,' he said. 'You steal from shop. I call the cops.' He had hold of her biceps. 'In there – stolen property.' He pointed at her sports bag. 'I watch you steal.'

'I've done fuck-all, you bastard,' she yelled into his face. 'If you don't let me go, I'll sue you for assault.'

She wriggled and squirmed and kicked out at him. Her Doc Marten boots connected with his shins and he emitted a yell of pain. Still, he hung onto her.

'Call cops!' he shouted to the woman behind the till, who had been watching the encounter with open mouth and no gumption. His shouts galvanised her into action, and she reached for the phone behind her.

Meanwhile, the little Asian shopkeeper discovered he had a tiger by the tail.

Claire spat horribly into his face. 'I've got AIDS, you bastard. Now you have!'

She wrenched herself free from his grasp. He lunged gamefully after her again. But, as Danny Furness had discovered, catching Claire Lilton was no easy matter.

She side-stepped him and picked up the charity box from the counter – which was shaped like a rocket – and swung round, holding it with both hands, rather like the movement an athlete makes when throwing the hammer. She did not let go of it, though. Building up force with momentum, she crashed it into the side of his head.

The box burst open spectacularly, sending a shower of copper coins into the air. More importantly, however, it felled the shopkeeper and gouged a deep gash into his head which spurted blood.

Claire hoisted the sports bag back onto her shoulder and dived out of the shop.

By the time the bloody-faced Asian looked out of the door, she had disappeared.

His Urdu was unrepeatable.

'Do you enjoy your work?' Steve Kruger asked the bodyguard to his immediate right.

There was no response. The guy continued to look dead ahead.

All five men were now on the first-floor level, walking down the middle of the concourse past the shops. No one took any notice of them. They were real professionals, the type of people who, somehow, never seemed to draw attention to themselves. A skill in itself. They simply made it look as though they were out for a stroll. All five of them, Kruger included.

Kruger looked at the members of the public close by. He acknowledged that what Bussola had said was true. If he did anything foolish at this stage, he would die, possibly others too, and these guys would simply dematerialise.

And as much as Kruger didn't want to die, he didn't want others to be killed because of him.

Even the security cameras, which he knew were all around, wouldn't be much use to him. They would never finger these bastards.

'How about you?' Kruger enquired of the man to his left.

'Speak once more and you get it here and now,' he said through the side of his mouth.

'Gotcha.'

They walked past the Disney Store.

'He's gotta be here somewhere,' Myrna Rosza gabbled agitatedly. She scanned the bank of TV monitors in front of her whilst the operator casually, but swiftly, clicked from shot to shot. 'He's gotta be here,' she repeated desperately. She glared at Mark Tapperman. 'This is your fault.'

189

The big Lieutenant shrank away from her eyes. He gave a pathetic shrug. 'He might not be here,' he said weakly.

'Don't kid yourself.' Myrna was caustic. 'Once he gets an idea into his stubborn head . . .'

'You sound like you care about him.'

'I do – he pays my wages.' She returned her attention to the screens. 'Now, where the hell is he?'

They were in the security control area of the airport, in the CCTV room, peering over the shoulder of the operator who flicked through the images received from all over MIA.

'There!' Myrna almost shouted, pointing to a screen. 'Focus in there!'

The operator did as instructed.

'Shit,' she said with disappointment as the high-powered lens zoomed in. It wasn't Kruger.

The frustration she was feeling could have been sliced open with a breadknife. Ever since Tapperman had called her at home with an hysterical edge to his voice and explained what had happened, Myrna had been on a high.

Suppose Kruger *had* gone storming to the airport? Suppose he'd got himself involved in a situation he couldn't handle? Suppose he was already dead meat?

Myrna had initially hung up on Tapperman and phoned Kruger. No reply. She called Tapperman again and instructed him to get a SWAT squad to the airport.

He had guffawed. 'Just on the off-chance – impossible!'

'At least get some cops up there.'

'Right. And do you know how many cops are on-duty at this moment in Miami as we speak?'

'No.'

'Well, I ain't gonna tell you. Suffice to say the public thinks there's hundreds. I'd be lucky to scrape a dozen unoccupied officers together. No resources, babe. Usual story.'

'Then you'd better get yourself there. I'll see you at the

190

meeting point in twenty minutes.' And she slammed the phone down without waiting for a response.

Myrna dressed in seconds. Tracksuit, trainers, her pistol around her shoulder. She kissed her sleeping husband and, grabbing her cell-tel on the way out, ran to her car. She constantly rang Kruger's home and mobile numbers as she drove at warp factor six to the airport.

There was no reply.

She and Tapperman came together as arranged and using his badge and contacts, got into the CCTV room, where they had been ever since.

Myrna rubbed her eyes. She had been having trouble sleeping, not least because she had cheated on her husband not many hours before and could not get her mind off it. She had secretly, and sometimes not so secretly, been attracted to Kruger ever since she began working for him. Personal and professional considerations and responsibilities ensured it never went further than banter or mild flirtation. The previous couple of days had put an end to those issues and it had been an absolute necessity for her to finish up in Kruger's bed. She had truly believed she could take it for what it was, keep it as a one-off, go back to equilibrium.

Instead she found herself completely disorientated. She couldn't get Kruger out of her head, nor the memory of him out of her body.

She had been fully awake, if exhausted, when Tapperman rang, and for a while after, the adrenaline flowed. Now, it was ebbing in despair.

Standing there, in front of the bank of TV screens, she had to admit to herself that she loved Steve, had done so for longer than she cared to recall, and the prospect of not seeing him again caused her to panic.

A little squeak escaped from her lips. Tapperman shot her a quick glance.

Then; 'There he is!' Tapperman proclaimed confidently. He rapped the appropriate monitor with his

191

knuckles. The camera shot in, focused. Myrna's heart shuddered so hard in her chest she nearly fell over.

The screen showed Kruger, surrounded by four tough-looking guys, stepping through a sliding door. There was an anxious expression on his face, as well as an injury of some sort which Tapperman could not define.

'Where the hell's that location?' he demanded.

Kruger, his four friends and a couple of other people were standing by a bank of elevators which would take them to the multi-storey parking lot.

The elevator arrived, the doors opened. A flood of people disgorged and dissipated. Kruger and the others stepped inside the large elevator, constructed to carry about twenty people plus luggage. A woman turned to him. 'Which level?'

'The top, please.'

She pressed her own selection, then his.

Just before the doors eased shut, a big hand stopped the process and forced the doors to re-open.

Two extra people stepped in. A man and a woman . . . a couple, bickering about something, like they'd been together too many years.

'C'mon, you godamned bitch, we're holdin' people up here.'

'You stop bad-mouthin' me, you asshole,' the woman replied, apparently fuming with anger. 'You ain't done nothin' but since we arrived.'

'Well, you deserve it, you lazy slut,' the man said. To the rest of the people in the elevator he said, ''Scuse us.' He yanked the woman between Kruger and the body-guard to his left. 'We'll carry this on back here.'

Kruger's expression did not change. His eyes showed no flicker of recognition. But inside, his stomach lurched. The hairs on the nape of his neck prickled with excitement. He hoped the guys behind him weren't staring at his neck, otherwise the game would have been given away.

The doors closed. The elevator rose smoothly, stopping at various levels, allowing people to step out. No one else got in.

Kruger heard snatches of the couple's argument which had been reduced in volume. It was clear there was a major domestic going on.

'You'll be tellin' me next it's healed up,' the man hissed. 'I ain't had it for weeks.'

'You don't deserve it, the way you treat me.'

'Nag, nag, nag,' the man said spitefully.

'An' you do nothin', nothin', nothin'.'

Eventually the only people remaining in the tin box were Kruger, his four buddies and the warring couple, all obviously destined for the top level.

When the elevator arrived, the doors slid open.

Kruger was about to step out when one of his captors grabbed his elbow and held him back. Another said to the couple, 'After you.'

'At last,' the woman said, 'a gentleman.' She smiled maliciously at her partner.

'Bitch,' hissed the man, shouldering his way out, pushing her ahead. They turned right.

Kruger got a shove in the ribs and stumbled out to the left. From the corner of his eye he saw the couple move towards a car.

Although they were on the top level, there was still a roof over their heads, and like most high-rise parking, the lighting was relatively poor.

Kruger led them towards his Chevy, parked at the very end of the level. His mind worked furiously, trying to decide what to do, wondering what Tapperman and Myrna, the perfect couple, had planned . . . if anything.

Shit, shit, shit, he said to himself, trying to make a decision.

The closer he got to his car, the more certain he was he would have to make the opening move.

Without further thought he went for it.

He stopped abruptly in his tracks. The bodyguard directly behind him walked straight into him. The ones either side went on a few paces.

As soon as he and the man made contact, Kruger swivelled at the hips and in a flowing, single motion, rammed the point of his elbow into the man's chest, connecting with the sternum. Kruger's arm rose and he smashed the back of his clenched fist into the man's face, making a wonderful, crunching sound, like a wooden ruler snapping.

The whole movement took less than a fraction of a second.

Even so, fast as it was, Kruger saw that guns were already appearing from nowhere in the hands of the remaining three team members.

'Move, Steve, move!' Tapperman bawled.

Kruger looked up, saw Tapperman and Myrna about twenty feet behind. Tapperman's body was fully exposed. Myrna was crouching over the hood of a parked car. Both had weapons drawn, ready for combat.

Kruger knew he had to keep going.

He grabbed the lapels of the nose-smashed bodyguard and swung him round into the gunman to his left, pushed and let go. They mangled together with spectacular success. Using the momentum generated by this manoeuvre, Kruger dived down between the two nearest parked cars, into cover, out of the line of fire. Tapperman yelled, 'Armed police! Drop your weapons!'

The two bodyguards who were not busy turned instinctively towards Tapperman, guns rising.

They moved instantaneously as professionals should when faced with a situation for which they had been trained.

The two bodyguards who had been positioned to Kruger's left side and were therefore not affected by this startling move, spun on their heels quicker than ice-skaters to face Tapperman and Myrna. Their firearms were rising and aiming as they did so.

The one who'd had his face broken by the back of Kruger's fist, though dazed by the blow, still had the presence of mind to drop to his knees so he would not get in the way. The fourth one, who'd watched Kruger disappear between the parked cars, threw himself to the ground between the cars nearest to him. He also had his gun ready and as soon as he hit the deck he was looking underneath the car towards where Kruger had landed.

This particular bodyguard was certain of one thing: even if this little task of theirs got flushed down the pan, Kruger would still die.

That was professionalism.

Tapperman saw them swinging around at an alarming rate. He noted the glint of firearms and did not intend to hesitate.

As both of the bodyguards were moving at roughly the same speed – lightning fast – there was little to choose, target-wise. So, because Tapperman was standing on Myrna's right-hand side, he chose to shoot the guy on his right.

Part of Tapperman's mind begged Myrna to bag the one on the left. He knew he could take out one of them – but only one. There would be no earthly hope of taking two.

Myrna had to act as quickly as he did – and go for the correct target.

'Shoot, Myrna, shoot!' he pleaded silently.

The pad of his right forefinger pulled the trigger back.

The wind whooshed out of Kruger's lungs as he thumped down onto the concrete floor. For a brief moment he did not move, other than to open his eyes and look underneath the car to his left where he saw the bodyguard, who had decided that, come what may, he would kill Kruger.

The man's gun was pointed directly at Kruger's face and his finger was on the trigger.

Myrna wasn't consciously going through any thought-process. She stood there, half her body protected by the cover provided by the car she stood behind. Her feet were positioned shoulder-width apart, knees bent, but flexible. The Sig was in her right hand, supported in the palm of her left.

There was a blankness in her mind. Yet, simply, she was aware – somewhere – that she had started to sweat from every pore in her body. As Kruger dived away, she saw the injured man drop to his knees, one of the bodyguards dive away too, and the other two start to turn . . . but in her mind it wasn't a fast twist because she slowed everything down right into its component parts without even realising she was doing it.

The two men as they pirouetted, their guns drawn from under their jackets . . . the weapons coming round to be pointed at her and Tapperman . . . the weight of the pistol in her hands . . . the high-contrast sights down the barrel. Her finger tightening on the trigger . . .

Three weapons exploded simultaneously.

The ones in the hands of Mark Tapperman and Myrna Rosza.

The one in the grip of the bodyguard who was aiming at the prostrate body of Steve Kruger.

Within the confines of the parking lot, the noise of the combined discharges was deafening. A huge reverberating, eardrum-smashing roar.

Having to run made Claire Lilton's cracked ribs hurt. When she thought she was out of catching distance, she slowed right down, dodged into a back alley and got her breath back. She reached into her sports bag and grabbed a cold can of orange Tango which she opened and gratefully gulped down. It was getting to be a hot day.

When recovered she tossed the can over a wall and wandered aimlessly around, until she was back on Dickson Road, about half a mile away from the shop.

She doubted whether the shopkeeper would call the cops, so she felt quite safe.

As it was approaching high season, Claire fitted in easily with the thousands of other kids thronging the streets of Blackpool, the single biggest holiday resort in the world. She knew that if necessary, she could mingle for weeks and never be noticed. All it required was a grain of common sense, some cunning and courage, a bit of luck and she would be able to survive indefinitely.

Within a few moments she had wandered onto Gynn Square, a large roundabout on the promenade in North Shore.

Wearily she went into a small recreation ground only yards away, off Warbreck Hill Road. She unhooked the bag and let it fall to the ground, slumped on a bench and stretched her tired legs.

She was dressed for the season in a cut-off T-shirt drawn tightly over her small, developing bust; then there was a gap showing her flat, white tummy; then there was a pair of Lycra exercise shorts clinging to her thighs. Nike trainers finished off her attire.

It had been Henry Christie's intention to get the team turned out onto the streets as soon as possible.

With Danny's efficient help, he succeeded.

He watched the last officer leave the briefing room, then turned to speak to Danny. 'They'll need all the luck in the world to catch this guy.' He nodded towards a window. 'And this weather won't help us at all. Tourists will be flooding in today . . . needle in a haystack job.'

'At least we're doing something. We need to catch him, otherwise he'll start again. Can you imagine what all those years cooped up could do to a pervert like him?'

Before Henry could reply he heard an angry voice behind him. 'DC Furness? Just what the hell do you think you're playing at?'

Jack Sands.

'My office – NOW!' he shrieked.

Danny looked up at Henry for support, fear in her eyes. Henry gave her a sly wink, and turned to Sands with a simmering anger. In a measured tone he said, 'Nobody calls people by their last names these days, and nobody says "my office – now" unless they want to come across as a real jerk.'

'Up yours, Henry,' Sands snapped back. 'She's my officer, not one of yours – not yet anyway – and I'll speak to her any way I want to.'

'Wrong on both counts,' Henry said crisply. 'Jack, we all need to sit down and chat – like now, if possible.'

'I haven't got time.'

Henry stepped up to him and snarled, 'You'd better make fuckin' time, if you value your job.'

Trent saw her sitting alone, a faraway look on her face. He knew instantly she was the one for him. She couldn't have been more than eleven years old, but looked older. Trent could see through that. He was good at judging a youngster's age and this one was just right for him. The age he liked. Their bodies beginning to develop, their womanhood not yet there. He looked again at this girl and experienced that old sensation, like someone had drawn a knife-blade down his back, triggering a sexual response in his genitals.

She had long slim legs, wore a minimum amount of clothing and was by herself. There was no one hovering nearby who could have been with her. She looked vulnerable, just right for plucking.

Trent seated himself at the far end of the bench. He opened his newspaper, crossed his legs. His eyes watched her reaction to his presence.

Initially there was no indication she had even seen him.

He coughed. That seemed to break her trance. She glanced at him. Her face was painfully beautiful. Trent sneered inside himself as he pictured her down on him. Outwardly he returned a smile.

She gave a wan, slightly pathetic grin.

'My name's Louis.' He folded down the newspaper. 'What's yours? I'll bet it's a pretty one.'

She told him.

'Take a seat,' Henry offered Jack. They were in Henry's small office where Henry had arranged three chairs on the 'public side' of his desk, ready for the encounter.

Sands sat with a great show of reluctance and impatience, sighing heavily.

Henry indicated for Danny to do likewise. She chose the chair furthest away from Sands which was also the one directly opposite him. Instantly she regretted two things – taking the seat and her choice of clothing.

She was in a pencil skirt which rode up her thighs as she sat down and crossed her legs. Sands's eyes homed in on the display and a look of wickedness flitted across his face. She pulled the skirt down and uncrossed her legs, sitting there with her knees pressed tightly together. It felt uncomfortable and unnatural and Sands knew it. She could tell from his face.

Henry hitched his trousers up with his fingers and thumbs on the creases and sat in the vacant seat. He crossed his legs.

Sands glowered cocksurely at him.

'As you know, Jack, Louis Trent did a runner from jail last night and he's almost certainly back in town. Obviously we need to try and recapture him as soon as possible. I spoke to Mr Fanshaw-Bayley this morning and he told me to use Danny to lead the team because she knows Trent so well. No doubt you agree with this thinking.'

Danny shot Henry a quick look of concern. To say he was distorting the truth was an understatement.

'Because it was such a rush to get things pulled together,' Henry added, 'I didn't have time to explain, so I apologise for that. At least you know now.'

'Well, now that your team are up and running, I'll have her back, thanks.'

Henry shook his head. 'As of now she's on CID.' He handed a rolled-up fax to Sands, rather like a Biblical scroll. Sands unrolled it and read it slowly. It was confirmation of what FB had promised Henry that morning, written and signed by the man himself. Danny was on CID as of now.

Sands's face looked like it would burst. 'This is completely out of order. He can't do this, not without consulting me.'

'He's an ACC. He can do mostly what he likes and usually does.'

'I'm going to go to the Detective Superintendent and get this blocked. She's on my Department until next Monday.' And Sands stood up to leave.

'Sit down Jack, there's more we need to discuss . . . I said, *sit down.*'

'All I'm doing,' Henry concluded patiently, 'is giving you the opportunity to say, "Hey, yeah, got a bit upset, bit obsessive and it won't happen again." That's all, Jack. Just hold your hand up, say sorry and we'll all walk out of here and that's that. Promise.'

'You can stick your promise right down your prick, Christie, because I've done nothing wrong and I'm not apologising to a paranoid bitch who can't bear the thought of me finishing with her.'

'We're not in the business of name-calling, Jack,' Henry said softly. 'We're trying to solve a problem, adult to adult, and swearing isn't gonna help.'

Sands held his hands up. 'Sorry . . . just got a bit

up-tight. Wouldn't you? What you've alleged is absolute crap and you'll never prove a thing because there's nothing to prove.'

Henry tutted. He hadn't wanted it to go this far. To Danny he said, 'Last night you said you received several phone calls of a distressing nature?'

'That's right, from about eight o'clock onwards. But whoever it was must have either dialled 141 before putting my number in to ensure the call couldn't be traced, or they were phoning through a switchboard.'

'How many calls did you receive?'

'Four that I answered. I took my phone off the hook then, but I checked with BT this morning. They told me I got twenty-five more calls up to midnight.'

'How did you feel about the calls you received?'

'Frightened. Scared. As if I was being violated in my own home.'

'Thanks, Danny.' Henry raised his eyebrows at Sands. 'Jack, did you make those calls?'

His answer was short and to the point. 'Did I fuck.'

'Okay,' said Henry, unflustered. 'Danny, what else happened last night?'

'Some creep,' she shuddered at the memory, 'stuffed a dozen red roses through my letterbox about half-one this morning.'

'I'll bet that had an effect on you, too?'

'I was absolutely terrified.' Her breath came in steps now as she thought about it. 'Someone prowling round my house, watching me, stalking me.'

'Jack – any response?'

He remained silent for a while, considering, lips pursing and unpursing. He breathed in and sat up. 'Yeah, just get to fuck, the pair of you. This is absolute shite. I'm off.' He pushed himself up again.

Henry said evenly, but with a deadly tone, 'You walk out of this room, Jack, I'll arrest you.'

The words struck Sands as heavily as a lorry. He sat

slowly back, eyes fixed firmly on Henry, who held the look, unwavering. Inside, Henry's heart was pounding dramatically. It was all he could do to maintain his composure. His mouth was dry, but his armpits were very wet. He knew he was in very dangerous territory.

Sands was the one to break the gaze between the men. He re-focused them immediately and savagely on Danny.

'Danny?' Henry continued. 'The night before last?'

'Someone smashed a window at my home, cut my face.' She placed the tip of a fingernail on the stitched cut on her cheek. 'They also damaged my car, scratched it and snapped the Mercedes badge off.'

'Jack?' said Henry, feeling like a facilitator.

Sands was tightlipped. 'Evidence?' he snapped.

'I saw you holding a Mercedes star in your hand when I left work last night,' Danny accused him.

Sands uttered a short, barking laugh. 'Your word against mine,' he said pityingly.

Henry reached for a folder on his desk. His hand slid into it and extracted a piece of paper. 'Our IT department ran this off for me,' he explained and handed it to Sands. 'It's a printout of all the phone numbers dialled from the extension in your office between 5 p.m. and midnight last night. You'll see that one number features pretty highly, wouldn't you say? In fact, it features twenty-nine times, Jack, doesn't it?'

Sands swallowed. His eyes were transfixed on the figures in front of them. His cocksure exterior crumbled slightly with the assistance of Henry's hammer and chisel.

'Wonderful thing, this IT lark,' Henry commented. 'Anything to say, Jack?'

'Proves nothing. I needed to speak to her on a work-related matter. She'd obviously taken her phone off the hook.'

'The work-related matter was what, Jack?'

'I'll think of something,' he said blandly.

'Fine, fine.' Henry's hand disappeared back into the

folder and pulled out another slip of paper. He gave it to Sands. 'This is a copy of the receipt from the florist on Elm Avenue. That's your Barclaycard number, your signature and your order for twelve red roses.'

Sands leaned back, his look of defiance wavering after his previous rally. 'Still proves nothing.'

'It can stop here and it can stop now, Jack. Believe me, trust me. This does not have to go on. You can say sorry and walk out of here and forget it.'

'You mean that's all you've got? It's crap and you know it, Henry. I have an answer for everything and I'm therefore not apologising for something I'm not guilty of.'

Henry pointed at Sands. 'Don't forget, Jack, I gave you the chance to save face.'

His hand went into his jacket pocket and extracted something. He held out his hand, turned it over and slowly opened his fingers to reveal a small, clear, plastic evidence bag.

In it was the famous three-pointed star seen so prominently on the front radiator grilles of Mercedes Benz cars.

A silence fell heavy on the three people in the room.

Myrna Rosza looked down at the two dead bodies of Bussola's bodyguards. The one sprawled to the right had been taken down by Mark Tapperman's double-tap. *Ba-bam!* The other on the left had been killed by herself. She was painfully aware that the first bullet which left her gun had basically removed the guy's throat and smashed through the back of his neck. He had been dead before he hit the ground squirming. Myrna didn't know that for sure, but she would happily have laid money on it.

She too had attempted a double-tap. The idea of that method of shooting was to put two bullets pretty roughly in the same hole in quick succession. Her second shot, however, had gone well off-target and disappeared to where only God knew.

She stared down at the dead guy, fascinated by the pool

of blood forming slowly underneath his grotesque body. It was going nowhere fast on the non-porous surface of the parking lot.

The first man she had ever killed.

Her jawline tightened.

Her time with the FBI had been concerned with more mundane matters – accounts, financial fraud, the occasional mob-related paperwork.

Nothing like this.

Never once had she faced a gunman, let alone drawn a weapon in anger. The only raids she had ever been on were the ones where she had been armed with folders, and were carried out during office hours – rifling through suspects' desks, drawers and computer files, arresting people possibly armed with a letter-opener at worst. The only real danger she had ever faced had been from paper cuts.

Now this.

What surprised her was how little it was affecting her, but she was intelligent enough to know about delayed shock. A reaction would come – and she would have to deal with it. For now, she was cool.

'Y'okay?' Tapperman asked.

She nodded. 'Yeah, thanks.'

Behind her, this level of the parking lot was a flurry of police activity. Why the hell did the emergency services love flashing lights so much? A migraine threatened. She closed her eyes and held the bridge of her nose with thumb and forefinger. 'Switch the damned things off!' she wanted to yell.

'You did good,' Tapperman said encouragingly. He patted her arm, squeezed it gently. 'There won't be any legal repercussions. I've already spoken with the DA and the Coroner. Nothing to worry about.'

She pulled her arm out of his fingers. Courts and the American legal system were a long way from her mind. 'You're still an asshole,' she said bluntly.

A crime-scene photographer pushed past and began taking shots of the two dead men. He was followed by another with a camcorder. *Crack!* With a noise like a firework, a huge arc lamp exploded into life, illuminating the scene, shining right into Myrna's eyes.

'Fuck!' she hissed angrily. She turned sharply away, blinking, literally seeing stars. Then, vision regained, she heaved Tapperman out of her way and walked over to talk to Steve Kruger.

She arrived at the moment before the plastic undertaker's bag was zipped up with him inside. Briefly she saw his horrendous head injuries. Kruger had taken three bullets smack in the face. They had been of a type designed to explode on impact, and succeeded in removing both the front and back of his head, splattering his brains everywhere. The man who had killed him had been good.

Myrna reeled at the sight. She had to reach out for a car to lean on to support her woolly legs.

With Steve Kruger dead she suddenly felt she didn't want to go on living. She cursed the cruelty of it all and wished she had actually told him she loved him when she had the opportunity. If only she hadn't been so pigheaded.

Now there was no chance.

She clung shaking to the car, tears pouring out of her eyes as a migraine dug cruel fingers into her skull, mercifully blocking out the scene.

Chapter Eleven

'I'm gasping for a drink and a fag,' Danny said. It was noon and not too early for either by any means. 'I need something to steady my nerves. I'm shaking like a leaf.'

'Right,' said Henry, 'let's do it. We deserve it.' He picked up his personal radio, turned it on and clicked the volume onto low – just in case.

They left his office and went to the lift. As the doors opened, the Police Constable who had taken the report of Claire Lilton missing from home again stepped out, almost barging into Danny.

'Been looking for you, Danny.' He waved the completed MFH report in her face. 'It's that little cow you've been dealing with . . . she's gone AWOL again. You know – that Claire Lilton.'

'When?' Danny asked, a little knot of concern in her stomach.

'Sometime last night or early hours of this morning. What do you want me to do about it? Circulate it or what?'

Danny's mind, which was really somewhere else, made a snap decision. 'Just drop the report on my desk. I'll see to it later – thanks.' She stepped into the lift next to Henry who was holding the doors open. They closed; descent commenced.

'Claire Lilton: shoplifter and persistent misper?'

Danny glanced at Henry, quietly respectful that a busy DI should know this. Henry prided himself on knowing most things.

'Yeah, that's the one,' she nodded. 'Been a real pain for a few weeks now, but I can't get to the bottom of why she's going. Something odd at home, I suspect.' She looked away from Henry, suddenly realising she was slightly in awe of him. Not only did he know things that most DIs wouldn't give a toss about, but there were not many police managers who would have had the bottle to do what he had just done on her behalf. Taking on Jack Sands – a tough, well-respected man's man so admired by so many gullible people – and confronting him head on. No, not many people would have done that. No wonder his team worked their backsides off for Henry Christie.

They walked out of the police station towards Blackpool town centre. It was a clear, sunny day. Danny breathed the warm fresh air into her lungs, expanding them to their full capacity. Out of the corner of his eye, Henry, the perfect manager, saw Danny's ample chest rise and fall.

Danny giggled. For a second he thought she had clocked him giving her the eye, but when he looked at her he saw he was mistaken. With her chin lifted high, she was staring dead ahead, a look of sheer happiness on her face.

'I don't know if it's done the trick, Henry, but I feel as if a great weight has been plucked off the top of my head – and it's all down to you. The look on Jack's face when you showed him the star and told him you'd found it taped under one of his desk drawers – and that you'd been accompanied at the time. He looked like he wanted to disappear down a plughole. It was a picture. Thanks, Henry.'

She grabbed his elbow, stopped him in his tracks and planted a kiss firmly on his cheek.

'Thanks,' she said again, genuinely.

'All part of the service,' he replied, colouring up slightly. He was very glad it was merely an innocent kiss of thanks. He knew that had there been anything more to

208

it, he would probably have been daft enough to try and follow it up and get himself into lumber yet again.

They carried on walking and reached the corner of Bank Hey Street, one of Blackpool's busiest shopping streets.

'What you got then?' the weasel-faced man asked. His name was Benstead. 'C'mon, I don't have time to fuck around. I'm a busy man.'

A slightly breathless and ruffled Trent glanced cautiously around the smoke-filled taproom of the pub. Although there were only a few people in it, every one of them, Benstead included, had a cigarette on the go. The ceiling was a dark brown, nicotine-stained colour. 'Here?' Trent asked Benstead.

'Yeah,' the little man nodded. 'Here. But, y'know – be discreet. Don't flash everything round for every Tom, Dick 'n' Arsehole to see. Show me under the table, out of sight. Right?'

Trent nodded and took a long draught from the pint of mild in front of him. He was very tense, hyped up. He wiped his mouth with the back of his hand, then took a small paper bag out of his pocket. He edged to one side and shuffled the contents out onto the space on the tatty benchseat between him and Benstead.

A driving licence and some credit cards.

'Is that all?' Benstead sneered. 'I thought you'd robbed fuckin' Barclaycard headquarters from the way you were talking.'

'Yeah, that's all,' Trent said. All but the ambulance-driver's cash card.

'Where'd you get 'em from?'

'Why?'

''Cos I want to know. It's all relevant to the price, innit? Things that're really hot, I don't spend much money on. You know – high-profile stuff. It's the bog standard things that interest me . . . things with a bit of a shelf-life.'

'Oh, right,' Trent said, understanding. He wiped his face with his hand, momentarily holding his fingers under his nose, inhaling deeply.

Inwardly he gasped. God! He could smell her! It was wonderful.

'Oh right,' Trent said again. 'These things are only lukewarm – almost cold, really. Come from a break-in down south yesterday.'

'Mmm.' Benstead picked up one of the credit cards by its edge and tilted it to the light. Suspiciously his eyes rose to Trent. 'You sure?'

Trent took another drink of beer. 'Very sure.'

'Hmm,' the dealer murmured dubiously. 'Even warm stuff' – he pronounced 'warm' as 'worm' – 'don't last long, a day, maybe two, in the right hands.' He dropped the credit card back onto the seat and picked up the driving licence in the same careful way. 'Now driving licences go on much further, and a driving licence and credit card in the same name . . .' He pondered and regarded Trent. 'How much?'

'I don't fucking know. Name a price.'

Benstead clicked his tongue thoughtfully. He already had a buyer in mind for this little lot, a guy who had a nice line – nationally – of defrauding car-hire companies by renting good quality motors and selling them on to a ringer. He would love this combination. Probably worth fifteen hundred.

'Fifty quid.'

'Don't take me for a fool. I may not have the sell-on contacts, but I know you do. These are worth good money to the right people. One-fifty.'

'Okay,' Benstead relented easily. 'One hundred.'

'One-two-five.'

'One-fifteen.'

Trent nodded. Benstead pulled a roll of banknotes out of his jeans pocket and peeled off the required number, handing them across under cover of the table. 'Now fuck

210

off,' he said, concluding business.

Trent grabbed the money and stuffed it into a pocket. He stood up and left the place through the back door.

Benstead shuffled the purchase back into the paper bag and dropped it into his anorak pocket. He picked up a copy of the *Daily Mail*, unfolded it and relaxed . . . for about a second . . . until he read the headlines and saw Trent's face staring dangerously at him from the front page.

A horribly nauseous feeling wrenched his guts. He placed the paper down on the table and reached for his drink. Christ! He'd just done business with the most wanted man in the country. His hand shook as he lifted the glass and missed his mouth. Then he groaned pathetically when the person he most detested and feared entered the taproom from the more salubrious snug next door.

Henry and Danny had walked along Bank Hey Street, Blackpool Tower rising above them to their left. The place was swarming with holidaymakers, bustling along, every single one of them with a smile. A whole range of people, young to old, slim to fat. Sober to drunk. Blackpool had something for everyone.

'I wonder how it's going with Trent,' Danny said.

'I'll be surprised if he stays here long and I'll be even more surprised if we catch him,' Henry said honestly.

'The very thought of him makes me shiver,' Danny confessed. 'I don't think I've ever met someone quite so evil. What he did to those little girls was appalling. It's a wonder he didn't kill them. I wouldn't normally wish death on anyone, but he should be hanged. I'd gladly put the noose around his neck.'

'Let's have a look in here.' Henry pointed to the door of a pub. 'Quick drink, then back to work.'

'In here?' Danny's lips curled in disgust as she looked up at the building. 'It's a dive.'

'Let's combine business and pleasure.'

Henry held the front door open, allowing Danny to enter first. They turned left into the snug and stood just inside the threshold of the bar.

Danny's words were accurate. The place was a dive, but both officers knew it was one of the main pubs in town where stolen goods from shoplifting sprees were often divided up and distributed or sold; a lot of minor drug dealing went down too. Both activities usually occurred without interference from management who were strongly suspected of being involved in both trades.

Henry liked to drop in unexpectedly now and again. Occasionally such visits produced results. More often than not they simply shook up the crims, something Henry took great pleasure in doing.

The snug was fairly empty. Henry could not spot anyone he knew, other than the barman, Fat Tommy.

'All right, Tommy?' Henry approached the bar.

'I was,' Tommy responded on seeing Henry. Tommy was not noted for his social skills.

'Kaliber for me . . . Danny?'

'I think my nerves are back in order. Coke please, with ice.' She pulled out a cigarette and lit up. She inhaled deeply and for a second or two went quite light-headed. She held the smoke in her lungs, then blew it out slowly. Bliss.

The rotund barman went about his tasks. Henry asked him, 'Anything doing?'

'Nope.' He banged the two drinks on the bar top.

'You don't like me, do you Tommy?'

'No, and I can't think why . . . two quid.'

'Shame, really . . . we have so much in common.' Henry handed him a five-pound note. Whilst Tommy was at the till, Henry stood on tiptoes and peered across the bar into the taproom where he saw Benstead. After checking his change he said, 'C'mon,' to Danny, led her out of the snug into the taproom and immediately saw the expression on Benstead's face.

He looked as though he'd seen the Grim Reaper.

Henry thought, Might've struck lucky here.

Benstead made a valiant effort to compose himself. He folded up his copy of the *Mail*, downed the last inch of his beer and tried to act as normally as possible in the circumstances. But he was agonisingly conscious that his face had probably conveyed a thousand words to Henry Christie. And that very same man, the bane of his life, the cop who harried him constantly, was now approaching. Fast.

Benstead rose unsteadily to his feet, tucking the tabloid under his arm, trying to give the impression he had not seen Henry.

As he moved off, Henry reached the table. Benstead feigned surprise.

'Well, well, well. What have we here?' Henry grinned maliciously. Actually he knew exactly what he had – one of the top handlers of stolen property in Blackpool, if not the North of England. Benstead was a career criminal who tried to keep a low profile in terms of his lifestyle. He lived with his common-law wife, her two kids from a previous marriage (not yet dissolved), his own two from a couple of brief relationships, and two German shepherd dogs in a semi-detached council house. He was unemployed, drawing maximum benefits, did not own a car and had very little to show outwardly from the money he made buying and selling other people's possessions.

Henry's intelligence-gathering on Benstead led him to believe the little scrote owned a large apartment in Tenerife and held several bank accounts in fictitious names. Knowing and proving were two different things, though. So far, all Henry's team had managed to do was convict Benstead once only for a petty job for which he got fined.

Which annoyed Henry.

And put Benstead high on his target-list.

A fact of which Benstead was painfully aware.

'You haven't got anything,' Benstead said in response to Henry's opening question, 'because I'm off.' He zipped up his anorak and side-stepped smartly.

Not smartly enough.

Henry side-stepped with him, blocking his exit.

'Know who this is?' Henry asked Danny, speaking through the corner of his mouth, his eyes remaining firmly on Benstead.

'Baz Benstead – disposer of stolen property,' she answered promptly.

'Someone we're always interested in.' Henry beamed down at the little man who had started to look very nervous indeed. 'Bit of a hot day for an anorak,' he observed. To Danny he said, 'Always wears one. Big pockets. Never quite knows what might come his way – do you, Baz?'

'Don't fuckin' hassle me, Henry, or I'll have my brief chasing you before you know what's hit you.'

'Oh, Baz!' Henry cried, feigning hurt. Then, 'Just who the fuck d'you think you're talking to? Come on, let's sit down and have a nice, pleasant chinwag.'

'I'm leaving – excuse me . . . ahhhh!'

Henry slammed his free hand into Benstead's chest and sat him down on the bench seat. 'Sit.'

Shit! Benstead thought. A well of panic rose from his feet to his neck.

Henry sat next to him, sipping his Kaliber.

Danny remained standing, glass in one hand, cigarette dangling from her mouth. Her eyes bore scornfully down on Benstead. She had heard much about him, but never met him until this moment. She was unimpressed.

'What're you up to?' Henry asked.

'Nowt.' Benstead put the newspaper on the table. The headlines screamed out about the most dangerous man in Britain on the loose. Benstead blinked rapidly as his brain

214

recorded the message again. He turned the paper over.

'You looked like you'd peered into your grave when we walked in.'

'Only 'cos I saw you. You always have that effect on me.'

'The look was there before you clocked me. I just made it worse. So, go on, what are you doing in here, Baz, ole buddy? It's not your local.'

Benstead shrugged. He measured up his chance of escape. All he needed was about ten seconds – or less – out of sight of Henry and his sidekick. Long enough to dump the boiling hot goods Trent had sold him.

Now £115 richer, there was hardly any space in Trent's pockets to squeeze in more cash. He had amassed over a thousand pounds and some loose change. Enough to see him over the next couple of weeks . . . and yet he wanted more money, here and now.

He walked towards Talbot Square where the Royal Bank of Scotland was situated. He was eager to withdraw as much money as possible from the account belonging to the dead ambulance-driver. To bleed it dry, like he had done to the man himself. He decided to try the cash machine again, firstly to see if the account was still operating and secondly if he could get any more cash out of it.

If the answer to both was no, he would find Benstead again and throw in the card for an extra £30.

Trent spent a couple of minutes checking the streets for lurking cops and fine-tuning the radio scanner he'd bought earlier from a high-street electrical retailer. It was tuned into the local police frequency. He inserted the earpiece and set the volume.

When he was satisfied, he crossed to the cash machine and slid the card into the slot.

He tapped in the well-remembered PIN code.

215

Benstead was a small man and could move quickly if he wanted to. Especially if the element of surprise was on his side.

Henry Christie, having shown disdain for Benstead and his threats, had allowed himself to drop his guard. He sat back and took a sip of the alcohol-free lager.

Danny took a long deep drag of her cigarette.

Without warning, Benstead reached for his empty pint glass. He took hold of it around the brim, twisted round and smashed the base of the glass across the side of Henry's head.

Henry screamed, more with surprise than pain as the bottom edge of the glass connected with an old wound on his temple, sustained in a car crash three years earlier. The skin split immediately, blood poured out. His hands went to the side of his head.

Fortunately, the glass did not break.

Benstead dropped it, lurched forwards from his seated position before Danny could react. He charged towards her, ramming his shoulder into her lower abdomen, bowling her back over a table. He then ran for the rear door of the pub.

Danny landed hard, legs akimbo, displaying her underwear. Her drink spilled all over her and the cigarette disappeared somewhere across the room.

Henry Christie had learned a lot of hard lessons in his time as a cop. One was that some of the things you expect to hurt badly are never quite as bad as imagined. Agreed, the crack on the head hurt, and the sight of pouring blood, especially your own, was frightening. But when it was all put into perspective, it wasn't as bad as being shot or knifed or having a broken glass screwed into your face. All that had happened was that a pathetic punk had given him a whack.

As soon as his brain assimilated this – within a split second – Henry was up and after Benstead, angry at having been caught offguard. He dived across the room at the fleeing felon and brought the little man crashing face-down into the liquor-stained carpet.

Benstead tried desperately to disentangle himself, scrambling, kicking wildly, with Henry holding on for dear life.

'Get off me, you fucking bastard!' Benstead screamed, squirming round and beginning to rain punches down on Henry's head. The DI tucked himself in and clung on tight, inching himself up Benstead's body as they rolled around on the floor.

Danny recovered quickly.

When she saw the two men fighting, she looked out for the opening which would let her in to assist her boss. It came when the two men separated briefly, Benstead on his back. She stepped astride him and dropped heavily across his chest, pinning his arms to the floor with her knees. Her skirt rode high up on her thighs.

From that position she curled her right hand into a tight fist, deliberately drew back her arm, ensured Benstead saw what was coming and – with a great deal of satisfaction – smashed the fist into the side of his face.

All the fight drained out of him.

His face started to swell within seconds of the blow, a huge red mound surrounding his left eye, which began to close and weep.

'Twat!' he hissed.

'You got it, pal,' she panted.

Henry let go of Benstead's legs and stood up shakily. He had an urge to kick the little bastard in the ribs, but the eyes of too many witnesses prevented him.

He picked up a beer mat and held it against the cut on his head.

'Turn him onto his front,' he told Danny.

She raised a leg and they both heaved Benstead over onto his chest. Danny pulled his hands back and cuffed him with Henry's handcuffs. Tightly.

'Here.' Henry looked round to see Fat Tommy, the

barman, holding out a bundle of something towards him. It was a bar-cloth. 'For your head. It's clean, don't worry.'

The detective smiled. 'Thanks, Tom. I didn't know you cared.'

'I don't. I just don't want a copper's blood all over my carpets.'

Henry dropped the beer mat and pressed the cloth onto his injury. The wound had been cracked open a few times since it had happened. One day, Henry thought, it would need a skin graft to close it, not stitches.

'Now then,' Danny said into Benstead's grubby ear. 'Let's see what all this was about.' She patted him down, went through his pockets. She pulled out the roll of banknotes and handed it to Henry. Conservative estimate, two grand. Then she found the bag.

Benstead moaned.

She stood up and peered into it. Her mouth popped open when she carefully withdrew the driving licence and read the name on it. She held it so Henry could see.

He raised his eyebrows and said, 'Oh.' To Benstead he said, 'Mate – you are under arrest.'

Any further conversation was halted when an urgent message came over the PR in Henry's pocket.

'All patrols, all patrols, make to the vicinity of Talbot Square, Royal Bank of Scotland . . . believed escaped prisoner Louis Vernon Trent has just attempted to use the cash machine there. I repeat . . .'

Henry and Danny looked at each other, then down at the their prisoner. Henry made the decision.

'You go. I'll stay and sort out Bollock Brain here.'

Even before he had finished speaking. Danny was out of the door.

Henry turned to Fat Tommy. 'How about a double whisky?'

The account belonging to the dead ambulanceman was still operating, but because Trent had withdrawn the maximum allowed for the day he was unable to steal any more money from it. He took the opportunity to confirm the present balance – £700. A nice, tidy sum of money which he hoped would be in his hands after midnight.

At the end of the transaction, the machine slid the card back out and Trent reclaimed it.

Feeling pretty buoyant, he strolled to the top of Clifton Street where it joined Abingdon Street. To his right, on Church Street, was the entrance to the Winter Gardens complex. A long queue of people were lined up patiently at the box office, buying tickets for that night's performance by a well-known TV comedian. He was doing a six-week stint of 'saucy' material and songs.

Trent had a sudden fancy to see him. He turned towards the Winter Gardens at the moment the scanner in his pocket picked up the police radio transmission and passed it to the earpiece.

Trent cursed his own foolishness and greed. He should have known the cops would have alerted the bank, who would reverse the process when the account got touched. The fact the account was still open should have been a warning beacon to him.

For a few vital moments he was rooted to the spot, unable to make a decision, even though he knew if he remained there he would very quickly end up in a police cell.

He took a chance, pivoted on his heels and headed quickly down Clifton Street towards the Promenade. Once on the sea-front he reckoned he could easily mingle and disappear, maybe into one of the big stores.

Danny spun out the back door of the pub, ran down onto Market Street where she intended to cut across to Clifton Street which was probably less than 100 yards away.

She zigzagged through crowds of people, thankful she had chosen to wear flat-soled shoes that morning. Part of her mind was still annoyed by Benstead who had caused

219

her to spill her drink all over her fairly new suit, one she quite liked and thought she looked pretty good in. The second outfit in the space of a few days ruined. They would cost a fortune to replace.

As she ran she pulled her PR out and turned the volume up high.

Other patrols were responding to the call, all descending on Clifton Street – until Henry Christie's impatient voice cut across them all with an instruction for the Comms operator: 'Get a grip on these deployments, will you? Don't let everyone race to the scene, otherwise we might miss him. Set up some checkpoints a little distance away. Get the Comms Sergeant to get it organised.'

The voice of the Comms Sergeant replied, slightly chastened, 'Will do, sir.'

Everybody seemed intent on holding Danny up. She had to dance around four kids, who, hands held, were skipping down the street; she skidded dangerously to avoid a woman laden down with a huge load of shopping who appeared from nowhere in her path; and physically rammed a huge, beer-bellied, T-shirted, drunken individual with a Scottish accent who did his level best to catch her.

Without checking for traffic she legged it across Corporation Street and into Clifton Street. She relayed her position to Comms and learned that she was the first officer on the street. Then she juddered to a stop and surveyed the area, fully aware that more often than not, by the time police receive such calls, ten minutes or more could have elapsed. Trent could easily be a quarter of a mile away now, making Henry's instructions to Comms a matter of common sense.

Her chest rose and fell, her nostrils dilated, as she panted heavily. She wiped the back of her sticky hand across her forehead, drawing several wide-eyed looks from passers-by. She looked like a scarecrow again.

A tingle of apprehension went down her spine as a sixth

sense of perception clicked in.

She knew Trent was nearby. Somewhere close by. Hiding.

Trent slammed himself flat against the side of a parked Ford Transit van when he saw Danny appear at the bottom of the street. He recognised her instantly as a member of that bastard conspiracy of individuals who had sent him to prison.

He shuffled along the side of the van until he was in a position to peep around the back of it. From there he could see Danny across the street, speaking into her PR. Trent could hear every word she spoke through his earpiece.

A surge of uncontrollable loathing, almost like a demon in his soul, coursed through his veins at the sight of the smug, arrogant bitch who had played such a pivotal role in consigning him to the torture of the last nine years. Danny Fucking Furness.

His lips drew back into a snarl.

At exactly the same moment these feelings surged through him, he saw a visible change in Danny's body language. She stood upright, stopped talking into the radio, cocked her head to one side. Suddenly she was ultra-alert, almost as if she knew where he was hiding. Yet he was certain she had not seen him.

Trent froze. *Godamnit, she fucking knows I'm here.*

Her face turned towards him. Trent pinned himself against the van, desperation rising. His earpiece told him two foot-patrol officers and two double-manned police cars were only literally seconds away. One of the cars was an armed response vehicle.

He would be trapped if he didn't move now.

The shop he found himself looking at was an estate agent's.

Her senses alive, fear making every nerve-ending electric,

Danny started to walk towards the Transit van parked across the street. She held her PR as if it was a hammer.

He was there. She knew it.

Suddenly he appeared, turned his face fleetingly towards her, and ran into the estate agency.

'He's gone into Lordson's,' Danny yelled into her PR. 'In through the front door of Lordson's.'

A middle-aged man and his wife browsed in the agency. Two female assistants typed away at their desks behind the counter.

No one even looked at Trent when he came through the door – until he drew the knife from his sleeve and slashed it across the man's neck as he ran past.

It was a lucky, but well-aimed stroke, slicing the carotid artery. Trent did not wait to see the effect, but leapt over the counter, plunged his knife into the shoulder of one of the women, withdrew it and made for the door at the rear of the shop.

He had torn through the shop in a matter of seconds with the effect of an out-of-control death-star. Behind him he had left a trail of bloody chaos, people screaming, confusion, injury, everyone wondering what the hell had hit them and what they had done to deserve this.

The Staff Only door was flimsy. He crashed through it to find himself in a small kitchen. Beyond was the back door of the premises; he headed straight for it.

Danny ran into the shop seconds behind him. She stopped and took everything in.

The man who had been slashed in the throat had collapsed to the floor, dragging some display boards down with him. He gagged and coughed blood in a fine spray, losing his false teeth as well. His fingers clutched the big vein in his neck which pumped blood. It was like trying to plug a damaged hosepipe on full flow. His wife stood next to him, helpless. Her hands covered her mouth

222

whilst she screamed hysterically.

The woman who had been stabbed in the shoulder screamed in tremendous agony coupled with terror as she watched the fast-spreading stain around her shoulder.

The other employee sat transfixed by the horror. Her fingers hovered above her keyboard, eyes wide, staring with disbelief, her whole frame immobile as a perfect still-life. She had been frozen into a statue by the flash of violence which had streaked by her.

'Get an ambulance to Lordson's,' Danny said into her PR. 'Two people down, injured, one very serious. Knife injuries . . .' She did not stay to tend the wounded, but vaulted over the counter in Trent's tracks.

By this time he was out of the back door, hurtling down the service alley which ran behind the shops.

Danny skidded out after him, losing her balance momentarily. 'Down Cheapside, heading towards Corporation Street,' she relayed over the PR. 'Armed with a knife, prepared to use it. Be careful.'

Trent stopped abruptly some twenty yards ahead of her.

Danny stopped too, puzzled, cautious.

Then she saw the reason why. A uniformed PC was walking up towards Trent, side-handled baton drawn.

A wave of euphoria hit Danny.

They had caught the bastard.

Trent crouched, left arm extended, hand palm outwards. His right arm was also extended but this hand held the knife in readiness to strike.

It was a slim knife, Danny saw. Blood dripped from it. There was blood on his hand and partway up his sleeve.

He slashed the air menacingly, the message clear.

Danny and the PC circled him cautiously, just beyond reach of an attack thrust. The PC slapped the extended portion of his baton provocatively into the palm of his left hand. The officer's message was pretty clear too: 'You are

223

going to get the full force of this right across your head.'

'Come on, Louis, put the knife down,' Danny said reasonably. 'This place will be crawling with cops in a matter of seconds. You don't have a cat in hell's chance, so just put the knife down. No one else needs to get hurt.'

Trent watched them both suspiciously. His gaze flickered from one to the other, his eyes afire.

The sense of Danny's words seemed to permeate through to him. He stood upright, let his arms fall to his side. A submissive, resigned expression crossed his face and he nodded. His shoulders drooped, he exhaled a long deep sigh. Beaten.

Danny knew better than to trust Trent . . . but the PC did not. She was about to tell Trent to drop the knife, kick it away, assume the position, and all that crap, when without warning the PC stepped confidently into the danger zone. His eagerness blocked all common sense. This was going to be one hell of an arrest.

Before Danny could yell out a warning, he was too close to Trent for her to do anything.

The escaped prisoner blurred into life, as fast and as deadly as a bolt of forked lightning.

The knife shot up.

Danny, standing side-on, saw the point of the blade touch the PC's blue shirt, then disappear up to the hilt behind the officer's ribs and into his heart. Trent rammed it home, stepped in close to his victim, grabbed the officer's shoulder with his free hand and pulled him even further forwards onto the knife-blade. He screwed and twisted the knife all the way, doing maximum damage. At the same time he turned and laughed at the horror-stricken Danny, throwing his head back like a maniac. He gave the knife one more massive – flamboyant – jerk before withdrawing it like a magician.

He stepped to one side, pulled the PC round and pushed him towards Danny.

She could not begin to describe the look on the young

officer's face. Pain? Shock? Disbelief? Whatever, it was a face she would remember for the rest of her life.

The PC staggered towards her, walking with the misco-ordination of an infant learning to toddle. He stared down at his shirt and the very fast-spreading stain.

Danny opened her arms to catch him.

He stumbled, dropped his baton which clattered use-lessly on the ground and went heavily onto one knee. He placed the palms of both hands over his heart, lifted his face pleadingly to Danny. He looked like he was propos-ing to her.

Then he toppled over and died at her feet.

Danny tore her eyes away.

Trent had gone.

Other police officers swarmed towards her from the top of the alley.

She lurched to a doorway, sank to her knees.

'Just tell me this, Henry – why is it that everything you seem to get involved in ends up with police officers being killed? Are you fucking jinxed, or what?'

The questions were asked by Fanshaw-Bayley. He was pacing up and down on the already thin carpet in front of Henry's desk, a return journey of no more than six feet. Henry watched him and decided not to respond. Instead, he pressed the paper towel against his temple. The cut appeared to have more or less stopped bleeding and maybe did not need re-stitching after all.

FB stopped mid-journey. 'Eh? Come on, Henry – why?'

Henry shrugged and remained impassive. It was hardly true, but he did not want to get into an argument. FB was very upset that an officer had died, murdered on duty. He had every right to be, and was simply venting some of his emotions on Henry whose shoulders were big and wide enough to take any rot FB cared to dish out.

'So, c'mon tell me what happened. What the fuck went

wrong? No, don't.' FB held up his hands and shook them dismissively. 'It's okay, Henry, don't tell me. It wasn't your fault the stupid young fool went out without his stab-vest on; it was his decision and unfortunately he died for it.' FB ruffled his own hair frustratedly, scratched his head, flattened his hair and eventually sat down. 'This man is a fucking mobile killing-machine. What the hell's our next move?'

Henry blew out his cheeks, glad they had returned to practicalities. 'It better be quick,' he mused thoughtfully. 'I doubt he'll hang round town now.'

'Come on then, brainbox . . . what do we do?'

'Chances are he's in a guest-house. What we need to do is increase the numbers of people on house-to-house, quarter the town and visit every guest-house physically. And I also think we should get a big switchboard installed and actually phone every guest-house and hotel too.' He pulled a face. 'It'll take a while to get that up and running.'

'How many phones are there in this police station?' FB asked, raising his eyebrows.

'Dozens.' Henry immediately caught on.

'There's your answer. Get the people you want in now. Sit 'em next to a phone each with a copy of Yellow Pages and an unlimited supply of coffee or tea, and get them phoning.'

There was a sharp knock at the door. A Detective Sergeant came in without waiting and handed a sheet of paper of Henry.

Henry's eyes closed despairingly after he'd read it. Without looking up, he handed the paper to FB.

Absently Danny picked up the Missing from Home report which was on the top of the pile of junk on her desk. She sat down slowly, read the name on top, and tossed it back. Claire Lilton could wait.

She leaned forwards and dropped her head into her hands.

Inside, everything was in turmoil. Guts, vital organs, brain . . . churning with a sensation never before experienced.

She had a terrible unshakable belief that she was totally responsible for everything that had happened. In particular the tragic death of the Police Constable, skewered and slaughtered right in front of her eyes. All because she had been too slow, had not shouted out a warning, had not pulled him away.

'Oh God,' she mumbled desperately. Tears formed in her eyes. She rubbed them angrily away as she tried to control herself. Not here, she instructed herself. You will not break down here. You will hold yourself with dignity and you will convey yourself home. Then, and only then, will you allow yourself the indulgence of turning into a slobbering, self-pitying jelly.

But not here.

A hand clamped on her shoulder. She jumped and landed back on earth.

'Danny, how are you?' Henry Christie.

'Not good,' she admitted. 'Dithering, almost on the verge of collapse. You know – woman stuff. What a bloody day!' She gave a short laugh and wiped the new tears away with a snuffle. Her nose had started to run. She blew it, making a very unladylike trumpeting sound. 'Sorry, sorry,' she said, embarrassed. 'Hell, what a mess.'

'It's okay,' Henry said. 'And it's understandable.' He did not patronise her with sympathy or empathy, even though he had been in similar circumstances himself previously. Danny knew this.

'How the hell do you deal with it, Henry?' She opened her arms and flopped them down in a gesture conveying complete loss. 'It's so damned awful and I just can't get my head round it at all. All I can see is that poor boy staggering towards me . . . his face . . . I feel so responsible. What do I do?'

Her eyes pleaded with him.

'You've been there,' she added.

'Everything sounds so glib and pat,' he said, 'but I suppose there's a couple of things, for what they're worth. Firstly, don't hold it in, otherwise it'll rot your soul like cancer rots a body. Take advantage of the Force counsellors; they do a good job. Secondly, don't get on a guilt trip. You couldn't have done anything, Danny. If it hadn't been him, it would've been you.'

'But that poor PC – and the other two people he stabbed!'

'They're both alive, so don't even consider them.'

The man whose throat had been cut had been saved by the officer who arrived on the scene behind Danny. His quick actions had staunched the bloodflow substantially until the arrival of the ambulance crew. The man had been very lucky, though.

'But, as I say, my words sound trite. That's my advice, anyway. Take it or leave it.'

She blew her nose again.

'Having said all that, Danny . . .' Henry paused, faltering slightly. 'I have some more bad news, I'm afraid.' He perched himself on the edge of her desk. 'I know I might well be making assumptions here, but I think there's an added dimension to Trent's escapades.'

Danny's eyebrows creased.

'It may only be a coincidence, but the body of a young girl has just been found in some bushes in a rec in North Shore. I've no further details yet – I'm going to the scene now with FB. It's your call here, Danny. If you feel up to it, you can come. If not, I'll understand.'

Danny's eyes flashed instinctively to the MFH report on her desk. Once again she referred to the Almighty. 'Dear God, please don't let it be Claire.'

Chapter Twelve

The lovers twisted into each other's arms as soon as the engine was turned off. They tore greedily at each other, their teeth clashing on first contact of their mouths. Even though there was a handbrake and gear lever between them, and the man's movements were impeded by the steering-wheel, within a matter of moments his trousers were unfastened, her blouse had been ripped open and her bra had been hoisted somewhere up around her neck.

'Oh my God!' they gasped together as the man's hand reached her vagina, and she grabbed his cock. She went onto him, making him writhe ecstatically in his seat, whilst at the same time he fondled her freely hanging left breast with his left hand.

She rose for air and looked out of the window.

'We need to do this properly,' she slavered, tasting him.

'You're dead right.'

'Come on, let's get out.'

They were parked on the grass verge of a narrow lane in the picturesque countryside above Darwen in East Lancashire.

They clambered comically out of the car in their state of undress. He shuffled along, holding up his pants precariously whilst she, having dispensed with her knickers, ran around the car and into the trees, covering her boobs with her arms. She led him into a small clearing a few yards from the roadside, but far enough to be out of sight of anyone passing.

They immediately started to ravage each other, dragging clothing off and tossing it away with abandon into the bushes. Moments later, both were naked, rolling around the cool woodland floor, screwing wildly, emitting animal-like rutting noises. They moved from position to position. To oral sex and back again. They finished up with him (a chartered accountant), mounting her (his secretary) from the rear.

When her hands sunk into some soft ground, she thought nothing of it. She was too busy concentrating on the timings of her reverse thrusts. However, when her fingers touched something hard, cold and dome-shaped, she wondered what the hell she'd found. Her fingers curled around the object and pulled it out of the ground.

It was the top part of a skull, without the lower jaw attachment.

She screamed, reared up and fell backwards onto her unsuspecting lover. For a moment he thought it was a new move and tried to ride with it. When he saw the skull circling up through the air where she had thrown it, he realised this tryst had ended before he had come.

Myrna Rosza walked noiselessly through the offices of Kruger Investigations, painfully aware that every single pair of eyes was on her. She had just ended a short meeting with the other execs from the firm and had volunteered to take on the task of formally announcing the death of Steve Kruger.

To most of them, at that moment, it was just a rumour. She faced the horrendous job of turning that into fact.

Five minutes later, everyone who was available that morning was gathered together in the boardroom, which was the single largest room. They were expectant, fearful, and totally silent.

Myrna did not know where to begin, but she knew the act of saying the words, 'Steve Kruger is dead,' would help her grieve, and start to come to terms with his loss.

She opened her arms in a gesture of helplessness. Croakily, she began to speak.

'Thank you all for coming,' she said stupidly, as if they would have refused. 'Early this morning Steve Kruger was involved in an enquiry at Miami International Airport, concerning the activities of Mario Bussola. You all know he is suspected of murdering Jimmy and Dale. So . . . to cut a long story short, a firefight ensued in a multi-storey parking lot during which Steve was fatally injured. He died of gunshot wounds at the scene.'

A gasp of horror went up from the staff. Several of them, men and women, began to cry.

Myrna licked her dry lips.

'What the hell happened, Myrna?' one asked.

'Look, I was there when he was shot, okay,' she responded, losing her hold. 'I know I should answer your question, George, but hell, I don't feel like it right now. Maybe later, huh? Sorry. I gotta go.'

Two detectives stood side by side and looked down at the pathetic body of a girl.

Henry James Christie and Danielle Louise Furness were silent, each in a world of their own.

From the position of her limbs and the way her clothing had been ripped off, it seemed fairly obvious she had been sexually molested either before or after her death. There were stab-wounds in her chest.

Henry ran a hand down his face, shook his head. In his career as a detective he had been involved in eight child-murder investigations: from the simple, but tragic, domestic murder to a serial killing. And he could not get used to seeing a young person dead, mainly because the images of his two daughters constantly flashed into his mind. How the hell he would ever cope if either of them came to such an end, he didn't know. Probably wouldn't. He would be destroyed, unable to operate as a fully functioning human being ever again. He knew

231

his wife, Kate, would be worse.

It was very hard for him to remain in control when faced with investigating such deaths. Hard to refrain from beating the offender – if caught – to a pulp. He squinted sideways at Danny, but was unable to identify the meaning of the expression on her face . . . mainly because she was experiencing conflicting emotions.

The first was relief.

At least it was not Claire Lilton lying there, having been dragged, beaten, mutilated, raped in the bushes, then horribly murdered.

The second was repulsion.

Who – WHO? – could have done such a thing? It beggared all belief and understanding in the human condition. To put someone through such suffering . . . The savagery people could stoop to constantly amazed her.

Henry's voice broke into her train of thought. 'What do you think?'

'I think we'd better step up the hunt for Trent. He's never killed before. He came close, but now I think we're dealing with someone who's gone right over the edge. Uncontrollable. He's my prime suspect.'

'I agree, but let's not blind ourselves to the possibility it might not be him.'

'Yep,' Danny said flatly. Her gaze returned to the dead girl. 'Let's make sure we do things right – and when we've identified her, let me tell her parents.'

'You sure? You've had a tough few days.'

She spun on Henry. 'Of all the people, I didn't expect you to patronise me, Henry.'

'Hey – whoa, sorry.' He retreated, taken aback by her anger.

She stormed away, leaving him open-mouthed.

Halfway across the Atlantic Ocean, a man called Charlie Gilbert sat in the first-class cabin in a plane travelling at

37,000 feet, Miami International Airport 1500 miles behind.

Even though the cabin temperature was quite fresh, Gilbert was sweating profusely, as grossly overweight men often do, whatever the circumstances. He had a wide seat with plenty of legroom but was extremely uncomfortable. He looked as though he'd been forced into the available space, like a hat hamster pressed into a tobacco tin. He had very little room to manoeuvre and there was only just enough space to drop his food tray in front of him.

He wasn't too concerned.

His business trip to America had been successful. Of course, there had been the little blip – namely, being arrested for taking part in the rape and indecent assault of a young girl – but that had been fixed. Mario Bussola assured him on that point. And when Bussola made assurances, they stuck.

The incident would be hushed up, he promised Gilbert. The press would not get to know about it. No further police would be taken, and appropriate revenge would be meted out.

Charlie Gilbert would be safe.

Thank God, because, after all, he had a reputation to think of.

Myrna realised what she had to do immediately was put together a strategy to ensure as much damage limitation as possible as far as Kruger Investigations was concerned.

Being Kruger's number two, and having taken on full responsibility for running the company, there were many things for her to do – not least reassuring jittery customers, some of whom had already called and were sounding extremely agitated.

To quote one: 'Just what the hell are Kruger Investigations up to, that their managing director has ended up dead in a fucking shoot-out with gangsters, for fuck's sake' – unquote.

Myrna quickly needed to soothe ruffled feathers. Then she needed to deal with the staff. They were shell-shocked – and rightly so. Within the space of a day, three employees had met very violent deaths, three people who were well-known and loved by everyone.

Myrna knew she had to act, hold it all together, otherwise she would lose other good people.

All thoughts of revenge, or mounting some sort of operation against Bussola needed to be shelved indefinitely. To hit out, strike back, was what she had desired to do initially . . . but that was a task for the legal process and if it failed, so be it.

It wasn't a job for a respectable company and Myrna wasn't about to put others at risk again.

She was in her office. It was an hour since the staff meeting. An hour since she had hurled up her insides.

She had just finished a phone call to Kelly, the comms van operator, who had returned home to Memphis whilst the Bussola threat was still in the air. Having given her the lowdown on the Kruger situation, Myrna suggested that maybe she would like to stay off work a little longer – on full pay. Eminently sensible lady she was, Kelly agreed to the idea.

Myrna's hand was resting on the phone when there was a knock on the door. It opened a fraction to reveal Mark Tapperman, the tall, well-built detective, standing there. He wore a forlorn expression making him look like a little boy, not the hard, uncompromising detective Myrna had become acquainted with and despised.

'Come on in, Mark,' she said softly, her instinct sensing something not quite right.

He entered the room and sat down.

She was perplexed by his whole body language. It was so incongruous to the usual swaggering macho stuff she had seen recently.

Then, without warning, it happened.

Mark Tapperman burst into tears.

234

'We're pretty sure he's called Patrick Orlove, at least as sure as we can be. He's got dozens of aliases, but the prints from the gun at the scene put up Orlove as his original name. We don't really know very much about his distant past, but recently he turned up in LA and did some work for the McGreevy cartel, which resulted in a murder one court appearance. He was acquitted: the usual witness problems. Next he turns up in the Big Apple, helping out one of the East Side gangs. Suspected of puttin' a gunload of lead into a junkie informer's grey matter, but mainly acted as close-quarter protection to a gang chief. From there, seems he got a recommendation to come south for Bussola, who we know axed and replaced a lot of his security since you and Steve were able to walk all over 'em and interrupt that gang-bang downtown. We think Orlove's still in the city, but by the same token he could be in Cuba.'

Myrna nodded as she listened to Tapperman telling her about the man suspected of killing Steve Kruger; the man they had allowed to escape from the scene of the tragedy.

The noise had been incredible when the guns in their hands discharged and the two men who had been turning and drawing their weapons had been hit. Myrna's mind saw it all again . . . the two men swivelled grotesquely and both fell down dead on the concrete floor, blood pouring out of their wounds. Tapperman raced to the third man, the one Kruger had punched in the nose before launching himself between the parked cars, and pointed his gun at the crouching guy's head. He yelled to Myrna. 'Cover him, I'm going after the other guy.'

Myrna had done as instructed, her arms locked in an isoceles triangle, keeping the man covered whilst he tried to stem the tide of blood gushing from his bust nose. Her eyes constantly flicked towards the two bodies close by. Both twitched like they were being tickled. She looked up towards Tapperman who was working his way methodically and cautiously down the line of cars, and she kept glancing to the gap where Kruger had thrown himself. She could see his feet. Why was he just lying there, not moving? Why didn't he get up? She knew, even then, something was wrong.

Tapperman edged back, still wary. He stopped at the gap Kruger had gone into, not far from where Myrna stood. He stared between the vehicles, his chest heaving. He knelt down out of sight for a few moments then rose back to his full height, grim.

Myrna was hopping on her toes, desperate to know, dying to run and see, but her job was to keep the bloody-nosed man covered.

Tapperman walked over to her. He stood about three feet away from the kneeling man. His face became a mask of rage. He stepped back, then kicked the man in the head, pitching him sideways across one of his dead buddies.

'Bastard.'

As quickly as it came, the anger subsided. Tapperman swooped down and cuffed the man expertly, hands right up his back. He threw him face-down. Then he stood up again and regarded Myrna.

'What the hell was all that about?' she demanded, shocked by his reaction.

'Steve's dead,' Tapperman responded simply.

And somehow the person responsible – now known to be Patrick Orlove – had escaped, and all they managed to find was his gun dumped in a trashcan when the scene was searched later.

Myrna shook her head and raised her face to Tapperman, sitting opposite her.

'He's on the wanted list now.'

'And the chances of catching him are . . .?'

'Zero, if I'm honest, especially if Bussola's looking after him.'

'What about the guy you practised your soccer skills on?'

236

'Saying nothing . . . but we've got him for illegal possession and he's wanted in Nevada for a serious assault with a deadly weapon. He's going nowhere, 'cept jail.'

'Bussola?'

Tapperman gave her a withering glance. This she interpreted as, 'Don't ask silly fucking questions.'

'What about the other guy, the English paedophile?' she persisted.

'Gilbert? Tucked up on a plane back to the UK.'

'You told the FBI about him?' she wanted to know.

'Should I?'

'Maybe they ought to know, maybe they can pass on the gen about him to the cops in England. If the cops over there don't know about this guy, it's time they did.'

'Aw . . . when I get round to it.'

'In that case, I'll do it. I know a guy at the London office, used to work from Miami. I'll tell him and he can pass it on.'

'Okay, whatever suits.'

'So that's it then – we're getting nowhere fast?'

'That's one way of lookin' at it, I guess. Myrna, you must be one o' those folks who always sees a half-empty glass.'

'I'm a realist.' She sounded sour.

'Right, sure.' Tapperman stood up. 'Just thought I'd keep you informed about things.' A bashful expression crossed his face, 'Er, about earlier. I . . . er . . . you won't tell anyone, will ya?'

'Lieutenant Tapperman, your secret is safe with me.'

'I owe ya, babe.'

For the first time in too long, a broad smile crept across Myrna's tired countenance.

Mark Tapperman's secret.

Behind all that macho bluster and bull, he was a big soft guy with real feelings and emotions. His outburst had astonished her. She was glad she had seen it because it made him human. To know he was grieving for Steve

Kruger, as she was, made her feel so much better.

She picked up the phone and asked her secretary to get the number of the American Embassy in London, England.

'Sorry . . . sorry, pretty please, forgive me.'

'Nah, no problems, you were quite right to jump down my throat. If you'd been a bloke I wouldn't have said it. It was patronising at best; at worst it was sexist. I'll hold my hands up.' Which Henry Christie promptly did.

Danny grinned. 'Can we forget it and get on with the job?'

'Forget what?' Henry smiled.

It was ten o'clock. He was surprised to see it was so late. It had been one hell of a day. A short time earlier he had returned from attending a double post mortem – first of a murdered Police Constable, then of a murdered girl. The pathologist had been pretty certain the same knife had killed both people.

He read the piece of paper in front of him, notes taken during the autopsies. 'She was sexually assaulted, as we expected, anally and vaginally,' he told Danny. 'The pathologist has taken samples of semen, so when we get Trent all we need do is match up the DNA and bingo! She actually died of a stab-wound to the heart, an organ which was horrendously damaged, as was the PC's. Trent gets the knife in and really rives it round.'

'Poor souls.'

Danny had been at the house of Mr and Mrs Tomlinson, the parents of the dead girl, for the last three hours since they had identified their daughter at the mortuary. It had been a difficult and testing time for her. 'I'll tell the girl's mum and dad tomorrow about the results of the PM. That's when they're expecting to be told. They've had enough pain and misery for today. Christ! All she'd done was pop out to play for a while. She'd just been recovering from flu. She was due to go back to school tomorrow.'

Henry said, 'Just for your information there's now twenty pairs of officers working through the hotels and guest-houses physically, another ten on phones. I've told them to crack on until midnight, then pack it in. All my available detectives are pubbing and clubbing it to see what they can turn up. There's a briefing at eight tomorrow and I hope to double those numbers at least for a couple of days.'

'How are the people from the estate agents?'

'The woman he stabbed has been sent home, no massive damage. The guy with the neck-wound is still in surgery – but he'll live.' Henry stretched. 'I'm going to call it a day. Fancy a quick jar on the way home? And it will be quick. I need to be back here by six-thirty to get everything ready for eight.'

'I'd like that, Henry. I've just got a couple of things to do.'

They made an arrangement to meet in a pub and Danny went to her office.

Henry headed straight out. He did not see the lurking figure in the doorway of an office nearby, a figure who had overheard their conversation.

Jack Sands stepped out of the shadow. 'Bitch and bastard,' he whispered.

Chapter Thirteen

Charlie Gilbert waddled through customs at Manchester Airport, having collected his hefty baggage and large Mickey Mouse from the carousel. He went down the green channel – nothing to declare, other than being overweight. In the arrivals hall he was greeted by a man called Ollie Spencer who looked and acted something like a wartime spiv: quick, sharp features, trimmed moustache and a look which said he could get anything, any time. He worked for Gilbert in the capacity of manager of some leisure facilities, and acted in close liaison with him in many spheres.

'Good trip?'

'Very good, Ollie. As a result of my little visit, our amusement arcades will soon be kitted out with the latest video technology from the States and beyond. We'll be streets ahead of the others. And not only that, for a very little effort, I'll be able to make another hundred grand – but I'll explain that one to you later.'

'Sounds good. Did you manage to have some fun as well?'

'Ollie – of course I did. Nice young fun.'

Spencer led Gilbert out through the sliding doors to where he had illegally parked the car – the vehicle in question being a stretch Rolls-Royce with darkened windows, hired for the occasion of Gilbert's return home. Spencer positioned the luggage trolley near to the rear of the car and opened the back door. Gilbert forced himself through the not-inconsiderable gap and plopped through onto the front-facing back seat.

The Rolls had been stretched to accommodate a rear-facing seat too, making it similar to one of those long limos often seen in America, but pretty unusual in Britain. There seemed to be acres of room.

Sitting coyly on the rear-facing seat was a girl.

Gilbert's face widened into a big smile of pleasure on seeing her. 'Honey Pot!' he beamed.

Spencer poked his angular face in. 'I hope you approve, boss. Bit of a coming-home pressie.' He handed Mickey Mouse to Gilbert who presented it to the girl; she took it with a giggle.

'I approve.' He slapped his thighs delightedly. 'Come to Daddy.'

The girl squeaked with peals of merriment. She rushed towards him and immediately fumbled for his flies.

She was eleven and a half years old.

Danny did not really feel like going for a drink, but she thought it would be churlish to refuse. After all, Henry had done a lot for her in a very short space of time and a quick drink wasn't too much of an inconvenience.

She tidied her desk, picked up Claire Lilton's Missing from Home forms and went into the Comms room. She ensured the circulation message would be sent that night. Danny knew how busy the following day would be and didn't want to forget Claire in the mêlée.

That task completed, she was ready to leave.

She hated the fact that the walk to her car had become such a big issue for her. Something she had done for years without a second thought had, in the last few days, become a nightmare journey. Although she was certain Jack Sands had got the message loud and clear from Henry, the walk down the dimly lit car park made her jumpy as hell. All the while checking the shadows, looking round over her shoulder . . . it was crap.

She pressed the remote and her car responded.

Seconds later she was in the driving seat, trying to get the key into the ignition . . . when the passenger door opened and a figure dropped into the seat.

Danny didn't even look for a moment. She closed her eyes tightly and said through gritted teeth, 'Jack, don't you ever fucking learn?'

'Jack? Who's this Jack?'

God, that voice! Danny's eyes shot open.

'I'm not Jack. My name's Louis Trent, but you know that, Danny, don't you?' He jammed the point of his knife into the side of her neck. 'Let's go for a drive.'

Henry Christie rarely drank alcohol before driving. For cops the drinking and driving game was far too dangerous to play. Too many had lost their jobs that way, and Henry wasn't about to join them. However, that evening, he was parched. He needed something long and cold to wash away the grit. He chose Foster's lager – a pint – and downed about half in one sustained slurp. It tasted wonderful and partly did the trick. He decided he would drink this, have one more with Danny, then head off home.

He edged away from the bar and sat in an empty alcove from where he could survey the pub. He spotted a couple of crims – low-level drug dealers – who didn't want to look at him, snorted a short laugh, sat back and waited for Danny.

Danny could hardly breathe. Like she was being suffocated. Like a pillow was being pressed on her face.

'Seat belt, Danny,' Trent said calmly. He pushed the knife further into her neck. Any deeper and blood would be drawn.

She drew the belt across her chest and clunked it in.

'Now reverse out of here and drive out of the car park. If you try anything, I'll skewer you and run. I'll stick this right into your heart and you'll fucking die here and now. Got that?'

She nodded.

'Good.' He lowered the blade so it rested against her left breast. He prodded and she jumped like a fork of static had jolted her. Trent laughed. Cruelly he said, 'I'll bet you've got nice tits, Danny. I'm going to carve them like Christmas turkey. Now drive!' He prodded her again.

She was unable to stop her right foot from trembling on the pedals. In consequence the car lurched backwards out of the parking space. She slammed the brake on, too hard, unintentionally, and the vehicle screeched to a swaying halt.

Trent reacted angrily. He whacked her across the face with the open palm of his left hand. He struck hard, making Danny's neck snap round. She glared at him. He held the knife up to her nose and inserted it half an inch into a nostril. 'Don't fuck about, Danny,' he warned her, 'or you're dead.'

'I can't stop my legs from shaking,' she explained, voice quivering.

'You'd better get in control of yourself,' he breathed, staring at her – and she could smell his body odour. It made her want to retch. 'Now drive away, nice and gently, and *in control*. Pretend I'm not here. Pretend I'm Jack.'

From one horror to another, she thought, taking a firm grip on the wheel when Trent removed the knife. She took a deep, steadying breath, exhaled shudderingly, slid the gear-stick into Drive and pressed the gas pedal with even strength.

'That's it, Danny,' he encouraged her. 'Nice . . . nice car, too.' He opened his legs and drove the knife into the seat between his thighs. 'Be a real mess when we've finished with it . . . sadly.' He made the opening in the fabric big and ragged by using the knife like a garden trowel. 'Let's got for a drive,' he laughed.

★ ★ ★

It was the cheapest Casio watch he could find – £4.95 at the time of purchase – but it had served him well over the years. The cost of replacement straps far outweighed the original cost of the watch. He looked at it and did not feel too happy. Almost eleven.

He had been in the pub twenty minutes. There was about a half-inch of lager remaining in the glass.

Where the hell was Danny?

He emptied the beer down his throat and made a return journey to the bar.

'Fosters,' he told the barman.

'Nasty cut, that,' the barman observed, nodding at Henry's temple.

They had been driving ten minutes, mainly in silence other than for Trent to give her directions. He told her to drive north up the Promenade, towards Fleetwood.

'Pussy got your tongue?' Trent sneered. 'You did enough talking when you interviewed me, didn't you? Do you remember what I said, all those years ago? That time we were alone together? Do you?'

'Yes,' she squeaked.

'Tell me.'

'You . . . you said you'd kill me.'

'No.' He jabbed her with the knife. 'The exact words, Danny. The *exact* words.'

She knew them. They were branded into her mind.

She spoke softly. ' "Guilty or not guilty, Danny, one fine day – or night",' – a tear of fear rolled out of her eye as the words came haltingly out – ' "I'm going to come back and kill you for this".'

'Yeah. Brilliant. Well done!' he shouted. He leaned across and spoke into her ear, his lips brushing her lobe. 'And now I'm here,' he said in a voice which sounded like the devil's. He sat back and drew the knife across the dashboard, slashing a line in the wooden veneer.

245

'Right, I've had enough of this journey. Turn round, head back to Blackpool.'

Henry found the second pint went down almost as easily as the first – and far quicker. Without much thought he had drunk it in five minutes. He must have been thirstier than he first imagined.

Still no sign of Danny.

'Ah well,' he said to himself. With a show of great reluctance for no one but himself, he pushed himself from his seat and plodded back to the bar. This was definitely going to be the last.

He presented the empty glass to the barman. 'Fosters.'

'It really is a nasty cut, that,' the man said, indicating Henry's temple.

They drove all the way back down the Promenade. All the way down the Golden Mile, past the amusement arcades, the Tower, Tussauds Waxworks, the Sea Life Centre, all still teeming with thousands of people. There was much laughter. Lots of rowdiness. They drove through South Shore, past the hotel where Claire Lilton lived, past the Pleasure Beach and the Pepsi Max Big One.

When the Promenade cut slightly inland and became Clifton Drive North and they drove through the Local Authority boundary into Lytham St Annes, Trent said, 'Pull in here.' He pointed across the road.

Danny veered across and stopped the car, facing oncoming traffic. She doused the headlights.

Only feet away to Danny's right, was Star Hill Dunes, an area of grass and sand dunes. On the opposite side of the road was a holiday camp. The dunes were popular with dog-owners, courting couples and, occasionally, murderers.

'Nah – too fucking busy here,' Trent blurted after consideration. 'Drive on.'

With relief, Danny accelerated away.

'I was going to kill you there.'

'I know,' Danny said – but to herself.

There was no reply from Danny's office phone, nor her home. Henry was perplexed. He hung up the payphone, drummed his fingers on the side of the wall-mounted, bubble-like kiosk which surrounded him. He picked up the phone again, dialled Blackpool comms and asked them. They knew nothing; Danny had not been deployed by them, but she had dropped a misper file off to be circulated about half an hour before. She'd said she was going for a drink.

He hung up and heard his ten-pence piece clatter away down the shute. He picked up his drink from the thoughtfully installed shelf next to the payphone and stepped back into the toilet corridor in which the phone was located. He took a sip from his third pint – almost gone – and walked back into the bar.

He was experiencing that old twinge of the sphincter. It told him, rather like an old woman's corns forecasting the weather, that something was a little off the beam here . . . and the towering spectre of Jack Sands loomed into Henry's thoughts. A man with a bagful of resentment. Someone who had already shown he was capable of violence.

Maybe he was being over-dramatic.

Yet Danny had clearly said she would come for a drink. Henry knew if she changed her mind she would have let him know, not just stood him up. She wasn't that kind of person.

His lager now tasted harsh on his tongue.

He threw the last of it down, wiped his mouth with the back of his hands. A quick visit to the toilet, then he was going to put his mind to rest one way or the other.

Danny knew she had to look for any chance of survival.

When it came, however slight, she had to go for it whether it meant physical confrontation with Trent or running away. Whichever, she would give it her best shot.

For the time being, she reasoned her best way forwards would be to talk and keep him talking.

'This is madness,' were the three ill-judged words which constituted her opening gambit.

Trent exploded.

'How dare you fucking-well say that, you stinking bitch!' he screamed. He plunged the knife towards her face. Danny braced herself. It slowed as it neared her and he stuck it against her cheek, on the stitches from her other bad night. With a quick nick, he drew first blood, reopening the wound. She almost cried out, but held back to a whimper. The warm blood trickled down her cheek. He removed the knife, then held it an angle across her neck. 'If I slice this now, you'll bleed to death and I'll just fucking watch you, like that ambulance-driver.' He breathed all over her. 'This, Danny, is not madness. It's revenge, a perfectly normal thing to do. People do it, governments do it, so how can it be wrong or mad? Yeah, revenge – for all that's been done to me over the years.'

'Yeah, yeah, I'm sorry. I was wrong to say what I did. I didn't mean it to sound that way . . . I just wanted to know why you were doing all this, Louis.'

'Now you know. I was betrayed by everyone, particularly those little angels who I cared for. They're the ones who must suffer – as well as people like you. People in the system who don't understand men like me.'

'But what about Meg Tomlinson?' she asked. That was the name of the murdered girl whose parents Danny had just spent several hours counselling. Danny needed to know if Trent had killed her. 'You didn't even know her, did you?' She asked the questions gently, so as not to antagonise him.

'Knowing is not the point.' Trent relaxed, removed the knife. He sat back and Danny breathed out. The cold line where the blade had been pressed throbbed. 'It's the principle of the matter. She was like them, one of them, really. I'm simply making a statement.'

'Why kill her, though?' She still needed a definite answer. 'I'm assuming you did kill her.'

'You assume right.'

Danny cast a quick glance at him. He stared ahead, eyes unblinking. She could hear his teeth grinding, a noise which made her cringe.

'I treated her with kindness and compassion, actually. But she didn't like it. She would have betrayed me like all the others – if she'd lived. She was going to die anyway, but she chose to do it without dignity. She could have been a willing martyr for me, but no. Instead of a dignified death, she struggled after we had finished making love . . . she was foolish, very foolish.'

He had said all this as if in a trance.

Danny shook as his words poured out. She had to blank her mind to how Meg Tomlinson must have suffered at Trent's hands. Making love! Jesus, Danny thought. Making love was not what the post mortem revealed, but a brutal, perverted assault.

It dawned on Danny, if it hadn't done before, that she had been kidnapped by a seriously deranged man who, for his own good and the safety of the general public, needed to be killed.

Danny knew she probably would not be the one to do the deed, though.

She fully expected to be his next victim.

Henry stood at the urinal. His water seemed to be passing for ever. He willed his bladder to empty quicker.

The toilet door opened behind him and someone came in.

Ahhh . . . finished. Henry looked down and shook off the drops and the image of his limp penis was the last thing he saw as his head exploded in a firework display

249

Guy Fawkes would have been proud of. His legs buckled and he crashed down, catching his chin against the bowl of the urinal before he hit the floor. A further broadside pummelled him into blackness.

The assault stopped abruptly.

Henry veered through that sickening twilight zone somewhere between conscious and not, fading in and out, whilst his mind blared like a siren, loud, then quiet, then louder.

Finally everything went quiet.

Henry lay there very still as the urinals flushed.

Trent made Danny loop round again, cut inland through Blackpool and eventually hit the M55, heading east towards Preston. His directions were as contorted as his thoughts. It became clear to Danny that he had no idea where to take her to finish her off. Obviously the prospect of dealing with Danny was unsettling him.

Before they had gone very far on the motorway, he instructed her to take the next turning off. She found herself being directed along country roads, towards Fleetwood. She knew exactly where she was, though, which made her feel comforted. She was pretty sure he'd be unable to take her anywhere within the county she did not know.

He made her turn right off the A586 and go across Shard Bridge, over the River Wyre. Now they were on narrower, winding roads, with Trent saying little, deeply engrossed in his own thoughts.

Soon they reached the coast again, well to the north of Blackpool, at a small seaside village called Knott End, and were driving down the short promenade towards the slipway near the river estuary. Fleetwood was directly opposite, across the water.

He told her to stop at the top of the slipway.

Fleetwood was lit up and looked prettier than it actually was. The tide was in, quite high, and the water lapped not many feet from the front wheels of the Mercedes. On this side of the water it was dark. No one around. In more ways than one, Danny had reached the point of no return.

'Switch off.'

She killed the engine. Silence surrounded them like a shroud.

'Keys,' he barked, holding out his hand. Danny took them out of the ignition and dropped them into his open palm. He slid them into his pocket.

Trent was now in a dilemma.

The very fact that Danny had to get out of the car gave her a slight opportunity to escape. He knew it, so did she.

As soon as he told her to get out, she was going to run. Trent's mind, already in turmoil, revolved furiously. Then he hit on a course of action.

He opened his door and placed his left leg out. With his right hand he grabbed Danny's hair, started to climb out and dragged her behind him over the handbrake and gearstick.

'This way. You come out this way and if you try anything I'll stab you.' The point of the knife wavered dangerously close as she succumbed to the situation. He pulled her across and dropped her onto the ground on her hands and knees. He stepped away from her, waving the blade threateningly.

'Come on, come on, get up, get up!'

She clambered unsteadily up, using the arm-rest on the inside of the door as leverage. Trent yanked her away from the door, back-heeled the door shut and propelled her towards the footpath which ran alongside the river, underneath the observation windows of the unmanned coastguard station and the golf club to their left. On their right was the River Wyre. The water lapped gently up the man-made riverbank.

Danny stumbled several times when Trent pushed her, but he was remorseless.

Two hundred yards down the path they approached a pretty white cottage at the water's edge, lit up, looking inviting and homely. Danny willed one of the occupants to come to a window. That did not happen as Trent frogmarched her quickly past. Ahead of them was a small sailing club with many dinghies drawn up on a slipway. Beyond were more cottages which Trent obviously did not know about.

'Shit,' he said on seeing them.

He pulled Danny around and marched her back past the white cottage and turned her onto the public footpath which sliced across the golf course. Within seconds the lights from Fleetwood docks were left behind. They seemed to walk into a shroud of blackness where it was impossible to see your feet.

A wave of panic coursed through Danny. This was the ideal place to finish the job. Drag her onto a fairway, into a bunker, then attack her. A hundred yards dead ahead of her, Danny saw the lights from a row of houses which backed onto the golf course, and to which the footpath led.

Trent shoved her, driving his open hand into the middle of her back, making her head snap backwards.

She stumbled.

And saw her chance.

She exaggerated the movement and turned it into a sprint.

She shot off like a whippet. Before Trent realised his error, Danny was five yards away. 'Bitch!' he shouted angrily. He lunged at her. The knife cut through the air with a *swish*.

Danny accelerated away. Having only recently tested her running skills when pursuing Claire Lilton, she knew her capabilities were limited, especially now with a sore ankle. But she had to put as much distance between herself and Trent as possible. She motored.

'No way! No fucking way!' Trent screamed behind her.

Danny's arms pumped wildly, her legs pumped, dismissing the pain in her ankle, her heart pumped to bursting. She knew she would get no help from adrenaline which had already overdosed her system. She had to rely on pure determination and the instinct to survive.

She willed herself to get to the houses ahead of Trent.

His footsteps crashed down in her wake, echoing in her ears.

He was only feet away, maybe only inches.

Danny surged on, motivated by the thought of his hands reaching out for her. She got to the point where the narrow footpath did a 90-degree turn to run directly behind the houses.

'Ahhh!' Trent cried. He had lost his footing at the turn and pitched headlong into bushes.

Danny forced herself to go even faster, racing to the point where the path ended and an avenue of bungalows began and street-lights blazed, house-lights burned . . . back to an environment of normality.

Before she could get to the nearest door and possibly safety, Trent was on her, having recovered quickly from his fall. He rugby-tackled her, driving her over a low garden wall, through a tangle of bushes, rolling onto a well-manicured lawn.

Trent landed on top, reared up with the knife rising in his right hand, glinting in the sodium lighting. It began a downward descent into her face.

With a superhuman effort, Danny writhed herself away from the weapon's arc of travel and Trent stuck the knife into the grass where, a split second before, Danny's eye had been.

Danny's right hand fell onto a large, hand-sized pebble on the rockery. She grabbed it immediately and with no thought process, just pure basic instinct, smashed it into the side of Trent's head. He sprawled across the grass, leaving the knife embedded in the lawn.

Danny crawled away from him, completely exhausted,

trying to get to her feet, but her whole body had given up responding to anything. Trent had already stood up. He staggered like a drunk around the garden, holding his head and searching for the knife.

'What the bloody 'ell's goin' on 'ere?' boomed a voice from the back door of the house. The dark figures of two burly, handy-looking men appeared and made towards Danny and Trent.

'Call the police,' Danny groaned. She slumped down. 'Please, call the police.'

Trent cursed. He stumbled on the hilt of the knife, extracted it from the grass, stared wildly at the two of them, then, inexplicably but wonderfully to the exhausted Danny, he turned and ran.

Chapter Fourteen

Monday morning, three days later, two battered and bruised figures hobbled into work.

Firstly there was Henry Christie.

He had a collection of swellings on his scalp of various sizes and configurations. Because he had been knocked into oblivion, he had spent Thursday night in hospital, under observation, even after X-rays on his thick skull had shown no fractures. He had then spent a long weekend at home, recuperating.

His brain constantly hummed and his left ear emitted a shriek every so often which, he was assured by the medical profession, would pass in time. He had to walk fairly slowly, though, because if he moved his head too quickly, lights exploded at the back of his eyeballs, making him feel like his brain was linked to a Van Der Graaf generator.

Other than that, he was feeling pretty steady.

Behind him came Danielle Louise Furness on the first day of her official promotion to Detective Sergeant. She dragged herself into the police station a few feet behind Henry because he had picked her up on the way in.

The first of Danny's days of sickness had been spent in the same hospital as Henry, where she had been checked over – again – by that same dishy doctor who had treated her before. He appeared to work more hours than she did. They became quite chatty under the circumstances and Danny filed him away for future possibilities.

Her next two days had been at her sister's house near

Preston where she had been fussed over and treated like royalty. Most of Danny's physical injuries were relatively minor. The weekend gave them some quality time to heal.

Now, as she limped in behind Henry, she was just stiff and sore. So pretty much, Danny's outer layer had been repaired.

It was her inner self, the psychological layers which concerned her. The chassis which held the bodywork together.

The night demons had been bad, sleep a problem. Each time she closed her eyes, whirling, frightening images came to her, where the faces of Jack Sands and Louis Trent overlayed each other to form a single terrifying monster with only one aim: to destroy Danny Furness.

But she had been determined to fight. She returned home on Sunday evening, resolved to sleep alone in her own house, get back to normal and get back into work to take up her new post.

And though she was suffering mentally, she knew she was tough enough to pull through it.

She and Henry rode up in the lift together.

It was 9 a.m. Louis Vernon Trent had not yet been captured.

Following the gruesome discovery of a skull in woodland near to Darwen in East Lancashire by two illicit lovers, one very decomposed body was dug carefully out of a shallow grave and transported to the mortuary. It turned out to be the skeletal remains of a young person and the pathologist called in for the job identified them as those of a young girl aged maybe ten or eleven years old; she had been buried there for about five years. The only way to make positive ID would be through dental records, as the jaws and teeth were well-preserved.

He could not specify a cause of death, nor whether the girl had been sexually molested. Even so, the police decided to set up an incident room, allocate half a dozen detectives to it and see where the enquiry led.

The first port of call for the detectives on the case was Lancashire Constabulary's Missing from Home files. These threw up three possibilities. One was quickly eliminated – she had actually returned home, but no one had cancelled the circulation. That left two girls, both having gone missing several years earlier and never returned.

The second port of call was to dental surgeries. This eliminated one of these girls.

The final port of call was to Blackpool police station.

Robert Fanshaw-Bayley, Assistant Chief Constable (Operations) was waiting impatiently in Henry Christie's office, sitting behind his desk, leafing through his things. Henry closed his eyes momentarily when he clapped eyes on FB.

What Henry wanted to do was sit at his desk, get his feet comfortably underneath it, take his time, get up to speed with the investigation, see where it was going, see where it was blocked, then get onto Trent's tail. It had been three days since Danny's horrific experience and Henry knew the trail was getting colder by the minute. It needed hotting up – but only after he had got himself up to scratch.

Henry had a pretty good idea that FB's presence would preclude the first part of the action plan.

'Henry, about time you got in here, for fuck's sake!' FB snorted, making a great show of looking at his watch and the wall clock.

Danny had followed Henry up to the office and was standing behind him. 'I'll catch you later, sir,' she said to Henry. She nodded at FB. 'Morning, sir.'

'No – you get in here too, young lady,' FB beckoned regally. Danny bristled, but came in and eased the door shut.

FB made no effort to vacate Henry's chair. The two lower-ranking officers sat on the seats opposite the desk.

'What's all this going off sick shit, Henry? Haven't I told you before it's a nancy-boy's trick?'

'I think you have, sir.'

FB grunted. His head reared back. 'Anyway, you both look like shite.' He glared at Henry. 'What's the story behind it?' He pointed at the DI's head. 'Who walloped you?'

Henry shrugged. 'No idea. Could've been any one of a number of people.' Deep down he believed he knew exactly who was responsible, but was not about to share it with FB. This was something personal.

'And how are you, missy?' FB directed the question to Danny.

She bristled again and bit her tongue. 'I'm fine.' She smiled primly.

'Good, good. Couple of days enough to get over it, I imagine?' It was a rhetorical question.

Henry regarded FB across the desk and thought he had become even more insufferable since his promotion to ACPO rank. He had been bad enough before. Now his management style resembled a steam-roller, riding rough-shod over everyone in his path, making no allowances for people's feelings.

Henry knew FB had recently been the subject of two grievances, one on the grounds of sexism, the other racism.

'You wanted to see us, boss?' Henry asked politely.

'Yeah, to make sure you don't do your normal thing, Henry – sit around all morning farting about getting nowhere. I want you to remember that besides a little girl being murdered by this bastard, he killed a cop too.' Danny winced visibly at the memory. 'And I am telling you that if you don't have this cunt – please excuse my French,' he said to Danny who winced again, 'in custody by the end of this week, questions will be asked in the big house. Get my drift? Jobs are on the line here, Henry – yours in particular. Remember, it gets bloody cold in uniform.'

Henry opened his mouth to utter something about being unfair, but thought better of it. FB was known for making rash statements before thinking them through, and not really meaning them; however, this did not stop his words from being unsettling.

'What I want you to do is come back to me in an hour and tell me exactly where this investigation is up to. I'm sure you can manage that. Right – that'll do for now. I'll see you later, back here, one hour.' He rose and left the room.

Henry slumped back and mouthed the word 'bastard' to himself, bitterly regretting coming back into work. He could, quite legitimately, have taken the week off. The discordant tunes in his cranium had escalated to full volume by FB-induced stress. He looked sideways at Danny.

'Is he always such a dick-brain?'

'That was his good side,' Henry said. 'You should see him when he really gets uppity.'

There was a knock on the door. Danny answered it. Two men came into the office and introduced themselves. They were detectives from Blackburn. Henry knew them by sight, not name.

'What can I do for you?' he asked. He sidled behind his desk and sat on his chair, noticing how warm it was from FB's sweaty backside. He swept his hand towards the chairs and the detectives sat.

One spoke. 'A body was found in a shallow grave a couple of days ago. Young girl, decomposed. We've managed to ID her from dental records and an MFH report.' The detective handed Danny a photograph of a family group with the face of the girl circled in red pen. Danny felt a chill. She handed the photo to Henry who saw the look on Danny's face. The detective carried on talking, revealing the girl's name as Annie Reece, aged fourteen. 'She went missing about five years ago, never turned up. Another girl disappeared at the same time. She never turned up either. You might recall?'

Henry did – but at the time he had been out of the country in Holland, on an operation with the Regional Crime Squad. There had been a big hunt for the two girls which eventually fizzled out. No clues, no leads.

'Does this mean something to you, Dan?' Henry asked.

Her face was bleak. 'I reported them both missing.'

'Does it link to Trent?'

'No. He was in prison by then.' She shook her head in disbelief. 'Funny how the past always seems to catch up with me.'

Henry's phone rang, cutting short any further time for Danny to reflect.

'Yep?' Henry answered it bluntly, nowhere near to Force instructions on how a phone should be answered. It was one of the officers from the incident room. Henry listened, his eyes on Danny.

'Yeah, right, thanks for that . . . Where exactly . . . What condition is it in? . . . Scenes of Crime, forensics on their way? Right, I'll be in shortly. Thanks again.' He hung up. 'Guess what? They've found your car,' he told Danny. This was a major leap forwards in the investigation because Trent had stolen Danny's car from Knott End after he had tried to kill her. Its description and registration had been circulated nationwide, but it had only just been found.

Danny perked up. 'Where?'

'Stoke-on-Trent, appropriately enough.'

'Stoke? What the hell's he doing going to Stoke? And the car?' She desperately wanted it back.

'I'm sorry . . . it was found by a couple of amateur divers in a flooded quarry just outside Stoke. Looks like it was torched before it went into the drink. I'm told it's a complete write-off.'

Danny wilted visibly. Despite its recent injuries, it was still her beautiful car. Treasured possession. Lovingly cared for, manicured weekly. First she was abducted in it, then it was stolen, now destroyed.

'Sorry, Dan. Look – oh, damn!' Once more the phone interrupted things. Henry picked it up, but continued talking. 'Why don't you go and get a brew for these guys and I'll join you in a few minutes to discuss how we can help them . . . Yep?' he said into the phone.

A voice he recognised instantly, but had not heard for about six months, said reprovingly, 'Is this always how you answer the phone, you godamned son of a gun?'

Henry brightened. 'Hey, Yank! How the hell y'doing?'

It was Karl Donaldson, former FBI Special Agent, now working in the FBI London Office as a Legal Attaché. He was a good friend of Henry's.

Henry shooed Danny and the two visiting jacks out of the office, leaned back in his chair, hoiked his feet onto the desk and said, 'What can I do for you, pal?'

'Remember Corelli?' the American's voice boomed.

'How could I forget?' was Henry's response. Indeed, how could he have forgotten the man who had dispatched a highly trained and paid assassin to do some dirty work in the North of England, and with whom Henry had become personally and professionally involved, nearly losing both his wife and life in the process. Henry knew Corelli had since been murdered. 'So what's this about? Surely he hasn't come back to life?'

'Not exactly, but he's been reincarnated in the guise of another Italian low-life, name of Mario Bussola. You know how it is: stamp on one cockroach and another one slithers out of the wall as a replacement? That's what Bussola's done, taken on the mantle of numero uno honcho in Florida's swampy underworld . . . but he's ten times worse, if that's possible.'

'Karl – all very interesting, but why tell me this?'

'Stick with me, you impatient git. Is that the right word, git?'

'Yeah – one of those quaint olde English expressions.' Henry smiled. He knew Donaldson liked to try out English slang.

'One thing I think Corelli never dabbled in was under-age sex. I know he was into prostitution, but never into little kids. Which is where he and Bussola differ. Bussola likes young girls, just on the turn from kiddie to lady, apparently. Our information also suggests he ain't all that choosy. Young male ass is also very acceptable. Still with me, or have you fallen asleep?'

'Still hangin' in there, buddy.'

'Good. The FBI in Florida have investigated Bussola frequently, but got nowhere. He is strongly suspected of shipping illegals in from all over the place – Mex, Cuba, wherever, you name it – and using them in his joints, porno films and also for himself. It's a big trade over there – bodies. Fuckin' phenomenal, really, but very underground. Something the likes of me an' you couldn't even envisage. They're just throwaways. Disposables. Makes me sick to ma stomach.'

'Karl, sorry pal, great story, but I'm busy, busy, busy . . . maybe I can phone you at home later? That bastard FB is really breathing heavily down my neck.'

'This is work and it affects you,' Donaldson said sternly.

'I'm suitably chastised.'

'You should be, Henry. That's the background. Last week Bussola was arrested indulging in a double-tap with an underage girl, a missing person.'

'Double tap?' To Henry that was a firearms term.

'A two-up, if you like.'

'I'm with you.'

'He was eventually released without charge. But now, here's the interestin' part from your point of view. Does the name Charlie Gilbert mean anything to you?'

'I know of a Charlie Gilbert,' Henry said cautiously. 'Why?'

'A fellow called Charlie Gilbert was the other member of the double-tap. Apparently he lives in Blackpool.'

'The only Charlie Gilbert I know is one who owns a fucking huge chunk of Blackpool. Numerous amusement arcades, a lot of pubs and restaurants, burger bars, a massive all-year-round fairground in North Shore. All sorts of stuff. He's a councillor, a member of the Rotary. Very high profile indeed and beyond reproach. Donates money to children's charities . . .' As he said the word 'children's', Henry's speech faltered slightly. 'Finances several youth clubs, junior football teams, netball teams . . . the guy's a saint.'

'U-huh?' said Donaldson. 'This will come as a bit of a shock to you, old buddy. He's also a child-molester. Released without charge, maybe, but I've spoken to a witness who saw him forcing his cock into the young girl's mouth while Bussola buggered her. He was also juiced up to the eyeballs, believed to be coke. Some saint, eh? One who mixes with la crème de la crème de la Florida underworld. Just thought you'd like to know.'

Henry came over all queasy.

Only three weeks earlier he had given Gilbert and several other dignitaries a guided tour of the police station during an official visit by the local council. Henry could see Gilbert's face now, very, very clearly. Large, round, flabby, but not ruddy. He was almost a sickly white, complexion-wise, and his skin hung in folds, rather like those unusual dogs, the breed of which Henry could never remember. Gilbert had been loud and ebullient. Full of himself, driven by his own self-confidence. Unusual for a fat person.

But Gilbert was an unusual person.

He'd begun his working life with nothing more than a roadside burger stall and over forty years had built up a veritable empire based in Blackpool, concentrating on cheap food and amusement . . . the areas which, on reflection, were attractive to young people.

Yes, Henry could clearly visualise Gilbert rolling down the corridors of the police station, voice booming above everyone else's. And all the while he hid disgusting secrets.

Henry wondered what else was hidden. He shivered at the thought, looked briefly down at his right hand – the one with which he had shaken Gilbert's. Instinctively he wiped the palm across his desk blotter.

'This is simply me acting in my liaison role, Henry, and passing you information,' Donaldson was saying. 'I haven't received anything on paper yet but I did check the facts before I called you. They are correct.'

'Cheers, Karl.'

They concluded the call with some quick family chit-chat.

Henry breathed out, puffing his cheeks. He was astounded by the news. He cursed as the phone went again – the bane of his life.

It was Danny. She sounded excited. 'Henry, we've got a possible location for Trent.'

'In Stoke?'

'No, here in Blackpool. In a guest-house.'

'Incident room, one minute,' Henry barked.

Mrs Bissell's guest-house – The Ronald, named after her dear departed – was a clean, well-run and fairly prosperous establishment in Charnley Road. Mrs Bissell was a robust lady, round, even-tempered and a whizz at cooking full English breakfasts. She had been running The Ronald for fifteen years, ever since becoming a widow. It gave her something to do and she found she was surprisingly good at it, having been a housewife most of her adult life. The majority of her guests were well-known regulars, but she always liked to keep a couple of spare rooms for passing trade; passing trade often became repeat trade.

Over the last three days she had received one phone call and one visit from the local police regarding Louis Trent. She knew all her guests personally and was adamant Trent was not one of them. The visiting officers accepted this.

Earlier that Monday morning, a few minutes before she had finished serving breakfasts, a man carrying a holdall called at the front door asking for accommodation. She immediately said yes, asked him to sign the visitor's book and pay a small deposit, which he did. He peeled a ten-pound note from a thick wad. She took him to one of the single rooms in the newly built extension at the rear of the premises. From the window there was a view of the southerly aspect of the Winter Gardens complex. Mrs Bissell offered her new guest a late breakfast, which he declined. After pointing out the amenities – there was no en suite but the bathroom was immediately across the passage – she left him in the room.

Walking back through the narrow, seemingly endless corridors, Mrs Bissell was a little perturbed. There was something not quite right about the man and this gave her a sense of unease. She was never 100 per cent happy taking in single men. Most of her custom came from older couples, usually pensioners. To her a single man often meant gay in Blackpool – not that she had anything against poofs . . .

She did not think this man was gay. So what was it? His reluctance to get into conversation? The large amount of money he openly displayed? Then it struck her.

She rushed back to the reception desk where she rooted through a pile of correspondence, eventually finding what she was looking for – the photograph and description of Louis Vernon Trent left by the police on their recent visit.

She peered at the image of the most wanted man in Britain, but couldn't be sure it was him. It looked like him, but then again . . . She checked the visitor's book and saw he had signed in as L. Blake, with an address in Stoke. Her lips puckered up. Again she peered closely at the photograph. She focused in on the eyes.

They were the giveaway.

With trembling fingers she picked up the phone, hoping she wasn't about to make a complete fool of herself, but deep down she knew that Louis Vernon Trent had just booked into her hotel.

'A guy has signed himself in as "L. Blake" from Stoke-on-Trent,' Henry said to the very quickly assembled

Armed Response Vehicle crews. Four officers had turned up – all in body armour, all overtly carrying their weapons. 'The name Blake is the surname of one of the inmates Trent is suspected of frying during his prison escape; Stoke is where he abandoned Danny's car.'

Other officers shuffled into the room. Six Support Unit, all having quickly changed into their riot gear.

'Come in, welcome,' Henry beckoned. 'We've only just started.'

FB then sidled in, joining Henry and Danny at the front of the room. Henry recapped on what he had said, then continued, 'According to the lady who runs the guest-house, Mrs Bissell, the suspect is in a single room at the rear of the building. Second floor with a view across to the Winter Gardens.'

A large-scale aerial photograph was Blu-tacked onto the wall behind Henry. It clearly showed the Winter Gardens and the surrounding streets. Because Blackpool hosts political conferences every year, the streets around the conference venue, the Winter Gardens, were well-documented in terms of photos, maps and plan drawings for reasons of security. Mrs Bissell's guest-house could clearly be seen and the picture was recent enough to include the new extension.

'This is the guest-house on Charnley Road.' Henry pointed to it. 'Most of you probably know it. Obviously we can't be sure that this is definitely Trent in the room, so we need to find out and play it softly softly just in case it isn't. I've roughed out a very quick operational plan and I'm going to run through it. If anyone has any better ideas, then please speak up.'

The heavy rain helped the initial approach. It was bucketing down remorselessly, driving in from the Irish Sea like fine rods of steel, almost horizontal.

This meant it was not exceptional to see two people, a couple, a man and a woman, jogging down the road against the weather, heads bowed against the onslaught, chins on chests, collars up, the woman with hat pulled down over her face, hiding her features, the man's arm around the woman's shoulders.

They turned into the guest-house, trotted up the steps and into the tiled vestibule where the proprietor met them with a sharp, 'We're full up.'

The man quickly flashed a badge. 'DI Christie from Blackpool police station. We talked on the phone a few minutes ago. This is Sergeant Furness.'

'Oooh, right,' said Mrs Bissell.

'Anywhere we can have a quick chat?'

She led them into the deserted TV lounge.

'Look, I don't even know if this is the right fella,' Mrs Bissell said worriedly. 'I don't want to upset him if I'm wrong. He is a paying guest, after all.'

'We understand that,' Danny said empathetically. 'We'll be tactful. Don't you fret yourself, love. As soon as I see him, I'll know. It's not as though we need to take a long time over it. In and out, whichever way it goes.'

Mrs Bissell held a hand across her ample bosom and sighed. 'Thank the Lord for that.'

'Is he still in that back bedroom, the one you described?' Danny asked.

'Yes.' She nodded. 'As far as I know.'

'Is there any way he can get out of the building without you knowing?'

'Only by the fire escape. It runs underneath his window.'

'Okay,' said Henry, 'can you show us to the room, point it out and leave us to it? And if you've got a master key, that would be helpful.'

Henry removed his raincoat and draped it across the back of a chair. He spoke into his PR and asked for positions. The reply came back: Three Support Unit and two firearms officers at the rear, on foot, out of sight, but with a view of the building; the remaining officers were

267

parked and ready in a van up the road.

'Right, we're going up,' Henry informed them. To Mrs Bissell he said, 'Please lead the way.'

Since kidnapping Danny, Trent had laid pretty low. He had escaped in her car, driven south on the motorway and come off at Stoke-on-Trent where he fired the car and rolled it into a flooded quarry. He spent that night in Stoke and the following morning bussed it to Manchester. He killed time there by drifting around porno cinemas, getting wind of some child-abuse films which he watched excitedly.

He found himself to be getting restless, though, with a sensation growing in him which meant he had to act again. He was tempted to strike in the city, but only felt 'right' doing it in Blackpool. He was comfortable there, knew the place well, the best spots to stalk and pounce, the best places to finish off his crimes.

To commit another crime was something he needed to do. It was building up inside him, burning through him and he had no control over it. He had to do much, much more. The little girl Meg Tomlinson was to be the first of many. Although Danny Furness had been a failure at least he had terrified her shitless. But putting fear into someone was not his intention. Killing them was. And Danny was still high up on the list for a knife in the ribs. Next time it would go straight in, no fucking about, no conversation. Just wham!

In – twist, in-twist, in-twist.

Trent slashed his hand at the water in his bath.

He sniggered, lounged back in the hot water and contentedly washed himself down.

Then came the knock on the door.

He shot upright. His right hand reached for the knife which lay on the bath stool.

Danny remained unconvinced that Henry's plan of action

was the most sensible in the world. To her, it would have been far better to have had a truckload of hairy-arsed bobbies thundering down the corridor, kicking in the door. No messing. Arresting whoever happened to be on the other side.

If it wasn't Trent, so what?

Brush him down and apologise.

If it was – all well and good.

But to have just the two of them tiptoeing down the corridor and knocking gently on the door Mrs Bissell had indicated, seemed plain stupid. Or was she being too sensitive? Perhaps being abducted at knife-point and having threats made to cut her breasts off had put things out of all perspective.

She took a firmer grip on her extended baton.

They reached the door. Henry gestured silently for Danny to back off, then he rapped his knuckles on the door and waited. No reply. He knocked again. No reply. Henry's hand went to the doorknob and turned it. The door was locked.

Danny swallowed.

Henry glanced quickly at her and pulled out the master key given to him by Mrs Bissell.

'Here I go,' he mouthed.

Trent rose slowly out of the bath, knife in hand. He trod quietly on the bathmat, took the single stride to the door and opened it a crack. The bathroom was directly across the corridor from his room. He immediately saw Henry Christie's unprotected back, his hand on the doorknob, turning it, while carefully inserting the key in the lock at the same time.

With a scream of rage, Trent raised the knife and threw himself across the narrow corridor, plunging the blade into Henry's back at a point between the right shoulder-blade and spine.

Danny yelled an agonised warning as she saw the naked

figure of Trent flash across the corridor and drive the knife into Henry.

Too late.

Henry managed a quarter-turn, saw the glint of the blade, tried to protect himself. Too slow. He and Trent crashed against the bedroom door, the lock splintering open on impact. Henry stumbled onto his knees under Trent's weight, then pitched forwards, smashing his forehead on the edge of the bedstead as Trent fell on him.

Danny's first instinct was to turn and run. To scream for assistance. She forced herself through that moment, took two long paces down the corridor and pivoted into the room behind the two men. Henry was prostrate and unmoving underneath Trent who straddled him. The knife was already slicing downwards towards Henry's exposed neck for the second blow.

Danny knew she had to react.

She stepped into the room, but because she was cramped for space, was not able to strike Trent as hard as she would have liked with her baton. Instead she gave a backhand flip, not dissimilar to a squash stroke. The shaft connected with Trent's left temple, knocking him sideways across the room. The knife shot out of his hand as he rolled over.

Danny glimpsed Trent's loosely hanging genitalia which made her want to retch.

She stepped over Henry. Trent was already on his hands and knees, scrabbling towards the knife, only inches from his fingers now.

This time she did have the room.

She took aim carefully . . . and the baton rose high.

She smashed him hard and deliberately on the back of his skull in a very controlled fashion. She did not want to lose her temper, but by the same token she secretly hoped she would kill him with the blows and fuck the consequences. It was a very satisfying feeling – once . . . twice . . . smack, crack.

Trent's whole body quivered and collapsed. His finger-tips were touching the knife-handle. Danny saw he was still breathing. She quickly pulled his arms round his back and applied a pair of cuffs, purposely ratcheting them too tight.

Then she turned to her boss. 'Henry, Henry, you all right?'

She heard him moan. 'Ohh, hell,' he spoke to the carpet, 'where did he come from?'

'Right behind you.' Danny helped him sit up.

'Jeez,' he gasped. He crossed his left hand over his right shoulder and reached for the shoulderblade. 'Feels like he hit me with a hammer.'

'No, just a knife. You were lucky.'

Henry nodded. It wasn't the first time that protective body armour – on this occasion a stab-vest – had saved his life.

'I need a fucking ambulance, you bastards.'

Danny and Henry looked at Trent. It was only then Danny saw her blows with the baton had split his scalp in two places, rather like knife-slashes across upholstery. She leaned over him with a delicious smile. 'You're fucking lucky you don't need a hearse,' she hissed into his ear.

She checked her watch. Eleven-thirty.

Not a bad day's work.

Most police officers believe, in principle, that prisoners should have rights. That principle usually goes crashing out the window when the officer gets personally involved in a case. Particularly child murders or abuse. Then they don't want to give prisoners anything – except a hard time.

Danny did not want to allow Trent to go to hospital. But the law is the law and off he went, handcuffed and escorted by three no-nonsense coppers and a driver. He wouldn't be going anywhere, other than straight back to the cells to be interviewed after he'd received treatment.

271

And in the meantime, Danny became very upset when Henry told her he had decided not to allow her to interview or have any further connection with Trent because of her personal involvement. He would allocate a team of four experienced jacks, working in pairs, to process, interview and charge Trent. Henry did not want any slip-ups. He wanted the prisoner to be dealt with fairly, correctly and above board. He knew Trent would be making counter-allegations of assault and the case would be difficult enough as it was.

Personal baggage would just make things more difficult.

He explained all this to Danny as she drove him back to the police station. She wasn't a happy bunny.

'You're rambling, Henry. That blow on the head's done you,' she said rudely.

'Don't argue, Danny. I'm right, you know I am.' He did have a hot zinger of a headache, additional to the one he had started the day with, but he was thinking clearly, planning the next twenty-four hours with Trent, or longer if need be. There would be a lot of people queuing up to see him and politics would no doubt rear its ugly head. The police investigating Trent's prison escape and the bloodbath which accompanied it would want first call on him; they had seven murders to clear up. But Henry wanted Trent to stay in Lancashire. He had killed a police officer up here and a child. Henry would fight them all the way.

At the back door of the police station Henry and Danny bumped into a couple of detectives rushing out.

'Is there a fire or something?'

'No, boss. Another body.'

'Any details?' asked Danny.

'No, not really, but according to the uniform at the scene, it looks like the girl who's been missing a few days.'

Danny's heart nearly stopped. 'Claire Lilton?'

'Yeah, that's the one.'

272

PART TWO

PART TWO

Chapter Fifteen

Since the death of Steve Kruger and the Armstrong brothers, life in the offices of Kruger Investigations in Miami had been very subdued indeed. There was no chatter, laughter or any of the lightness Kruger had brought to the workplace when he was alive. A shroud had descended, seemingly impossible to lift.

Myrna Rosza spent most of her time walking around, speaking to the employees. Sitting down over a cup of coffee, listening, encouraging and attempting to get everyone back on track, to get the place humming again, people motivated.

All to no avail.

And, God, Myrna missed him dreadfully. She could empathise with the way in which every employee was feeling, except for her it was a million times worse.

Kruger's funeral had been one of the most testing occasions of her life. Of course she was allowed a little tear and her husband accepted that. Only natural. All she wanted to do, though, was let herself go; prostrate herself over the coffin, wailing and hysterical, and make a complete fool of herself.

She didn't. She stood with dignity and poise and denied herself the outburst she really needed.

She had not realised how much she loved him. Standing beside her husband whilst watching the coffin disappear slowly beyond the purple velvet drapes at the chapel only magnified those latent feelings. By the same token, it revealed to her how much she did *not* love her husband, Ben. Not that she disliked him, nor had any axe to grind with him – because he was a good husband, even if his work often took him away for long periods. She simply did not love him any more. They were more like friends, these days, and it was many weeks, maybe months, since they had last made love.

During the service Ben had reached for Myrna's hand in a gesture of support and comfort. She pretended not to see it coming and wiped a tear away instead, avoiding contact. On the same night, Ben had tried to cuddle her. She rolled away, pulled herself into a tight ball and rocked gently to sleep.

Myrna had also attended the double funeral of the Armstrongs at their home town in Virginia. At least she had not been in love with either of them, though the crimson-vivid memory of the walk down that hallway could not be shaken from her mind as their coffins were carried past her.

How had they reconstructed the bodies?

Were they in little pieces, fitted into their coffins like a jigsaw? An arm up here, the head down there?

And now, two days after Steve Kruger's funeral, Myrna was sitting at her desk, alone in her office, the staff having gone home. Silence was everywhere. It was Wednesday, 7 p.m.

Myrna stared with growing disbelief at the telephone on which she had, only seconds before, finished a conversation with her husband.

'Wha . . .?' she blurted to the wall. 'I can't believe . . . Christ!' She could not stop her head from shaking as the words tumbled over and over through her mind. 'The asshole, the bastard,' she uttered and slammed the desk hard with her fist. Everything rose a millimetre and fell back into place, blotter, phone, pen-stand, laptop, everything.

She rose to her feet and stalked around the room, fuming.

'Hello, darling, it's Ben . . .' the conversation had started. There was a crackle of static on the line and it was difficult to hear, yet immediately Myrna could tell something was not quite right. 'How are you, honey?'

'Under the circumstances, doing okay,' she answered guardedly.

'Look, dear, I have some sad news for you . . . something to tell you . . .' And with those words, Myrna knew. 'As you know, I'm out here in LA. I . . .' he hesitated.

'Spit it out, Ben.'

'There's no easy way to say this. I won't be coming home.'

Myrna remained silent as an icy blast of chilled air wafted over her.

'Are you still there, Myrna?'

Yes, she was. Her voice was brittle. 'Who is it? Somebody I know?'

'No, no, it's someone I met at a convention in Salt Lake last year, a fellow surgeon.'

'A fellow surgeon! That's a nice way of putting it. What's her name?'

'No, Myrna, you don't understand. When I say "fellow" surgeon, that's exactly what I mean.'

Bombshell number two. A crackle of static on the line. Myrna sat there, wide-eyed, as the meaning struck home. 'You're leaving me for a MAN?'

'Yes, I'm sorry. We are very much in love. You'd like him.' Ben sounded weak and contrite.

'I doubt it.'

'He's a heart-surgeon, too. Married, couple of kids. We're setting up over here, both got positions in the best private hospital around. Chief surgeons. You can have the house and the cars. I don't want anything from you, Myrna . . . just your understanding and maybe one day your blessing.' His words tumbled out. 'I know you haven't really loved me for some time and I think this coincided with two things: Steve Kruger, and me discovering my sexuality. I think you've secretly been in love with Steve for a long time, haven't you? I just wish I'd had the courage to let you go to him sooner . . .'

It was on these words that Myrna slammed the phone down.

She stood at the window. Miami was in darkness, a million lights on in buildings. She rested her forehead on the glass and cried as the heavens opened and torrential rain sluiced down over the city.

Without any financial recompense, merely accumulated days off which she would never find the time to take, Detective Sergeant Danny Furness had put in sixteen hours a day since the Monday-morning arrest of Trent and the subsequent discovery of Claire Lilton's pathetic, battered and sexually mutilated body on the perimeter of the public golf course in Stanley Park.

'Welcome to life on CID,' as FB might as have said.

What Danny had hoped to be a smooth change of career had been anything but. By the time midnight came on Wednesday, she was, once again, mentally and physically a wreck.

She crept into her bed after a long cold drink. Her newly installed house alarm was set, and the panic button on the wall within reach from the bed, glowed a dim, reassuring red. She lay naked under the cool sheet, legs and arms splayed wide, constantly searching for the next cool bit, loving the sensation of lying in a bed she had not seen for seventeen hours. She had not even bothered to have a bath, so desperate was she to get in. She was aware of the dried body sweat, the stale hair, the make-up and the rather obscene knickers she'd had to toss into the washing basket with a grimace of disgust on her face.

A deep sigh lifted her chest and she explored her physical sensations.

She had leg-ache, like she used to get when she was a kid; no doubt varicose veins were a real possibility. Her stomach gurgled in protest at the junk food she had consumed thoughtlessly for the last seventy-two hours, food she would not normally have even looked at. Her eyes were heavy and dark patches grew daily underneath them.

Suddenly the desire to sleep came over her. She reached out, clicked off the bedside light. As she drifted off she thought about the last three days . . .

Danny had immediately recognised Claire Lilton, though the youngster's face had been smashed to a pulp and was bloated horrendously by the ligature around her neck. Once the work at the scene had been done, Henry went with the body to the mortuary whilst Danny went straight to see Claire's parents. She had delivered numerous messages in her time and it seemed that always – *always* – the receiver of the message knew what the bad news would be even before she opened her mouth. Danny could see the knowledge in their eyes, and Ruth Lilton's eyes had been no different.

She knew her daughter was dead as soon as she saw Danny.

As she delivered the tragic news, Danny kept one eye on Joe Lilton, the stepfather. Danny knew never to judge a person's grief; grief was an individual thing, dealt with by people in their own way. Sometimes they were hysterical, other times they reacted with cold detachment. No two people were ever alike, but something crept up Danny's backside when she witnessed the shifty look of discomfort on Joe Lilton's face. He squirmed where he sat. And it caused Danny to wonder . . . Joe, what the hell do you know about Claire's death?

Before leaving the Liltons' that day, Danny did everything she could for Ruth.

The work of investigating then began, even though the prime suspect was already in custody.

During the course of that first day, Danny and Henry had little contact with each other. They managed to get together late to have the drink they had missed a few days earlier, when things had taken a bad turn for both of them. Unfortunately, their meeting brought about the second argument Danny had ever had with Henry.

The chat was innocent enough to begin with. They discussed their experiences on 'the night of the missed drink', as they called it between themselves. It was probably the tenth time of going over it, but both needed it, Danny in particular. She was grateful to Henry for listening. Each time she spoke, it got easier. The fear lessened; the horror subsided, though still lurked in a dark corner of her mind. But Danny was nothing if not resilient and she was determined to work herself through it.

'So, Henry,' she said eventually, 'any idea who might have cracked you? You didn't let on to FB.'

'I know . . . but I reckon we both know who is favourite, don't we?'

'Jack?'

'Just his kind of trick, I'd say. Not that he would have done it himself. He's been a detective in this town for a lot of years and he knows a lot of toe-rags who'd do it for the price of a pint. I've bumped into him a couple of times today and he has a sort of knowing look on his face. Supercilious, even.'

'And it's all my fault. Should never have got involved with him.'

'No,' Henry corrected her, 'it's *his* fault. But it'll all come out in the wash one day, in the not too distant future. He'll come a cropper and someone will fettle him.'

A minor, but pleasant silence descended on the couple whilst they considered their drinks.

Danny looked at her watch: 11.45 p.m. 'I suppose Trent'll be sleeping like a baby now,' she observed. 'He's spent most of the sodding day giving them the runaround at the hospital. He's only got a scratch on his head . . . boy, I enjoyed hitting him.' She curled her hands into tight fists and said, 'Yeah,' through gritted teeth.

'And the interviews have been bloody slow,' Henry whined. 'He's a tough one, saying very little other than being a clever dick. It doesn't make one jot really. We've got enough forensic and other evidence to convict him of . . .' Henry held up his fingers and counted off, one at a time: 'Theft from the old woman on the train, Meg Tomlinson's murder, your kidnap and assault, theft of your car, the murder of a police officer, the woundings in the estate agent's . . . He's been a busy man. Tomorrow we'll get into his ribs about Claire Lilton; that's not even been mentioned to him yet. He probably doesn't even know we've found her body – and there's all the other stuff concerned with the prison escape. That's seven more bodies. He'll never see the light of day again, other than from a prison yard. He'll probably end up in Broadmoor . . . something wrong?'

Danny had been frowning as Henry spoke. She looked as though she was building up confidence to say something.

'I don't think he killed Claire,' she said flatly. Henry sat back, aghast.

'Course he effin' did.'

'She was strangled. Trent's been using a knife.'

'But he used to half-strangle his victims when you caught him last time. He's obviously reverted to that.'

'Yeah, half-strangle is right. He never actually killed them back then. Now he's gone over the top into murder, it's not his hands he's been using, it's that knife. It seems to give him that extra feeling of power. Why would he revert to manual strangulation . . . doesn't make sense.'

'Nothing in that bastard's mind makes sense.'

'I know, I know . . . but to me, it doesn't seem to add up right.'

'I think you're wrong.' Henry was adamant.

'Look – we can't simply assume he killed Claire, become blinkered to it. That's not fair or just.'

'What happened to Claire wasn't fair or just,' Henry argued.

'Henry, you don't need to tell me that, but does it mean we railroad him, just because we've closed our minds to the implications of what I'm saying?'

Henry bridled. He had been convinced of Trent's guilt. Now the belief was being challenged, he was uneasy. 'No,' he said sheepishly. He took a swig of beer. 'I'm not happy with the thought it wasn't Trent who did it. It's just too much of a coincidence for him NOT to have done it.'

'So do we get him convicted just because of a coincidence?'

'No, I'm saying that—'

'What are you saying, Henry?'

'Don't you want him done?' he almost shouted. He took control of his voice, lowered it, leaned across the circular table and pointed a finger at Danny. 'That guy abducted you at knife-point, was probably going to rape you, was definitely going to murder you – and yet you seem to want to protect him.' He shook his head, confused. 'I don't get it.'

Now she leaned forwards. 'I want justice done, Henry. I want to see him inside until he dies, but I don't want him convicted of something he didn't do. That's too good for him. It makes us as bad as him. Everything we do needs to be spot on and he needs to know it's spot on, because if it isn't he'll always be one-up on us, and I don't want that.' She sat upright and rubbed her eyes. Her face softened and she smiled. 'Let's not fall out – I don't like arguing with you, but I'm sure true justice is really what you want too.'

He exhaled a long sigh, nodding. 'Yeah, you're right, I do. But if he didn't kill Claire, you know what that means, don't you?'

Danny shivered. 'I know exactly what that means.'

They had another quick drink and left the pub. The night had a chill to it. Danny instinctively linked arms

282

with Henry as they strolled amiably to his car which was parked some way down the road, under a street lamp and not in the pub car park. Both had developed phobias about car parks. A little shimmer of pleasure glittered through Danny when she touched Henry.

'That was a nice drink, Henry.'

'I enjoyed it too, even though you made me think. I don't usually like to think too deeply with a beer in my hand. The two activities don't seem to correlate. I usually talk football or sex, or both.'

Henry drove her home, pulling up outside.

'Thanks, Henry.'

'Pleasure.'

She looked at him. There was only a small distance between their faces. Danny felt a rush down between her legs as her eyes flicked across his face. She swallowed, giggled and broke the moment.

'It would be nice, wouldn't it?' she said, a hint of regret in her voice.

'It would be wonderful,' he conceded.

'But it won't happen.'

'No. I'll watch you walk to your door.'

'Good night, Henry.' She was out of the car quickly, in the house moments later, giving him a quick wave from the threshold.

He drove off, failing to notice the black figure in the shadows at the end of the road, stepping out to watch Henry's tail-lights disappear around the corner.

As Danny expected, Trent subsequently denied murdering Claire when the allegation was put to him on Tuesday morning. Although he had denied everything else, even in the face of overwhelming evidence, his denial of Claire's murder seemed to be true. With increasing anguish, the police concluded that maybe, possibly, probably . . . then *definitely* . . . there was another child-killer on the loose.

★ ★ ★

When Danny eventually fell asleep it was half-past midnight. Thursday morning. In Miami, it was seven-thirty in the evening.

Myrna Rosza finished crying for the moment.

She was in her personal restroom adjoining her office, glaring at herself in the mirror over the wash-basin. Emotions tumbled across each other inside her, but she had regained outwards control of herself. She flicked on the tap, filled the basin with hot water and washed her face, removing the stained make-up from around her eyes and cheeks.

Then she spent almost twenty minutes carefully reapplying it, after which she felt more positive about things and life in general. She completed the process by brushing and spraying her hair into place.

When she reviewed the new woman, she attempted a smile which lapsed fairly quickly at the prospect of the immediate hours ahead of her. Home was not a place to which she desired to return. It would be empty, cold and forbidding. On the spur of the moment she darted back into the office, picked up the phone and dialled the Fontainbleau Hilton on Collins Avenue, Miami Beach, booked a room, and a table at one of the restaurants. She slammed the phone back down, put on her top coat and walked purposefully out of the office.

The elevator to the basement was empty. It stopped with a bump and opened its doors to reveal a vast, deserted, underground parking lot. Since Kruger's death, the building superintendent had allowed her to park there – at a cost.

Moments later, the tyres of the Lexus were squealing across the concrete floor. She hit the exit ramp, suspension bouncing, drove through the raised security gate, then out onto the road where the rain hit the hood and windshield like a bucket full of grit. Myrna fumbled for the wiper control, then felt the thud of a body on the front of the car. She slammed on, unable to see properly, but aware a person had rolled off the hood onto the road.

'Shit,' Myrna cried. She leapt out – and at the back of her mind thought she could be stepping into a heist, a robbery, God knew what. At the front of the car lay the crumpled form of a female who was already rising to her hands and knees. She was totally drenched. In her hand was a rolled-up newspaper.

'Good God, are you okay?' Myrna bent low to assist.

The female looked up.

'You!' Myrna exclaimed.

To have had that long white wine and soda immediately before coming to bed was a pretty big mistake, Danny discovered not long after falling asleep. Her bladder called to her pitifully, 'Empty me!' in such a pathetic tone she could not ignore it.

With a grunt of frustration, she rolled out of bed, padded to the loo and back. When her head hit the pillow, she expected to return to sleep immediately. No chance.

Uncontrollably her mind clicked into gear and refused to get out of it. She found herself tossing and turning, desperately trying to get to sleep. She constantly re-ran images and conversations of the week through her mind's eye and it began to drive her mad.

She pictured herself sitting next to Ruth Lilton on their settee, clasping the woman's delicate hands in her own, offering support and reassurance, whilst at the same time bringing her up-to-date with the investigation.

'We initially believed the man we had in custody for the other matters was responsible for Claire's death. He denied it and, quite honestly, it looks as though he may not have killed her.'

'He must have, he must have,' Ruth Lilton sobbed.

'I can appreciate how you must feel like that,' Danny said softly.

'You can't appreciate fuck all,' Joe Lilton snarled into

Danny's face. 'You don't know fuck all about how we're feeling; we've lost a daughter. Murdered. How can you have the bottle to sit there and say "I can appreciate"?' He mimicked Danny's voice.

'Joe!' Ruth said. 'Please.'

'Well, bloody police . . . you're telling us that bastard who's locked up didn't kill her.'

'Yes, that's what I'm telling you,' Danny said stonily, trying not to rise to him, even though her blood had passed boiling point.

'Well, who did kill her? C'mon, tell us. Do your job.'

Danny's eyes played over his face. 'We don't know yet, but it's only a matter of time. We will be able to get a DNA profile from the bodily fluids her attacker left in her. We'll catch whoever did it, never fear. That's a promise.'

Joe went silent at these words. Then with a snort of contempt he threw up his arms and stormed out of the room.

'I'm sorry. I'm so sorry,' Ruth apologised.

'Its okay. He's upset and angry,' said Danny.

Danny rolled over in bed. Sweat started to dribble where her thighs met. The bed was hotting up the more she was unable to sleep.

And the next image that came to her mind was the meeting she and Henry had had with the pathologist who had performed Claire's post mortem. His name was Baines and it was apparent he and Henry knew each other well.

'Quite a few things of interest to you, H,' Baines said.

'Go on then.'

'Old sperm in her uterus – probably about four days. On its last legs, or flippers, as you might say.'

'Wow,' Henry said.

'Mmm, she was not a virgin. Probably hadn't been one for some time, by all indications.'

Danny closed her eyes. 'She was eleven years old.'

Baines nodded.

'Anything else?' Henry asked.

Baines opened his mouth and reeled off other interesting things which were lost on Danny who sat through the rest of the meeting numb, the voices of the two men simply a meaningless background to the physical sickness she was feeling on Claire's behalf.

Suddenly Danny cut back into the conversation. 'Can you pinpoint exactly how old the sperm is, Doctor?' she demanded to know.

Her eyes flipped open. 'Damn,' she said out loud to the bedroom ceiling. 'Why the hell can't I get to sleep? What have I done wrong? Come on, God, tell me.' She flicked off the duvet and went to the loo again.

Myrna stood by the door of the restroom next to her office and knocked tentatively.

'Some towels for you,' she called.

There was a murmur from the other side of the door which Myrna took to be some form of permission to enter. She opened the door and stepped in. The shower was hissing and steam rose towards the extractor fan. Through the frosted glass Myrna could see the naked, but indistinct shape beyond, soaping down.

'They're just outside the shower door.' She dropped them onto the floor.

Another murmur was the response.

Myrna retreated from the restroom. Back in the office she sat on her leather chair and tried to work out what the hell was going on. On the desk-top lay the newspaper the female had been carrying. It was soaking wet, near to deterioration. Myrna considered tossing it into the wastebasket. Before she did, she unrolled it carefully.

It was a five-day-old edition of the British *Daily Mail*. Not an unusual sight in Miami, where British newspapers were common on the streets and sold at many stores. Myrna flattened it carefully so the sports headlines were uppermost. She turned the paper over and read the news headlines.

The irony of it was that, through snoring loudly, Danny woke herself up. She cursed. She had been to sleep and then, fuck it, she had woken herself up. This, she thought, was going to be one of those nights.

She rolled over, tugged the duvet tight around her head and shut her eyes. It was one o'clock. In six hours she had to be up. Six hours . . . if only she could get six hours, that would be bliss – almost a normal night's sleep. Six lovely hours . . .

The restroom door opened and Myrna looked up.

The sex-chatline telephonist, who had been a vital witness against Bussola, the girl by the name of Tracey Greenwood stood there, one of the bath towels folded around her, another smaller towel around her head. Myrna had to admit she looked a thousand times better than she had done an hour before when Myrna had brought her into the office.

'Hi. How are you feeling?'

'Okay.'

'You should really go to hospital.'

'I'm fine, nothing's broken; you didn't run into me, I jumped onto your bonnet.'

'Bonnet?'

'Bonnet – hood – you know.'

'Oh yeah, I see. Bonnet's English.'

'Yeah, summat like that.'

Myrna stood up. 'Come on, sit over here.' She pointed to the sofa. 'I've got some coffee on, but I've only been able to find some cookies to eat. There's not much food around the office.'

'It's okay, I'm not really hungry.'

The girl pulled the bath towel tight and tottered across the office to the sofa. Myrna watched her out of the corner of her eye whilst she fixed two cups of steaming coffee from the filter machine. The girl was deadly thin, her legs seemingly no fatter than a ballpoint pen; her shoulders protruded bones and her arms were like twigs, dry-looking and capable of being snapped. She looked anorexic and like a drug addict. The mainline marks on the inside of her arms and the backs of her knees were prominent. Some had scabs on them, where blunt, rusted or pre-used needles had been inserted. It would not be long before she was dead.

Myrna handed her a coffee. She took it gratefully, hands a-quiver. She piled numerous lumps of brown sugar in then added cream.

Myrna drank hers back. She lowered herself down onto the opposite end of the couch.

The girl sipped her sweet brew. Her eyes traversed the office and the view across Miami. 'Nice office,' she commented.

'Thanks.'

'I suppose you're wondering why I threw myself at you.'

'You could say that.'

A massive shiver suddenly convulsed the girl's whole body. She almost spilled her coffee. 'Oh God,' she gasped, 'I really need a fix.' She looked hopefully at Myrna.

'Coffee's as far as I go.'

'I really wanted to see Kruger.'

'He's dead.'

'I know.'

'So why have you come?' Myrna demanded because she suddenly remembered that Kruger's death might have been prevented if only this girl hadn't disappeared. 'You're partly responsible for him dying. If you'd stayed and testified in the first place, Bussola might still be in the can.'

'No way. Don't try to pin that one on me.'

289

'Okay – so I ask again: why are you here?'

'I know something,' she said. A look of horror crossed her face and remained there. Myrna studied her carefully and thought the girl's expression was the result of seeing something so painful that even its memory brought back terror. The girl's head flicked quickly towards Myrna; her opaque, lifeless eyes produced tears which tumbled down her white cheeks. 'I know something,' she repeated with a sob of anguish. 'Something terrible.'

Danny was in a sort of dream-filled twilight zone, somewhere between sleep and deep sleep, images of fifteen years ago zipping through her mind. She was walking towards a door. From behind the door were voices. Angry. Raised. Arguing. Danny was in uniform. Her police car was parked behind her. There were white chippings underneath her feet, scrunching as she walked. She got closer to the door. The voices became louder. A man and a woman. The words had meant nothing to her. Merely jumbled. A big disagreement, possibly the first stages of domestic violence.

At the time she only half-listened to what was said, yet the words must have lodged themselves into her mind subconsciously. Like someone half-seeing a numberplate and subsequently dredging it out of the recycle bin of the memory whole and complete.

But the mind is a curious organ. Often it stores things the owner doesn't even know are there. The skill is in the process of recall. Sometimes it is a skill which can be acquired. Other times it is pure luck or circumstance which is the catalyst.

And that night it was a dream, because Danny had fallen asleep thinking about poor Claire Lilton . . . and the coincidence was that fifteen years before she had visited Joe Lilton's home on the outskirts of Blackburn to do a firearms enquiry and had stumbled into a domestic dispute, but at the time had not really heard the words which were being said as she walked to the door of the house.

In her dream, Danny was back there. It was a perfect reconstruction. All her recall was superb, even down to the words which passed between Joe and his then wife.

Danny woke abruptly and for once did not lose the dream. It was there with her, vivid and exact.

'Jesus, Jesus.' She threw the duvet off and got into her dressing-gown. She dashed downstairs, cursing herself for not keeping a pen and paper next to the bedside. She found both in the kitchen odds and sods cupboard and scribbled down the words.

Suddenly they all made sense.

The memory must have hurt the girl. Since speaking those last words she had lapsed into a vague silence, blankly staring through the window.

'What do you know, Tracey?' Myrna asked softly, unable to stand it any longer.

Tracey jumped like a charge had been passed through her. She raised a thin finger and pointed to Myrna's desk. 'The newspaper . . . can you get the newspaper?'

Myrna placed her coffee down, crossed the office and peeled the wet paper from her desk blotter and carefully carried it back, handing it over to Tracey. She took it and laid it on the sofa. She did not open the paper, as Myrna expected her to, simply pointed to the headlines.

'What? You know something about that?'

Tracey nodded.

Myrna twisted her head and skimmed through the story underneath the headlines. It was all about the discovery of a girl's body in some woodland in the North of England. It was a fairly run-of-the-mill story in national newspaper terms and had only made headlines because other good news was scarce, and the way in which the body had been discovered was obviously of great interest to many people. Lovers frolicking in a woodland glade don't often find bodies – but when they do they can rest assured the whole world will want to know and so will their legal partners.

'What do you know?' Myrna asked.

'I know the girl who was murdered . . . Annie Reece. She was my friend.' Her voice faltered. 'And I know who killed her.'

'Go on,' said Myrna

'His name is Charlie Gilbert. You know him too . . . he was one of the men who were defiling that girl the other night.'

Chapter Sixteen

'A sodding dream?' Henry exclaimed with mixture of contempt and amusement. 'You want to go and investigate something because you had a dream? I need you here, not gallivanting across the county on some cockamamie goose chase.'

Danny rubbed her face and held her thumb and forefinger at the bridge of her nose in an effort to alleviate the monstrous headache she had as a result of the lack of sleep. 'I know it sounds whacky, Henry, but I think it's worth following up.'

'Tell me what the dream was and I might let you go.'

'It was . . . oh God,' she began hesitantly. The images which had been so alive had now faded away to nothingness. It was a good job she had written some of the words down. 'Words. I just remembered some words I'd heard years ago and I think there might be some connection with Claire.'

'And how many years ago did you hear those words?' There was a hint of mockery in his voice.

'Fifteen.'

'And Claire was only eleven, right?'

'I know it sounds completely stupid and my mind is like a little ball of cottonwool at the moment, which doesn't help matters.' She was pacing Henry's office. 'But humour me. Give a sucker an even break.'

She stood across the desk from Henry. Pale, tired, drawn. She had not even bothered to put on make-up, which was very unusual. She looked ill.

'Okay,' he relented. 'Although I don't know how I'll justify it if anyone asks me – "my DS is following up a lead from a dream". Sounds like something from *The X-files*.'

'Thanks, Henry. I'm grateful.'

'You've got until five today, then it's back to reality, Danny – and take a mobile with you, just in case we need you back here.'

She shot out of the office before he finished speaking.

Tracey was sleeping now, curled up on the sofa with Myrna's overcoat laid over her thin body. She twitched constantly and moaned, sometimes fearfully, as though demons were chasing her.

Myrna leaned back in her big office chair, feet on the edge of the desk, her half-closed eyes on Tracey, working through the horror story Tracey had spent a couple of hours relating in minute detail.

The sound of police sirens on the streets below permeated through the triple-glazed windows.

The big question for Myrna was – what was the next step to take? Or even, did she believe what Tracey was saying? Or was it simply revenge?

Myrna believed it was true. It was other people, she guessed, who would have to be convinced. She flicked open her electronic organiser and tabbed through the directory to find the phone number she required.

Within thirty minutes of leaving Henry's office, Danny, in a plain CID car, was leaving the motorway and heading east towards Blackburn. She bore left towards Clitheroe and passed British Aerospace at Salmesbury, the classic English Electric Lightning guarding the gates like a huge Airfix kit. Even compared to jet-fighters today, the Lightning still looked the biz.

Minutes later she turned left off the main road and cut down towards Osbaldeston.

In fifteen years the place had changed little. She drove straight to the large house which had once belonged to Joe Lilton. Apart from a new colour for the woodwork, the house looked exactly the same. A large Mercedes was on the driveway, the same colour as Danny's somewhat older model had been. She experienced a tinge of sadness at the thought of her lovely car, but was thankful the insurance meant that in the not-too distant future, there would be a brand-spanker on her drive.

As she walked to the house this time there were no sounds of people arguing. A couple of dogs barked when she rapped on the door, which opened after a short wait. Two black Labradors bounded out and surrounded her in a friendly way.

'Can I help?' asked the lady with them.

She was in her fifties with a ruddy complexion, a large aquiline nose and sharp, angular face. Danny knew instantly it was not Joe Lilton's former wife. She sighed inwardly, knowing she'd been a bit optimistic to hope to still find her here.

'I'm looking for an old friend,' Danny said, thinking that introducing herself as a cop might complicate matters. 'She lived here, ooh, a good fifteen years ago. We lost touch when I moved south. Her married name was Lilton.'

The woman considered the information, then shook her head. 'No, doesn't ring a bell. We've been here five years; bought the place from a family called Rice. I think the house had been through several hands before that. Sorry.'

'Okay, thanks. It was a long shot.'

Danny drove away and pulled up under some trees in a country lane. Even for a cop, finding someone fifteen years on is not necessarily easy. She thought for a few minutes, then had a brainwave. She used the mobile phone Henry had made her take (bless him) and dialled Lancashire Police HQ and asked to be put through to the pensions department in Human Resources.

She explained who she was and what it was she wanted.

Less than five minutes later, the woman gave Danny the information she required: Robert Neville, Police Constable, had retired eleven years ago. She gave Danny his address and telephone number. Danny was pleased to discover he still lived in Blackburn.

Neville was the officer who had regularly worked the mobile beat covering Osbaldeston fifteen years before – the beat Danny had been allocated for that one day when he had been off sick.

It took Myrna two hours to contact Karl Donaldson at the FBI office in London. He had been in a breakfast meeting with the Commissioner of the Metropolitan Police and the head of the Maltese Police, discussing a particular drugs problem involving an American gang.

When he returned to his office, he had skimmed through his messages, saw the one from Myrna timed at 8 a.m. and was immediately interested. He put her message to the top of the pile, then went to get a coffee. First things first.

'It was really nice to see you after all these years,' Robert Neville said with a wave. 'Sorry I couldn't help you.'

'That's fine,' Danny said, trying to mask her disappointment. It had been a wasted journey because Neville had no idea where the first Mrs Lilton had gone after she moved away from Osbaldeston. He had just been glad she had gone.

Danny walked away from Neville's house towards the CID car, giving a quick backward glance and saying, 'It was nice to see you too, Bob.'

'There is one thing that might help, actually . . . it's just come to me.'

Danny tried not to let her shoulders droop. It had been an effort to get away from this man who had been divorced about six years, seemed to be leading a fairly solitary existence, and was reluctant to let the sight of a skirt leave his house without giving it a good long ogle. She turned, firmly believing this to be a delaying tactic.

'Yeah, there is one thing. I seem to remember that when the Liltons split up, she got a fair percentage of the business. They had a few of those shops that sell everything dirt cheap – toiletries and stationery, stuff like that. They had five shops and I think she got two of them, one in Accrington and one in Burnley. She had to change the name of them, though.'

'Can you remember what they were called?' Danny smiled sweetly.

Neville wracked his brains. 'Something like "Everything You Need" or "Just the Ticket" or "Cheep 'n' Cheerful". I'm not sure, sorry. Something tacky. I think the shops are still there. The one in Accrington is on Broadway, I think.'

At five-fifteen in the morning it could only be one person calling the office. Myrna lunged for the phone on her desk and picked it up before the first chirp had been completed. Tracey moved, disturbed by the noise. She did not wake.

'Karl?'

'Yeah, it's me, Myrna. How ya doin'?' came the voice from 3000 miles away, loud and clear.

'Good,' she whispered into the mouthpiece. 'Can you hear me okay?'

'Yeah – but you sound like you don't want anyone else to hear.'

'I don't. Just hold the line while I transfer you.'

She put the call through to Steve Kruger's office and slipped across the hallway, closing the door behind her. It was a strange sensation to sit in Kruger's chair, but she felt comfortable and warm doing so, almost as if he was still there and she was sitting on his knee. She picked up the phone. 'That's better. Now I can talk.'

'What can I do for you, Myrna? I passed on that last piece of information you gave me to a detective I know in Lancashire Police.'

'Thanks, Karl. This is about him again, Charlie Gilbert.'

Donaldson did a quick calculation in his head re time-zones. 'In that case this must be important if you're phoning at this time of day.'

'It is, I think. I want to get something moving, only I'm not sure how. I reckon I need your knowledge.'

'I'm flattered. Shoot.'

'The cops in Lancashire have dug up a body, young girl, maybe a week ago now, I'm not sure. It made national headlines because it was found by a man and a woman having sex.'

'I read about it.'

'I got some information which points to Gilbert as the perp.'

Ahh, the word 'perp' made him smile nostalgically. 'Offender', which they used in England, was just so . . . dull.

'Gilbert? How good is the information?' Donaldson wanted to know. 'I don't want to bother the cops with gossip.'

'It's better than information, Karl.' Myrna declared her hand. 'It's a witness. I've got one here who says she knows for sure it was Gilbert. I believe her, and from what I know of Gilbert I'd believe he'd easily be capable of murder. I just don't know how to take this forwards . . . and there is a further complication.'

'Yep?' He tried to sound positive.

'The girl will only talk to one person. It's a cop she met a few years ago, some guy called Danny Furness.'

And that 'guy', Danny Furness, was at that very moment strolling through the rather grimy streets of Accrington, an East Lancashire town with great tradition but little else to show the modern world. Broadway was the main shopping street, now pedestrianised with the open market on one side and shops on the other.

The one Danny was looking for was at the end of a row of shops. Its huge plate-glass window was garishly covered in brightly lettered words which declared brashly, *Everything-U-want – under 1 roof* and that everything was *permanently reduced*. Danny went in and walked directly to the first member of staff she could identify. She flashed her badge and warrant card and asked to speak to the manager. She was led to the back stairs and up through an assault course of stock boxes to a first-floor office, where she was introduced to a woman who she immediately recognised as the former Mrs Joe Lilton.

The woman looked like Danny felt. She was a mess. Her stringy bleached hair was pulled back into a pony tail; her blotchy skin, puffed up around the cheeks, looked like too much alcohol had taken its toll; the smell of booze was one of the things Danny recalled from her previous encounter with this woman. She had a mouth which was permanently turned down at the corners and the skin around her thin lips was corrugated with age.

'You probably don't remember me,' Danny said, presenting her warrant card which the woman peered at suspiciously.

'No, you're right. I don't.'

'Look.' Danny glanced quickly round the room. 'I'm really sorry to barge in on you unexpectedly, but I'd like to talk to you. I need about half an hour of your time, but I don't think talking in here is appropriate.' She indicated the office. It was no place to sit and talk, particularly as Danny knew it would be a conversation of great delicacy. The room was a complete mess of papers, invoices and more stacked-up stock. And there was only one chair and a phone which rang constantly.

'I'm busy,' the woman barked sharply.

Danny held her hands up placatingly. 'I know you are, but so am I; I'm here doing some enquiries about the murder of a young girl in Blackpool. Her name is Claire Lilton. Her stepfather is your ex-husband, Joe Lilton.'

'I won't make any apologies for this. He was a complete, utter, fucking bastard.' She leaned over her cup of tea and hissed the words across to Danny. They were sitting in a café in the shopping centre, facing each other at a corner table. Danny had learned that since her divorce from Joe, the woman had reverted to her maiden name, Turner.

'In what way, Jackie?'

'Used to really slap me about. I should've got out years before, but the money was good . . . y'know?' she admitted. 'The money was hellish good.' She sniffed.

'Why did you split up?'

Jackie Turner shifted uncomfortably, did not reply. Danny saw she had struck some sort of chord. 'What happened after the divorce?'

'He was a right bastard, but I screwed him as best I could.' She lit a cigarette and Danny took a light from the match. 'We had six shops then, all selling rubbish, mind, but little gold mines they were. He made sure I got the two least profitable ones and I even had to change the trading name, f'God's sake. I sold one immediately, and ploughed the money into this one which has turned into a real good 'un; I also got the house, but I couldn't afford to keep it on, so I sold that and got myself a bungalow instead – in Wilpshire. Nice 'n' snobby . . . haven't managed to find a bloke with much money yet, but I do all right.' She gave a wistful smile. Danny warmed to her.

'And the kids?'

A shadow crossed her face momentarily, then cleared. 'Kid – my daughter Julie.' Danny's eyes narrowed at the mention of the name. Then: 'She's twenty-four, married, got two kids of her own now, but it's a marriage made in hell, if you know what I mean?'

Danny considered the woman sitting opposite and was quite impressed. She was obviously a fighter and a survivor. Danny hoped she would turn out to be the same.

Jackie Turner's eyebrows rose, what was left of them, that is. They had been plucked almost to oblivion, replaced by an unsure line. 'What do you want from me?'

'Because it's a murder investigation, we follow up all sorts of leads, so don't think it's unusual to be asked a few questions. Joe's not a suspect, but we like to know as much as possible about families, backgrounds, all that kind of stuff.'

'I'd suspect the bastard,' Jackie said vehemently. 'He could be really violent.'

'Even with kids?'

Jackie clamped her mouth shut tight, accentuating her corrugated lips.

'Jackie, when I came to see you all those years ago, you and Joe were having a real humdinger.'

'Yeah, I remember now.'

'What was it about?'

She shrugged. 'The usual shite. Drink played its part. I'm not sure what sparked it.'

Danny looked directly into her eyes. Jackie's dropped and she inspected her smouldering cigarette end.

'I don't think it was the usual, was it, Jackie?'

'I don't know what you mean.'

The detective's eyes closed briefly in an expression which told Jackie that Danny thought she was a lying bitch. 'It's only just come back to me, Jackie. Literally only last night, but I think I've put two and two together. When I turned up at your house, I wasn't really listening to the words of your ding-dong, but they must have sunk into my thick head.' She tapped her skull. 'And only now have they come out the other side.' Danny opened her shoulder bag and took out the scrap of paper she had written on in the early hours after that vivid dream. She glanced at Jackie, who looked very unhappy.

'Joe said, "I never touched her",' Danny read out. 'You said, "You did, you bastard. You had it off with her. She told me".'

Jackie stared past Danny's shoulders, her jaw set tight. Her eyes were moist. Danny was aware of the other woman tapping the floor with her feet.

' "I never, as God is my witness", or something like that, is what Joe then said. And you said, "You got into bed and . . ." ' Danny's voice swooped to a whisper, ' "fucked Julie". That's what I remember, Jackie. What was all that about?'

Jackie's head fell into her hands. A huge sob thudded through her body and Danny touched her shoulder. Then Jackie sat upright and wiped her face which was streaming with tears. 'Snot rag, I need a snot rag.' She patted her pockets desperately and stopped when Danny handed her a tissue. She blew her nose with a loud trumpeting sound and looked at Danny with a forlorn expression. 'Oh God – Jackie, Joe and Julie, the three J's . . . a perfect family by all accounts,' she spat bitterly. 'Money, businesses, big house, big bloody Jag and a father who couldn't keep his filthy rotten hands off his only daughter. She was ten years old when he did it to her and then denied it. That's what really split us up. I don't even need to start explaining why, do I?'

Danny shook her head.

'No bloody wonder Julie's own marriage is on the rocks. She's completely dysfunctional where sex is concerned, even though she's had two kids.'

'Did you have any proof about Joe?'

'Julie's word. A doctor's examination.'

'Why didn't you go to the police?'

Jackie stared contemptuously at Danny. 'Because I didn't trust you to do anything other than put Julie through hell – and she'd gone through enough already.'

Jackie's hands fumbled with her cigarette packet in an

302

attempt to get one out. Danny laid her hands over Jackie's and took the packet from her, tapping one out and handing it to her. Jackie lit it from the one she was already smoking.

'Thanks, Jackie. I'm sorry to have brought up such painful memories.'

'You haven't.' Jackie uttered a short laugh, a sardonic curl on her lips. 'It's with me every single day, every hour of every day and I can't shake it off. It will never leave me and I'm not sure I want it to, perverse as it may seem.'

Danny nodded, rose to leave.

Jackie reached out and grabbed her arm. 'There is one thing?'

'What's that?'

'Please don't approach Julie and ask her anything. She has to forget.'

'I won't,' Danny promised.

It was only a very short appearance at Blackpool Magistrates Court for Louis Vernon Trent. He was flanked by two large policemen, one of whom was handcuffed to him, the other standing slightly behind him in the dock, his hand rubbing the knob of his baton almost sensually, willing Trent to behave badly so he could whack him. As it was, Trent remained meek, mild and compliant.

There was no application for bail and Trent was remanded in custody to reappear before magistrates on the following Thursday.

Twenty minutes later he was in the back of a prison bus which turned out of the rear yard of Blackpool police station, only to be met by a crowd of jeering onlookers who pelted the vehicle with eggs and rotten tomatoes.

Henry Christie yawned and stretched. He had been chatting to the CPS solicitor who had handled the short hearing, but had now gone, leaving Henry alone in the court, which was now deserted.

Henry was pleased Trent had been boxed off. It took a lot of pressure off him, particularly from FB who seemed to relish giving Henry grief. Now, other than the paperwork side of things, Henry could concentrate on Claire Lilton's murder, which in a lot of respects was even more worrying than Trent's escapades.

At least they knew they had been after Trent.

Now they had another murderer on the loose who they did not have a clue about. It was going to be a tough one to solve and he had to get a squad up and running from nothing again and motivate them to success.

As he walked towards the court door, it swung open and a breathless DS Furness stood there.

'I've got something.'

'What? From this dream nonsense?' Henry laughed.

'Yes, from this dream nonsense.'

'Sit. Tell.' Henry waved to a seat at the back of the court. She did both.

When she'd concluded, she said, 'Well?'

Henry nodded slowly. 'Let's give it a run. Let's pull him in.'

They walked out of the court, across the mezzanine and into the door of the police station.

'Danny!'

She turned to the enquiry desk where the Public Enquiry Assistant was tapping on the toughened glass screen, beckoning Danny towards her. The woman pointed across the foyer to the waiting area. 'He wants to see you.'

Danny looked.

It was Joe Lilton.

Chapter Seventeen

It was with a great deal of pleasure that Danny 'laid hands' on Joe Lilton and arrested him on suspicion of murdering his stepdaughter. She cautioned him to the letter and he replied, 'I don't blame you for arresting me, but I didn't kill her; that's what I've come in here to clear up.'

Danny led him down to the custody office.

Henry came along for the ride, switching off his pager which was irritating the hell out of him by vibrating in his pocket. Downstairs he phoned comms and they passed a message to him to ring Karl Donaldson at the FBI office in London.

A call that would have to wait.

Danny presented Joe Lilton to the custody officer who went through the computerised booking-in system which automatically checked all incoming prisoners on the PNC. No previous convictions were thrown up for Lilton, but reference was made to his firearms certificate. He still held one. The custody officer pointed this out to Danny, who said, 'I know.'

They went through the full kit and caboodle with Lilton.

His clothing was seized and bagged up for forensic; swabs and hair were taken for DNA sampling. He was given a paper suit and slippers, then Danny booked out a set of tapes and she and Henry took him to an interview room.

He had indicated he did not wish to have a solicitor present.

As they left the custody office, there was the sound of an incredible ruckus from outside in the yard. Three police officers were fighting a young girl who was going berserk, scratching, spitting, kicking, screaming.

Henry caught sight of the rumpus as it tumbled through the custody office door. He gave a short laugh before following Danny down to the interview room.

'What's going on, Karl?' Myrna demanded to know.

'I've done what I can – left a message for the guy I know in Lancashire to contact me. I can only wait for his call, Myrna.'

'Yeah, sure, you're right. Ring me as soon as you hear something, okay?'

'I will, Myrna, promise.'

'Promise?'

'Promise.'

She hung up and looked across the room at Tracey, still sleeping and twitching. Myrna folded her arms on the desk, laid her head on them, closed her eyes.

'I want to get this straight from the word go: I did *not* kill her. No way are you going to pin that on me.'

'Why are you here, then?' Danny's tongue flicked her bottom lip as she regarded the man sat opposite her in the paper suit. She hoped she was keeping a sneer off her face; probably it was a forlorn hope. Danny detested everything about Joe Lilton from the colour of his eyes to the fact he breathed the same air as she did.

'Because of what you said the other day, and that I know you lot will get round to me sooner or later.' He shrugged. 'I mean, you always pick on the father or stepfather, don't you? First port of call, usually.'

'That's because they've usually done it, Joe,' Henry observed.

Lilton raised his face towards Henry in a challenging manner. 'Not in this case.' His voice was hoarse.

'What did I say the other day, Joe – to make you come in?' Danny asked.

'It was when you were talking about how the investigation was going and you mentioned DNA.'

'Go on,' Danny encouraged him.

'Is it right that if you get DNA samples you can match them up to offenders?'

'It's very true.'

'How, like, accurate is it?'

'Foolproof,' Henry said.

Joe's head dropped. He studied his thumbs as they circled each other.

'For example, Joe,' Henry began, 'in the case of Claire, she had semen inside her that is estimated to be four days old. It's a piece of piss to match that up with a suspect. It's also piss-easy to prove that someone ISN'T involved.'

Joe's cranium remained pointing towards the detectives.

'So, Joe,' Danny sighed, 'why *have* you come here?'

Joe looked at her. 'You fucking know, don't you? You fucking know you bitch, don't you?' He jabbed a finger at her. 'You fucking know why I'm here.'

Danny remained impassive as the end of his finger hovered near the tip of her nose; she willed him to hit her. Instead he sat slowly back, dropped his head into his hands and sobbed.

'I didn't kill her. You've got to believe me,' he slavered through his fingers.

'What did you do?'

Joe looked up again. 'Made love to her.'

Danny seethed. It was the second time a child-molester had referred to making love to his victims. 'You made love to her?' she demanded with a snarl.

'Yeah, she was willing.'

307

'She was eleven years old,' Henry pointed out. He too was holding himself back from pitching over the table to strangle the bastard.

'You put your penis into her vagina and you ejaculated. Is that what you're trying to say, Joe?' Danny persisted.

'God, you make it sound so clinical,' he snapped. 'It was nothing like that.'

'What exactly was it like, Joe? Eh? Screwing your eleven-year-old stepdaughter? Go on, did the earth move? Was it all passion? Do you expect us to believe this shite?' Danny's voice was rising uncontrollably, particularly as she remembered Claire's face when she drove her back home that day of the storm, back to a home where she was suffering abuse of the worst kind. That look on her face . . . 'You screwed your daughter, for God's sake! A forty-four-year-old man, screwing his eleven-year-old daughter. That is not making love, as you so eloquently put it. It's a serious criminal and moral matter, not a moment of passion between consenting adults.' Danny stood up, pushed herself away from the table and walked to the corner of the room.

'DS Furness has stood up and walked across the interview room, away from the suspect, Lilton,' Henry said for the benefit of the tape.

'But I didn't kill her. That's the bottom line.'

Henry spoke into the microphone in a steady tone. 'I suggest, Mr Lilton, you take on the services of a solicitor. I feel it is inappropriate for this interview to proceed without one being present.' Henry concluded the interview as per the Codes of Practice, sealed one of the tapes and got Joe to sign across the seal.

Danny remained tucked away in one corner, arms folded, head down, silently scuffing a shoe across the carpet.

Without warning, Henry's hand shot out and grabbed Joe Lilton's throat. He heaved the man to his feet, sending the chair underneath him spinning across the room with a clatter. He shoved Lilton into the wall, on which his head smacked hollowly. Lilton had fear flittering in his eyes. Henry's face was only inches away from Lilton's.

'You are a fucking pervert,' he growled at the man. 'In the past you would've been bounced around the cells and sometimes, just sometimes, I hanker for the good old days, Joe, because more than anything, I want to beat you to an inch of your life – and then kick you some more – whether or not you killed Claire.'

He released Joe with an exaggerated flick of the fingers, like he was dropping something horrible. Then, grabbing Joe's arm, he said, 'Come on, let's go and see the Custody Officer.'

'There was no need to do that, Henry.' Danny's voice was strained. She was sitting on the examination couch in the police surgeon's room in the custody complex, her feet swinging. Lilton was in a cell, awaiting his brief.

'Yeah,' he conceded, slightly embarrassed. 'I suffer from the "red mist" syndrome occasionally. It gets me into trouble now and then.'

'He's not worth it.'

'Hey, okay, nuff said.' Henry held up his hands in surrender.

Danny looked down at the floor and suddenly it came out. 'I saw her face, Claire's face, the expression on it,' she choked, 'and it's only now I realise what it meant, and I made her go back home and it was obvious to anyone with half a brain she had good reason not to want to go back.' A torrent of tears welled up and flooded over the edge. Her face rose pleadingly to Henry. He crossed to her. She slid off the couch and her arms went round him. 'Her dad was sexually assaulting her. No wonder she went off the rails . . . and I didn't spot it. Someone with my experience – I must be thick as a brick. And she even came in twice to see me, but didn't have the courage to

309

stay and speak. And what did I do? Nothing. I deserve to lose my job for this.'

'No.' Henry held Danny at arm's length so he could see her. 'You cannot blame yourself for this. Every cop in the world would go bananas if they blamed themselves for things going wrong in other people's lives.'

She closed her eyes sadly and wiped away her tears with a flourish of both hands. 'Yeah, right,' she muttered. 'What are we going to do about Joe Lilton?'

'Do you think he killed her?'

Danny shook her head. 'No, I don't.'

'Let's interview him with a solicitor, then bail him to come back here in a week. We'll probably have a better picture of things by then. What about Mrs Lilton? Should we arrest her too?'

'I don't think she will be involved, but I suppose we need to speak to her at some stage.'

The door swished open. It was the Custody Sergeant. 'Henry, Danny, need to have a quick word.'

The detectives exchanged a glance, both thinking the same thing: Joe Lilton had made a complaint of assault against Henry.

Both were wrong.

Myrna stirred. Her head was still resting on her forearms. She was stiff and aching. For a few moments she did not move, keeping her eyes closed and breathing in deeply through her nostrils. She sat up and stretched the feeling back into her blood-starved limbs. The crinkle of pins and needles was painful and pleasurable at the same time. She rolled her neck and winced as her back muscles protested.

The clock on her desk told her that ninety minutes had passed since her last phone call to Karl Donaldson in London. Dawn had already revealed itself across Miami; soon the office cleaners would be in, followed shortly by the more enthusiastic workers amongst the staff.

310

She rubbed her eyes, cleared her throat and glanced across to Tracey.

'Holy shit!' were the first words Myrna uttered.

The girl had disappeared.

The custody officer pulled the custody record out of its plastic wallet.

'We don't know who she is – she won't tell us,' he said to Danny and Henry, 'but she's about eleven or twelve; she's as pissed as a rat, glued up to the eyeballs, as violent as any girl that age can be and basically a real bitch to deal with. I gave her a drink of tea which she promptly threw all over me. Luckily most of it missed; now she's stripped herself stark naked and is prancing about in the buff in a juvenile detention room, having urinated and then shat in one corner. She's now smeared excreta all over the walls.' He raised his nose. 'Can you smell it?'

Henry inhaled. 'Ahhh, yes, the smell of shite.' He smiled empathetically at the Sergeant; Henry was pleased to announce that his spell as a custody officer had been brief but horrible, done a short time after his promotion to uniform Sergeant, somewhere in the dim, distant past. The role was unenviable, having to be a kind of unloved intermediary between the investigating officers and the prisoners. Always a no-win situation. It was a job Henry had quite happily left behind.

'So it's a crap job you've got,' said Henry. 'What's it got to do with me?'

'It's probably all balls, I suppose, but she said she knew who killed Claire Lilton, but she wasn't going to tell us – then she stuck two fingers up at me and lobbed a turd in my general direction. I'm getting too old for this,' he whined, rubbing his neck. He was twenty-seven. 'Just thought you'd like to know, that's all. Take it or leave it.'

'Nothing lost having a word, is there?' Danny said.

Myrna shot out of her chair and crossed quickly to the

restroom. Tracey was not there. She began a systematic walk through the offices of Kruger Investigations. Ten minutes later she returned to her office, pretty certain Tracey had gone. She sat down heavily and reached for the phone to call night security down at the front entrance. As her hand drew the receiver to her ear, she noticed her purse was open. With a curse playing on her lips, she grabbed the black bag and rummaged through it.

Tracey had beaten her to it.

She had been cleaned out.

Juveniles are not detained in normal cells, but in juvenile detention rooms which, instead of cell doors, have thick wooden ones with toughened glass windows. There are no toilets in such rooms and every time the occupant wishes to pay a visit, they have to ring the bell. Henry hated dealing with kids. Give him a hardened professional criminal any day. Much simpler.

He and Danny stood outside the DR and tried to peer through the layer of faeces the young lady had smeared over the window. They could just see her, sitting cross-legged on the floor, naked, singing at the top of her voice, then shouting obscenities between verses. They could smell her very well.

The cell was covered in it and so was she.

Danny turned to the custody Sergeant. 'Why was she arrested anyway?'

'A nothing of a job really. Caught shoplifting in W H Smiths. The store detective chased her, she ran away down the Prom and she kicked off when she was collared. She gave the store detective a real shiner, I'm told. Took three bobbies to bring her in.'

'And we don't know who she is, yet?'

'No.'

'Yes, we do,' came a triumphant voice, interrupting the Sergeant's reply. It was one of the arresting officers. 'Been leafing through the Missing from Home reports, just in case – and *voilà*!' He flapped a message switch. 'I think it's this girl.'

'Well done,' the Sergeant commented.

'What's your plan of action?' Danny asked.

'Hm . . . got to get her cleaned up before we do anything with her. Going to have to get a couple of policewomen into overalls, drag her out and dump her under a shower. This DR'll have to be steam-cleaned now – little madam. Danny?' He looked questioningly at the DS. 'Don't suppose you'd be interested in grabbing a pair of overalls and helping out?' It was a fairly rhetorical question. 'No, supposed not.'

'We'll come back and speak to her when she's clean – and sober,' Henry said.

The custody officer looked severely miffed at the problem. Bloody kids, he thought. Should be shot at birth.

'Just got off speaking to the States again. A woman named Myrna Rosza, remember? She was the one who originated the information on Charlie Gilbert.'

'Yeah, I remember.' Henry had the phone cradled between his ear and shoulder, sipping a cup of tea, dunking a ginger biscuit at the same time, saturating it to the point of near-disintegration before dropping it skilfully into his open mouth. Gorgeous.

'Done anything with that yet?'

'No,' he mumbled. 'Filed for the moment. Too busy with other things.' He reached for another biscuit and dunked it.

Karl explained the phone call he'd had from Myrna.

'Sounds very interesting,' Henry commented. 'Why does she want to speak to Danny Furness?'

'Dunno, but that was the gist of the message; she's supposedly a witness to that murder and she'll only talk to this Furness guy.'

'This Furness guy happens to be a girl, actually.'

'So be it.' Donaldson took a breath. 'But having said all

313

that, there's a bit of a sorry twist in the tail. The girl has now disappeared.'

'Oh, that's handy. What do you reckon to the story anyway?'

'Myrna is ex-FBI, very bright, don't take no shit, and wouldn't bother me if she didn't think it was worthwhile. I think the girl is genuine.'

'But she's done a bunk?'

'As you say – done a bunk.'

'I'll speak to Danny Furness for a start, Karl.'

'You know him – her?'

'Yes. I'll see what she knows about this girl, if anything. Let us know if she turns up again. I don't really see us getting too excited until then. At the same time I'll liaise with the murder team over in Darwen and let them know what's happening – oh shit! Sorry, Karl. Just had an accident here.'

Henry had misjudged his timing and whilst in mid-air, on the journey from cup to lip, his ginger biscuit disintegrated all over his shirt and tie.

There was, undeniably, the smell of shit in the air: disinfectant, cheap soap and shit.

Danny's nostrils dilated as she sat down opposite the girl. A woman from the social services sat next to the girl, a stern look on her face. Her nose twitched.

The girl slumped in the plastic chair, a sneer slashed across her face, contempt oozing from every pore in her body. The white zoot suit was far too large for her, made her look stupid and vulnerable.

She peered closely at the girl's face and saw the redness around her nostrils and top lip, symptoms associated with glue-sniffing. Danny's eyes looked into the girl's which were wild, pupils still dilated. Danny speculated how far gone she was, whether it was recoverable or had her brain and vital organs been irreparably damaged by the fumes.

Danny pitied her. She made a note to get the police surgeon to check her out.

'How're you feeling?'

Sullen, no response. Expected.

'You've cleaned up quite nicely.'

She shook her head sadly as though this was all crap and she did not need to be here. Her eyes – dilated, watery – showed nothing but hatred for Danny.

Danny inspected the faxes in front of her. A Missing from Home report from the police in Huddersfield told her the girl was called Grace Lawson, that she was eleven years old and had been missing from a children's home for three months. It was a long time, but not unusual, particularly for kids who could fend for themselves.

'What're you doing in Blackpool, Grace?' Not that Danny needed an answer. Second to London, Blackpool, during summer months, was a Mecca for kids on the run. The girl's eyes flickered.

'Yeah, that's right. We know who you are.'

She sighed disdainfully and raised her eyebrows.

'Cat got your tongue? Not talking will do you no good at all.'

'Oh, just fuck off, bitch.'

Water off a duck's back. 'What are you doing here in Blackpool? How long have you been here and who have you been with?'

Grace closed her eyes, opened them slowly. Defiance.

'Earlier today you were caught shoplifting in Smiths. You assaulted the store detective, then hit three police officers.'

A smile now, pleasure and remembrance.

'You think it's funny?'

'Yeah, very fuckin' funny.'

'Is that because your brain's rotted with glue? Does that make you see things differently? Can you see anything at all?'

315

Grace leaned on the table. 'I can see an old bitch whose mouth is opening and closing and spewing shite. That's what I can see.'

Danny grinned, thought, *less of the 'old'*. 'You've been on the run a long time,' she said aloud. 'Three months. How have you survived?'

'Easy – when you've got a cunt.'

Danny flinched inwardly. Outwardly she did not blink or show shock. The social worker blanched, her tight lips parting in shock.

'And that's how you've survived?'

'Hand jobs, blow jobs, fucks. Yeah, you name 'em. The cash keeps rollin' in.'

'You know what sexual intercourse is then?'

Grace grunted in amusement.

'And shoplifting?'

'Bit of that, sure.'

'Who puts a roof over your head?'

'None of your business, Mrs Busybody, nosy-cow bitch,' she spat, sat back and folded her arms.

'How do you know Claire Lilton?'

'Who?' Her face curled up. Danny repeated the name. 'I don't.'

'You mentioned her name when you were brought in here.'

'I probably mentioned Robbie Williams too. But I don't know him.'

'You're a smartarse, aren't you?'

'I could outwit you any day of the week.'

Danny paused, leaned back and eyed Grace, not surprised by the responses she was getting. She'd had worse from eight-year-olds. There was quiet in the room and the slightly metallic hiss of the tape spools rotating could be heard.

'Let me tell you a story, Grace. It's about a little girl very much like you.'

'I'm not little!' She was affronted by the insinuation.

'Oh yes, you are. Little in every sense. Body, mind, brain, intellect. You only think you're big. You talk big words. You do big girl things. But underneath you're a little kid. A child. Nothing more than a child. I'll bet you still have a teddy, don't you?'

Grace swallowed. She blushed.

'Do you hold it every night? I'll bet you do. Anyway, I was telling you a story. Just a short story, because it's about a little girl like you. Same age, same height, same braveness . . . and she went missing from home, but she didn't last three months or even three days, because I found her strangled to death.'

Grace was listening, riveted.

'Ever wonder what it's like to be strangled? No air. Can't breathe—'

'I say, is this really necessary?' the social worker interrupted. Danny fired her a look which had the effect of clamping the woman's mouth up. Grace was transfixed by Danny.

'Squirming, trying to get away, being held down, throttled, maybe even more than one person doing it . . . screaming, a hand over your mouth and nose so you won't make a noise and that rope tightening around your neck, tighter and tighter and your tongue grows in the back of your throat and your eyes bulge because they feel like they're going to pop out . . .'

'Don't!' Grace screamed, covering her ears. She started to sob all the way up from her guts, almost retching, then she vomited all over the table, over the tape deck, then jerking her head and covering the lap of the social worked. Danny saw it coming. She moved in time.

Grace choked, bent double, head between her legs, spitting out the last of her stomach contents.

Danny walked round the table and laid a hand on the back of her head. 'There, there,' she muttered softly. 'Everything'll be all right, Grace, but you need to tell me about yourself, don't you? Then tell me about Claire

Lilton, because you know about her, don't you? You know who killed her, don't you?'

'Yeah . . .' she gasped.

'Who?'

'Charlie and Ollie.'

Same old story, Danny thought whilst listening – in a different, vomit-free interview room – to Grace. Abused by a succession of 'uncles' (her mother's lovers), social services become involved, goes into care from the age of seven; the short forays home result in more abuse; behaviour worsens, the homes become more secure, better supervised. Ends up in one, aged ten, abused by the staff and the older kids . . . it becomes part of a dark life, part of her day-to-day existence. She runs, returns, runs some more, but this time vows not to return. Blackpool sounds good. She's been there on several day trips. Lots of life, sounds and people. And that's where she ended up. Sleeping rough, cruising the arcades, stealing food . . . and then being spotted and watched, eventually approached. A meal provided. A bath. Somewhere comfy to sleep. Some cash. Build up trust, something which didn't take too long, and then she was hooked . . . and introduced to the man who had done her so much good; it was no surprise when his cock came out and it tasted like all the others had done, felt like all the others had done. And soon she was on the lookout for him – other vulnerables, mispers, day-trippers even – bring them in, make promises . . . but something horrible happened to one of them. Her name had been Claire. She didn't want it, didn't want the sex, not for anything. She fought and was subdued. Fought again, subdued even more and then she was dead.

And now something else: Danny was being nice to her and getting something from Grace, something for nothing.

Cleaned up, but smelling of sick, the social worker listened in silence.

318

Danny coaxed, reassured, probed as she pulled out a tangled web of emotion, fear, hatred and a million other things because this was the first time Grace had ever talked. Danny had to deal with all the excess baggage. That was the way it had to be, like plaiting fog, as they say. Only then, when it had all been faced and talked through, could the questions begin to flow, slowly at first, about Claire Lilton.

And yes, Danny had to admit, she was not really interested in Grace's story. All that was blind alleys. She wanted to hear about Claire Lilton.

Grace talked for three hours.

Every single operational operative from Kruger Investigations was out on the bricks searching for Tracey. Photos in hand, descending on as many likely places as they could think of.

Myrna, meanwhile, was on to Mark Tapperman.

Under pressure he refused to yield. 'No, I cannot spare any of my officers to go looking for a reluctant witness who's probably regaled you with the most bullshit you've ever heard, just for a bed for the night and the opportunity to steal from your purse. And it worked!'

Myrna silently mouthed numerous cuss-words at him from her end of the phone.

'And it's a godamned good job we don't have video conferencing otherwise I'd be able to see your lips bad-mouthin' me,' Tapperman laughed.

'How in hell . . .?'

'I'm a cop. People are always cussin' me silently down the phone. Hey, look, Myrna, sorry, but we can't afford the manpower. Tell you what I will do – I'll get a radio message out to all mobiles, ask 'em to keep their eyes peeled, okay? That's all I can do. We're chasin' our tails here.'

'Fine, thanks,' Myrna conceded. 'Any progress on Steve's killer?'

'Patrick Orlove? No, nothing. We're trying our best.'

'I believe you.' She hung up.

'He calls me his little honey pot, but I don't really know why. Because I'm sweet, I suppose.' Grace managed a weak smile. The effort of self-revelation had taken everything out of the little girl. All her own important stuff had been about herself, not Claire; her past, present and unspeakable future. 'I met Claire in one of the arcades and I could tell she were alone, like. I talked to her and said I could get her somewhere to sleep for the night. I took her to see Ollie and he give her a couple of quid for some chips an' me an' her went for some an' came back when the arcade had closed. We got into Ollie's car and he drove us to his flat an' Charlie were there waitin' for us. I got pissed on wine – I like wine. Claire had a bit to drink and she got smashed easy, like. Then Ollie asked me to give him a suck an' he got it out an' I started. I had to close me eyes 'cos I don't really like lookin' at it and the wine takes the taste off.

'While I were doin' this,' she went on, 'Charlie took Claire out the room and into the bedroom. Going for a shag. Everythin' were all right and Ollie'd cum in me mouth an' he made me swallow it an' then all hell broke loose. There's a loada shoutin' an' screamin' from the bedroom and Claire ran out . . . she had no clothes on and Charlie were chasing her. He were fuckin' angry. He grabbed her and thumped her in the face and sez to Ollie, "Come an' 'elp me with the little bitch." They both grabbed her then an' dragged her back into the bedroom an' slammed the door behind 'em. Well, the door don't close proper and it just sorta bounced open a bit an' I sneaked a look.' Tears welled up in Grace's eyes.

'Go on,' Danny said gently.

'I were frightened. Claire were strugglin' an' fightin'. They were both holdin' her down and Charlie was trying to get his dick in her, but she were really fighting and kickin' and they were gettin' really mad. Charlie had a rope or somethin' round her neck, pullin' tight an' next thing Claire weren't moving at all.'

She fell silent.

Danny touched Grace's trembling fingers.

The social worker was white.

'They said she were all reet, just sleepin'. I could see she wasn't. They'd been smashing her in the face too and it were a real mess. I've never seen a dead person before. It were 'orrible . . . I can still see her now.'

'What happened then?'

'They carried her into the shower and washed her, I think. They told me not to look. I just ran out and glued meself up . . . I haven't been back.'

'Who were the two men?'

'Like I said. Charlie and Ollie.'

'Do you know their last names?'

'Charlie Gilbert. Ollie Spencer.'

'What do Charlie Gilbert and Ollie Spencer have in common?' Henry Christie pondered out loud. He knew Gilbert was one of the most respected figures on the Fylde, and Spencer was a purveyor of porn and perversion across the Northwest. 'Other than their sexual interests, that is.'

'The fact is, they are together and I want to go and arrest both for murder,' Danny stated categorically. She could hardly contain herself after listening to Grace's story and recording the subsequent statement. Grace was still in the police station, being held on the assault and shoplifting charges whilst a decision was made about what to do with her. In many ways it was out of the hands of the police. She had to be handed over to Social Services for safekeeping – not something either Henry or Danny was happy with. They would rather have kept her under lock and key.

They were in the incident room at Blackpool police

station, scrumming down with FB and other members of the murder squad.

'Just hold your horses,' FB said impatiently. His jacket and tie were off. He paced the room, taking up the tension more degrees than necessary. 'Tell me where we're up to exactly.'

He looked at Henry, who, never afraid of delegation and empowerment, looked in turn at Danny.

She cleared her throat.

'Okay, we've boxed off Trent. He's out of the picture, back on remand next Thursday, charged with numerous serious offences. If he ever sets foot out of prison again, it should only be in a pine box.

'Claire Lilton: missing from home. Turns up murdered, and initially we think it's down to Trent, but it doesn't quite match his murder MO – the knife. So we agree we have a problem – another child-killer on the loose. Then Grace Lawson turns up, a witness from nowhere, also a misper, eleven years old who says she saw Claire get murdered by Ollie Spencer and Charlie Gilbert. Describes the whole event in gory detail and it matches everything we know medically and forensically about Claire's death.'

'Thanks – very succinct,' FB said. 'Anything else?'

'Yes. Claire had four-day-old sperm in her. Her stepfather gave himself up and admitted having sexual relations with her. We've DNA'd him and at present he's on bail, returning here in a week's time. We're pretty sure he didn't kill her, but we are going to fettle him good and proper. Unfortunately there are no further forensics or DNA; as Grace told us, Gilbert and Spencer washed her body off. They were very thorough.'

'Do we know where the crime took place?' FB asked.

Danny nodded. 'Spencer's flat.'

'In that case we need to hit it quick and go for bedsheets, et cetera, et cetera, down the plughole – everything,' FB decided. 'Let's just see how thorough they've really been. Anything else?'

'Yep,' said Henry, 'and it concerns Gilbert, bastion of society. It's an American angle. Remember Karl Donaldson?' Henry raised his eyebrows at FB, whose face went sour at the mention of the FBI operative. FB and Donaldson had a history and did not match well. 'Gilbert was recently arrested in Miami on child-molestation allegations and released without charge. Seems he's involved with some American gangster called Bussola, very big crimewise in Florida. His legal business side includes amusement arcades, where it's believed he deals drugs. The amusement side is probably where Bussola's connection with Gilbert comes in, a man who made most of his fortune from kids' pennies. Gilbert apparently buys Bussola's arcade cast-offs. That's how they know each other, I believe.'

'Where's this leading, Henry?' FB asked impatiently.

Henry did all but ignore him. Their history gave Henry some rights not normally available to Detective Inspectors. 'The dead girl found over in Darwen, actually: the five-year-old murder. Don't ask me how – I'm sure it'll come out in the wash – but a girl over in the States read about the murder and came forward to say she knew who'd done it . . .' he paused for effect '. . . Charlie Gilbert. Then she clammed up and said nothing else, except, and this is the killer' – his eyes turned to Danny – 'that she'll only talk to Danny, who she met some years ago. The girl is a Brit, working over in the States.'

'She'll only speak to me?' Danny was puzzled. 'What's her name?'

'Tracey Greenwood. Ring a bell?'

'Not offhand.'

'She also insisted on something else too – that Danny goes to the States and brings her back to England and she'll give evidence against Gilbert. But only Danny.'

'Out of the question,' said FB. 'She's pulling a fast one for some reason.'

'There is another thing too.' Henry pulled a face. 'She's done a runner.'

'They've lost her?' FB said incredulously. 'Typical bloody Donaldson.'

'So I'm waiting to hear,' Henry said.

'Okay, thanks, Henry. We'll see what comes of it – if anything. But for the moment, let's concentrate on the here and now – Gilbert and Spencer.' He looked squarely at Danny. 'Go get 'em.'

Chapter Eighteen

They had to do it right and they needed the manpower to get it right.

FB, unusually magnanimous, gave the go-ahead.

First up, the Surveillance Unit were hurriedly called in and briefed by Danny: their task to pinpoint the suspects, keep them in sight and report their whereabouts.

Secondly, the Support Unit were roused and, again, briefed by Danny. Their job was to follow arrest teams in and, under the instructions of a team leader, to search, seize and secure evidence. That meant at Spencer's place the bedclothes, the sink, the drains, the shower – anything which could be useful for forensics and could link Claire Lilton with the address.

Then there would be a forensic and Scenes of Crime team behind them, supporting and bagging any evidence for further examination.

It had been decided that Danny would lead one arrest team, Henry the other. They would hit both men simultaneously and bring them to Blackpool nick. One at a time. Ensure no contact – eyeball, verbal, physical, whatever, their cells were to be at opposite ends of the complex so they would not be able to even shout to each other.

Once both men were incarcerated, given their rights and everything else they had to be given, Danny would lead the interview teams whilst Henry took a step backwards to supervise the process.

They tossed up to see who would arrest whom.

Henry flicked the 2p piece with his thumb. 'Heads I take Gilbert, tails you take him.' Both wanted him badly.

The coin rolled up through the air, slow motion almost.

Danny prayed: Let it be tails.

Henry moved out of the way of the falling coin. It clattered on the floor.

Danny smiled grimly.

Four hours later and Myrna had heard nothing. She helped herself to a strong black coffee from the machine in the main office and stared through the window across the cityscape, a vacant look in her eyes but her mind churning angrily because she felt such a fool on two counts.

One, she had been used by Tracey, the little bitch.

Two, Karl Donaldson must have thought she was an annoying little tick who could not do anything right.

Damn the girl.

The two detectives waited patiently as the Surveillance Unit coasted into action. There was nothing to do now but be patient.

'How's things on the Jack Sands front?' Henry asked conversationally.

Danny's skin crept at the mention of the name. 'Okay. No hassle. Haven't seen him, actually. How about you?'

'Me neither. Seems to be keeping a low profile.'

'Think he's got the message?'

Henry shrugged. 'Don't know. He's not thick, but he's stubborn.'

A personal radio stood on its base on Henry's desk, tuned into the encrypted channel dedicated to the arrest operation. It crackled. A message passed from one member of the Surveillance Unit to another. It was nothing for Henry or Danny or the arrest teams, who were biding their time by playing snooker upstairs in the recreation room.

Danny's heart jumped, but she remained calm.

Soon, she thought. *Soon*.

'Any progress?'

'Zilch.'

'Not to worry,' Karl Donaldson said reassuringly. 'She'll turn up.'

'Yeah, yeah, sure,' Myrna moaned. 'Look, I'm really sorry if I've caused any problems over there. She was right here when I spoke to you.' Myrna gestured to the empty seat in her office as though Donaldson could see. 'Then I dozed off and when I woke, she'd skedaddled.'

'Just keep me posted.'

'Yeah. Hey, Karl, thanks for phoning. I've felt such a barf.'

'Forget it.'

'Got him! Target Two in sight, walking down the Promenade. Dressed in a pale blue suit. Grey shoes. Completely un-fucking-mistakable. Stands out like a prick in a nursery.'

Danny grabbed the radio before Henry could.

'Good job. But remember there's more than just you and your team listening, so maintain strict radio discipline. Received?'

'Roger,' grunted the glum reply, knuckles rapped.

'Whereabouts on the Prom?' Danny asked.

'Just outside Tussaud's, walking north. There's a two-man follow behind him now on foot. We've got him. He's not going anywhere without us knowing, especially in that suit.'

'Keep us informed.'

Henry gestured for the radio.

'Arrest squad two,' he transmitted over it. 'CID office, two minutes, ready to roll, please.'

'Already there, boss,' came the reply.

'I'll see you later.' Henry pointed at Danny, stood up, and clicked his thumb.

'Henry?' She rose slowly and looked at him.

Another of those stomach-churning, 'Do we? Don't we?' moments flipped between them. Both caught it, both held back. Instead, Henry squeezed her hand and less than romantically said, 'Next time I see you, make sure it's in the custody office.' It was probably destined to be one of the great romantic lines of all times. They laughed, parted and Henry was gone.

The Promenade was bitter cold, the usual icy wind driving in from the Irish Sea. Henry danced a jig and rubbed his hands to keep warm. His jacket collar was turned up high around his ears, his shoulders hunched low. He was near the entrance to North Pier, looking across the wide Prom towards a row of amusement arcades on the opposite side of the road, just south of the junction with Talbot Square. He was chatting to a member of the Surveillance Unit.

Ollie Spencer – Target Two – had been seen to enter 'Ollie's Amusements' and go into the back room of the arcade. As arcades went in Blackpool, it was one of the less salubrious ones, fairly grotty, but still able to attract the penny-droppers. From the short opportunity Henry had had to do some research into Charlie Gilbert, he knew the fat man owned this business.

The front and rear of the arcade were covered by the surveillance team. At any one time, using a tried and tested rotation system, there could be up to three members of the team in the premises, playing the bandits and video games. All on expenses, of course.

Once Henry had been briefed as to the situation, he walked back to his car parked a safe distance away. A member of his arrest team was driving for him.

The surveillance officer he had been talking to rejoined his team.

Henry crashed back into the passenger seat and smiled at his companion, a Detective Constable named Dave

Seymour. Henry turned up the heater and said, 'We wait.'

Seymour nodded. Waiting suited him. He didn't like moving unless absolutely necessary.

The other members of the arrest team – two uniformed officers driving an unmarked police car – were parked nearby.

'He's coming out of his office now,' a voice came over the radio. 'Leaving via the rear door. Get ready guys, 'n' gals, he'll be with you in fifteen seconds.'

There was a silent delay on the airwaves. It seemed interminable.

'Got him,' came the next voice eventually, 'heading towards Talbot Square.'

Henry breathed out, not realising he had been holding his breath in the first place.

They followed him unobtrusively, sometimes even brushing past him, even actually making eye-contact with him on occasion. So Spencer actually saw members of the surveillance team, yet never once suspected remotely they were cops and he was being tailed.

'Up Talbot Road, away from the Prom.'

'He's going to take them to his flat,' Henry mused out loud. Where, if their information was correct, Claire had been murdered.

'Turning left onto Dickson Road.'

Henry looked at Seymour. Yes, Ollie Spencer was taking them home.

The other surveillance team were not having quite the same measure of success. The whereabouts of Target One, Charlie Gilbert, eluded them. They set up an ob-point near his house in Poulton-le-Fylde, but no one was home. Another ob-point was at his usual place of work – a grand, restored building, formerly a warehouse of some sort which had been refurbished as offices and storage facilities. But Gilbert could have been anywhere. He owned a chain of arcades down the Golden Mile on the sea-front, restaurants, cafés, shops selling cheap tack; and not only in Blackpool. There probably wasn't one large town in the Northwest of England which did not have one of Gilbert's arcades in it. They were everywhere. His other recent business moves included out-of-town developments where, several years before, he had bought cheap land and then as the out-of-town shopping boom burst open, he began to develop the land, making vast amounts of money in the process.

In Henry's office, Danny grew impatient, wanting to get going. She tapped her teeth with the tip of her pen as she listened to the movements of the team tracking Spencer.

Her PR crackled. 'Target Two now entering the flat above the electrical goods shop.' She heard Henry acknowledge this piece of information. Then: 'Unit One interrupting!'

Whoa! Danny's heart quickened.

'Target One's vehicle now pulling into the driveway of his home. DS Furness received?'

She jumped for the radio. 'Sit on him, don't let him see you and wait for support . . . Arrest Squad One, meet me down in the garage.' She spun out of the office into the corridor and collided, body to body, face to face, with Jack Sands.

She tried to heave him out of the way.

He took hold of her, his big powerful arms circling her body, and he literally carried her back into Henry's office, slamming the door behind him with his heel. Danny squirmed and wriggled herself out of his grasp.

'I haven't got time for this shit, Jack,' she snarled angrily. 'Just get out of the way.'

His tongue ran along the inside of his lower lip, like a reptile was slithering about in his mouth. 'You think you're so fucking smart, don't you?'

'Jack, I need to get out fast. I've got important work on. Please.'

'That's exactly what I mean. You think you're some high-fuckin'-falutin' detective now, working on some very important cases.' He mimicked Danny with these last three words, shaking his head and sounding like some kind of Hooray Henry. 'But you're not.' He poked his finger right in the middle of her cleavage so forcefully she staggered backwards against the desk, holding it for support. 'You're just a fuckin' no-good bitch that doesn't know anything except what I've taught her, and what have you done to me? Eh? Dumped me – like that.' He clicked his fingers with a snap and a jab forward of his face.

'Let me go, Jack.'

She pushed herself away from the desk and tried to walk round him. He took hold of her again and pulled her to him.

'No – I won't let you go. Ever. I love you. Don't you see what you're doing to me?'

Her eyes softened for a moment. Jack released some of the power of his grip, giving her space to manoeuvre. Just enough room to twist slightly and, once again, drive her knee up into his testicles.

He roared in agony, released her, doubled up in pain, and reeled away, clutching his privates, cursing and swearing. His eyeballs were ready to pop out.

Danny left him hobbling around the office, no backward glance.

Fifteen minutes later.

'In position,' Danny transmitted.

'Received.' Henry acknowledged Danny's radio message. This meant everyone was ready to roll – the initial arrest teams, backed up by the evidence-gatherers.

Henry breathed deep. 'Let's hit 'em,' he said, his mouth dry in anticipation.

When the 'Roger' came from Danny, he opened his car door and moved.

Gilbert's house had a huge sweeping driveway, the house itself set in two and a half acres of landscaped gardens. There were wrought-iron gates at the entrance to the drive, but they were open. A convoy, led by Danny and her arrest squad, drove at a sedate pace and stopped outside the front door of the house.

Danny rang the bell. She had decided this arrest was going to be made in a dignified, adult manner . . . at least, that's how it would start out. This approach didn't stop her sending two cops around the back of the house to ensure there was no chance of a back-door dash.

Gilbert came to the door. Danny had never been close to the guy before, but had seen photos of him. She was astounded – and repulsed – by his enormity. He was like an overweight walrus, with broken capillaries all over his face, tiny piggy eyes and a girth which needed a chalk-mark to measure it. He was so hideous she almost giggled.

'Detective Sergeant Furness, Blackpool CID.' She wafted her warrant card and badge under his nose. 'Are you Charles Gilbert?'

He nodded, perplexed.

'I'm arresting you on suspicion of the murder of Claire Lilton.' Danny cautioned him and waited for his reply.

He blinked rapidly a few times. Then, patronisingly, said, 'Dearie, you are making one hell of a mistake here. Do you know who I am?'

'I know exactly who you are, Mr Gilbert.' Danny smiled sweetly and waved the search team into the house.

'What the hell's going on here?' Gilbert demanded. He moved his bulk and wedged himself into the doorway. 'You're not coming in here. Where's your warrant?'

Danny regarded him, rotating her lower jaw as if chewing gum. 'Under the Police and Criminal Evidence Act, we don't need one.'

The officer leading the Support Unit search team was standing at Danny's shoulder, his troops behind him, eager to get on with the job. He poked his chin over Danny's shoulder and said, 'So if you don't get out of the way, you big fat tub of lard, we'll happily move you.'

Gilbert nodded, beaten. He moved aside and whined, 'I want a solicitor – now.'

'You'll get one when you reach the police station,' Danny told him. 'Now what I'd like you to do is accompany these two officers to that van, get in and be taken to Blackpool police station.'

'I said I want a solicitor now.'

Danny remained pleasant in tone. 'Sooner you get in the van, sooner you get to the station, sooner you get a brief.'

One of the uniformed officers on the arrest squad reached out and tried to grab Gilbert's upper arm. It was too big and fat for his hand.

'Don't you dare touch me,' Gilbert said, shaking him off.

'No more delay.' Danny's voice hardened. 'Get in the back of the van, *now*.'

Gilbert eyed her dangerously and pushed past her.

As an aside, the uniformed officer said to Danny, 'I honestly don't think he'll fit in. We should've brought an HGV for the fat bastard.'

Danny sniggered. Stage one over. With a sense of satisfaction, she prepared to send Henry a message over the airwaves: mission accomplished.

Her boss had decided on a less subtle approach for Ollie Spencer. A rapid entry was needed in this case, because if the police took too much time getting in, Spencer might be able to dispose of vital evidence; with his flat being the supposed scene of the murder, Henry wanted as much from it as possible.

The entrance to the flat was by way of a door at the rear of an electrical shop, leading directly to some stairs and up onto a landing; the doors of the flat were off this landing.

Henry's team had to get in, get up the stairs and locate Spencer before he knew what had hit him. To assist the team they had a map which had been drawn initially by Grace, then improved by a detective. According to this floor plan, once on the landing, there was a bedroom door to the left, bathroom, toilet and kitchen through doors on the right and dead ahead, a living room.

The Support Unit were going to do the entry, race up the stairs, split like the Red Arrows and hit each door virtually simultaneously. Maximum fifteen seconds from going in the door to locating and neutralising Spencer, they promised.

The officers gathered around the outer door with the 'Ram-it' in the hands of one of them.

He shuffled his shoulders, flexed his fingers on the handles of the thirty-inch, thirty-five pounds of solid metal tubing with a flattened end. He swung it backwards about two feet to gain the necessary momentum, then let it swing towards the door.

Fourteen thousand pounds of kinetic force burst the door open with one blow. The officer pivoted out of the way.

The Support Unit teams raced in and bounded up the stairs in a well-practised drill.

At the top of the stairs they split and hit the doors.

Twelve seconds after entry the shout went up: 'Suspect located – neutralised – bedroom.'

Henry Christie jogged up the stairs to the bedroom where he saw Spencer, naked, lying spreadeagled on the bed, a rather flaccid erection meandering up from his ginger pubic hair. A young boy who looked no more than nine, also naked, was sitting next to him on the bed.

'Found this one, too.'

Henry turned at the voice. An officer was holding another youngster, this time a girl, who had only a towel wrapped loosely around her.

Henry looked at Spencer and arrested him for murder.

★ ★ ★

'One arrested – no problems,' Danny informed Henry over the radio, just moments after he had cautioned Spencer and thrown a pair of trousers at him.

'Received,' he replied. 'Ditto – no problems either, just a couple of house-guests, probably mispers.'

'Understood.'

'We'll probably be at the nick before you, so we'll book our chap in, then I'll call you when the coast is clear.'

'Roger,' Danny replied.

Henry turned his attention back to Spencer, who was making a meal of getting dressed. 'Get your fucking clothes on,' the DI growled, 'or I'll drag you naked through the streets of Blackpool and show everyone what a pervert you are.'

Spencer eyed him unsurely; decided he was probably telling the truth.

He was fully dressed within a minute.

Spencer was processed into the custody system fairly smoothly. He was quiet and easy to deal with, saying little, exercising none of his rights until he found out where he stood. When he was sitting in a cell, Henry radioed Danny to bring Gilbert in.

By this time he had been sitting in the back of the van in the rear yard of the police station for about fifteen minutes, getting increasingly restless.

Danny opened the van doors, then the inner cage door. Gilbert eased himself through the gap.

'You are going to look so stupid,' he told Danny.

'Yeah, right.' She pointed to the back door of the police station. 'I believe you made an official visit here a few weeks ago, so you'll know the way to the cells.' She pushed him gently. He snapped her hand away.

'Don't ever touch me.'

'Don't make me have to.'

He walked to the door. Behind him one of the uniformed officers imitated his rolling gait, blowing his cheeks out like a trumpet-player and forcing his belly out. Danny laughed silently . . . but the smile dropped from her lips as, right at the back door, the one and only police witness in the case appeared in the company of a social worker and literally walked straight into Gilbert.

'How could that have happened?' FB demanded furiously. 'Your most vital witness walking right into the main suspect. Come on – *how*?'

'I don't know, sir,' Danny admitted. 'It just happened – one of those things. I feel bad about it. It should not have happened . . . just an unlucky coincidence.'

'Someone should swing for this,' FB blazed.

Henry had watched him browbeating Danny for long enough. 'What's done is done,' he said reasonably. 'No one's to blame for it. Grace had been handed over to Social Services and was leaving the station.'

Danny slumped heavily onto a chair. They were all back in Henry's office.

'I've really cocked up again, haven't I?' Danny admonished herself. She was close to tears. 'I did it with Claire, now I've done it with Grace.'

'What do you mean?' FB asked.

'I mean I promised Grace we'd protect her if she gave evidence and look what happened.' Danny shook her head in frustration. 'Slap-bang into him. You should have seen his face. As soon as I get the chance I'll visit Grace, spend some time with her, reassure her. She'll need all the support we can give her now.'

'Fine, do that,' FB said. 'Now, where are we up to?'

'Gilbert's in with his solicitor; Spencer hasn't requested one. Danny and a DC are going to interview Gilbert first,' Henry explained.

'No,' FB said firmly to Henry. 'I want you and Danny to interview them both.'

'Why?'

'Because I say so, that's why. I want the best interviewer on this, and that's you.'

Henry didn't know whether to be pleased or pissed off. On the one hand he was glad FB had said something nice about him for once; on the other, it wasn't his job to interview.

'I want those bastards charged and convicted of murder, Henry.'

'Is this place bugged? Can they hear what we are saying?'

Gilbert and his solicitor, Maurice Stanway, were in the solicitor's room. Stanway had been Gilbert's brief for almost twenty years. They knew each other well.

The room was basic. One table screwed to the floor, three plastic chairs. They faced each other across the table. Gilbert's bulk overflowed his chair and the thin metal legs sagged.

'It's always possible, but I doubt it,' Stanway said. 'Believe it or not, they're pretty ethical these days.'

'Fools,' Gilbert laughed. 'So, what's going to happen now?'

'You'll be interviewed, probably fairly cursorily at first. They'll establish a few facts, ensure you know why you've been arrested, things like that. Then they'll start asking you questions, probably hoping you'll crack before they declare any real evidence at this stage.'

'In other words, they'll offer me the chance to confess?'

'In other words, yes.'

'And if I don't?'

'They'll start to declare evidence, bit by bit. Forensic, direct evidence from witnesses . . . hoping you'll admit.'

'What forensic do they have?'

'I don't know yet. We'll have to wait and see.'

'They won't have any.'

'You sound certain.'

'I am.'

'They may well have witnesses.'

337

'They have. I saw her when I came into the station.'

'All it takes is one witness,' Stanway stated.

'I think they'll rely heavily on her.'

'Her testimony may well be enough – at least to get you charged and put before a court. But let's see how it pans out, shall we?'

'Okay.'

'Will the police find anything at your house, Charles?'

'Books, videos, magazines, photographs . . . you know the sort of thing.'

'Anything to link you to the dead girl?'

'No.'

'Well, that's good. Let's go and see what they've got.'

Ninety minutes later Gilbert and Stanway were back in the solicitor's consulting room. They were buzzing, feeling very confident.

'You handled the questions skilfully, Charles. I applaud you.' They shook hands and sat down. 'So,' Stanway said, 'that was the opening salvo.'

'And pretty tame it was, too.'

'If you're sure about the forensic side of things, I'd suggest they will have only the girl's eyewitness testimony. And, of course, Ollie Spencer, who has not been interviewed yet, nor requested a solicitor.'

'In that case, you should offer your services. I would hate for him to say anything stupid.'

Stanway nodded.

'When will I be out of here?'

'Oh, they'll keep you in as long as possible. They always do in cases such as these.'

At midnight Henry Christie and Danny Furness were sitting on a bench on the promenade, near to Central Pier. From having been a cold day, the night had become idyllic and still. The tide was way out. The sky was clear and the moon almost full. It was even quite mild, verging on warm.

Henry rubbed his neck and rolled his head. His bones creaked and cracked. 'God, I'm whacked.'

Danny stood up and walked behind him. She began to massage his shoulders through his jacket. Her fingers probed into his muscles. He groaned, not far short of ecstasy.

'That is wonderful,' he murmured. His toes tingled. He dropped his chin onto his chest and revelled in the sensation.

'In another time, on another planet, I'll lay odds we could have been good together,' Danny whispered into his ear.

'It's a nice thought,' he responded, taking one of Danny's hands and squeezing it.

Danny kissed his neck, sending a shiver of absolute pleasure down his spine. 'Come on, Henry, let's get some sleep. Busy day tomorrow.'

They strolled back to the police station car park, arm-in-arm, Danny with her head resting on Henry's shoulder. He drove her home and dropped her off. On the way to his own home he was quite proud of himself. Not very long ago he would have been in bed with her – or at least he would have tried to be. It wasn't that he did not like the idea of it, but he was a reformed character where women were concerned. Too many close shaves had made him see his family was more important than his libido. Never again did he want to hurt his wife or children.

Meanwhile Danny undressed and wished she was climbing into bed with him, but knew it would never happen. She was glad Henry had been strong for them both. She knew that if he had laid a hand on her, she would have been unable to resist and then she would have been in the fire, just having jumped out of the frying pan.

Chapter Nineteen

'The search teams and forensic have ripped that flat apart, been down the toilet, up the U-bends, down the drains, everywhere. They worked through the night and are still beavering away as we speak, but early indications are that there is nothing, nothing at all, which will be of evidential use to link Claire Lilton to that flat and those two men.'

Danny had returned to work at 6 a.m., having cadged a lift from one of the early-turn officers. She had liaised with the specialists, checking on the progress of that side of the investigation; it was eight now and she was briefing the murder squad, Henry and FB included.

'What have we recovered from Gilbert's house?'

'Child pornography – videos, magazines, books, hard copy from the Internet . . . possibly some cocaine, but only a small amount . . . sexual aids and several little black books containing names and addresses of people who, we believe, are his associates in the aforementioned areas. They contain detailed information on sexual preferences, likes, dislikes. My feeling is that Gilbert and Spencer are part of a paedophile ring; my guess is Ollie Spencer does the legwork, finding the kids – probably like the two we found in his flat yesterday – and once he and Gilbert have finished with them, they get sucked into the ring. There's a lot of codes in his books. If we ever crack them, or he tells us that they mean, I think it'll tell us the story of some poor kids.'

'But right now we want to hang a murder on him, don't we?' FB said. 'So let's concentrate on that for the time being. Where the hell do we stand on that?'

Danny shook her head sadly. 'It's looking more and more like we're going to have to rely on Grace's evidence. Gilbert and Spencer have obviously been really thorough as regards cleaning up after their wrongdoings, and the only thing they didn't deal with properly was Grace. She's all we've got for the moment, and I'm not happy with that. It puts too much pressure on her and makes our case very weak.'

Henry checked the time. 'Better get going. They've both been in custody over twelve hours now; another twelve and we'll be after a Superintendent's extension.'

Gilbert and Spencer were interviewed all day, sometimes for extended periods, sometimes in short bursts. All the time Danny and Henry kept an eye on their rights, ensuring they got adequate breaks and refreshments and the interviews were conducted fairly and without oppression.

All in all, very frustrating.

Being polite to people suspected of murdering kids did not come easy to either detective and as the day wore on, the veneer cracked occasionally. Particularly when they could see they were getting nowhere fast.

Neither prisoner admitted anything which would incriminate them in the murder, not even when the detectives – reluctantly – played their best hand and dropped Grace's evidence on their laps.

At 6 p.m. that day, decisions needed to be made.

'Let me get this straight: as it stands at the moment, the only thing that will convict me now is the evidence from that little girl.'

'That's true, but the task of discrediting her story would not be too onerous, I would suggest.'

342

Gilbert spread his sausage-like fingers on the table. 'The only problem is, she knows some things only an eye-witness would know. She saw us bashing the girl's face and she saw us drag her into the shower and wash her; she also saw us get rid of the bedding. It's little things like that which make her story all too real.'

'You're right,' Stanway agreed.

'I think,' Gilbert pointed at Stanway, 'it would be better for all of us if that young lady were unable to give evidence, don't you, Maurice?'

Stanway went icy from head to toe. His throat constricted. He squeaked, 'What do you mean? You want her paid off, or something?'

Gilbert chuckled evilly at Stanway's misconception. His pig eyes bored into Stanway's. 'No, I mean that for all concerned, she would be better off dead.'

Stanway's rectum squinted as he held back a fart of fear. 'You mean . . .?'

'Are you fucking thick, Maurice? I thought you had a law degree.'

'I . . . I do. I . . .' He was dumb for a moment, then blurted, 'What are you suggesting?'

Gilbert leaned on the table which creaked under his weight. His voice was just above a whisper, but was dangerous nonetheless. 'Go and see my co-defendant, Mr Spencer, and tell him to give you the name of someone who will, for a fee, be happy to go and visit our young ladyfriend, wherever she may be, and put a pillow over her face, or whatever is most appropriate.'

'I can't do that.'

'You can and you will.'

Stanway's bottom lip flapped uncontrollably like an awning in high winds as he babbled nervously, 'I'm a solicitor, not someone who organises contracts on people. And anyway, we don't know where they're keeping the girl. She's in secure accommodation somewhere.'

'And that's a problem for you?'

'It is.'

Gilbert's voice did not change, but to Stanway's ears it became more and more menacing.

'Are you telling me you cannot walk out of here, pick up a phone and speak to one of our like-minded colleagues in the Social Services – and they would be unwilling to give you that information? Is that what you're telling me?'

'No, but . . .'

'But what? Now let me spell this out for you, Maurice. In more ways than one I am very big in the Northwest of England. Very rich, very well-connected. I'm sure I'll be able to ride out the storm caused by the material the police have found in my house, but facing a murder charge is a very different kettle of fish.' He lifted an eyebrow. 'I know you have a predilection for putting your twinkle into the bottoms of little boys . . .' The solicitor started to babble a protest; Gilbert held up a hand to shut him up. 'I don't have a problem with that, Maurice, as you know, but what I'm leading up to is this: many of my friends and business associates have the same bent, shall we say. I could reel off a list of names of businessmen, councillors, school governors, all sorts of people – solicitors, even. So, what I'm getting at is this – if I get done for murder, lots more heads will roll, Maurice. Including yours, my friend.'

Maurice Stanway, LLB, was stone grey and feeling bilious.

'If she dies, and it's made to look like a coincidence, then I'll be very happy indeed. Have I made my point?'

Henry's office: Danny replaced the phone. 'Nothing further from the forensic team.' She relayed the news grimly to Henry and FB.

Henry tapped his bottom teeth with his thumbnail. It was 6.30 p.m. 'No supporting evidence,' he said bitterly. 'This is shit.'

'There's not even any point in going for a Super's extension,' Danny said. 'An extra twelve hours only gives us until tomorrow morning. They'll be spending eight of those asleep.'

'Charge him,' FB said. 'Put him before court in the morning and get a three-day liedown so we can get into his ribs about the other murder in Darwen.'

'Based on what?' Henry enquired. 'A witness in the States who's done a runner? And not only that, we don't know one hundred per cent that it *is* a murder. The post mortem was inconclusive.'

'He has to be questioned about it at the very least. And we need chats with him about all the stuff in his house. I think we've stumbled onto something very big here.'

'What about Spencer?'

'He's going nowhere. Charge him with murder too, get a three-day liedown and let's have a nice long chat with him about the two mispers we found in his place – and Grace's allegations about him sexually assaulting her.'

Henry and Danny nodded. Henry crossed to the computer in his office and logged into the custody system.

He started to prepare a murder charge.

'Do you wish to make any reply to the charge?' Danny asked Gilbert. 'If so, you may like to write it in the space here on the form, or I'll gladly write it for you.'

'Only that you'll all regret your mistake, but I don't wish to have that recorded, so no – no reply.'

Danny turned to Spencer. They had been jointly charged. He shook his head, said nothing.

Danny completed the charge forms and handed the defendants their copies. They immediately gave them to Stanway who stuffed them into his briefcase. Danny thought he looked decidedly agitated. His hands were shaking as he closed the case. He appeared near to collapse.

'Are you okay, Mr Stanway?' she asked with concern. 'You look peaky.'

345

'I'm fine, thanks,' he said tightly. 'I'll see you all at court in the morning.' He turned to leave, only to find he had not locked his case properly. It flipped open, scattering the contents across the floor, papers, pens, forms, everywhere.

Danny helped him collect them together. She was unaware that the last piece of paper she handed to him only had one bit of information on it. A telephone number given to Stanway by Ollie Spencer.

The number of a killer.

Stanway waited in the dark in his car in one corner of a deserted coach park near to Blackpool football club's increasingly dilapidated ground. The beat of his heart seemed to be taking place in his throat.

A movement in the shadows made him gasp.

He peered through the windscreen into the darkness. A man was standing there. How he had got to that position, Stanway did not know. On his hands and knees perhaps.

There was the flare of a match, briefly illuminating a face, the features of which were difficult to make out. The match died, the end of a cigarette burned.

Another match was struck, flared, tossed to one side.

Two matches. The agreed signal.

'Oh God,' muttered Stanway. He opened his car door and had to lift his numb legs out of the footwell and onto the ground with his hands. He was sure he would fall over as soon as he put any weight on them. But they held him up. Only just, but they worked.

Stanway teetered across to the man in the shadows, stopping about six feet away from him. The end of the cigarette glowed as he took a drag. Stanway smelled booze and body odour as well as the smoke.

'Got the money?'

'Half now, half when it's done.'

'That wasn't the arrangement.'

'Oh yes it was.' Stanway tried to sound assertive.

A hand appeared. Stanway fumbled in his pocket and

slapped an envelope into the waiting palm.

'Do I need to count it?'

'It's all there.'

'It better be.'

'The job needs to be done soon. Tonight if possible. Are you sure you can do it?'

The man sniggered. 'Piece of piss. Where is she?'

Stanway told him.

'Tomorrow night, back here, same time,' the man said. 'Make sure you come alone again and with the rest of the money. If you don't, I'll come for you, Mr Stanway.'

The man moved into deeper shadow. Stanway saw the butt of the cigarette drop to the ground, heard the scrunch of a heel, then there was no sound. The man had gone.

Danny worked for two hours on the preparation of the remand file for Gilbert and Spencer. She wanted it to be exactly right and continually read and re-read it until she saw double and her head throbbed.

Finally she completed the front sheet, copied the file and pinned it all together.

She walked wearily to Henry's office where he was still transcribing one of the interviews from tape to paper. A tedious task, usually carried out by a trained civvie. Unfortunately they didn't work after five and urgent files don't wait until the morning. He removed the head-phones when Danny came in.

'Done,' she said, and dropped the files onto his desk.

'Excellent.'

'Now I'm going to have a word with Grace, which I should have done yesterday.'

'Don't spend too much time with her tonight, Danny. Just a quick hello, how are you, we're still with you, then get yourself to bed. It's been another long day.'

'Yeah, yeah, yeah,' she said, leaving the office, giving

Henry a tired wave over her shoulder. 'See ya in the morning.'

She nipped into the CID office, commandeered the keys for one of the cars and five minutes later was heading north out of Blackpool.

St Jude's was a former primary school, saved from certain demolition about twenty years before when an overflow problem at various juvenile detention centres and children's homes saved it from the bulldozer. Little money had ever been spent on it and much of its refurbishment was merely cosmetic.

Danny parked in front of the building and went to the huge double doors. She rang the bell and heard it echoing somewhere inside. Footsteps drew nearer and the door was opened by a very formidable-looking woman. Danny knew this to be the matron, named, appropriately enough, Miss Steele.

Danny flashed her badge and introduced herself, already having phoned ahead in advance to warn of her arrival.

'She's in room number four.' Miss Steele answered Danny's query and gave her directions.

'Is there just yourself on duty?'

'Aye, me and nine kids. Want me to take you down to her room?'

'I'll find my own way, thanks. I'll see you on the way out. Only be about ten minutes.'

'I'll be in the office, just here.' She pointed to a slightly open door.

Danny thanked her and walked down the corridor. She passed a common room, which she glanced into. Several young girls were lounging around, watching TV. Danny walked on, turned right down a hallway, off which were the private rooms. Grace's room was the last on the right.

As she walked she felt a distinct chill from a draught blowing thinly down the corridor. At the far end she could see a fire door which was open, banging in the breeze. Danny thought it was unusual, but nothing more than that. She decided she would tell Miss Steele on the way out.

She stopped at Grace's door and tapped. 'Grace, it's me, Danny Furness,' she cooed. 'I've come to see you.' Her fingers wrapped around the handle, Danny pushed the door open.

Inside the room, the man sub-contracted by Maurice Stanway looked up. He had not quite finished the job and he forced the pillow down with all his weight onto Grace's face and at the moment the door opened, she ceased squirming.

Danny could not believe her eyes, but incredulous though the image was, she reacted instantaneously. She threw herself across the room screaming, 'Get off her, you bastard!' Her arms flailed as she launched herself over the last few feet.

The man fended her off with the pillow, held like a shield before him, taking all the blows Danny rained down on him.

But he was big and mean and the concept of striking a woman, particularly in this predicament, did not play on his conscience at all. Using the pillow he forced Danny away from him, pushing her roughly. She staggered back.

He dropped the pillow, bunched the fingers of his right hand into a large, hairy fist and drove it towards Danny's face. It caught her hard, sent her spinning back against Grace's bed, over the prone figure of the dead girl. Danny knew she did not have the strength or the fighting skill to win here, but she had one thing going for her – long fingernails.

Though dizzy from his punch, she spun round like a panther and lurched towards him again, willing herself to get her claws into his cheeks and dig them in as deeply as humanly possible.

She succeeded. Dramatically so.

Eight fingernails gouged down both his cheeks, drawing rivulets of blood and flesh with them and a howl of pain from the attacker, who reacted by whipping up both his forearms, flicking her hands away and leaving her very open for his next onslaught.

He pummelled her down to the floor and would have gone on, probably to kill her, if Miss Steele hadn't appeared at the door and shrieked something incomprehensible.

He leapt over Danny, punched Miss Steele out of the way and hurled himself down the corridor towards the open fire escape, which had been his means of entry, and was gone.

Blood dripping from her nose, Danny dragged herself up by the edge of the bed. She looked at Grace's pale face and placed the tips of her first and second fingers onto her warm neck, checking for the beating of a pulse which she knew she would not find.

Danny then inspected her own fingernails and hoped she had got enough of the man underneath them to identify him through DNA.

350

Chapter Twenty

In comparison to the previous evening, Saturday morning found Maurice Stanway in his element. He stood before the three magistrates on the Bench in the specially convened court and carefully stacked the files on the table in front of him, adjusted his spectacles and cleared his throat. He squinted contemptuously at the CPS solicitor sitting a few feet away from him; Stanway believed he could run rings round the bugger. He smiled benignly at the magistrate's clerk and the Bench beyond.

'If it may please Your Worships,' he said with a mouth full of syrup, 'I represent the defendants in this case, Messrs Gilbert and Spencer . . .'

In the dock, sitting mutely side by side behind the high brass bars, were the two named persons. Four cops hovered behind them. Neither prisoner was handcuffed.

'You have heard my learned friend,' and there was a slight sneer as Stanway emphasised the word 'friend', 'and I have several submissions to make on behalf of my clients this morning. Firstly, as you know, both are charged with murder, a serious allegation. My first submission is in respect of this charge. It is within my knowledge that the police do not have any evidence to substantiate this charge whatsoever. As you are aware, a dreadful, dreadful incident occurred last night which resulted in the death of the only police witness to this case. It was an incident, I hasten to add, purely coincidental and unrelated to my clients being in custody . . .'

'My arse!' hissed Danny Furness through clenched teeth. She, Henry and FB were seated at the rear of the court. Henry quickly laid a hand on her arm. He sensed she was about to stand up and heckle some very unprofessional points of view. She was convinced, as was Henry, that Grace's death was no coincidence.

'Shush,' Henry admonished her.

'The prosecution evidence, as I understand, relied one hundred per cent on this unfortunate girl's evidence.' Stanway sounded sad. No one could have guessed he was the one responsible for sending her killer round. 'There is no supporting evidence – nothing. And, to put it simply, the prosecution no longer has a case. To proceed on the evidence of one dead witness would be ludicrous and a criminal waste of public money. On those grounds, I submit to the court that the charge is withdrawn and the case dismissed.'

He paused for effect, then went on: 'The prosecution have also stated their desire to interview my client about other matters. What are these other matters?' Stanway took a breath. 'Let me tell you: in relation to Mr Gilbert, one of Blackpool's most respected businessmen, a man who supports many local children's charities, these are matters concerning certain documents found in his house. Yes, Your Worships, documents. I ask you! Does that require a further seventy-two hours in custody? No, I submit it does not. Mr Gilbert will gladly make an appointment to come to the police station and be interviewed at any time suitable to the police, not himself. It is imperative that Mr Gilbert is given his liberty today. He has many businesses to run, many people to employ who depend on him . . .'

'God give me strength,' Danny blurted, unable to contain herself.

Stanway stopped talking, swivelled slowly and glared at

Danny, as did everyone else in court. He pulled his spectacles down his nose and looked over the frames at her. Danny stared defiantly back. Fuck them, she thought.

'Please keep quiet, Officer,' the clerk of the court warned, 'or I shall have to consider you to be in contempt of court.'

Danny breathed impatiently down her nose.

Stanway resumed his address, but Danny did not hear another word of it. Her mind suddenly felt as if an express train was roaring through it, whilst reliving last night's horror at the children's home. Henry kept one eye on her, fully responsive to her tension, knowing she was close to explosion.

When Stanway had finished his submissions, the CPS solicitor asked for a short adjournment.

'We are *not* going to let those bastards back out on the streets!' Danny smashed a fist onto the table in the police room at the court. 'No fucking way.'

'Danny, Danny. Calm down,' Henry tried to cool it. 'We've no intention of doing so, but we've got to get the submission to the court correct. If we shout at them, they'll just let them go.'

She took a deep drag on her cigarette, defying the No Smoking signs.

FB addressed the CPS solicitor. 'That murder charge stands. We are not going to withdraw it. Understand?'

The man nodded.

'And,' FB went on, 'we don't want him to have bail, even with conditions. There's lots more than just documents to talk to him about, such as that other death in East Lancashire and the controlled drugs found in his home. You've really got to lay it on thick.'

'Right, right.' The man scribbled on a pad.

'Henry – brief this guy up properly, but don't forget, we don't want to give away too much in court.'

* * *

The court reconvened.

The CPS solicitor stood up nervously. This was his biggest case so far and he wanted to do well.

'Your Worships,' he began when the three men had settled, 'the charge of murder will not be withdrawn and neither will the application to keep the defendants in custody for further questioning.' After he'd said those opening words he relaxed into solicitor mode and delivered the half-truths, half-lies Henry had fed him. 'In relation to the charge of murder, whilst it cannot be denied that the dead girl was a vital witness, we believe it is only right and proper that these two defendants face and answer the allegations in a court of law. Whilst the witness may be dead, her evidence remains valid. Also, as I speak, scientists are still working on the forensic side of things and fully expect to have evidence which supports and complements the evidence of the dead girl.' That was – almost – a lie. 'Secondly, not only do the police wish to interview Gilbert about documents found in his house, but also about many other items which point towards other serious offences, and also the police need to question him about another suspicious death, the details of which I do not wish to divulge in open court as they would prejudice the police investigation. If Gilbert did get bail, there is a real possibility of him absconding. He spends a great deal of his time abroad and we believe he would immediately leave the country, together with his co-accused, Spencer, about whom I have the following submissions to make . . .'

Stanway subsequently countered all the prosecution arguments and then the magistrates adjourned to consider the matter over a cup of coffee.

Danny paced the corridor outside the courtroom door. Nerves, like little electric shocks, flickered around her stomach walls.

354

Henry sat and watched her until he could stand it no longer. He pulled her into an empty witness waiting room. 'Danny, you're driving me up the wall!'

'Well, I won't apologise for it. That bastard – those bastards – are going to be out on the streets again. I can feel it. I just know. And we're powerless to do anything about it.'

'Danny, sit down . . . I said *sit*.'

Meekly, she obeyed.

Henry sat next to her and tenderly pushed a strand of her hair back from her forehead. 'You've been through a tough time these last few days.'

'You don't know the half of it,' she snapped.

Henry was hurt by the remark, but kept a cool head. 'No, I know I don't. But you need to take a step back from this and get it into perspective. We have done everything and more that's expected of us. We've put away Louis Trent for the rest of his life and we're on track to sending those two bastards down the corridor behind him. Now, if we don't succeed, then we'll have to accept it, okay? Let's just make sure we do everything right, to the book, and keep a professional head on – just like you told me the other day, remember?'

'The book! Those two swines should be shot!'

'Maybe so, but they won't be and that's life.' He shrugged. 'Now, Danny, you are a very caring person. I know it sounds trite and corny, but it's also true. I want someone on my team like you, but I also want you to be more realistic in your approach. I do know some of the things you've been through over the last few days. They've been pretty horrific. I know I—'

'No, you don't know. Don't even try to know.' Then Danny caught his wounded expression. 'Oh God, I'm sorry, Henry.'

'It's all right. All I'm saying, in a pathetic kind of way, is you're going to have to deal with things one way or another. Try to work out what'll be best for you. Might

355

just be a chat with a friend, or me, or the Welfare Department, but whatever you do, Danny, deal with it. I speak from experience.'

She gave a wan smile and draped her arms around his neck, touching her forehead onto his, sighing deeply. 'God, if only you weren't married . . .'

'Danny, if I wasn't married, I'd shag you here and now!'

They burst apart, laughing uproariously. 'And I'd let you.'

The door opened and FB strutted in. 'And just what the hell are you up to? They've been up and dealt with while you've been getting all touchy-feely.'

Danny stiffened.

'And?' Henry's voice was cautious.

FB dug his fist like he was punching some poor sucker in the solar plexus. 'Stuck it up 'em!' he announced jubilantly. 'Bail refused – three-day liedown.'

Danny shot off her seat and danced around the room, madly waving her arms up and down, jigging on the spot. Then she astounded FB by throwing her arms round him and placing a big wet kiss on his cheek.

Henry stayed seated, a smirk of satisfaction on his face.

Danny's joy subsided when she pulled away from FB who wiped his cheek distastefully with his pristine clean hankie.

She exchanged a glance with Henry. 'Now the work really begins.'

Chapter Twenty-one

Two days later there was nothing further the police could do. Having charged Gilbert and Spencer with Claire Lilton's murder they were not, by law, allowed to question them any further about that matter.

All they had for Gilbert was the material found at his home, which in the grand scheme of things was pretty insignificant. He was questioned at length about the dead girl in East Lancashire, but denied all knowledge when faced with the paltry evidence against him.

Finding two naked runaways in Spencer's flat meant there were many long conversations with him, but nothing more on the murder front and he denied sexually assaulting Grace.

Forty-eight hours, therefore, failed to produce anything worthwhile.

All the while, Danny and Henry had vague hopes that America might be the key, but nothing happened on that score. Henry phoned Karl Donaldson, who in turn phoned Myrna, who had no further information.

So, two tired detectives, having spent all those hours in each other's pockets, came to realise they would have to put the defendants back before the court before the three days was up. There was no way they could justify keeping them in police custody any longer. They had to go back to court, hopefully to get the two defendants remanded in custody and then commit the case to Crown Court.

Which is what they did on Monday morning.

And the magistrates went along with them and denied bail.

Stanway was astounded by the decision and immediately stated his intention to appeal against the decision to a High Court Judge in chambers.

Meanwhile, Gilbert and Spencer were transferred, like common criminals, to Risley Remand Centre.

On the next day, Tuesday, at 10 a.m., Stanway appealed to a judge in chambers – a course of action which often resulted in the magistrates' decision being overturned.

Lancaster Crown Court was in session, presided over by High Court Judge Constance Ellison. At the age of seventy-two she was as quick and nimble in both brain and body as a forty-year-old, and unlike most other judges her age, she was very much in touch with modern trends and thinking. She would never have to ask who Oasis or The Spice Girls were.

She had scheduled the appeal before the start of the day's court proceedings and was waiting in her chambers, dressed in full regalia, looking absolutely splendid and very imposing. She sat behind a large, highly polished mahogany desk.

A court usher led in Stanway and his opposite number from the CPS.

'Good morning, gentlemen,' she greeted them. 'Please be seated. I may have the full kit on, as they say, but let's not be too formal in here.' She smiled a warm, pleasant smile.

They both sat, shuffling their papers nervously. Both knew she had a formidable reputation for chewing up and spitting out solicitors and lawyers.

Stanway began . . .

. . .And outside in the chilly corridor, Henry and Danny waited tensely for the result.

Half an hour dragged by as slowly as creeping death.

Neither spoke.

Danny sat there unmoving, consumed with her innermost thoughts. Henry, on contrast, fidgeted constantly. Standing up, sitting down, patrolling the corridor. Bored to death by doing nothing.

It was a relief for both when Henry's pager vibrated against his pelvic bone, summoning him to make a phone call. He wandered away to find the nearest one. Danny was glad to see him go. He was getting on her nerves this time.

He had been gone less than two minutes when the door to the Judge's chamber creaked open. The usher poked his head out. 'DI Christie? DS Furness?' he called enquiringly.

'I'm DS Furness.' Danny stood up.

'Where is DI Christie?'

'Gone to make a phone call. Why?'

'The Judge wants to see you both.'

Over the last few days, since Tracey had disappeared, the operatives of Kruger Investigations had been getting nowhere fast. The streets of Miami had been constantly combed, particularly the areas notable for street hookers and drug abusers.

They drew a blank.

Myrna had got the girl's last known address from Mark Tapperman; two of her best investigators had visited it, but the place was empty. It looked as though she had done a quick getaway, leaving several items of personal belongings behind.

Myrna called her people off.

There was no guarantee Tracey was even in Miami. She could have been anywhere, or even dead, so Myrna resumed normality – or at least the normality of life without Steve Kruger and a gay husband.

Too much time chasing shadows would have been unproductive for a firm still reeling from its founder's death.

Myrna needed to devote herself to jittery customers.

That was what she did.

She worked from very early each morning until late into the night, calling customers worldwide, chatting, reassuring them in the same way she had done very soon after Kruger's death. She spent most of her waking hours next to the phone in her office, feeding the fax and writing letters. It was a hell of a task, but needed the personal touch, she believed. She contacted, one way or another, every single customer and supplier, past and present, and the response she got was brilliant. She firmly began to believe that Kruger Investigations had a future, even without Steve, but it had to be driven by her.

And in the early hours of that Tuesday morning, she put the finishing touches to a couple of letters, slotted them into envelopes and dropped them into the out tray.

She was tired, yeah, but it was the fatigue which came through constructive hard work. She blinked the grit out of her eyes and yawned. What to do with the weekend was the question playing on her mind. She was adamant she would take Friday off and make something of it.

The prospect of heading down to the Keys with no particular aim in sight kind of appealed to her. Maybe she'd get the old Thunderbird out – the one her husband had so recklessly bought her a couple of years before, probably in a fit of guilt – and see how that performed.

Mmmm . . . She closed her eyes, imagined the warm wind in her hair, the straight road, a beachside guest-house, a drink or two . . . she was almost asleep at the desk when the phone rang, loud and shrill in the stillness of the morning. She leapt out of her skin and fumbled to answer it.

It was Jake, the security man, down in reception.

'Sorry t' bother ya'll Mizz Rosza, but I knew you wuz in or I woulden a rang . . .'

'It's okay, Jake. What is it?'

'Like, normally, I'da thrown her out on her ear, but she

sez she knows ya and wants t'see ya an' apologise.'

'Who does?'

'Whazz y'name, gal?' Myrna heard Jake ask. There was a mutter. 'Sez she's a-called Tracey Greenwood. Sez y've prob'ly bin lookin' f'her.'

'Put her in the elevator, Jake and send her up.'

Myrna waited for the arrival of the elevator. When the doors opened Tracey was huddled in a foetal ball in one corner, big eyes staring up fearfully at Myrna, thumb in her mouth. She looked dreadful, just like a bunch of rags.

Myrna helped her to her feet. She was pathetically light. Brittle.

'I'm sorry, I got scared – lost me bottle' she said with a cough.

'Not scared enough to steal my purse, girl,' Myrna rejoined with a snap.

When Tracey had been seated down in Myrna's office and given a coffee, Myrna said, 'You here to stay now?'

She nodded dumbly.

'Why the hell did you go off like that?'

'Don't know. I was frightened. I needed a fix too.'

'And now you've run out of money, I suppose,' Myrna said scornfully. She did not wait for a response. 'Are you planning to leave again?'

'No.'

'In that case, sit there, don't move. I've got a phone call to make.'

From Kruger's office she dialled Karl Donaldson's home number, having worked out it was only 8 a.m. in London and there was a chance he was still at home before setting off for work. Donaldson's wife, Karen, answered. A baby screamed in the background. 'He's just about to leave. I'll get him. Hold on.'

'This is Karl Donaldson.'

'Karl, she's back.'

'You gonna keep hold of her this time?'

361

'I am.'

'Right, good. Call you back soon.'

Donaldson immediately phoned Henry Christie at home but was told he had already left for work. He then rang Blackpool police station to be told he had not yet turned in, but was expected to be in later after attending a special hearing at Lancaster Crown Court. Donaldson asked for a mobile or pager number, but no one could actually put their fingers on one at that moment. Cursing, Donaldson hung up and flipped through his organiser. The number of Henry's pager was not there either. He knew he had it at work, so he decided to wait until he got there before trying to get hold of Henry.

Meanwhile, Myrna returned to her office, ready to get some answers from young Tracey, the girl who had stolen her credit cards.

'Hey, I've got some great—'

'Come on, Henry!' Danny waved him urgently back down the corridor. 'The Judge wants to see us – now!'

'Eh? Why?'

'How the hell should I know? Come on, hurry up.' Danny knocked on the chamber door.

'Please, please, sit down,' Mrs Ellison said to them. Two extra chairs had been brought in and placed directly in front of her desk. The two solicitors were sitting apart, on chairs at an angle to the corners of the desk. Henry and Danny sat in between. The Judge peered down her nose at Henry.

'Mr Christie – I thought I recognised the name. How are you?'

'Your Honour, I'm fine, thank you very much.'

Danny gazed incredulously at him. Stanway almost groaned. The last thing he wanted was for Henry Christie to be on intimate terms with the Judge.

'I seem to remember you were in pretty bad shape last

time we met – dodging bullets and Mafia hitmen, as I recall.' She recalled correctly, having presided almost four years before on a very high-profile trial, here at Lancaster Crown Court, in which Henry had been one of the main police witnesses.

'I'm well recovered from then, thank you, Ma'am.'

'But still in the wars, I see.' She chuckled, nodding towards his recent facial injuries.

'Trouble follows me everywhere,' he shrugged modestly.

She gave him a tight smile which indicated the pleasantries were over and business was about to begin. 'Now, you may be wondering why I've asked you both in here,' she said, gearing smoothly into the meat of the day. 'The fact is, I've listened to these two gentlemen arguing their individual points of view and it seems, overwhelmingly, that I should give the defendant, Gilbert, bail; Spencer, on the other hand will stay in custody. However, I don't wish to rush any decision if there is a chance of getting more perspectives on it. I was aware you were out there and I believe it only right you should be able to talk to me about the matter.'

'Thank you. That's very thoughtful,' Henry said.

'Before we commence, though, I would like you both to take the oath.'

The usher moved in silently and handed Henry a Bible which he took in his right hand and swore to Almighty God to tell the truth, the whole truth and nothing but the truth. Danny did likewise.

'Mr Christie, why don't you want these men to get bail?'

'Firstly, they are charged with murder, an offence for which I believe bail should not be granted under any circumstance. Both men are wealthy people with huge liquid assets. I believe that if given bail, both would abscond and by abscond, I mean leave the country.'

'I object!' Stanway interrupted loudly. 'My clients would be more than happy to surrender their passports.'

'It's very easy to get forged passports,' Henry said patiently. 'Your Honour, I know for a fact that the defendant Gilbert has connections with the underworld in the United States. He was recently arrested for indecent acts with a child whilst in Miami, but was released without charge. The person he was arrested with is an active member of the Florida underworld – a gangster in other words. The forgery of passports is common to such people. I believe we would never see either defendant again.'

'Is it true you have little evidence against them for the murder charge?' the Judge asked.

Henry wondered how to flower it up. He decided to go straight for the jugular – and sod it. 'It's true our evidence, at this moment, relies substantially on a statement taken from a witness who is now dead. I do not believe it is a coincidence that this young girl was murdered as a result of giving the police a statement. I firmly believe Gilbert ordered her murder.'

It was the first time Henry had openly voiced such an opinion. He watched Stanway's non-verbals and thought he saw the whole of his body wobble.

'This is an outlandish suggestion,' Stanway retorted. His face was red. 'My client has absolutely no connection whatsoever with this incident and to suggest it is so is preposterous and, were we not in a court of law, scandalous.'

'Quiet!' Mrs Ellison snapped.

Stanway drew in his neck, like a tortoise into a shell.

'We believe,' Henry went on, 'that if released, Gilbert will continue, in whatever way he can, to pervert the course of justice. He's a powerful man who rides roughshod over people to get what he wants. I am also sure he is involved in a paedophile network which may be international in its scope. Several items the police have seized point to this as being much more than supposition. There is no doubt he is heavily involved in child sex-abuse and

364

his release will only allow him to continue his activities.

'Finally, there is the murder of another young girl. Her body was discovered recently in a shallow grave near Darwen. We suspect Gilbert to be involved in this.'

'Evidence?' Mrs Ellison asked.

Henry coughed. He glanced at Stanway, then back at the Judge. 'Could I speak to you privately, Your Honour?'

'This had better be good, Mr Christie. The fortunate thing for me is that I have the power to administer appeals as I see fit. Mr Stanway is not impressed at being ejected from the chamber.'

'I understand – but it is good.' Henry went on to detail the story of the disappearing witness in America and the fact that if this witness could be found, Gilbert would definitely be facing another murder charge. Henry concluded the story by saying, 'I have just received a phone call to say the witness has turned up again and is willing to give evidence.'

'So what are you saying?'

'I'm saying that if Gilbert gets bail, we have a good chance of never seeing him again. If he stays in custody – on remand – and we bring this witness back from America, we can arrest him and deal with him without any problems. From what I can gather, this witness is very jittery indeed. We need to act with due speed.'

Mrs Ellison nodded thoughtfully. 'I'll give you until Thursday to get this witness back into Britain and accordingly I shall remand both defendants until that day . . . then it's back to the Magistrates' Court. If you haven't got a witness by then, you will have to appeal to the lower court again . . . and there is a very good case for releasing Gilbert on bail.'

'That doesn't give us much time,' Danny observed bleakly. 'Two days. How are we going to manage it?'

'It's better than nothing.'

They were on the M6, Henry driving south towards Preston. The CID Mondeo was touching a hundred and beginning to reek of burning oil.

'You're such a pessimist, aren't you?' he said.

'Just answer me this – how the hell *are* we going to manage it? A reluctant witness, one who'll only speak to me . . . come on, how?' Danny's hands made a gripping gesture.

'That's what we're going to sort out now when we see FB at Headquarters. I'm going to put to him that we send you on a plane to Miami today and you can bring her back and at the same time take a statement off her in mid-Atlantic. We'll get her into protective custody as soon as she lands and then slap Gilbert with a—'

'Hang on, hang on!' The implications of what Henry had just said struck her. 'So you want me to go to America? Drop everything – just like that! Henry . . . hold your horses!'

He swerved into the fast lane to avoid a lorry which pulled out unexpectedly.

'Henry, all I plan to do this week is crash out. I am absolutely knackered and the last thing I want to do is fly to Miami and back in a day. It's an eight-hour flight each way!'

'Would you rather see Gilbert walk?'

'You know I wouldn't. That's not the point.'

'I'll arrange first-class seats. You can stretch out and sleep all the way over. You might even get to do some sightseeing. It won't be that bad.'

She shook her head, unimpressed. 'I'm not going. Why don't you just get her dumped on a plane at that end and we'll meet her over here. That would make more sense and it would be cheaper.'

Henry fell silent. 'You've got a point, I suppose,' he said eventually. 'We can't make you go.'

'But I want to go.'

'What?'

'I really, really want to go and bring her back and charge Gilbert with another murder . . . part of me, a big part of me wants to do that. But I'm just exhausted. I'm probably on the edge of a nervous breakdown too and I don't want to have it three thousand miles from home.'

'Tell you what,' Henry began persuasively, 'you go, bring her back, then leave her with me. Then take a few weeks' leave from Friday. Go away – out of the country for a while. Crash out in Spain or the Bahamas.'

'But you're short-staffed. Other people are on leave.'

'We'll manage. Just do this last thing for me. I know you're completely shell-shocked and I know you'll be even more knackered with two long flights under your belt in quick succession, but do it and then take as much time off as you need. I'll square it with FB. I would really appreciate it.'

'Shit! You could talk the knickers off a nun. I'll do it.'

'Brilliant! Now all I have to do is convince FB to send you. As you said, it won't be cheap.'

'You mean this conversation could have been for nothing? You don't even know if he'll pay for me to go?'

'Well, I certainly don't have the authority to spend probably well over five grand in air fares, do I?'

'Henry, you are a real bastard.' She punched him on the arm. Hard.

He came off the M6 at junction 29, and cut across south of Preston to Police Headquarters at Hutton.

He did not notice the grey Jaguar which shot past him, motoring south, driven by Maurice Stanway who was carefully rehearsing the words he would be saying to his clients down at Risley Remand Centre, near Warrington. He knew Charlie Gilbert would not be a happy man.

'That is one hell of a lot of money.' FB read the figures again and again and did some calculations in his brain, subtracting the amount from some budget or other. 'Anything cheaper?'

'Yeah.' Henry's lips were pursed like a cat's bottom, his annoyance beginning to show with FB's penny-pinching ways. 'There's no doubt a three-hundred-quid return on a charter flight, cramped up like a sardine, no legroom, no space to sleep, shit food, swollen ankles.'

'And there's something wrong with that?'

'With respect, sir – yes, there is. This is, after all, a business trip, not a holiday flight.'

'But the price! We could buy another helicopter for this.'

Henry shook his head impatiently. 'It's either that – Business Class – or she won't go. Will you, Danny?' He turned unexpectedly to her, bringing her into the conversation.

Up to that point Danny had simply been a spectator. She was thrown for a few seconds. 'No,' she said finally.

FB glowered at her. Then *his* lips pursed into the shape of a cat's arse. He knew he was being railroaded. With dignity, he conceded defeat. 'What must be, must be,' he shrugged.

'If nothing else she deserves a bit of pampering after what she's been through,' Henry said patronisingly, wishing his words unspoken when he saw Danny's angry face.

'When can we get her on a flight?' FB asked, a note of resignation in his voice.

Henry consulted his notes, taken during a conversation with a travel agent with whom the Force often dealt. 'There's one tonight, arriving four a.m. our time, eleven p.m. theirs.'

Danny quickly worked that one out. 'I don't fancy that,' she said disgustedly. 'That means leaving here at eight tonight. No, thanks. I want a decent night's sleep before I go.'

'Shit,' Henry said under his breath. 'That starts cutting things a bit fine then. There is an eight a.m. flight tomorrow, landing in Miami at 4 p.m. our time, eleven a.m. their time. That means you'd have to pick the girl up and do a quick turn around, catch a six p.m. flight back from Miami, which would land back in Manchester at seven a.m. our time on Thursday morning.'

'Jesus,' Danny said. She closed her eyes and sighed. Sixteen hours, two eight-hour flights almost back to back. Not recommended for anyone in any condition. However, Henry's promises about the days following made her decision. 'I'll do it. Just make sure that when I land back in Manchester on Thursday morning, you are waiting for me, probably with a hearse, because I'll be all but dead.'

They both looked at FB whose face wore the mask of pain of a man who was having to fork out money from his own wallet. 'Okay, get it booked.'

Henry reached for the phone.

'Oi! What do you think you're doing?'

'I was going to use your tele—'

FB was shaking his head. He jerked his thumb towards the door. 'Find another.'

Out in the corridor Danny remarked, 'You don't let FB walk all over you, do you? He usually flattens people.'

'He's done that in the past, but since he pulled a particularly dirty trick on me a while ago, which nearly got me shot to pieces, I don't take any shit from him, ACC or not. And that's not meant to sound like bragging. He owes me a lot . . . now, where can I find a phone? I know, let's go out to the Divers' hut. We can get a brew there as well.'

'The Divers' hut?'

'Yeah. I used to be a police diver donkey's years ago. Did a couple of years on the branch when it was a part-time thing; there's people on it I know well.'

Ten minutes later Henry had booked Danny on the flight to Miami and, over a cup of tea, was showing her the intricacies of some diving equipment, boring her to death in the process.

'I'm sorry to say bail was refused.' Stanway's voice was weak.

'On what grounds?'

'Likely to abscond, interfere with witnesses, but the Judge said the case must be reviewed on Thursday and every week thereafter if necessary.'

'What exactly does that mean, Maurice?'

'It means, Charles, that if the police have found no further evidence against you, you will be released, probably with bail conditions.'

'I sense a "but" at the end of that sentence.'

'I think they will have evidence, but not concerning Claire Lilton. It'll be evidence about the body of the girl they found in Darwen. I did some checking on the way down, via the mobile in the car, with a friend I have in the CPS. They're sending an officer to the United States to bring a vital witness back who will give evidence against you.'

Gilbert's head dropped into his hands.

They were in yet another consulting room, this time at Risley Remand Centre. Gilbert's big, round, football of a head rose. He stuffed a little finger up his nose, rooted around and extracted a ball of snot which he wiped underneath the table.

'Who is it?'

'Some girl or other. I don't have details.'

'Fuck! I know who she is. It can only be one person.' He gazed at the ceiling for inspiration. 'This puts me right back to square one, because if she turns up, I'll face a murder charge . . . and I don't want that to happen, Maurice.'

'We'll defend it,' Stanway declared resolutely.

'No, Maurice. I said I didn't want it to happen at all.'

'What are you going to do then? Have another witness murdered?' Stanway's voice rose. 'I mean, she's in America. It's not as though we can send that dumb gorilla

370

round we paid the other night, can we?'

'No, that's true – and keep your voice down, Maurice. Walls have ears.'

'What do you intend doing, then?' Stanway re-enquired. 'I think we should defend it.'

'I will not appear in court on another murder charge.'

'Charles,' Stanway breathed with exasperation, 'she's in America, presumably in police hands. She'll be handed over to the Lancashire officer and brought straight back – in police hands. There is no way you could pull a stunt of any sort.'

'Maurice,' Gilbert began in a tone of voice which was losing patience, 'I want you to do something for me.' He wiggled a forefinger to bring Stanway's face closer and he whispered in the solicitor's ear.

When he had finished, Stanway stood up and paced the room. 'No, no, I will not do it – you cannot make me do it! First I meet and pay some bloody lowlife to commit a murder and now you ask me to do this. I am just digging myself in deeper and deeper . . . I will not do it. Ethically, morally, legally, it is against all my principles. The answer is no, Charles. A definite no.'

Gilbert listened to the tirade, almost expecting Stanway to stamp his feet.

'Finished, Maurice?'

Stanway nodded and licked his dry lips.

'You don't have a fucking choice.'

Hyperventilation: breathing at an abnormally rapid rate, resulting in increased loss of carbon dioxide.

Maurice Stanway put the dictionary down with dithering hands. That was exactly what he was suffering from. His breathing was out of control; his heartrate astounding. His was light-headed; grey flecks were whizzing in front of his eyes. In fact, it was a miracle he had made it from Risley Remand Centre back to his office in the car. It was only sheer willpower which had prevented him from blacking out on the motorway.

The office was deserted. All the staff had gone home.

It was 7 p.m.

Stanway tried to control everything by sitting at his desk and getting a firm grip on his bodily functions. Without success. In the end he yanked open his bottom drawer and reached for the quarter bottle of scotch he kept there. Normally it languished unopened from Christmas to Christmas. He unscrewed the cap and put the bottle to his lips, gurgling down the fiery liquid. Almost half the bottle went down within seconds. He almost choked.

'Christ, Christ, Christ.' His current predicament was beyond his comprehension, but he knew it was solely down to one thing – his weakness. From his experience as a solicitor he knew that weakness was the usual downfall of most people, whether it be a fondness for drink, drugs, money or power, or, as in his case, young boys. Preferably around the ages of seven or eight.

For the millionth time he asked himself why. Why did he like it? Something he knew was completely unnatural, immoral and illegal. But he did. He loved the texture of their soft flesh; he loved causing pain and loved holding them down whilst he completed the act. That too, was a power thing.

But why?

A married man, kids of his own who he would have defended with his life from the advances of someone like himself. A good, moderately successful career. Nice house, two decent cars, money not a problem.

Perhaps his longstanding friendship with Gilbert was one reason. They had known each other since Grammar School, where the brutish Gilbert had led him astray then . . . and the relationship had continued in the same vein for thirty odd years.

Maurice Stanway, the man who was so easily led.

Now he was trapped in a cage of his own making.

Gilbert had such power and personal influence over him it was impossible to resist. For his own survival he had to help Gilbert again.

He pulled his briefcase onto the desk and snapped it open. In his notebook he turned to the page where he had jotted down the number Gilbert had dictated to him. The very private number of a very dangerous man.

Stanway squeezed his face in the palm of his hand, breathed in, held it and exhaled slowly. Then he picked up the phone and dialled quickly so he would not stop halfway through.

Despite the long distance, connection was made immediately.

On the second ring, the phone was answered by a woman.

Stanway quickly explained who he was and asked to speak to that man.

After the rain, Miami was boiling hot again.

However, Felicity Bussola, previously known as Felicity Kruger and before that, Jane Creek, was sitting in the shade of a large umbrella, laid out full-length on a sun lounger by the pool.

She answered the cell-tel as soon as it rang. It had been left on the drinks table next to her. After listening for a few moments, she pressed the 'secret' button and shouted across the pool.

'It's for you, darling, she called. She held the phone out between her first finger and thumb.

Mario Bussola was sitting at a table in the full sunshine, working on a laptop. There was a fax machine by his side, a small copier, a shredder and two other phones, all within reach. He was stripped down to his boxer shorts and the heat of the sun was making his rippling fat glisten and perspire.

Bussola sat up. He frowned. Few people ever called him on this number because it was only divulged to selected and thoroughly vetted individuals. 'Bring the fucking thing here,' he said. There was no way he was going to get up.

'Okay, babe.' She rose to her feet stiffly because the broken ribs had not really begun to heal, and shuffled around the edge of the pool. Not only did the ribs still hurt, but also the base of her spine which was sore and bruised. This particular injury meant she walked like an eighty-year-old.

On the way round the pool she had to walk past two of Bussola's new bodyguards. One was on duty, sat up at a table, reading in the shade of a tree. The other was off-duty, laid out on a recliner in his boxing shorts, browning himself in the rays. Guns and holsters were very much in evidence. They both watched Felicity from behind the dark lenses of their Ray-Bans.

Even though she was injured and probably incapable of anything more than very passive sex, Felicity could not help noticing the bulge in the guard's boxers. It looked a dangerous packet. She longed to reach out for it.

Her husband was gesturing impatiently with his fingers.

She handed the mobile over.

'Why don' you just fuck off inside? I'm sicka lookin' at cha hobblin' around like a witch all day long,' Bussola suggested.

'Okay, babe,' she murmured. 'Anything you say.'

She shuffled away.

Bussola stuck the phone to his ear.

'Is . . . is that Mr Bussola?' Stanway stuttered.

'You rang the number, you tell me.'

'I'll assume it is . . . My name is Maurice Stanway and I'm very sorry to disturb you, I know you are a busy man.'

'How did ya get this number?'

'I . . . er, represent Charles Gilbert. I'm a solicitor – lawyer, if you like. He gave me the number and I'm phoning on his behalf.'

'In that case stop friggin' about and get on with it. You're right – I am busy.'

Felicity crept up the stairs which wound their way up the rear of the house. A first-level landing gave her the chance to rest. The window there looked over the terrace to the pool where she could see her husband on the phone.

Had her eyes been pistols, they would have shot Bussola to pieces. She perched the corner of her bottom on the low window-ledge and opened the window quietly. Just below her were the two bodyguards, unaware she was hovering above them. Bussola was talking gruffly on the phone. The bodyguards were whispering something to each other. Felicity craned her neck and strained to eavesdrop.

'She deserved it . . . no fucker pisses with Mario,' the on-duty guard was saying.

'He made a classic mess of her,' the other observed. Felicity knew his name was Gus. She did not know the other's name.

'Yeah – she used to be a good-lookin' piece a tail. Now her face is so outta line she couldn't even blow a candle out.'

Felicity choked back a sob at the words. They were true. She was horrible to look at now. Face swollen, body bruised to hell and back – was she ever going to recover? Her husband had made a mess of her and she hated him for it.

'Shit!' Bussola roared. He threw the phone down in a fit of temper and it smashed to pieces on the terracotta floor.

The bodyguards shot to attention, nerves showing.

'Ira!' the Italian bellowed. 'Get your stinking Jewish ass out here now.'

Bussola rolled up to his feet and waddled over to the bodyguards quicker than they anticipated. They jumped to their feet.

Felicity dodged behind the cover of the drape.

'Siddown, you assholes,' Bussola instructed them. 'Ira? You heard me, or what?'

'I'm here, I'm here, keep your big Italian mouth in check.' Ira Begin, Bussola's lawyer and adviser in all matters of law, strategy, finance and tactical operations, scuttled like a beetle out of the house, where he had been busy on paperwork. He was the only person who could get away with talking back to Bussola, but even he judged it carefully. Sometimes Bussola needed to be treated with kid gloves and Begin generally knew when. He had been with Bussola many years and though he was a small, insignificant-looking man, he wielded great power and influence in Bussola's empire. He was ruthless when necessary, having cold-bloodedly murdered four people in his time and assisted Bussola to murder or dispose of eight others, including the Armstrong brothers; mostly, though, Begin liked to keep timidly in the background, using his various skills to assist in the acquisition of money and power for his boss. He slid his John Lennon-style spectacles on and blinked in the sunlight. 'What's up?'

'Got an issue.' Bussola perched himself on the edge of the table the bodyguard had been sitting at. He always used the word 'issue' rather than 'problem'.

'Shoot.'

'Gilbert's been arrested in England.'

'How is that an issue?'

'Let me finish, you twerp. In two ways. Firstly, the equipment we are shipping over to him – you know, the video games – need to be dealt with by him. He's going to hand over the little extras we have secreted in them to our other contact in Manchester.' Bussola was referring to the two kilos of cocaine that were going to accompany the arcade games; Gilbert was due to deliver them to a drug dealer who was handling Bussola's North of England operation. If Gilbert was not there to receive the games,

376

there could be major complications, not only of a financial nature. 'And secondly, the English cops are coming across here to pick up a witness against him and take that witness back to testify. It's about a murder five godamned years ago! I mean, who the hell gives a shit about something that old? Anyway, it's that stupid little girl who spoiled some of our fun.'

'Tracey Greenwood – the English girl.' Begin knew immediately; it was his job to know.

'Yeah – that junkie piece a shit. She could damage me – possibly,' Bussola complained. 'And not only that, Gilbert is a friend. I look after friends.'

'I take it you would rather she did not testify?' Begin said fussily.

'It would simplify things all round. Make some enquiries, find out where she is and then just fucking waste her.'

In the window Felicity drew back again when Begin turned and walked back into the house.

She had heard everything that had been said.

Maurice Stanway replaced the phone. His hand shook. His palms were sweating. For the second time in a matter of days he had arranged the murder of an innocent individual.

He stood up, drained emotionally and physically, walked out of his office and found his way to the cloakroom, where he filled a wash-basin and ducked his face into the cold water until his lungs almost burst. He pulled up, spluttering, looking scornfully at his image in the mirror.

'You bastard,' he breathed. 'You absolute bastard.'

... one could be sure I might ... sure of a ...
old nature. And so nothing the Bradleys are content ...
... back to reality. No which a murder is ... pollarded ...
... a dead man, who are full even a she who ...
... Anyway it might until body for she
... some of our love.

"Poor little poet," the English girl began faint-
"... was all you do know," ...

"Yes — and under such a ... should damage me —
wisely fluent ... and no ... one that Clifton
is a friend I feel also friends." ...

"... it is young and rather she did not really," Begin
to it finally.

"It was, and all things it could make, into showing
... and her often she is and that just talking wash and ...
to the window. Prick's slow feet upon, where Lewis
turned and walked back, one tip below.

She had heard something that had been said.

Monster Clinton ... given, the upon like body find,
the middle was wonderful of the about us and a narrow
... on days he had cramped his arms to ... on important
business.

He stood up, dashed eye, comber and placed in
... out of his place. Then, behind the scenes, the
... thin finger, settled a red beam and darted the
... into the side, so each on long silent arms. He
pulled up, waterproof, losing something or nervous in the
... uptown.

"My friend," he finished, "I'm done in beauty."

Chapter Twenty-two

Henry leaned across, flicked the handle and pushed the door open for Danny who walked down her short drive and dropped into the passenger seat. She was dead-beat and looked it. Her bleary eyes could hardly stay open even though she had slept well that night.

But five in the morning is no time for anyone to get up. It reminded her of days gone by when she worked shifts. On reflection she was amazed she handled them so well.

It was now 5.45 a.m., Wednesday morning, and Henry, as promised, was bang on time to pick her up. He estimated a good hour to get to Manchester Airport because even at that time of day, traffic around the city's motorways could be horrendous.

He was wide awake and pretty buzzy. 'Morning!'

'Urumph,' Danny responded, smacking the recliner button and jerking backwards into a nearly prone position. She tossed a holdall into the back seat, then settled as comfortably as possible after turning up the heating a few notches. She was a very warm-blooded animal and needed heat, especially at this time of day, and particularly in her extremities, which were like blocks of ice.

Henry, perceptive as ever, picked up the body language: DO NOT DISTURB. He drove in silence and within minutes they were on the motorway. The radio was tuned into Jazz FM, so Danny closed her eyes, mentally rolled to the beat . . . and fell asleep.

★ ★ ★

'Here we are.'

'What?' Danny shook her head and rubbed her eyes, unable to believe they had arrived at the airport already. 'Is this a Tardis, or what?'

'No, just sounds like one.'

Henry handed her a package which contained a visa for Danny and an emergency passport for Tracey Greenwood. Both had been sent by courier, arriving at midnight at Henry's house. He also handed her a wad of dollar traveller cheques. She stuffed the whole lot into her holdall.

'Got your own passport?'

She shot him a withering glance.

They walked to International Departures where Danny checked in without having to wait. She was told to go directly to passport control.

'Okay, Danny, try to get some sleep on the flight because you'll need it if you're going to do a quick turnaround. Grab the girl and get her back here for tomorrow. I'll be waiting.'

She took hold of Henry's lapels and dragged his face down to her. They kissed briefly.

'Look after yourself. See you tomorrow.'

Danny gave a quick wave and trotted away towards passport control. She didn't glance back.

Thirty minutes later she was settled in the most luxurious airplane seat she had ever been in and was back asleep before the plane left the ground.

Following her rash decision to employ Steve Kruger to tail her husband, Felicity Bussola had learned some hard lessons.

The first was that no one messes with Mario Bussola without getting hurt . . . and that included his wife.

Bussola had beaten up on her remorselessly, enjoying every minute of it. He had smashed her face in, initially

380

with his big fat fists and by pounding her on the edge of the grand piano, breaking her cheekbones. The instrument had subsequently to be cleaned to remove all the blood and snot and two teeth Felicity had dribbled into its workings.

Bussola had not been content with the face. Next he pummelled her body, but not with his hands or feet. He carefully selected a lamp-stand, and wielding it like a baseball bat, whacked her repeatedly with it, following her round the house as she cowered in terror behind any cover she could find. After this he dragged her back to the piano, forced her fingers onto the ivories and slammed the lid down at least a dozen times. But he only actually broke two of her fingers on her left hand.

Then, loving husband that he was, he arranged private medical treatment for her at a clinic he owned.

Very much linked to the first lesson was that it was in her interests not to take any more interest in her husband's whereabouts. He ran businesses which operated twenty-four hours a day and he had to be in a position to supervise them appropriately. So of course he would be away nights. It didn't mean he was being unfaithful to her.

Yeah, right.

The final lesson was that she should be grateful to be married to him. She should be grateful he came home at all and even more grateful if he deigned to fuck her. She learned this lesson, because he told her.

Those, at least, were the direct learning points from hiring Steve Kruger.

She learned a few indirect ones too. One was to never – *ever* – trust the staff. Whatever they said, she would never again take any one of them into her confidence, like she had done with the two bastards who had kidnapped Steve Kruger for her. In the end, Mario employed them, and their first loyalty was to him, not her.

She had also become aware that the house was riddled with listening devices and miniature cameras, monitored from a control room at the gate-house, into which she had never been allowed. She had been under the impression the gate-house was simply a place where Bussola's heavyweights just crashed out. Now she knew it was far more sinister.

Her personal objective now was to find all the surveillance devices and then never to say or do anything further to incriminate herself or any other person in any way. It might get someone killed.

She believed she had located all the bugs. The only rooms which appeared to be free of them were the bedrooms, Mario and Ira Begin's offices and most corridors and landings. She had no idea why the bugs existed and did not dare ask.

The main lesson she had learned from recent events, though, was that she was a stupid, naïve bitch who had been blinded by money and lifestyle and was now more unhappy than she had ever been in the whole of her life. She felt trapped, with no way out . . . and she still didn't know if Bussola was cheating on her.

Not that it seemed to matter any more.

'It took a little time,' Ira Begin said apologetically, 'but he came through in the end.'

Bussola looked up from his desk at Begin who was leaning against the door jamb of his boss's study. It was 9 a.m., on the day after Begin had been given instructions to start making enquiries into the current state of play and whereabouts of Tracey Greenwood.

'Sit down,' Bussola nodded. Begin came into the office and took a seat on the couch, pushing the door to behind him, though it did not close properly.

'I had to pull in some goodwill on this one, Mario. It'll cost.'

'Pay.'

Begin nodded. 'Apparently Tracey Greenwood presented herself to Myrna Rosza at Kruger Investigations and stated she wanted to testify against Gilbert in some old murder case in England.'

'Why Kruger Investigations?'

Begin shrugged. 'Maybe she doesn't trust the authorities. Anyway, she's now with that black bitch Rosza, who's babysitting her until the English cops get here. There's a detective due to land at MIA later today to escort the girl back to Britain – a guy called Danny Furness.'

'Where's the girl now, as we speak?'

Begin heaved a sigh. 'With Rosza, place unknown.'

Bussola gave his assistant a withering look. 'Make it a place known.'

'Working on it as we speak.'

Bussola ran a hand through his hair. 'I want her dead, Ira. If you can negotiate a hand-over with Rosza, then all well and good.'

'I have an idea, a leverage tool we might use.'

Bussola waved a hand dismissively. 'I believe in empowerment, Ira. Do it your way, but if it doesn't work, kill the girl and then kill anyone else who causes any obstruction, cops included.'

At the study door there was the faintest whisper of a sigh, a movement . . . Begin leapt to his feet and jumped to the door.

No one there.

He gave a short laugh and closed it.

Felicity had been watching and waiting for Begin to go in and see her husband, and had then sneaked up to the door and listened to every word spoken between the two men. She had remained still, completely rigid, during the conversation, her ear literally at the crack in the door. Then her ribs twisted slightly and she could not prevent the squeak of pain escaping from her lips.

She spun out of sight in the dog-leg of the hallway just a moment before Begin poked his head out of the door, amazing herself how quickly she could move when she needed to, despite the present condition of her body.

Now she needed to get to a phone which wasn't wired up. Something easier said than done.

Felicity's activities had been very much curtailed since her recent blunder, and getting out of the house alone was now a major operation. Bussola was deeply suspicious of her, wanted to know where she was going, what she was doing, who she was seeing; he also made sure she was accompanied all the time.

Had she not been almost crippled by his beating, slipping away from a chaperone would have been relatively easy. Now she had to think up some other strategy, and double-quick too, for if she could not get away from the house, she'd be unable to warn Myrna of Bussola's plans for the witness and possibly Myrna herself.

Ten minutes after his conversation with Begin, Bussola was again working by the poolside, his laptop connected up to the Internet where he was surfing the pornography pages. Felicity hovered with a complete lack of assertiveness, just in his view.

'Yeah?' he said at length, not raising his head from the screen.

'Sweetheart, I need to get out,' she said humbly.

Bussola stopped tapping at the keys. He regarded her sternly and she prepared herself for the 'why' question.

It came. 'Why?'

'I just wanna drift around a few clothes shops, cheer myself up a little, maybe try on a few things. I won't buy anything.' Not that she could. As part of her punishment, Bussola had chopped off all her credit. 'Honey, please can I?' she pined.

He then shocked her. 'Yeah, you can. In fact, go and buy yourself something.' He delved into his briefcase and extracted a wad of cash. He did not count it, just handed it over.

'Gee . . . thanks honey,' she said genuinely, seduced by

the sight of greenbacks. There must have been about fifteen hundred dollars.

'Pleasure, babe.'

Then she remembered who he was, what he had done to her and others, but nevertheless maintained her gratefulness. 'You are really good to me.'

'Hey!' he clicked his forefinger at her. 'And don't you forget it. Now get lost.'

His attention returned to the computer. Felicity limped painfully away, hearing Bussola's voice call behind her. 'Gus, you take my wife shopping, y'hear?'

Gus stood up. 'Okay, boss.' Felicity saw it was the bodyguard with the rather substantial appendages. It was horrendous to be horny and unable to do anything about it.

Ira Begin had not reached his exalted position in life without proper planning, taking into account all the imponderables of a situation, always making back-up plans for any contingency and ensuring they were in place should his initial course of action not succeed.

As was the case with the situation concerning Tracey Greenwood and Myrna Rosza.

He had quickly established how he was going to approach the problem. It would, as Bussola had suggested, be through a process of negotiation. If that failed, other tactics would drop into place. But what he needed to know before anything happened at all was the exact holding position of the girl.

Once he had that, he would swing into action.

'Captain Crenshaw, Homicide, please.' Begin said into the phone.

'May I ask who is calling?'

'I'm his chiropractor.'

'Thank you. Please hold the line.'

A series of clicks, a slight pause, then, 'Crenshaw, Homicide.'

'Ahh, Captain, this is your chiropractor. I was just wondering if you'd made that appointment yet.'

'Hey, I haven't forgotten.'

'It is urgent. You know how tight your spine is.'

'Yeah, I'll get back to you soon with details.'

'And, of course, you will feel great benefit.' Begin hung up, slightly frustrated. He desperately needed to know where Tracey was being held, otherwise he might start to look stupid.

He picked his phone up again and dialled a zero. He ordered someone from the gatehouse to bring a car up for him. He had to get out and see someone, pronto.

Gus was sticking to Felicity like a limpet, not difficult in her present condition. Dark glasses covering her bruised face, she was moving slowly around the Bal Harbor shops on Collins Avenue, Miami Beach, where high-class names were in abundance – Saks, Cartier, Hermès *et al*. Not much was priced below four hundred dollars and an average price in some shops was four thousand.

'Gus, why don't you fuck off?' Felicity suggested. 'I'm staying in and around these shops, going nowhere else. What about you and me meet back here in an hour, say? I ain't gonna tell Mario . . . but you're going to be bored shitless because all I'm going to do is drift around dress shops.'

'Uh-huh. With respect, but no way, Mrs Bussola. Boss says I've got to stay with you and I'm going to do just that.'

Felicity shrugged.

Gus was a simple son of a bitch and she doubted if she could shake his dog-like determination to follow orders to the letter. She would just have to look for another opportunity and grasp it when it came.

Henry Christie's early start that day did not deter him from going into work to catch up with everything. He drove from the airport, arriving at the station about seven-thirty. Accompanied by a wonderful cup of tea, he took full advantage of the early hour to get some clearance work done at his desk.

At 2 p.m. he was still busy, not having stopped for any refreshment other than of the hot liquid variety. He was really motoring on his paperwork and didn't want to interrupt his momentum.

Blackpool is a town where nobody gets noticed. The extravagant and outlandish are the norm. The normal is the norm too. Being the worse for drink is not unusual; inebriates abound and unless they are fighting drunk, do not raise an eyebrow.

That particular Wednesday afternoon, no one noticed the unshaven, slightly smelly figure of a man who, stinking of booze, staggered and rolled through the streets. Occasionally he bumped into people but muttered apologies. He wasn't looking for trouble. Sometimes he crashed into walls or shopfronts and apologised too. Though he was unsteady on his feet, he did not fall over.

The only thing which perhaps set him apart from the usual drunk was his standard of dress. Though tie-less, his suit was obviously expensive, his shoes too, and his silk shirt was definitely made to measure. Even so, he was paid no heed. People just tried to avoid him.

When he stumbled into the Tower complex, slapping down his cash at the pay desk, he wasn't even acknowledged by the staff. Just another customer, just another drunk.

It was 3 p.m., British time. Henry sat back, interlocked his fingers behind his head and thought about Danny.

Seven hours since she had taken off. The plane, no doubt, would be staring its gradual descent into Miami International, somewhere over the Atlantic Ocean. Henry did not particularly envy her, but thought that nevertheless it would be quite nice to have a taste, however brief, of some Florida sunshine. The weather in Blackpool had not been too bad for a couple of days, but didn't have the warmth Henry remembered from his holiday in Florida a couple of years earlier.

He shook his head. His brain was slowing down now, becoming a nebulous mass after the morning's marathon of paper shifting.

Time for a break. He peered out through the office window and decided on a brisk stroll up the Prom. Clear his head, maybe buy the kids something useless, maybe buy Kate something too. Now *that* would surprise her.

He slid his Barbour on, dropped his PR into a pocket and quit the office. A few minutes later he was on the Promenade. The sun was shining brightly, but it was still extremely chilly.

The drunken man reeled slowly through the Tower amusement complex. He dallied in the Hall of Mirrors, staring angrily at each reflection, particularly the one which made him look very small. He dawdled in the aquarium, staring up at the sharks, detesting the smug way in which they glided smoothly around with no effort whatsoever, masters of their environment, their small, piggy, emotionless eyes with a bead on him, like they were telling him something.

Well, fuck them! There was nothing they could tell him about himself he didn't already know.

For half an hour he sat on the balcony overlooking the Tower ballroom, watching the dancers slide around the floor. He had a couple of large whiskies whilst he watched the, in the main, elderly couples dancing the afternoon away in a ritual more reminiscent of the thirties than the nineties. He went to the bar and gulped a further Scotch which really seemed to hit the mark.

Then he made his way to the lift which would take him all the way up the Tower.

With unusually helpful tailwinds, Danny's plane touched down half an hour ahead of schedule at Miami International, 10.30 a.m. US time. She had been in the air seven and a half hours but it was only like the blink of an eye to her because, with the exception of devouring the rather delicious meal provided, she had slept all the way.

Very refreshed, she made her way off the plane, straight through customs with the only slight hitch being the diligent checking of her visa at passport control. In the arrival lounge she expected to be met, but not by Arnold Schwarzenegger. Or to be more accurate, Mark Tapperman, who bore a card with Danny's name on it.

'That's me,' said Danny, approaching the big man.

Tapperman looked at the name on the card, then up at Danny.

'It's short for Danielle,' she explained.

'Oh, right, yeah.' Tapperman was completely thrown. 'They didn't say I was going to meet a woman.'

'Is that a problem?'

'No, no, no.' Tapperman regained some sort of control of himself and thrust out his right hand which Danny shook. 'Welcome to Miami. I'm Lieutenant Mark Tapperman, Miami PD. Here.' He flashed his badge.

'I'm Danny Furness, as you already know. Detective Sergeant, Blackpool CID.' She showed him her warrant card.

'Lemme take your case. Come on, follow me. My car's waiting.'

'I'll carry it myself, Mark. Thanks.'

'So . . . good flight?'

'Excellent.'

'Blackpool? I heard of that place. Guess it's pretty

389

quiet. Not much going on – not much excitement cop-wise, I guess.'

Danny smiled inwardly. 'I guess not.'

Henry Christie could not resist Robert's Oyster Bar. He dived in and bought himself a tub of potted shrimps which he proceeded to eat whilst leaning against the sea-wall railings and looking across to the Golden Mile. The shrimps tasted wonderful.

Henry's eyes followed the Tower upwards, 519 feet to the pinnacle. It was a clear day and the view from the platform would be superb.

The last of the shrimps went into his mouth. It was time to head back to the office and maybe have an early dart home.

'Gus, you cannot follow me in here, no matter what Mario told you. I am a lady, this is a ladies' changing room and if you try to come in, I'll scream the place down.'

'Uh, I dunno about this,' he said dumbly.

'You'd have to shoot the security guards,' Felicity said. 'Now, I'm going in there to try these two dresses on.' They were folded across her arm. 'And I'll probably be about fifteen minutes, okay? There's nowhere I can go, so relax and go choose something sexy for your girl from the lingerie department.'

'Lingerie?'

'Underwear to you – panties, brassières, you know the kind of stuff. Over there.' She spun him round and shoved him in the direction of the department. He tottered away unhappily, giving several backward glances.

Felicity went into the changing area and chose the booth furthest away, locking the door behind her.

Once inside she sat down and relaxed. Then she began to undress.

Henry Christie was correct. The view from the platform almost at the top of the Tower *was* magical. No one was allowed to go to the very top these days, however; too many people jumped off. Now visitors were restricted to the covered platform at 380 feet, from which there was a 360-degree view of Blackpool and its environs.

The drunken man walked around the platform, feeling the fresh wind in his hair, looking at the view, not really appreciating either.

Above the head-high railings was a wire-mesh cage to dissuade people from climbing up and over and launching themselves into oblivion. The man walked round, inspecting the mesh above his head, noting the location of the joins, where the weak points were.

It did not take him long to find what he was looking for.

He clambered up the metal railings and reached for the mesh, pulling it apart at one of the seams. Within moments he had broken through and clambered up onto the cage, sitting on the edge with nothing now between himself and the roofs of the shops below. He shuffled right to the edge, dangling his legs over. One last push, and he would be over.

It would be over.

'What do you think of this one, Gus?'

Felicity emerged from the changing room, displaying the thousand-dollar creation she was trying on for size. And also to reassure Gus, who had spent no time in lingerie; he had been sitting on a chair at the entrance to the changing rooms, agitatedly tapping his feet, peering in for a sight of Mrs Bussola.

'It's really nice, Mrs B,' Gus said. He tried to sound enthusiastic.

'Thanks, Gus. You're obviously a connoisseur.'

'A what?'

'A thick cunt,' Felicity said under her breath. She

twirled back into the changing area, accompanied by an attentive member of staff, to try on the next outfit.

Before she closed the door, she spoke briefly to the sales assistant. 'Darling, do you have access to a mobile phone? I seem to have left mine at home and I need to phone my husband. Of course I'll pay for any calls and any extras.' She gave a knowing nod to the woman and crushed a fifty-dollar note into her receptive palm.

'I'll see what I can do, Mrs Bussola.'

'Oh, and by the way, don't let on to that goon, will you?'

'You can be assured of my discretion.'

Ira Begin was on edge. Everything was now ready. He had been to see the person who would act as the last line of attack if the worst came to the worst. Now all he needed to be told was where the girl was.

He was in the rear of a car being driven back to Bussola's house in South Beach. His cell-tel was on his lap and he prayed for it to ring. If it didn't, then a certain police officer would have more than just his annual retainer cut off.

He bounced the small phone in his hand, desperately holding himself back from calling Captain Crenshaw. From past experience, Begin knew it would not speed matters up.

Then it rang and Begin jumped. He fumbled to answer it.

'Yeah.' He listened. 'Got that. Consider your efforts to be a good investment.'

Begin ended the call.

Now he had everything he needed.

'Patrol to attend the Tower: report of a possible jumper. I repeat.'

Henry Christie, normally so poor at using the PR other than for his personal benefit, had actually tried to develop

392

some good habits since becoming a Detective Inspector. He actually listened to it these days and even while he had been out eating shrimps, he'd kept one ear on the comings and goings of police activity around the town.

'DI Christie received. I am literally outside the Tower now. I'll attend.'

'Roger. Thanks, sir. Any other patrols to assist?'

Several called up, by which time Henry was running across the Promenade, looking up as he did so.

It was a very long way up. And down.

It was one of the biggest cars Danny had ever seen in her life, and was like sitting in a mobile living room. Typically American, she thought; all the same, lovely and very comfortable. But not a patch on her beloved, now deceased, Merc.

She looked discreetly sideways at the big detective who was driving. His left elbow rested out of the window and he was steering using his left little finger, occasionally holding the wheel with his right when necessary. He whistled tunelessly, looked laid back and cool in his dark glasses. Danny had not thought to pack sunglasses, but did not mind the bright sun in her eyes. It made a change from Britain's pathetic effort.

'Not far now,' Tapperman informed her.

'Fine.' They had not travelled far anyway.

Ten minutes later they pulled up in the driveway of a large white house in a fairly exclusive development.

'I thought we'd be going to a cop shop.'

'Naw,' drawled Tapperman, releasing his seat belt. 'This girl's got an aversion to cops.'

Danny grabbed her holdall and got out of the car, which was still bouncing on its soft springs from stopping. As they walked up the drive, past another large vehicle, some type of people-carrier, the front door opened and a black woman stood on the threshold, right hand extended.

'Hi, I'm Myrna Rosza. You must be Danny Furness. I'm pleased to meet you.'

'And I'm pleased to meet you, Myrna.'

They shook hands and appraised each other critically, both liking what they saw. Somehow there was something between them immediately. A connection. A closeness. Both sensed this would be a harmonious relationship.

'Come in, you must be bushed.'

'I'm not too bad. Where's Tracey?'

Myrna's eyes flickered upwards. 'Asleep, like she's been for most of the time. I don't intend to wake her, if that's okay. I think she needs all the rest she can get. Maybe you'd like a shower, get freshened up? Then I'll do us a meal and we can talk.'

'Sounds good.'

They smiled at each other.

Behind them Tapperman said, 'I'll leave you to it. If you have any problems, bell me anytime.'

'Sure, thanks Mark.'

When he'd gone, Myrna said conspiratorially, 'Bit soft dumbass, but a heart of gold. Here, let me take your bag.'

Henry barged his way through the tourists of the day, unceremoniously heaving them to one side where necessary. He arrived at the lift to find a long queue of people waiting to go up the Tower.

'You a police officer?' somebody shouted.

'Yeah.' Henry turned. He recognised the manager of the place.

'Come with me.'

He led Henry to the service lift which was ready and waiting and empty. Henry peered through the window as the lift rose, watching in case the jumper decided to fly before he got there.

Felicity was standing in her underwear when the sales assistant returned with a mobile phone. The woman's mouth sagged open in shock when she saw the bruises all over Felicity's torso. The gangster's wife caught the expression and with a sneer said, 'It's how my husband shows affection.'

Stunned, the woman held out the mobile. Felicity banged in a number and waited impatiently for the connection. The sales assistant withdrew.

'Kruger Investigations? I want to speak to Myrna Rosza. *Urgently.*'

It was wonderfully fresh, brilliant up here. The drunken man was sitting on top of the mesh, looking at a view inland across Lancashire, towards the Pennines. Then he looked down between his legs and swallowed. There was a flat roof below on which he would surely land.

For a split second there was hesitation. He wondered if he had the courage to do this thing.

Someone on the platform shouted, 'Don't do it, mate!'

But he had to.

For what he had done, he would never be able to live with himself again.

Myrna, Felicity was informed, could not be contacted. 'This is a matter of life and death,' Felicity pleaded. 'It concerns the girl she is protecting. Please let me speak to her. I *need* to speak to her. It's vital . . .' And here Felicity made a guess. 'Bussola knows where they are and he's going to kill the girl – *and* Myrna, if she gets in the way. I've got to speak to her! I'm Steve Kruger's ex-wife. It's imperative . . .'

'Just hold the line,' the polite telephonist said.

'Fuck!' Felicity closed her eyes, which flipped open when the changing-room door clattered open.

Gus appeared, breathing heavily, the sales assistant behind him, remonstrating. 'You cannot barge in here like this!' Gus rammed the palm of his big hand into her face, scrunched it up like a piece of paper and said, 'Go away, please.' He pushed her with such force that she crashed through the closed door of the changing booth opposite.

Gus lurched across to Felicity, a hurt and disappointed look on his face. He pulled the mobile out of her hand and threw it to the floor, ramming his heel down on it.

'You shouldn't ought to have done that, Mrs B. You lied to me, so get dressed, please. I'm gonna take you home.'

The service lift doors opened, Henry stepped out and immediately saw the man sitting on the overhead mesh.

All the way up Henry had been sifting through the possible openings he might use to begin the process of talking the man down.

He strolled to the left of the man, who looked down and showed recognition in his face. Henry recognised him too.

Before Henry could open his mouth, the man gave himself a push and went over the edge.

Chapter Twenty-three

'This is a lovely house,' Danny commented to Myrna. They were standing in the kitchen. The refrigerator was open and appeared to be crammed full of Hurricane Reef Lager, row upon row of bottles. Danny saw them. 'Somebody seems to like this.'

'Yeah, try one.' Myrna slid a bottle out, flipped the cap and handed it to Danny. She took a drink.

'Gorgeous,' she said approvingly.

'Come on, let's walk out here.'

Myrna led the way to the terrace at the rear of the house where they sat by the pool. The sun was bright and hot, the sky crystal clear. Danny closed her eyes and tilted her face upwards. 'Fantastic . . . you don't know how lucky you are.'

'Good weather, bad criminals.'

'Bad weather, bad criminals,' Danny rejoined.

Myrna smiled. She let her eyes wander around the pool, dreaming of the moment, not many days before, when Steve Kruger had entered her whilst they balanced precariously in the shallow end, her legs wrapped around him. She blinked away the beginning of a tear. It had been wonderful, intense . . . made her feel so alive. She sighed.

'It is a nice house, belongs to my employer Steve Kruger who is now dead, murdered. I think you know the full story.'

'Yes, I got a telephone briefing from Karl Donaldson

before I left. He filled me in on everything.'

'Why does Tracey wish to speak to you only, Danny?'

'Not sure. When the murdered girl went missing all those years before, I interviewed all the friends we could find, but the files I re-read before I came don't have a Tracey Greenwood as being one of them. So I don't know why she wants to speak to me. She obviously knows me, but I don't know her.' Danny sipped her lager, revelled in the sunshine on her face. 'If she can come up with what she claims, we have a very good chance of nailing Mr Gilbert – but we'll have to protect her. The last witness we had against him has ended up dead. Coincidence? I think not.'

'I've seen Gilbert in action. He was disgusting.' Myrna shuddered.

'And there are possibilities of more stuff from her once she gets talking, I suppose. There's the American angle, for example. When we get back, Karl Donaldson will be coming up to interview her about what she knows about Bussola – but that's for the future. My priority now is to get her home in one piece, get a statement from her on the way, and get Gilbert charged with another murder before he walks free. If I'm late returning and he's out on bail, there's a good chance we won't see him again. I don't want that to happen.'

Myrna looked towards the house.

A bare-footed Tracey plodded out of the French windows towards them.

Danny's eyes narrowed as she immediately recognised her.

Twenty minutes after discovering Felicity making an illicit phone call, Gus dragged her back to the Miami Beach mansion and paraded her in front of Bussola.

'Who were you calling?' Bussola demanded. 'Tell me now, or I bust you up again.'

'Just a friend, that's all. A girlfriend – someone to talk

to. Women's things. I've been like a prisoner in here. I need to get out, I need some company. Honestly, that's all. I wouldn't do anything stupid. Not again, not ever. I've learned.'

Bussola was unsure. He looked at Felicity with a deadly glint as he considered what she had said. He spoke to Gus, the bodyguard. 'You did well, very well. Now fuck off and have the rest of the day off.'

'Thanks, boss.'

'And as for you, I'll think about what to do with you.' He hovered and hesitated before eventually leaving Felicity on her bed.

She held her breath and could not believe how fortunate she had been.

She had another chance.

Better not blow it this time.

Maurice Stanway's body had to be scraped off the roof with shovels and put into a plastic bag. He had landed head first and his skull was no more, other than a pulp of brain, skin, bone and blood. His shoulders and the upper part of his body had also been crushed to a mush; only his lower abdomen and legs remained intact.

Henry thought it was a good job he had seen Stanway's face just before he jumped, otherwise there was a good possibility that identification would have been a problem.

What the hell drives a man to this? Henry pondered, as he watched the gruesome task of body recovery take place. Fortunately it wasn't a job for CID. Suicides were dealt with by uniform. Henry was happy to hand it over to the patrol Sergeant.

Was it anything to do with Charlie Gilbert? Henry thought, then dismissed the idea. Enquiries would probably reveal money troubles, a complex personal life and a myriad of other things, none of which were Charlie Gilbert-related. Henry imagined that working for Gilbert would have been quite lucrative and not something for which you'd chuck yourself off Blackpool Tower.

'If you don't mind,' Danny said to Myrna, 'I think it might be worthwhile getting a few things down on paper now. The return flight isn't until later this evening and I might as well make use of these hours, even though I'd rather be shopping in the city.'

'Tell you what, then. You spend, say, a couple of hours doing this. In the meantime, I'll arrange for another member of my staff to stand in for me and look after Tracey and later this afternoon I'll drive you into Miami, maybe do some shops, hit a restaurant and then pick Tracey up on the way to the airport. How's that sound? Tight, I know – but possible.'

'Sounds great. It would be a sin not to get a feel of the place, wouldn't it?'

'It certainly would.'

They had been chatting by the French windows whilst Tracey lounged on a chair by the pool.

Danny went over and sat next to her. She had decided not to mince her words. 'Your name is not Tracey Greenwood, is it?'

Danny knew she was right. The girl in front of her was not called Tracey Greenwood, but Tracey Higgins. She had been a resident at Mowbreak Children's Home in Blackpool some five years earlier. Danny had reported her Missing from Home on several occasions and she had always returned, until the last time when she reported her missing and she never came back. On that occasion she had gone missing with her best friend, Annie Reece, whose remains had been recently discovered by two frolicking lovers.

Things began to slot slowly into place for Danny.

'No, you're right,' the girl admitted. 'My last name isn't Greenwood, but I am called Tracey.'

'Tracey Higgins,' Danny interjected. 'I remember. But why the name change?'

400

She shrugged. 'Because Charlie Gilbert said it was the only way to get me out of the country. I didn't have a passport in my real name and Charlie gave me a new one. I was only thirteen at the time, but the date of birth on the passport said I was eighteen. And I looked it. I could get away with that easy if I was dolled up.'

'So Charlie obtained a forged passport for you?' Danny asked, wanting this confirmed in her own mind.

Tracey nodded. 'And a US work permit, visa, all the immigration crap you need to get into this country. Everything to start a new life.'

Danny almost permitted herself a smile. So it hadn't been too far-fetched to claim in court that Gilbert could obtain forged travel documents after all. She was relieved.

'A new life at the age of thirteen?'

'The old one was shit anyway and Charlie promised me loads of things.'

'Why?'

'Why?' Tracey snorted. 'Because I saw him kill Annie and he panicked and this was his way of shutting me up, I reckon.'

The Bussola household was unusually quiet.

Felicity paused on the stairs and looked out across the pool. Her husband was at the poolside, working away at his computer. One bodyguard lounged in the shade, reading a thriller.

Felicity trod quietly downstairs and wandered from room to room, finding no one else around, not even Begin, which was odd. He was usually creeping around somewhere. She went outside and hobbled around the gardens, looking for more bodyguards. All she found was one lonely soul in the gatehouse, playing patience.

Like a bolt of lightning, it suddenly struck her why they were all missing.

They had gone to get the girl, kill her and anyone else who got in their way.

401

* * *

It took time and not a little coaching and coaxing, a lot of patience and a good deal of skill to get Tracey talking. Her story was not much different to the one Danny had heard from Grace and it did not shock Danny to hear it. Nevertheless it expanded the picture of Charlie Gilbert and his lifestyle.

Tracey was a girl local to Blackpool and had ended up in care through the usual series of mishaps, bad parenting and abuse so very common with children in her social sphere. She was put in a home, from which she frequently absconded. Most of her time was spent around the arcades where she met Ollie Spencer and subsequently Charlie Gilbert. She was lured by money, food and drugs and enjoyed every minute of it.

She had only just begun her story properly when the chimes of the front doorbell echoed through the house, interrupting the conversation. Tracey stopped talking and sat back. Myrna, seated at the far end of the pool, out of earshot, pulled a face, but got up and walked through the house to the front door.

She froze when she saw who was standing there. It was Ira Begin, Mario Bussola's right-hand man. She recognised him immediately.

'Mrs Rosza,' Begin said with a nod. 'How do you do? My name is—'

'I know exactly who you are.'

Begin gave a supercilious smirk. 'In that case there is no need for introductions.'

'What do you want?'

'I'd like to talk to you about a mutual acquaintance of ours.'

'I don't think we have one.' Myrna's mind raced frantically; panic crept through her being. How the hell did he get to know where I am? she demanded of herself. Myrna started to close the door.

Like a bad door-to-door salesman, Begin jammed his

foot behind the threshold, preventing closure. 'Oh yes we do,' he said. He reminded Myrna of a slimy reptile. 'And I suggest you spare some time now to discuss the matter with me.'

They eyed each other, cat and mouse.

'Okay,' Myrna relented, 'but first let me close the door and come back to you in a couple of minutes.'

'Is that a promise?'

'It is.'

'In that case . . .' Begin lifted his foot out of the door. Myrna closed it, whirled round and ran out to the pool.

'What is it?' Danny asked, seeing Myrna's worried expression.

'Er, nothing to worry about, I hope, but we need to talk. Tracey, will you give us a few minutes? Go upstairs to the bedroom you've been using? Danny and I need to discuss something.'

'Yeah, sure, whatever.' She failed to pick up any of Myrna's tension. She was thinking about her next fix and where it was coming from. She calmly trundled inside the house.

Danny, however, could feel and almost see Myrna's agitation. 'What is it? What's wrong?'

'Look, I don't know – but Mario Bussola's right-hand man is on the doorstep. I smell big trouble here. Danny, will you just hang back out of sight? It might be better if he doesn't know you're here – unless he knows already, of course.'

The doorbell chimed again.

'Time's up,' Begin said when Myrna opened the door.

Mark Tapperman was at the scene of a murder. One of a series of drive-by shootings which had sprung up from an inter-gang dispute in downtown Miami. Two gang members had been splattered whilst sitting on the sidewalk terrace of a coffee shop. Problem was, two civilians had also been struck and one had died. Three bodies, blood, guts, overturned tables, chairs, shattered glass and lots of cops.

Tapperman surveyed the carnage. If only the civvie hadn't bought it, he was thinking. Two gang members gunned down was easy to deal with. They deserved what they got for living like they did. But a civilian down put another angle on it.

Now the cops had to go all out to solve it, otherwise there would be a major outcry.

As if he didn't have enough on his plate, not least of which was the small matter of hunting down Patrick Orlove, the man responsible for blowing Steve Kruger's brains out. That was a trail that had gone ice-cold very quickly. Tapperman suspected Orlove had been whisked out of state, possibly out of the country. He despaired of ever laying his hands on the bastard.

Tapperman shook his head, refocused on the three dead bodies and lots of blood.

His mobile chirped.

'Is that Lieutenant Tapperman?' the worried female voice enquired.

'Yup.'

'I'm Erica from Kruger Investigations. I'm really sorry to bother you, but I thought you might be able to help me.'

'I'll try.' Tapperman eased a toecap under the shoulder of one of the dead gang members and lifted him slightly to get a look at what remained of the face.

'We've been trying to get hold of Myrna Rosza for some time, but no one here knows where she is. There's no reply on her home number, or cell-tel. She hasn't told us where she can be reached and we need to pass an urgent message to her. I know it's a long shot, but—'

Tapperman pulled his toe away. 'I know where she is – at Steve Kruger's house. But you won't be able to call there because his phone has been disconnected since he died. If you don't mind me asking, what's the message?'

Erica relayed the message she had taken earlier from Felicity Bussola.

'Jesus Christ!' Tapperman gasped. 'Leave it with me . . . Harry!' He called over to another detective. 'Take over, I gotta go!'

'I'll come straight to the point,' Ira Begin said. He and Myrna were in the dining room, sat at the table opposite each other. He lifted his briefcase onto the table and took out a plastic wallet. 'You are presently protecting a witness by the name of Tracey Greenwood?' It was a statement and question combined. He raised his eyebrows to invite a reply. None came.

Begin shrugged amicably. 'I know she is here, whether or not you wish to admit it.'

How, you bastard? Myrna's mind screeched. Who could have told you she was here?

'Now you know as well as I do that I could simply walk in here with a show of force and take her away, probably hurting people like yourself in the process. I don't wish to do that because I like win-win situations, where everybody comes out with some profit. The lawyer in me likes to negotiate, so I have a proposition for you.'

'I can't wait.'

'In this wallet I have copies of certain documents that, if they were made public and sent to the right people – the IRS, the FBI, CIA, your customers, even . . . would destroy Kruger Investigations.' Begin opened the wallet and shook out a sheaf of papers. He placed them on the table and fanned them out. 'They relate to a very illegal business transaction in which Kruger Investigations acted as agents to supply certain goods to enemies of the USA.'

'Cut to the chase.'

'Hand the girl over and I will ensure you receive the originals of these documents within the hour. Then we shall both be happy. You won't have this hanging over your head like the Sword of Damocles and the girl will not be a thorn in our side.'

'And what about her? Where does she stand in this win-win situation?'

'She loses.'

'And if I don't agree?'

'I'll take her by force, kill you if necessary, but if I don't kill you, I'll ruin Kruger Investigations just for fun.'

'Shit, Myrna, answer the godamned phone!' Tapperman was driving maniacally, steering with one hand, mobile crushed to his ear by his free hand. He swerved dangerously, in and out of traffic, accelerating and braking madly, yelling obscenities at all other road-users.

'How much time do I have to think?'

Ira Begin made a show of checking his watch. 'Not long.'

Myrna stood up. 'Let me have a few minutes. I need to go over this in my head.'

'Sure, fine, Mrs Rosza, but don't do anything rash like call the cops.'

'As if.'

She left the room and walked quickly into the kitchen where Danny waited apprehensively.

'Where the hell's my phone?' Myrna demanded.

'Out by the pool, I think.'

She ran out and picked it up off the coffee table and started to dial. Danny was behind her. 'What's going on, Myrna?'

'Why the hell is this thing not working?' Myrna looked at the machine and realised the battery was dead. She did a quick exchange for one in her purse. Immediately, she thumbed the power button, the phone rang.

'Yes?' she answered cautiously.

It was Mark Tapperman. Myrna listened as he shouted to her to get the hell out of the house.

'It's too late, Mark. Begin's already here and by assumption he's probably got back-up stashed away nearby.'

'I'll try and get a team there myself,' Tapperman yelled, then, 'Oh shit!'

There was a loud crash and Myrna held the phone away from her ear. 'Mark, you okay?'

'Yeah, yeah, f'Christ's sake. I've just hit a parked car. You try and get outta there, Myrna. I'll do my best to get a SWAT team to you, or something.' He ended the call.

Myrna eyed Danny. 'Bussola wants Tracey, the easy way or the hard way. I can't give her to him, Danny. I don't know what the hell to do.'

'You go back and keep Begin talking,' Danny said, getting her brain into gear. 'I'll nip upstairs and get Tracey. Have you got the keys for that car on the drive?'

'The Chevy? Yeah – hung up in the kitchen.'

'Right – I'll get Tracey into the van while you talk to Begin. When she's there I'll come and get you and we'll make a run for it. How does that sound?'

'Like shit, Danny – but it's better than anything I can think of at this moment in time. Can you use a gun, Danny?'

The English detective nodded unsurely as Myrna told her where Steve Kruger kept the firearms in his bedroom.

'This was supposed to be a jolly,' Danny said to herself as she sneaked quietly upstairs and went into Steve Kruger's bedroom. 'Not a fucking Wild West show.' She opened the drawer in the bedside cabinet as instructed and found Kruger's snub-nosed .38 special. She tucked it very carefully into the waistband of her jeans at the small of her back.

Next she went to the wardrobe where she found two more weapons, shaking her head in astonishment on seeing them. 'Just what sort of a country have I come to?' she asked herself.

One of the guns was a pistol, the other a Heckler & Kock sub-machine pistol, very light, accurate and deadly. It looked thoroughly evil to Danny. She put the small pistol down her waistband next to the revolver and dropped the HK into her holdall.

Then she went to collect Tracey.

'I want the originals in my hand before I give up the girl,' Myrna bluffed to Begin.

'That will not be possible,' he said. 'I am a man of honour; as I said, you will have the originals delivered to you within an hour of me taking possession of the girl. Trust me.'

Myrna leaned back, pretending to consider this. In reality she was straining to hear outside the dining-room door, trying to judge where Danny was up to with Tracey.

'You keep very, very quiet,' Danny hissed. 'Believe me, your life depends on it, so does mine and so does Myrna's.'

The girl was compliant, terrified.

Danny crept downstairs ahead of her, into the hallway and to the front door, passing the dining room on the way.

From the front door it was less than twelve feet to the Chevrolet. Danny looked at the keys in her hand and her heart sank when she saw the remote-control locking fob. She pointed it at the car and held her breath, hoping it would not make too much of a noise.

There was a loud squeak as the alarm was deactivated and the doors unlocked.

Danny paused, expecting a reaction. Nothing happened.

She walked confidently to the car, her eyes taking in everything there was to be seen up and down the cul-de-sac – including the two sedans parked a hundred yards away, each packed with muscle. Danny swallowed. She opened the rear door and beckoned Tracey to get in.

'Lie down across the seat and don't move,' Danny instructed her harshly. She jumped into the driver's seat, threw her holdall into the passenger footwell and started the engine.

Once she was happy it was ticking over nicely, she ran back to the house.

Myrna winced when she heard Kruger's car squawk like a parrot, and eyed Begin in readiness for a reaction.

He simply sat staring at Myrna, not in the least suspecting what was going on.

'Okay,' Myrna said with a sigh, apparently reaching a decision. She leaned forwards. 'I'll do it.'

Begin beamed the smile of the modest victor. 'You've seen sense,' he patronised.

The door crashed open and Danny came into the room like a whirlwind, snub-nosed revolver in her right hand, pistol in her left.

'Here – catch!' she shouted and tossed the pistol across to Myrna who caught it expertly, rising from her chair, pivoting round and pointing it at Begin.

'Actually I'm not interested in your fucking deal,' she said. 'It stinks.'

'You fool,' Begin said calmly, sitting back.

'No, I don't think so. Now you sit there like a good boy, otherwise I'll blast your fucking head off.'

The women backed slowly out of the room, their guns aimed dangerously at Begin. He did not move, other than to shake his head deprecatingly.

Once out of the door, Danny shouted, 'You drive!'

They turned and ran out to the Chevrolet which Myrna slammed into reverse. She stood on the gas and released the parking brake. The wheels spun and the car lurched backwards.

Begin appeared at the front door, beckoning towards the two cars parked down the road, wildly flapping his

409

hands to get his message across.

'Scrotes ahead,' Danny yelled.

'Seen 'em,' Myrna retorted, gritting her teeth.

As the car swerved out of the driveway, Myrna yanked the gear-stick into Drive and gunned the gearbox into 'kick-down'. It surged forwards.

Up ahead, both cars moved away from the kerb and stopped side by side, effectively blocking the road. Men jumped out, took cover behind open doors and aimed weapons at the Chevrolet.

'Get down!' Myrna screamed. 'And hold on tight!' In the back seat, Tracey whimpered pathetically.

The first bullet crashed through the windshield. Danny felt it whizz inches away from her head. The next one embedded itself in her headrest. She ducked. Myrna grappled with the wheel. She pulled it down to the left, mounted the kerb with a thud, putting the Chevrolet at an angle to the shooters. Bullets slammed into the side. Danny's window shattered into a million pieces and the bullet passed right in front of Myrna's eyes, exiting through her side window which also shattered.

A second later Myrna powered the Chevrolet through a low, perfectly manicured and cultivated hedge, into a front garden. This was the only way past Bussola's men.

Whether it was braveness or stupidity, Danny wasn't sure – probably a combination of both – but she sat up, having pulled the HK out of her holdall. She rested it on the doorframe where the window had once been, aimed it in the general direction of the men and pulled back the trigger. Even though there was hardly any recoil, her shooting was wild and inaccurate but it had the desired effect of making Bussola's men dive for better cover as the Chevrolet roared past.

Myrna pulled back onto the road, unable to stop a smile cracking on her face.

Danny slumped, feeling the crumbs of the broken glass all down her back. She looked at the bullet-holes in the windshield, the remnants of the two side windows, twisted to see the bullet-hole in the headrest and then looked at the weapon in her hands which was literally smoking. Unbelievably a sensation of pure exhilaration went through her.

'That was amazing,' she said to Myrna. 'Fucking amazing.'

everybody, the beginning of the term. He studied
better to read the different in the subject and the
looked at her reason in her hand which we would
might... Unfortunately a question of view children
were (though are...

F.S. — As expected, she will be liked. Thatlong
amount.

Chapter Twenty-four

It was a thick, buff, legal envelope. On the front of it were written two names – Henry Christie and Danny Furness. It had been lying, still sealed, on Henry's dining-room table ever since the Constable investigating the suicide of Maurice Stanway had dropped it off at his home address.

There had been no obvious suicide note amongst Stanway's papers at his office, the Constable told Henry. Just this envelope with the two names on it. It could well be the suicide note, but the PC was handing it over to Henry for him to do whatever he wanted to do with it that evening, so long as he returned it the following day.

The police were actually under strict instructions from the Coroner not to open and read suicide notes if they were sealed; only the Coroner was allowed to do that.

Henry tore the envelope open.

A neatly bound file of papers slithered out. Handwritten, probably by Stanway.

Henry began to read: *This is for the two detectives investigating the case of Charles Gilbert. By the time you read this, I, Maurice Alan Stanway, will be dead, having taken my own life. I decided to end my life, simply because I could no longer bear to live with myself, having consigned two other people to death. I will tell you about that in a while. But I detest myself utterly. I am a weak, pathetic individual, easily led and influenced. And the main influence in my life has been Charles Gilbert. I know everything there is to know about*

Charles Gilbert and the last thing I want to do is die without revealing these details to other people.

Henry stopped reading and flicked quickly through the pages. There were eleven. It would take him some time to read them. He poured himself a large Bell's with a dash of soda and settled down.

The house was quiet. His wife, Kate, and his two daughters, Jenny and Leanne, were tucked up in bed asleep. They were more exhausted than he was by the long hours he'd been putting in.

It was 11 p.m.

Myrna, Danny and Tracey spent the rest of that afternoon under guard, courtesy of Mark Tapperman and the Miami Police Department, at Miami International Airport. Tapperman had arranged for the use of an executive lounge and posted uniformed, armed police officers at every entrance and exit.

No one seriously thought Bussola was stupid enough to try anything, but better safe than sorry.

It was a tense afternoon for the women. They said little to each other, even less to Tapperman. When it was announced their flight would be delayed another hour, it only served to make them more jumpy than ever.

At 7 p.m., passengers were called to the boarding gate.

Surrounded by armed cops, Danny and Tracey were escorted all the way to the gate, jumping ahead of the queue of passengers, right up to the door of the plane.

Myrna and Tapperman were with them all the way.

At the door, Danny turned to Myrna. They embraced.

'It'll be a tight schedule at the far end,' Myrna said.

'Yes, I know,' Danny said. There was an 8 a.m. landing, British time. Very tight, especially when the court sat at 10 a.m.

'Look after yourself,' Danny told Myrna. 'We'll be safe from here on in, but you'll have to watch your back.'

'I'll be fine,' Myrna said. 'I've got this big oaf watching

over me, even though he keeps crashing cars on the way to help me.' She thumbed Tapperman. He gave a lop-sided grin and shook hands with Danny, who ushered Tracey onto the aircraft.

Tapperman and Myrna walked back against the tide of boarding passengers. Tapperman bumped into one guy who had a vaguely familiar look about him. Tapperman thought no more about the encounter.

Felicity suppressed a giggle. She did not even need to have her ear to the door to listen to this one: Mario Bussola going ape-shit with Ira Begin for letting three women outwit and outrun him. Bussola's angry voice boomed down the hallway outside Begin's office and all Felicity had to do was stand in the doorway of the living room and try not to laugh too loudly.

They had done it, Felicity thought triumphantly. The girl was now on her way to England safe and sound.

And Mario was left with a face full of scrambled egg.

The office door opened and Begin stormed out. Felicity stepped back out of sight.

'It's not as bad as you think, Mario,' the under-pressure Begin defended himself.

'Why not? Go on, tell me. I'm very fucking interested.'

'Two things. Firstly with those papers on my desk, we will smash Kruger Investigations. And secondly, the girl is still going to die.'

'Oh? And how have you arranged that one?' Bussola sneered. 'Bomb on the plane?'

'No – even better than that. You wanted to get Patrick Orlove out of the country – well, I've arranged it. He's on that plane, with a new passport, new name, different-coloured hair, and with orders to kill Tracey Greenwood when the appropriate moment comes. Then he can disappear, firstly into Britain, where I've opened a bank account for him with two grand in it; then he can hop across to Europe, where I've deposited a quarter of a

415

million in a Paris bank for him – activated when the kill is confirmed, of course.'

There was a silence while no doubt Bussola absorbed all this.

'Mario, you should know me by now,' Begin's voice said persuasively. 'I always have a fall-back position. I *never* take anything for granted.'

Felicity took the news like a blow to the stomach.

So it wasn't over yet.

Felicity could not sleep. She heard Bussola return to the house just after midnight, then crash into his bedroom down the hallway. His snores more or less immediately permeated through the walls. Big, loud, disgusting ones, just like him. They made Felicity's lips curl in distaste.

She could not help but think this was the time to get out of this mess. She hated her life, she hated her husband and she needed to break free. Otherwise she would crack up or die.

Other than the sound of snoring, the house was quiet.

Begin was not back – he slept in a room next to his office – so there was only herself and Bussola in at that moment.

Time to take a chance.

She dressed quickly in light clothing, filling a small valise with other clothing and some of life's essentials.

She stepped into the hallway, which she was fairly sure was not observed by surveillance cameras. A dozen strides and she was outside Bussola's door. It was unlocked. Felicity crept into the bedroom. A dim bedside light illuminated the massive, jello-like form of Bussola lying spreadeagled and naked across the bed like a beached whale. She tiptoed up to him, any noise she might be making masked by the deafening snores emanating deep from his throat. Alcoholic fumes and stale sweat wafted up from him.

He squirmed. His body wobbled.

416

Felicity remained still, confident he would not wake.

Bussola's clothes were scattered drunkenly around the room. She picked up his jacket and rummaged through the pockets, finding two keys on a chain. She pocketed them.

'What the hell's . . .?' Bussola blurted out and sat upright.

Felicity dropped like a stone at the end of the bed. The bedsprings bounced, Bussola groaned . . . then the snoring recommenced.

Felicity exhaled falteringly.

On her hands and knees she crawled around the bed to the cabinet in which she knew her husband kept his own personal gun. It was a .25 Beretta, just like James Bond used to carry.

It was fully loaded.

She rose to her knees and found herself face to face with her beloved. Spittle dribbled out of the corners of his mouth. Oh, how she hated him. She stood up, reached over him and picked up a pillow. Holding the gun in her right hand, she held the pillow over it so the end of the barrel protruded slightly and pointed the weapon at her husband's temple.

Not close enough.

She forced herself to touch the muzzle to his skin, braced and pulled the trigger twice in quick succession. The sound was dreadful in the confines of the bedroom. People must come running . . . she waited, listening for the sound of running footsteps, ready to bring down the first one through the door and die fighting the others.

No one came.

Before leaving the room she grabbed the wrist-watch on the bedside cupboard; it was a Rolex, once owned by Steve Kruger. Felicity pocketed it, a lump in her throat. With one last glance at her husband, whose brains now made a pattern on the light-shade next to the bed, she left the room.

A minute later she was downstairs outside Begin's office. She unlocked the door with one of the keys she had just appropriated from Bussola. As Begin had boasted, the documents which would smash Kruger Investigations were on his desk – the same documents Felicity had stolen at the time of her divorce from Steve and which had subsequently played a big part in his death.

Well, she was making amends now, as best she could.

With a great deal of pleasure she fed them one by one into the paper shredder next to Begin's desk. Twelve sheets, shredded in three minutes. But that wasn't all she planned to do in his office.

She moved to the small wall-safe set behind some law books on a shelf. She wasn't certain what it contained, but she had an inkling there was something worthwhile within.

The other key on the chain opened it. Her jaw sagged in amazement when she clapped eyes on the contents. Felicity estimated she was looking at somewhere in the region of a quarter of a million bucks; she immediately transferred the bundles into her case.

Now all she had to do was make a quick phone call and get the hell out.

As she replaced the telephone, the figure of Ira Begin loomed in through the open door of his office. He was not expecting to see Felicity, but when his eyes fell on her and the open door of the safe, he quickly made the addition.

Felicity was on her feet. She hadn't heard his car pull up.

Begin said, 'What are you doing, Felicity? You don't seriously think Mario will let you get away with stealing from him, do you? He'll probably kill you this time.'

'Yeah, no doubt he would – if he was alive to do it.'

Begin's face registered shock.

Felicity reached calmly into the valise and pulled out the revolver.

Begin's hands rose instinctively. 'Hey, if he's dead, I don't have any argument with you. I'll stand aside. You can go.'

Her mind whirred. Yeah, she thought, and I'll never get past that gate-house alive.

'Okay, Ira, I believe you,' she lied, 'but I want you to do one thing for me – phone those greasy bastards down at the gate and tell them that in a couple of minutes' time you'll be driving out and for them to get the gates open now, because you're in a hurry.'

'But I'm not,' he protested.

'Ira – that's not the point, is it? I have a gun and I'm telling you what to do. If you don't do it, I'll shoot you . . . and don't think for a moment I won't. I've just got a taste for blood.'

He eyed her nervously and nodded.

'If you try or say anything stupid, I'll put a bullet in your skull and take my chances with those no-brain wonders anyway,' she warned him.

'Okay, I'll do it.'

He crossed to the phone. Felicity circled away from him, covering him all the time, not trusting him an inch. She knew how sneaky and deceitful he was, and how violent when the need arose. At that moment in time she was feeling good, completely in control for once in her life. She had made a decision about her destiny and it put her on a high operating plane.

Begin replaced the phone. 'Done.'

'Thanks, Ira – now get on your knees and put your forehead against the wall.'

He started to protest and she levelled the gun at him. 'Ira, don't worry, I'm only gonna put some cuffs on you.'

Unsurely he knelt down, facing the wall.

Felicity stepped quickly up to him, placed the gun at the back of his head and shot him. She ran out of the

419

room before he toppled over.

Begin's car was outside the front door of the house. Unlocked, keys in the ignition, as were all cars left within the grounds. Headlights blazing, Felicity skidded down the gravel driveway and out of the gates with a loud 'Yahoo!' on her lips.

'I'd better be going.' Tapperman indicated the wall clock. It was 2.30 a.m. He and Myrna were sitting in the living room of her house, having drunk endless cups of coffee. 'There'll be a black and white right outside the door twenty-four hours per day until you feel safe.'

'I feel pretty safe now,' Myrna said. 'Just tired, that's all.'

'Hey, my fault. I've kept you talking too long.'

'No, it's okay. I've enjoyed it.' And she had, because the main topic of conversation had been the memories both had of Steve Kruger.

'Fine, see ya,' Tapperman waved. He stood up, his head almost brushing the ceiling. His mobile phone rang. He unhooked it from his belt. 'Tapperman.'

Myrna collected the cups and wandered wearily into the kitchen, a burnt-out case. She returned as Tapperman finished his call. His face was white, because he was suddenly remembering the familiar face he had bumped into at the airport. Now he knew who it belonged to.

'That was the office. An anonymous called just left a message for me.' He gritted his teeth and found himself short of breath. 'Patrick Orlove is on board that plane with Danny and Tracey. He's got orders to take Tracey out and then disappear into Europe.'

Both their eyes turned to the clock.

'The plane's due to land in half an hour,' Myrna said. 'We need to get a message to the cops in England.'

'Do you know any cops in England?'

'No – but I know a man who does.' She reached for her phone.

★ ★ ★

Since reading Stanway's letter, Henry Christie had been far too excited to sleep. He had re-read the thing several times and spent the night agitatedly wandering about the house whilst upstairs his wife and two daughters slept soundly.

He must have dropped off around 3 a.m. because he awoke in a contorted position on the settee just before 6 a.m. with a stiff neck and dead arm. Then in a panic, he rushed round, brushing his teeth, grabbing a quick shower and getting into his work suit, waking the whole household as he did so, before leaping into the car and heading off towards Manchester Airport.

He arrived at the terminal building at 7.45 a.m., parked up and walked into International Arrivals. According to the screens, the flight from Miami was slightly delayed. He cursed, he was looking forward to seeing Danny.

At exactly that time, the first of three cells on the Solitary wing at Risley Remand Centre was unlocked by four prison guards. The door was pulled open and the inmate was found standing there ready prepared.

Louis Vernon Trent smiled amiably at the guards and compliantly held his hands out for the cuffs to be clamped around his wrists. His eyes watched everything that was happening, and everyone. He knew this would be his last chance to escape from custody for a while. After today his remand hearings would take place without his presence. The next time he would be at court would be for his committal hearing, and after that his trial.

This was the first of three chances to effect an escape and if the opportunity arose, he would be on his toes because he knew that, most probably, after the court appearances he would never be released for the rest of his life.

He was prodded along the landing to the next cell, opened by one of the screws.

421

A mean-faced, impatient Charlie Gilbert was also ready and waiting. A pair of specially widened handcuffs were ratcheted onto his fat wrists.

He was dressed very well and expensively. He fully expected to walk out of court a free man, or at the very least on bail today. Bussola would see to that, he believed. And if he did leave as a free man, he would show the cops a thing or two. He would tighten up his network and continue to abuse young girls and if they were difficult, he would kill them; more and more he wanted to kill them anyway. It gave him a great sense of satisfaction. If he walked out of court on bail, he would flee the country, he had decided.

A prison guard's hand propelled him to the next cell from which Ollie Spencer was extracted.

He was a man with no dreams or expectations. What happened, happened. He was content to take things as they came.

All three men were led out to the yard and bundled into a converted mini-bus with armoured windows and toughened body panels. The prisoners were put into an inner cage, the guards took up positions on seats outside the cage. The driver was in a protected cabin.

When they were ready the mini-bus pulled out of the remand centre.

'Would Henry Christie please attend the information desk to take an urgent phone call?'

Henry was standing under the Meeting Point with a cup of coffee in his hand. His mind was retracing the words of Stanway's letter again and again. He was in deep thought. The letter was very much on his mind, everything else simply background.

I know that Charles has always loved little girls, Henry remembered reading, *and he has always directed his energies to being in a position where he could meet them – or arrange to meet them. His amusement arcades were always a good place*

*for this to happen and he frequently lured girls aged around
eleven (because that's the age group he loved the best) and
then he would ultimately abuse them. Most he discarded back
onto the scrap heap they came from (many were missing from
homes, many never got to know his name), but some became
regulars, being paid to perform the most disgusting sexual acts
with him and his friend Spencer – who was always there.
Some liked it. Some didn't. Some fought him and he overpowered them. Some he could not overpower . . . and these he
would kill.*

'I repeat, would Mr Henry Christie please attend the
information desk for an urgent message . . .'

At this mention of his name, Henry snapped back into
the here and now. He threw his coffee down his neck and
with a quick glance at the arrivals screen, which told him
the flight from Miami had touched down, he went to the
information desk.

The flight had been peaceful. A couple of good films were
shown. The food was passable and the service excellent.
Some people even managed to sleep.

Danny and Tracey spent a long time talking about
Charlie Gilbert and Mario Bussola. Tracey knew a great
deal about both and their activities, and her story was
pretty typical of a young person's involvement with them.
Gilbert often arranged to take 'likely candidates' across to
America where they were inducted into Bussola's porn
empire. It was easy, Tracey said, to arrange forged
passports, work permits, social security numbers. Bussola
did that for Gilbert so that all the Brit had to do was
bring the right sort of kids over.

Gilbert would promise his girls a chance in films. Most
were under his power and influence and believed anything
he told them anyway. The reality of the 'films' soon hit
them. Once Bussola had abused them to his own personal
satisfaction, he passed them down the line where they got
roles in poorly made, but expensive to buy, blue movies.

They then passed on into prostitution and subsequently burned out on drugs and booze.

Gilbert had promised Tracey stardom. She had 'it', he told her. Looks, presence, potential, the body . . . everything.

But she knew he was lying. All he was trying to do was shut her up because she had witnessed him murder her friend; he'd whisked her off to America, where he handed her over to Bussola and his organisation. It was doomed from the start. She could not even pretend she liked being fucked in front of a camera, or that it was a pleasure fellating a guy with a lens pointed at her. She tried, because the cash and dope payment was good . . . but she hated it, her eyes could not hide it and the camera saw it.

She didn't last long before she was turned out onto the mean and dirty streets of Miami.

Eventually she gravitated into one of Florida's most notorious motorcycle gangs – like Hell's Angels, only a million times worse. Her life became a series of scenes from a movie: guns, robberies, shootings, drugs, one-man rape and then a gang-rape – fifteen of them – and being left for alligators to eat in the Everglades.

Somehow she survived.

She even got a job, on the sex-line, unaware that the business belonged to Bussola. And that night, when she saw the two of them together, Bussola and Gilbert, she flipped and attacked them – with the assistance of cocaine.

The cold light of dawn made her realise that by testifying against them, her life would be in danger; that was why she disappeared. By pure chance she had seen a copy of the *Daily Mail* with its coverage of the discovery of her friend's body – Annie Reece, whom Gilbert had killed in her presence. An urge to do something for Annie had spurred her on to go and see Myrna, but then she got frightened again and ran out.

She returned a few days later when she discovered she

had nothing to lose by giving evidence against Gilbert and, possibly, Bussola.

Danny frantically recorded everything on a witness statement form. It took four hours to write. When the statement had been completed and signed, Danny sat back and thought for a moment. At length she said, 'There are a couple of questions which are nagging at me, Tracey. They're not really answered in the statement and I haven't pushed you – but one is *why* didn't Gilbert kill you as well as Annie? He's a ruthless bastard.'

Tracey squirmed uncomfortably.

Danny kept quiet, using the weapon of silence to her advantage, putting Tracey under pressure.

'I don't know.'

'Yes, you do,' Danny said quietly.

Tracey closed her eyes. A look of self-loathing crossed her thin, drug-ravaged face. She swallowed and then admitted: 'I helped him to bury her body. Me and Ollie – we both helped him.'

'Shit.' Danny sighed. She was going to need some advice on that one. 'Right,' she said slowly. 'The other question is, you said you had nothing to lose by giving evidence against Gilbert. What does that mean?'

Tracey took a long juddering breath. 'When I ran out on Myrna I learnt something.' Her voice was weaker than it ever had been. A tear appeared, clung to her eyelid, then rolled tiredly down her cheek. 'I've just found out I've got full-blown AIDS. Gilbert and Bussola can't do anything to hurt me now. If they killed me, they'd only be doing me a favour. I don't have long to live anyway.'

'Oh, Tracey,' Danny cried. She twisted in her seat and closed her arms around the young girl.

The remainder of the flight was spent dozing, eating and movie-watching.

And three rows back, Patrick Orlove's slitted eyes kept observation on the back of their heads. In the flight bag by his feet was the pistol which Ira Begin had thoughtfully managed to have placed in the life-jacket pocket, by one of the airport cleaning staff employed on a casual basis by Bussola. It was a good gun. Light, accurate and would do the trick.

But when? Orlove had to think this one through.

To shoot someone in a pressurised aircraft cabin, so the movies would have one believe, could have extremely dangerous consequences. Orlove was no martyr; he didn't want to cause the plane to plummet to earth. To strangle her when she visited the toilet was one option he considered, but it was messy. There could be witnesses and no doubt cops would be waiting to greet the plane. So that was ruled out.

He knew he had to hit her at the airport. Somewhere between customs and the arrivals lounge would probably be ideal.

As the flight touched down, Orlove was calculating how far a quarter of a million dollars would go. He had heard Portugal was inexpensive. Maybe he'd crash out there for a few months and reassess his future then.

The plane finished taxiing and linked up to the terminal. The 'fasten seat belts sign' was extinguished. The doors heaved open.

Hello, Manchester, Orlove thought. So long, Tracey. Whoever you may be and whatever you may have done.

Henry slammed down the phone. Near hysteria gripped his voice when he said to the woman at the information desk, 'What stage are the passengers at from the Miami flight?'

'Should be collecting baggage very shortly.'

Henry ran towards the doors which led to the customs channel. In his ears, the words of Karl Donaldson rang out. 'Shit!' Henry burbled repeatedly as he ran to the doors – which he found to be automatic sliding doors which only opened when approached from the opposite side. Henry inserted his fingertips between them to try and prise them apart. They refused to respond.

There was, of course, no need for Danny and Tracey to wait to collect luggage. They had none.

Once clear of passport control, and after a slight delay when the customs officer carefully read Tracey's emergency documentation, they were en route to the baggage reclamation area which they had to pass through to get to the green channel.

Patrick Orlove was right behind them, having been first in the queue for holders of non-EEC passports. He had presented a passport bearing the name of Daniel Harrison; it was forged, but good enough to fool even a close inspection by a customs official.

'What do you think you're doing? You can't go through there, mate.'

A hand crashed down onto Henry's shoulder and spun him away from the automatic doors. He was ready to punch whoever it was.

'Jesus, thank God for that!' he breathed in relief when he saw the heavily armed police officer staring sternly at him. An MP5 was draped across his chest, a handgun was in a holster at his side and he wore body armour and a peaked cap. The epitome of a friendly, helpful bobby.

Henry pulled out his warrant card.

They were so far ahead of the other passengers, having gone through the green channel unchallenged, that when they hit the corridor between the customs and the international arrivals hall, there were only the three of them walking down it – Danny, Tracey and Patrick Orlove.

This is easy, Orlove thought. Portugal, here I come! Pop her here, and the other one, then I'm away and two dead bodies will be lying there ready for collection.

He was only a matter of feet behind his targets. His hand went underneath his jacket and withdrew the gun from his waistband. He upped his pace slightly.

The women were strolling casually along, totally oblivious to his presence.

He concentrated on the spot at the back of Tracey's head which, when penetrated by a bullet, would take the girl down as effectively as a vet shooting a horse with a captive bolt.

The firearms officer could not believe this was happening. The moment for which he had trained so hard, for which he'd been put through his paces so many times. And now, just like the cinetronic screen, it was being enacted in front of him. But this was no video clip. *This was for real.*

He clearly saw the gun in Orlove's hand.

It was coming swiftly up.

There was no time to shout a warning, as had been drummed into him, time after time in the training environment.

He was learning at supersonic speed that no amount of time on a firing range, or dealing with situations in a training environment, could prepare someone for the real thing. Fuck the psychological tests. They meant nothing when you were actually faced with a life-and-death decision right in front of your eyes.

If he did not shoot now, an innocent person would die.

Orlove increased his speed. He was right behind the intended victim. The gun was almost there, at the back of her head. The officer needed to shoot, to bring him down, to kill him, if that's what it took to stop the bastard.

And if he missed there was an awfully good chance of killing one of the females.

The time for considered thought was over.

It was a sound, not unlike someone slapping a table top with the flat of their hand. Smack, smack.

Danny turned to look.

The male passenger walking behind her crumpled to the ground and the gun in his hand clattered across the tiled floor.

Behind him was an armed cop, of the type seen so often in British airports these days, except his MP5 was in his hands, having just been fired. Beyond him stood the figure of Henry Christie, now moving towards her.

Tracey turned and saw the tableau.

She did not scream, cry, become hysterical. She just looked through tired eyes at it all.

A dead man and a cop with a gun.

So what else was new in her life?

'I'll swear out a warrant this afternoon,' Henry said quietly to Danny. She lifted her head from Stanway's letter which was in her lap and looked at him, her eyes glazed as she thought of all the misery, suffering and death wrought by Gilbert and Spencer over the years. 'Then,' Henry went on, 'I'll get some search teams together and start digging up his lovely garden. Probably first thing tomorrow.'

They were heading north on the M6, filtering into the lane which would take them west towards Blackpool.

'He claims at least twenty bodies,' Danny said, referring to the letter. '*At least*,' she said, stressing the words. 'I can't get my head around that.'

'Fred West, eat humble pie and God rot your soul,' Henry said. He nodded back towards Tracey, splayed out asleep across the rear seats. 'She was one of the lucky ones.'

Danny snorted. 'That's a matter of opinion.' She closed her eyes and sighed. 'At least twenty . . . and that's only in his garden. What about all those buried elsewhere?'

'I imagine they'll stay buried and undiscovered, unless Gilbert or Spencer start blabbing, which I doubt. Twenty'll do for a beginning.'

Danny felt silent. Then she touched Henry's thigh.

'Thanks for saving her life, and mine probably.' She negotiated her seat belt and leaned across, pecking him on the cheek.

'Pleasure . . . but I do want payment in kind, you know.'

'Henry, you can have me any time. I'm too knackered to resist anyway. Just pull my nightie down when you've finished.'

The prison mini-bus trundled laboriously up Richardson Street towards the rear doors of the police station yard at Blackpool.

A killer lurked near the pay and display car park which overlooked the street, waiting for the chance to strike, but not really knowing where. Just looking for the right moment.

The 'why' was known and fixed in the killer's mind. That was no problem.

The 'how' was in the killer's pocket. That was no problem either.

The mini-bus transporting the three prisoners pulled up at the entrance to the police yard, and waited for the roller door to rise. And now the killer saw a chance. The door rose slowly; controlled by a button in the comms room and when there was enough headroom, the vehicle moved slowly forwards into the yard.

The killer ran down the steps from the car park and strolled casually in behind the bus, all the way to the top of the yard where it stopped.

The killer walked to the front of the vehicle, trying to look confident, not out of place.

The side door of the bus opened. A prison guard stepped down, closely followed by the first prisoner, Ollie Spencer, wearing rigid handcuffs.

Next came the immense figure of Charlie Gilbert, wearing the specially ordered cuffs which fitted his enormous wrists.

430

Then came Louis Vernon Trent, also cuffed, looking as nasty and as evil as ever.

All three were made to stand in line behind each other.

The 'where' now became real easy.

The killer stepped quickly forwards. There was a fully licensed .38 Smith & Wesson in the killer's right hand, loaded with wad cutters.

It was over in seconds. No one reacted until all of the six bullets had been discharged into the prisoner in the middle of the row.

Then, Mrs Ruth Lilton dropped her husband's weapon and stood there waiting to be taken into custody for the murder of Charlie Gilbert and of her husband Joe Lilton, who was lying dead at their home, another six bullets in him.

Ruth Lilton felt good. The two men who had destroyed her daughter Claire were now incapable of doing the same to any other child.

Louis Vernon Trent was the first person to take advantage of the situation. Handcuffed though he was, he was always on the lookout for any chance, slim or fat, to escape. He turned and ran for the rear door of the police station yard, his instinct to be free driving him on.

He fully expected to be brought down by a flying rugby tackle at any moment.

It never happened.

He ran through the pedestrian entrance, out across Richardson Street, up the short flight of steps to the car park and, keeping low, ran for his life and freedom.

Seconds later, Henry Christie turned his car into Richardson Street, Danny's hand resting on his thigh, blissfully unaware of anything that had just taken place in the back yard of Blackpool Central police station.

Epilogue

Danny stood underneath the shower. Jets of hot water cascaded down her body and she soaped herself again and again, luxuriating in the sensation which was making her tired body feel alive.

Henry Christie had been as good as his word and, with FB's blessing, had said she could take as much time off as she wanted to recuperate from the rigours of the last two weeks. But, because circumstances had changed so dramatically today with the death of Charlie Gilbert and the escape of Louis Trent, it was typical of Danny that she did not want to miss any developments. She knew that if she was sat on a beach on some Greek island or other she would be bored, lonely and consumed with curiosity about what was happening at work.

'I'll be back next Monday,' were her parting words to Henry. She needed a few days to recharge her batteries and she also wanted to price up a new car, maybe a little sporty thing this time. She had decided she would use the insurance money from the Mercedes and take out whatever else was required in the form of a loan and treat herself.

Having spent the day interviewing and feeling very sorry for Ruth Lilton, murderess, Danny had arrived home – dropped off by a police car – at ten that evening.

Her guts told her to hit the sack straight away.

But she was stale from the long, overnight flight, a little clammy, and although totally whacked, she wanted to go to bed accompanied by a pleasant perfumey smell, not body odour.

She compromised and showered instead of having a bath. The action of washing herself, letting her hands run up and down her body, almost like a massage, was wonderful. She would have preferred Henry's hands, but that would never happen, she knew.

She stepped out of the shower and dried herself. After wrapping a huge fluffy bath towel around herself, tucking it under her armpits, she made a turban for her head from a smaller towel.

Suddenly the lights went out though the extractor fan continued to hum.

She swore, opened the door and stepped out onto the landing to find that light out too. She tried the switch. Nothing. Obviously a fuse gone. She groaned, annoyed. Just when she needed it. She flicked the switch again. Still nothing. Damn!

Angrily she tried the bathroom light switch, which was outside the bathroom itself. The light came on immediately.

Danny frowned, puzzled, her brain still in neutral. She fingered the switch thoughtfully until it dawned on her. Someone had actually been up here and switched off the light. Someone was physically here, in the house. An intruder.

Her eyes rose to the landing light. There was no light bulb in the socket. A sudden, nauseous dread overcame her. Louis Trent, she thought dizzily. He's here, in my house. He's been outside the bathroom while I was in the shower and I didn't hear him because of the water.

She turned and made a dash for her bedroom, aiming to press the panic alarm button next to her bed.

She lurched for the button as she veered into the darkened bedroom, but her hand did not reach it. Another, stronger one clamped down on hers and she was thrown across the bed with such force that she rolled off the other side and crashed to the floor. Next thing, she was being dragged by her hair back onto the bed.

A bedside light was switched on.

The figure towered over her, a terrifying look on his face.

He bent down and picked something up that was leaning against the wardrobe. At first Danny thought it was a broom-handle. When it was pointed at her face she saw it was a single-barrelled shotgun that Jack Sands was holding.

He perched on the end of the bed. Danny sat near the headboard with her legs drawn up. He had made her throw the towels away so she was naked and starting to shiver. The shotgun rested across his lap, his left hand holding the barrel, his right the stock, his forefinger curled around the trigger.

They had been talking for well over two hours, going round and round in circles.

To Danny he sounded demented and very dangerous.

'I just can't give you up,' he informed her for the hundredth time. 'You're part of my life, part of me.' He shook his head sadly. His eyes had a faraway look. 'I won't give you up to anyone, let alone that bastard Christie.'

'Henry Christie is my boss. He is not my lover, and never will be.'

'Bollocks! I've seen you two together. I've seen him drop you off at your house, groping you before you get out of the car. I've seen it happen, Danny. He's shagging you, isn't he?'

'No – no one's shagging me, as you so pleasantly put it, Jack. I don't have a lover and I don't want one. Not you, not anybody. And your imagination is running riot. Henry has never groped me, either.'

'I don't believe you.'

Danny shrugged. 'Can I put my dressing-gown on? It's cold here.'

'No.'

'Fine.'

'He deserved that crack on the head. I wish he'd got brain damage from it.'

'You did it?'

'I arranged it. Put a couple of toe-rags onto him who owed me past favours.'

Danny took in the information. 'So what's it going to be, Jack? We've been talking here for ages now, getting nowhere.'

He cleared his throat. A tear rolled out of one eye. 'I can't bear the thought of anyone else touching you. And if it can't be me, no one else will ever touch you because I'm going to kill you now. Then I'll kill myself. Ha! I know this is only a single barrel, but you'll have to trust me. This is a suicide pact. You'll die and then I promise I'll reload and put the gun to my head. I'll only be seconds behind you. I've even written a suicide note.' He produced it from a pocket and flapped the envelope at her and dropped it on the bed between them.

Then he took a shotgun cartridge from his pocket and placed it upright on the dressing-table. 'That's for me. Yours is already in the gun.' He lifted the weapon and pointed it at her.

'You're mad, Jack. A fucking raving loony.'

'No. Don't think that of me. I'm obsessed, yeah. I'm in love, but I'm not mad, Danny.'

'Well, let me tell you this,' Danny said falteringly, fear rising through her. 'If there *is* an afterlife, I'll be going to it with that thought in my mind. Jack Sands is fucking mental. A pathetic, spineless bastard who—'

'Shut it!' he screamed. The gun shook in his hands. He hoisted it to his shoulder and looked down the barrel at Danny. She stared straight back, transfixed like a rabbit in a poacher's torchbeam.

'Go on,' she snarled, 'pull the fucking trigger and have done. You've made my life a misery anyway. Go on, pull

436

it, then kill yourself, Jack. The world will be a far better place without you in it.'

'I will! I will!' he threatened, right on the edge. His finger wrapped around the trigger. Danny could see him forcing himself to pull it.

Her face wore a mask of contempt. She shifted slightly on the bed, an inch nearer to the panic button. 'It's over, Jack. You and me. It would never have worked in a million years. You can't have your cake and eat it. You're married on one hand, having a longstanding affair on the other. Something had to break sooner or later and that something was me. You were never going to leave her, so I had to end it, don't you see?' Then she added desperately, 'What about your kids? Jack, they need you, they need a father. Stop this now . . . please. For everyone's sake.'

'I've got enough love for everyone.'

'Oh, Jack, don't be a fool. No one has that much love. Killing me and killing yourself is not the way to see this through. Come on,' she said softly, 'please see sense.'

There was a long silence. The gun was still pointed right at Danny's nose.

'You're right,' he said. He stood up and without a further word he walked out of the bedroom, head held high, shotgun in his right hand.

Danny leapt to her feet and slammed the door behind him, locking it.

She heard his footsteps on the stairs.

Everything drained out of her. She slumped onto the bed, holding her head.

Then she heard the bang of the shotgun being discharged somewhere downstairs.

In deep shock she rolled onto the bed, curled up like a baby in the womb, jammed a thumb into her mouth and rocked and cried.